ECHOES OF ENVY

A PARANORMAL ROMANCE MYSTERY

J. K. GRUEBER

MYSTIC RIDGE PUBLISHING, LLC

Mystic Ridge Publishing, LLC

Mysticridgepublishing.com

ISBN: 978-1-965796-07-8 (Hardback)

ISBN: 979-8-9878673-5-8 (Paperback)

ISBN: 979-8-9878673-4-1 (Ebook)

Cover design by: Anne Graff, Andrew Grueber, and William Grueber.

Contributing cover photo editor: Sanderson-Decello Design, LLC.

Printed in the United States of America.

Also By J. K. Grueber

The Envy Series:

COLORS OF ENVY: A Paranormal Romance Mystery
FACES OF ENVY: A Paranormal Romance Mystery
ECHOES OF ENVY: A Paranormal Romance Mystery

The MacDade Brothers Mysteries:

EXPOSED IN THE SHADOWS: He Who Plays.
A Paranormal Mystery Rekindling Lost Love
The MacDade Brother's Mysteries (Book One)

EXPOSED IN THE CROSSHAIRS: He Who Rides
The MacDade Brothers Mysteries (Book Two)

EXPOSED BY THE RIVERSIDE: He Who Lives
The MacDade Brothers Mysteries (Book Three)

The Vampire Tales:

CURSED AT CONCEPTION:
The Vampire's Henchman

Dedication

In memory of Suellen Brady, May 2023. My sister, my friend, my biggest fan, and most respected critic.

May the road rise to meet you.
May the wind be always at your back.
May the sun shine warm upon your face.
May the rains fall upon your fields.
And until we meet again,
May God hold you in the hollow of His hand.

PROLOGUE

"Re'd for me . . ." the words slipped through his mind, mesmerizing, "Re`d for me, bab`be boy."

"Nooo! Pleeease nooo. . . Not again, Mom`ma . . . Pleeease not again," he pleaded as he looked up at her slender face.

Flawless, her alabaster complexion was as smooth as a bisque statue, from her high intelligent brow to her aloof tipped chin. Hair, as black as onyx, framed her face and tumbled over her shoulders, down her back in stunning contrast to her scarlet blouse. Delicate, her soft full lips almost always curved in a gentle smile, but she wasn't smiling now. Pensive and determined, her gypsy-black eyes held fast on the white silk, deliberately avoiding his gaze, ignoring his plea. Meticulously, she'd splayed the monogrammed handkerchief in front of him. In sharp contrast, it lay innocently on the mosaic-tiled table. Her desk.

Like any businesswoman, she professed, she needed a desk, but not like an ordinary desk. This one was round and large enough to seat five chairs . . . like the five points of a pentagram. Around the room, the tools of her trade decorated the walls, from star charts with countless symbols to tapestry-covered shelves laden with a wide array of jars, urns, and colorful inlaid boxes.

A parlor had occupied the room in another era. A parlor where a dozen or more courtships of the DC elite had begun. If he tried—even if he didn't try—he sometimes saw them, young men and women dressed in fabulous gowns and dinner jackets, laughing and chatting, shy and outrageous as they waltzed around the parlor. He knew those styles now, knew the fashions of the 19th century. He always saw them in candlelight or aglow in sunbeams to pour through the tall narrow windows. The scents of candlewax and oil touched him more swiftly than the incense and perfumes trapped within the dark parlor of his mother's office.

Heavy drapes covered the walls, and not a single sliver of outside light filtered through the layered cloth. Darkness. Always in darkness. Five Tiffany lamps offered a kaleidoscope of color against the twilight, like the tiles surrounding the white handkerchief. A single embroidered 'J' faced him. The corner point aimed at his center. The black thread appeared to ripple like a snake in wicked contrast to the glowing silk.

'Painless,' a low soothing voice chanted. 'Nothing to fear . . . I don't want to hurt you, really . . . But you are mine . . ..'

The ill-omen touched him, sending a shiver through his slight frame, and without a thought, he started a backward step. Faster, like a lightning strike, the slender fingers caught his wrist and froze him, rooting his tennis shoes to the floor, but his fingers fisted, recoiling in the iron grip.

"Mom`ma, nooo," he whined, looking up at her, begging her to look at him. Sometimes, just sometimes if he looked into others' eyes, he could get his way. Nanna said it was a gift; Mom`ma said it was his curse.

She wouldn't look at him. Not ever. He was different. She knew it. Nanna knew it. No playing ball like other boys. No walking to the park with Nanna now. Different. He was different. Like his pap`pa, he was a warlock. That's what his mom`ma told him, but sometimes she seemed proud or pleased with her profession. He wasn't like other boys. Things he touched, talked to him. The dead talked to him. He had to read . . . learn to read. *A monster* . . . and they would come for him. The Necromancer.

A single gunshot echoed, lost in the rush of the wind to surf across the choppy black water. The wood planks vibrated underfoot, barely visible with the illumination of a single bulb at the entrance of the boat ramp. Even in the dim light, the muzzle flash was blinding. A bright white flash, a circle of death on an alabaster forehead . . .

But this wasn't his mother's face. The face of an angel, his angel, his guardian angel.

2,1,4 . . . a perfect seven.

A moan slipped off his lips as he tried again to withdraw his hand, but he was no match for his mother's grip.

In his mind's eye, he saw the stricken blue eyes, blue diamond eyes. The slender body propelled, the force of the blast snapping her neck, lifting, launching her off the planks.

"Forgivvve meee . . . I haaad nooo chooice . . ." A voice cried out in the night. No choice. If she was here, then she knew more than she should. She knew, and she would never stop digging, not now, not with her husband gone. She would need answers . . . and she could destroy them. Everything they'd worked for would be lost. If not him, then someone else would need to stop her! They'd come too far!

A cry of outrage—of terror—ripped through the aether, and he knew that voice. His own voice screamed as he watched the blue diamond eyes sinking, fading rapidly in the murky water with black hair scattered Medusa-style, twining in the current.

A monster . . . he was a monster to be feared . . . to be afraid. And he was afraid . . . More afraid now of living . . . than of dying. What they could do to him . . . would do to him. What they'd already done to him? *What they were doing to him now?*

"Do you want them to take you, bab`be boy? Is thot whot you want . . . If they knew whot you were . . ."

In confusion and fear, he strained to keep his fist from lowering, meant to keep his fingers locked, but his mother's hand was so much larger, stronger. "Mom`ma, nooo, please. She's touched the hand of the devil," he heaved softly, tears springing over his emerald eyes. "Nooo," he moaned as the images swirled in his young mind. He'd been here before, at this moment, knowing a catalyst lay before him, knowing too early what that word meant to him—for him. Things would change, but he would be the same.

. . . 2,1,4 . . . a perfect seven . . .

Before his knuckles bruised on the ceramic tabletop, the long red fingernails clamped into his wrist, springing his fingers open. His palm slammed down over the black J.

As if a window burst open before him, glass shattering, the images erupted, clearing as sounds of screams echoed through time. Drawing a breath, stifling a cry, he suffered the severance, seeing himself as younger—then older. His own young face was animated, pale, and gaunt. His eyes haunted in stop-action frames captured on endless reels of film . . . He saw himself, his lean body twisting, turning within cotton bands to hold his wrists, his waist, his chest, and crying out when the torment and pain became unbearable in his wasted young body. Dreams within dreams, nightmares within a nightmare . . . but so few were illusions. None, imagination. From the outside looking in, through the eyes of an adult, from the face of a child. He understood himself viewing a film, a film of himself viewing a film. On dual planes, he hovered, confused and terrified . . . on the outside looking in, on the inside looking out . . .

The husky American voice came at a low volume. "Put both hands on the side of the car. No one needs to get hurt here. We're just going to take a little ride and have a chat."

"Reassuring, sir, with a gun in my back. A telephone call would have been more appropriate," he commented indifferently, but he placed his hands on the car door. Even anticipating the quick jab at his hip, he jolted, rising in reflex before the heated flash started through his system. "Bassstard." The word hissed off his lips as his tongue swelled and the world rippled.

"Just relax," the man stated and clasped his arm as he staggered against the side of the car. "Let's go . . . just a few steps."

No choice. His knees buckled as hot liquid raced through his muscles and veins. Stumbling and collapsing, he reached the backseat. Not total darkness, nor relief from the consciousness. He fell over on the stiff bench seat, vaguely aware of the voices droning, the engine igniting. That he would reach his intended destination, alive—barely—he harbored no doubts . . .

"Mayday! Mayday!" *Harry Windell shouted into the headsets. The instrument panel lit up like a Christmas tree in front of him, screaming every kind of mechanical failure from the engines to the landing gear. They were going down!* "Buckle up!" *Harry shouted to his passengers, but if either man heard, neither responded.* "We're going down! . . ."

CHAPTER 1

The federal surveillance sedan remained—unmanned—in the hotel parking lot.

Three floors above, Veronica Bryson-Laquette peered through a crack between heavy drapes and window, verifying the car's presence, along with its vacancy. The inhabitants, the two gentlemen who'd occupied the front seat last evening, had apparently opted for a room and comfortable bed where they could spell off watching her from a lower floor. Considering her recognizance mission last evening, sneaking through shadows and behind bushes to collect a license plate number, she shook her head. The equivalent of cat burglary wasn't her usual approach to an investigation, but it worked.

Whether she should be relieved or irritated with the official vehicle stationed below, she couldn't decide. Four spaces away from the sedan, past a gray Beetle, a red Taurus, and a darker gray Chevy wagon, the fancy little Ford pickup stood out like a black rose among thorns. Her husband, Jade Laquette, did nothing halfway or understated. Across the shiny black doors, in bold English script, the words boasted, 'Olden Time Antiques and Collectables, LLC.' In a smaller script, the shop address and phone number remained clearly visible from three stories away.

Her wily husband was up to something—likely something dangerous considering the company he was presently keeping in Cleveland. Federal agents, homicide detectives, and politicians had appeared in brief quips and replays throughout the early morning broadcast on the national news station. Not surprisingly, Jade had avoided the media. This soon after the circus in Bentwood months ago, his name, if not his face, would hike the ratings on every station, but she suffered no doubts that he was in Cleveland.

While she, on the other hand, stood in a hotel more than a hundred miles away.

The little college town of Elmview wasn't a hotbed of crime, although, in a few days, it would probably rate a half-column in a national tabloid. Possibly sooner if the news out of Cleveland triggered the local chapter of *White Supremacists Anonymous.*

A shiver skittered down her spine, and unconsciously, Ronnie stepped back from the window, not touching the curtain. In twenty-twenty hindsight, without the angry adrenalin rush that had fueled her last evening, she understood Donna Spencer's fear. Threatening to blow the nuts off a skinhead twice her size probably wasn't her most rational decision, but the idiot shouldn't have messed with her pumpkins—or her and Donna.

No—probably not her smartest move.

At the first flutter at her center, Ronnie settled on the edge of the bed, fluffed the pillows, and flopped onto her side, prepared for another bout of nausea. At four months, Tad affectionately dubbed Tadpole, with his size in mind, was generally active at the crack of dawn, and according to Dr. Blackwell, the motion would continue, although the morning sickness should subside soon. Until leaving Bentwood the previous morning, however, Tad's rocking and rolling had gratefully remained a morning affliction. And Ronnie preferred not to dwell too deeply on that change regarding her mission—or Jade's mission, as she suspected.

'You have one mystery to solve, love, and apparently, I have another.'

Those words he'd spoken only yesterday morning when changing his plans to accompany her to this little college town.

As she knew, now, thanks to Tim Spencer, Jade had departed Bentwood less than a half hour after her, in the company of two federal agents . . . one of whom had stood at a podium last evening, fielding questions of a serial killer running amuck in Cleveland, Ohio. Special Agent Mark Jarvins wore a camera-friendly presence, but the irony remained. A blond-haired, blue-eyed agent—no matter his tailored dark suit and tie—attempting to defuse an angry mob on either end of the racial supremacy spectrum might not have been the FBI's best choice. Len Devinio—tall, dark, and Italian-handsome with an air of lofty indifference—might have served that purpose to appear neutral.

From the snippets of news from the evening and early morning broadcasts, the murders were racially oriented, and two notorious, extremely verbal supremacists were in custody though the details were sketchy. A viciously mutilated body had been found two nights ago, the fourth victim discovered in a similar condition. Frances Cummings, age 25, a lovely young Caucasian woman—which made no sense regarding a racial connection—had been found via an anonymous tip to the authorities. And somehow, Jade was involved; that much Ronnie knew. But she wondered . . . if he'd admitted his intentions to assist in that investigation, how would she have reacted?

She might have engaged her female wiles—either to stop him or to join him—and therein, the clue to her current location. A red herring, nothing more. And she'd fallen for it, hook, line, and sinker. If she'd considered the details when her wily husband had sent her—with Donna Spencer, full-time mom, part-time Interior Designer—to Elmview to investigate a possible homicide with his blessing, Ronnie probably would have anticipated the uneventfulness of her trip.

And the federal agents currently watching her truck—hence, her—were only further proof.

Lenny had sounded relieved when she'd asked him to check into that official license plate number, but that, too, presented a curiosity considering Len's proximity to Jade. Unless something was off in her suppositions, Jade should have enlisted Len to order surveillance on her if a danger existed, and Len should have already known why she was under guard.

If her blasted husband would call as promised . . . she wouldn't be lying around, twisting in the wind. By now, one would think, he'd know better than to attempt evasion. Even though he claimed ignorance regarding the future where she and Tad were concerned, he damned sure knew she had a nose for news. Her traveling to Cleveland was inevitable. Whether she traveled in his company or solo remained the only question.

Well, maybe not the only question. She had no idea what she'd do there.

Investigating a murder—any murder, much less multiple murders—was no longer an option.

Ronnie had decided hours if not months ago, to forgo her career as an investigative journalist considering her current condition. No way would she subject Tad to the horrors of a serial killer, not when he was surely his father's son. Still, she needed to reach Cleveland—

So why the hell was she lying around like she had all day to get there?

With the quietus spreading at her center, Ronnie wondered if her tiny passenger might agree with her decision. The little dickens had given her more than a few fits since the break of dawn when she'd first viewed those broadcasts from Cleveland. Now, however, he seemed content.

Rather carefully, Ronnie pushed off her side, testing the water, so to speak.

Just past the end of the bed, the TV—muted—flashed the latest craze in laundry soap, and Ronnie sent a scathing glance at the set, recalling the riot scene to greet her at the crack of dawn. No relief came with the memory of her husband suffering a wicked night of tossing and turning only two nights past—the same night Cummings had been murdered. And the preceding nightmares leading to that night should have warned her in advance. When a man like Jade Laquette starts tossing, turning, growling, and sweating throughout the night, it was a good bet he wasn't suffering from indigestion.

He was either in Cleveland or had been in Cleveland if the two neo-Nazis presently in custody were any indication.

And she was still wasting time without a single good reason.

Nearly two hours had passed since she'd persuaded the Spencers to take off on a buying spree. Morning sickness had offered a fine excuse to avoid that excursion, and it wasn't a lie. Tad had been swimming Olympic-quality acrobatics even before that newscast.

Damn it, even that—Officer Tim Spencer's unexpected arrival last evening—should have tipped her off to her husband's intentions, although that detail created another quandary.

On the one hand, Tim's presence suggested that she and Donna might need protection from something, or someone, involved in Jack Trumble's early demise. On the other, Tim had forfeited the investigation of a possible homicide far too easily. He hadn't needed much persuasion to accompany his wife on a shopping spree—with a focus on music boxes, no less. Even though Elmview wasn't his jurisdiction, Tim's police sense should have kicked in along with his curiosity.

Only the morning past, Tim had spoken with Jade . . . and if she thought about that too long or too hard, she might be tempted to hurt her wily husband when she caught up to him.

He was in good hands, or so Jade had assured Tim, allegedly intending for Tim to impart those words as a comfort to her. In Len's company, Jade should be safe . . . . . . and yet an odd sense of dread touched the edges of her mind.

Something was wrong. Terribly wrong. She knew it. She felt it on every blasted level, from the prickling at her hair follicles to the quiver starting in her gut. Tad felt it too, and that certainty only disturbed her more. Between her own and her unborn child's gifts, she might go mad before her ninth month . . . and was that the price she would pay for falling madly in love with a psychic?

"Dammit," she muttered and pushed off the edge of the bed, hesitating to make sure her passenger agreed before she began collecting her personal items. Right or wrong, it was time to go.

Considering her precarious balance, she called for a bellhop, musing over the irony. When she finally aspired to pamper herself, no one stood to witness her good sense. Only her husband seemed to realize she could carry their child without mishap, and that revelation drew a smirk on her lips. If she had a nickel for every time one or another of her family or friends cautioned her to be careful, she could probably outfit an entire nursery. And her blasted husband thought nothing of sending her off to track down a killer.

No doubts remained; Jack Trumble, the local realtor, had been murdered because of a conspiracy, but the proper authorities were already involved in the investigation. There was no point in sticking around.

Overnight bag packed, Ronnie waited for the bellhop and chitchatted en route to the lobby with the young bellhop, a college student with a shock of red hair to give the makers of L'Oréal a coronary. At the front desk, on a whim, Ronnie paid for another night for the Spencers, jotted a note on a piece of hotel stationery, and slipped the young woman a five to be sure they received her message when they returned.

Solo. It was the way she worked. The way she had always worked and worked best.

Despite the sun sprinkling through the near barren branches of trees circling the lot, a chill prickled under Ronnie's sweater collar as she strode across the lot. Surreptitiously, she spied the black sedan, still vacant, but she sensed rather than saw the curtain shift on a first-floor window.

She probably shouldn't be surprised or worried despite Len's curiosity. After all, she should be accustomed to picking up shadows. In some circles, her father was a little too well known, and like any successful lifelong politician, his family sometimes suffered. A fact of life. A way of life. She'd lived with contingency plans for everything from nuclear war to a hit squad of foreign terrorists. Robert Bryson Sr. had forfeited the mundane life of a bureaucrat dictated by his father to ride the tides of economic trends, political hotspots, and global manipulation. If he wasn't her father, doubtful she would even like him. He was, without a doubt, the most demanding, egotistical, manipulative man she'd ever had the displeasure of knowing, and the son-of-a-gun got away with it.

That was the phone call she could have made to learn why these two slightly inept watchdogs were on her heels. Unfortunately, phoning Robert Sr. would inevitably involve informing him of her location and current endeavors. He wouldn't bother sermonizing or ranting; he'd simply spare a word with Fiona, who in turn would spare a litany with their only daughter. In life, Ronnie's mother Fiona's sole mission, other than epitomizing the perfect hostess and wife to the revered Robert Bryson, was to keep their headstrong daughter in check, and the woman could be relentless. No sense igniting that crusade. Robert had probably sighed his relief and thanked the Almighty with the news of a grandchild on the way—and bouncing another babe on his knee would be the furthest thing from his mind. Ronnie could nearly imagine him praising God like a tent-star evangelist for providing a reason for her to forfeit her chosen profession. He might even genuinely accept her marriage and his son-in-law for that same reason. Bursting his bubble wouldn't wear well on their familial detente.

She'd been sitting too blasted long.

Muttering a curse, Ronnie ignited the engine and pulled from the parking space, catching a glimpse of a black-clad man hurrying from a side entrance. Definitely, the FBI. Classic black suit and tie.

Pulling under the carport entrance, Ronnie climbed from the cab and stood aside as the redhead loaded her bag onto the passenger's seat. As she tipped the bellhop, she glimpsed a shadow behind the lobby glass and then returned to the driver's seat.

At the mouth of the hotel entrance, paused to await a break in the sporadic traffic, Ronnie glimpsed the sedan in her rearview mirror as it zipped under the carport to collect a passenger.

"It's going to be a long hot afternoon for you boys," she muttered while pulling into a narrow break in traffic, heading toward Elmview's business district. "Hope you stocked up on a few gallons of bottled water . . ." Or a thermos of coffee, she added silently before considering the multitude of antique shops that she and Donna had skipped the day before.

Shopping. A buying spree . . . 'Be sure to take time out to shop,' Jade's words echoed in her inner ear, and almost as if she heard something unspoken now added to those words, she understood a weird significance. Shopping. Innocuous and mundane as it sounded, shopping seemed like the most important enterprise of her life . . . almost as if there was something she truly needed to find, to buy. Something of vast importance. A treasure hunt of mega portent . . . and uncomfortably dark. If only by the shiver down her spine, she realized her accuracy. Whatever this wily husband of hers intended for her to search and find . . . it was most definitely not a piece of wood from the Crucifixion of Christ.

Even Tad squirmed slightly within his safe cocoon, startling and distracting her from her internal kibitzing. Odd, very odd, that her thoughts seemed to genuinely affect this little spark of creation no larger than her fist. Ridiculous, of course. Even conceding to the latest theory that a child in the womb could be influenced by external stimuli—like reading medical journals and giving birth to another Dr. Spock—the idea of this tiny flicker of life grasping external or internal thought was absurd. And for her safety, her sanity, she refused to debate that issue further.

If anything, her emotional roller coaster had affected her physical system, and the little fellow was suffering from a physiological influx of adrenalin through the umbilical cord. She would need to be careful. She could just imagine giving birth to a neurotic with stomach ulcers from day one.

Shopping. She was the wife of an antique dealer, a partner in that uneventful, rewarding enterprise. Nothing could be more natural than spending a morning in search of treasures.

At the first stoplight, Ronnie turned off the main avenue, unconsciously glimpsing the sedan navigating the turn two cars back. Protection or threat? She had yet to decide, but as long as she knew they were there, she couldn't find fault in dragging them around.

That didn't mean she intended to make their job easy. At the last possible moment, she switched on her turning signal and braked, nearly wearing the front grill of the car behind her, sliding the pickup into a slot at the curb.

Torture, raw torture, the ancient projector reel clattered and clinked in a monotonous rhythm as the scratchy old film scrolled across the wide screen. Larger than life, the black and white images jerked like broken marionettes through a natural fog. In his mind, he heard the click of the projector and saw the gray-on-gray figures shuffling in the mist, their animation distorted by the time-worn quality of the film. White spots, black streaks of imperfection, but the procession was clear . . . heads lowered, hats, scarves, heavy coats, and long skirts. The beat of a train engine hammered at the edges of his mind, and he heard himself moaning as he tried to drag his focus away.

He knew this place, felt the panic and fear beneath the surface of the eyes that ducked away from him, fearing to look at him . . . he'd been here before, pushed and shoved through the crowd and feeling the uncertainty in the bodies around him. A factory . . . the train . . . the click of the camera. Voices, then, shouting orders and shoving at the bodies, tearing children from their father's arms, shoving mothers against mothers. He knew what they intended to do, and it sickened him . . . but he couldn't pull away. The showers . . . they had to strip off their clothes . . . and those pictures came to him, spindly men, stout men, sagging women, and young girls, children . . . into the showers . . .

And he saw him then, the face behind the film, coaching, issuing orders, marching the half-starved bodies . . . eins, zwei, drei . . . zehn. Into the pits, they were marched ten at a time, and he watched them following commands to lie down upon the dirt . . . a line of soldiers stood on the rim of the pits, swilling vodka, loading rifles. Music blared, crackling from overhead speakers . . . and the weapons opened fire.

On dual planes, boy and man, observer and participant, he watched the film scrolling through his mind, heard his sobs, and felt himself buckling from the images splashed on the screen, but no escape existed from those inside his head. He heard the screams and terror as poison gas sprayed from the vents, and he viewed the faces of the soldiers, rigid and unmoved, refusing to leave their posts outside the door as the cries of slaughter and fists pounded on the doors. Inside, outside, and in his mind now, he knew he'd touched this place, touched . . . someone from this place. The evil he'd brushed inside these walls . . . outside these walls . . . transcended time, carried to him . . . And in an odd moment, he saw his mother's face above him. Her eyes searched him, sparking with the strange fervor that reflected her interest and excitement as she listened to the soft rambling words off his lips.

". . . Touched the hand of the devil . . ."

And the face of the devil appeared in his mind's eye, an ordinary face except for the eyes, eyes as black and empty as pitch. A smile twisted on his thin lips as he admitted to using human subjects to evaluate the effects of chemical warfare on Nazi troops. Within the small soundproof room, the monster spoke of the benefits of human experimentation, severing arms to perfect procedural repairs on their soldiers, and the effects of blood loss from the same. To his small audience, he spoke of freezing bodies, injecting diseases, testing chemicals . . . and the test subjects wouldn't necessarily need to know, he professed to a select few. Soldiers could be used as easily as Jews and Roma. Average citizens could be lured into mind traps. So, it had begun and not ended.

Trapped in the mind of the monster, he couldn't pull away but rather watched as the madness continued. But this wasn't Auschwitz . . . this was Arlington, Virginia, USA . . ..

In a fierce grip, his mother held his shimmering palm to the silk, and the lacey edges fluttered around his small white hand as if attempting to escape.

"Nooo, Mom`ma," he heaved as the images flashed faster, flickering now like tiny stars exploding in his mind's eye. In one flash, he saw himself strapped and writhing within a leather chair; in another, he saw himself sitting within a vault, his head caught in his hands, elbows on his knees. And still faster, he saw the pockmarked young face . . . blue eyes transfixed and fascinated by the images flashing on the screen, the young scrawny body growing excited by the horrors and intriguing the keepers. And still more, the faces of the madmen who would entrap innocent souls—

At the bloody red bust of a human face, a face without flesh, eyes bulging like bloody marbles from the mass of red tissue, the scream exploded off his lips.

Breaking free of the grip on his wrist, he fled from the table, searching blindly for an escape. Any escape. He slammed into the wall, staggering, stumbling, slamming the laden shelves with a force to topple a kaleidoscope of urns into his path, and still, he continued. Ramming the corner, he collapsed into himself, aware of his mother, aware of another—his lover, his friend, rising and reacting to his terror, coming to rescue him. His angel . . .

Sobbing, heaving breaths and sounds, he cowered in the corner, his small body compacting as the words sailed through his mind. The hand of the devil . . . and the devil was alive. Protected. Working his wicked deeds. "Here, Mom`ma . . . he is here. She knows him; her husband knows him, knows what he's done. So many dead . . . blood on his hands. Oh, Mom`ma, what he's done and still doing. The madness . . . and they let him continue. . . He's still experimenting. Only . . . only now, he's wasting American lives, and they're protecting him . . . He murdered hundreds . . . thousands . . . and they let him come here . . . to this country. . . to continue . . . and they're creating another—"

"Heartbeat's accelerating. Blood pressure's climbing . . . He's waking up, doctor!"

"Not possible!"

Possible or not, he was waking and fully aware of the medical apparatus surrounding him for the second time in his life. A repeat performance, like an encore, and at a base level, the circumstances amused him. He wasn't a child, and whether hovering on the brink of death or swamped under a drug-induced stasis, he would grant them no more than he deemed necessary.

A psychic . . . they wanted proof positive of his abilities. And the irony struck him even more amusing as the mad scientist issued orders for more sedation, and the three attending assistants questioned his orders.

"Doctor, we've already—"

"Do as I say! Stat!"

Ah, medical terms. Stat. No differently than the mad doctor of yesteryear, this one failed to grasp the simple fact laid before him. Attempting to study psychic phenomena without the psychic's consent was rather like trying to catch time in a bottle.

With a whisper of a smile haunting his mustached lips, he faded under another injection.

CHAPTER 2

Elmview was an antique dealer's delight with its multitude of tiny shops and private enterprises set up in storefronts or garages with a single rustic shingle tacked to a lamppost or door ornament. At one time or another, this small shop had probably been a corner pharmacy or hardware store. Hardwood floors creaked underfoot, shelves sagged under the weight of too many stacked dishes, and dust clung to wicker baskets tucked under a collection of chairs and tables, which would demand a great deal of attention to repair and refinish. With an eye for detail, Ronnie spotted a set of Candlewick candlesticks so covered in grime that the milk glass looked more like gray marble.

The young woman, who'd hustled from behind the sales desk—a college student, apparently killing time and making hamburger money—bubbled incessantly alongside Ronnie as she meandered through the narrow aisles. If nothing else, the young lady conveyed her enthusiasm for business as clearly as her ineptitude in the antique trade. She probably majored in Economics, which had no bearing on the intrinsic value of a hunk of glass from the pre-Depression era. After a thorough, if somewhat swift perusal, Ronnie found a few more pieces of china and crystal, mentally calculating the quick sales to a few of her choice customers. On a whim, she added one of the wicker baskets, thinking it might clean up nice and offer a pleasant touch to the nursery . . . a diaper pail.

If the girl wondered why Ronnie smiled a little wryly, she was too polite to ask, more than happy to bustle the basket to the counter and diligently add another discounted value to the tab.

Remembering how she'd refrained from using 'antique dealer' as her cover when entering Bentwood four months prior, Ronnie offered the genuine tax number card, smiling even more wryly. Jade would have known her lie long before asking for her tax number. Collector, she'd admitted, refraining from boasting about her profession, which, in twenty-twenty hindsight, would have put him off instantly. A premonition then that she'd eventually carry an official, legitimate card to buy antiques at dealers' wholesale prices. As an added benefit, the card spared them from paying taxes twice on any given item.

Her husband, she'd discovered, was a stickler for bookkeeping, a detail which undoubtedly stemmed from some undisclosed distrust of the government. He refused in no uncertain terms to pay one cent more than his due to the IRS, and considering his bank account, his due amounted to more than an average citizen earned in a year. She saved less than five dollars, she noted while tucking the receipt in her purse, but it was five dollars less than she would need to charge to break even on the ultimate sales.

Big business, she mused while collecting the basket into which the girl had tucked the glassware—carefully rolled and mounded in newspapers. Hurrying, the young woman rounded the makeshift counter and held the door, bidding Ronnie a pleasant day before ducking inside to continue reading the latest fashion magazine.

Placing the basket close to the cab, Ronnie glimpsed the sedan parked down the block, wondering if her pals were bored yet. Surveillance had to be the dreariest lot of a federal agent, not to mention the most oppressive. To spend one's morning governed by the whim and whimsy of another could rank right up there with cleaning johns in a train station. Life passing them by.

Behind the wheel of her pickup, Ronnie sped past the sedan, navigating the first right turn before the sedan even ignited its engine. Maybe she would be kind and run a stop to give them a thrill. On second thought, she would rather not run into a certain police chief of questionable character. The Trumble case was closed.

Maintaining a reasonable speed and exercising safe driving practices at every turn, Ronnie considered her passive-aggressive antics, keeping the speedometer at the exact required speed limit, whether 15 mph in a school zone or 25 mph on a secondary. If she hadn't spoken to Agent Len Devinio about this surveillance, doubtful she would be taking it so lightly, but until these fellows offered her a reason to worry—or Len called with the same—she determined to enjoy herself.

Stopping, browsing, kibitzing, and socializing, Ronnie visited a half dozen more shops, accumulating a dozen more boxes, crates, baskets, and bags. With the pickup half full and a warehouse load of new friends and acquaintances,

Ronnie considered heading for Bentwood, but the niggling thought that something else existed, something she needed to find, veered her course yet again.

Something . . . another shop. Another . . . a smaller shop. One of the backdoor vendors, she considered and nearly cursed aloud with her frustration. If there was another man like that farmer, Monty Montgomery, who'd added insight to Hank Ryder's character while producing a wooden trunk of ancient tools to be purchased, at least her wily husband could have lent her a few blasted clues.

Curiously, the sense that he might have done exactly that, fleeted through her mind.

Jack Trumble—real estate agent deceased by a questionable auto accident.

Hank Ryder—a ninety-plus-year-old farmer deceased by natural—or unnatural causes—with his heirs manipulating his last will and testament, which might have led to Trumble's demise.

Rich Logan—a crooked sheriff, possibly involved in the scam.

As the names continued to scroll through her mind, Ronnie halted at a stop sign, tempted to head toward the highway and home.

Whitman—a former chief of police. Probably on the take.

Finn and Lucy Briggers—antique dealers and old timers with a colorful history. Old timers with a great deal of local history and a distrust for the government to rival Jade's?

Consciously or subconsciously, Ronnie dispatched her turning signal and glided smoothly on course. Finn and Lucy Briggers. She and Donna had visited their shop—Finn's Corner—yesterday afternoon. Like every other blasted place that she and Donna had stopped the previous day, this elder couple had known Jade as Zack, and clearly, they'd met him more than a time or two.

A good story, Ronnie considered. The zany older couple had freely offered information concerning a successful realtor's early demise, along with the rumor about a toxic dump coming to town. As an encore, they'd wound a comical whopper about a local celebrity, Ethel Savrel, a rowdy, fire-spitting madame who'd plied a trade that any law-abiding, God-fearing farming community would find slightly undesirable. Considering Finn's age and the youthful zeal he'd displayed during that nostalgic interlude, Ronnie estimated Ethel's crime spree had spanned the Prohibition Era and might have limped through the Depression and World War II. The lady had passed away more than twenty years ago, but her stay on this earth had made an impression on a few good men—and boys. What more could a woman ask in a lifetime?

A scent of chalk dust and sunbaked glass swirled within the bright streamers slanting through the slits in the half-mast blinds . . . and he knew himself, here, at this moment. His classroom in St. Augustine's Academy

Squinting against the brightness reflected on the yellow paper in front of him, he scrolled another number, his attention lifting to the blackboard where Miss Andros jotted another problem on the slate. Like every boy in the class, Jade worked extra hard for this young teacher who could warm him with a smile and touch him with her gentleness . . .

But his head hurt suddenly. His hand lifted and rubbed his throbbing temple as a shiver skittered down his spine. A mild panic touched him with the knowledge of what could be happening to him, what would happen . . . no control. The headaches came on too suddenly, and they were getting worse, frighteningly more frequent. Heavily, his elbow skidded on the desk, wrinkling the paper as his head dropped more leaden in his palm. It hurt. His head hurt, pulsing against his palm as if something alive pounded against his skull, trying to get out. Uncontrollably, the tears lifted as the pain increased. Dying. He was dying. His head would explode.

His head sank more. A moan slipped off his lips as he buried his face against his folded arm. He lost his grip on the pencil and heard it plink on the wood floor as he clasped his skull with his vacant fingers. The headache had him . . . no control. He understood the hand touching him, but suddenly, all other images shattered with the crease of pain lancing his forehead.

"Mayday! Mayday!" *the pilot shouted into the headsets. The instrument panel lit up like a Christmas tree in front of him, screaming every kind of failure from the engines to the landing gear. They were going down!* "Buckle up!" the "We're going down . . .!"

". . . And I'm telling you, director, this is not Laquette! I believe those reports coming in from Kentucky are far more accurate."

He woke resting on a too-familiar bed in the nurses' office at St. Augustine's Academy. Barely he blinked and gasped when the blood erupted as terrifying as the smell and salty taste in his mouth. He was falling—then running. He ran blind, battling the hands trying to stop him, racing and slamming open the glass doors, launching into the blinding afternoon light. He heard the shouts behind him. Panic only drove him faster. His smooth leather soles barely skimmed the sidewalk as he gulped against the blood in his mouth, on his lips. Through the red haze spilling over his eyes, he followed the path that he walked every morning, every afternoon. St. Augustine's Academy . . . his private school.

The beginning.

By the time he pushed through the cast iron gates, something had happened inside him. Slowly, every step forced, he climbed the steps to the front door . . . the main entry. He never entered by the main entry— preferred the kitchen entrance where he wouldn't cross paths with his mother's clients. The inside door stood open. Open just a half foot, he noticed, while pulling open the storm door where the letter "L" was scrolled ornately within the black screen guard. Leaded glass skylights stood to either side of the door, spilling a kaleidoscope of color into the vast main entry. With the animation of a manikin, he pushed open the door, and his attention halted, riveted.

He'd seen her like this before, sprawled in the center of the bright tile. Black chiffon wings swelled from her spread arms like a black angel in flight. Forever, it seemed, he stood staring at her long legs covered meticulously in the sheer cloth, her silk slipper-covered feet pointed toward him from opposite poles.

This image he'd seen and understood. Not natural this pose. Her hands lay open, palms up, both positioned to fill the side points of a pentagram. He understood those symbols. He'd seen them thousands of times in his mother's books, on her star charts, in her doodling in the margins of notebooks. She lay in the pentagram, now, and it seemed a mercy. But a conflicted mercy. From the doorway, the light at his back, the kaleidoscopic hues blinding against the tiles around him, he stood looking at the pale face turned upward. The gypsy-black eyes stared at the teardrop crystals of the chandelier directly over her head, and he followed that blind gaze to the wide circle under which she rested. The circle and the pentagram—and a star splatter of blood in the center of her forehead. One thread spiraled at her temple and vanished into the dark flowing waves forming a halo around her slender face, and another trail slid into the pocket of her eye socket. A mere trickle of crimson slipped from the corner of her parted lips.

And he'd seen all of this before.

Resigned, he nudged the door closed behind him and walked past her feet. In leaden steps, he reached the living room, lifted the telephone receiver, and spoke with the automation of a robot to the operator. The message conveyed, he settled at the corner of the couch and studied his blood-smudged fingers folded on his lap. Unsurprised, he watched the crimson hue begin to fade. Chalk dust turned his fingers white; he'd cleaned the blackboard for Miss Andros during recess just before his math class.

He was still sitting in the corner of the couch when the voices erupted, first hushed. Then anxious and rushed. To the strange tense faces, he spoke his name, but it was a lie, that name. No truer for him than the "L" boasted on the front door. Just a name, his name of the moment. Nothing more needed said, not until the homicide detective led him up the back stairwell, sparing him the rush of voices and strangers, the crude irreverence of the coroner mentioning the staged position postmortem.

"What happened here, son? What can you tell me?" Det. Max Hagen's voice carried a quiet quality of confidence and reassurance, lulling in its rhythm.

"Mom`ma's dead," he answered as he gazed at his creation of clay monsters standing in a neat row on his dresser. Monsters. Little clay monsters dressed in 1940 uniforms. Monsters in lab coats pretending to be doctors. Monsters like him, pretending to be human.

"Son, I need you to tell me whatever you can," the deep voice coaxed and cajoled. A warm hand touched his shoulder.

In lightning flash illumination, other images erupted, from bloodied faces and hands to weeping and wailing mothers and children . . . but the face of an angel intruded, overwhelming the violent images conveyed through the palm pressed at his shoulder. "Did you see anyone here? Were you here when this happened?"

Staring blind, he found voice. "You won't find her killer, sir. But that's okay," he admitted softly. "I will," he confided as he lay down on his colorful quilt, a quilt Nan Duncan had given him not long ago. 'Fresh from the factory,' she promised, but still, he'd seen the faces of weavers and factory workers, of delivery men. Lying on his side, he gazed at the closed drapes.

Outside, the sunlight glowed brilliantly, but the dull brown glow in his room eclipsed that light. Always on the outside, the light. "I'll know what to do when the time comes, and it's all right." He found the familiar face of the police detective hovering above him and managed a sad smile. The immense hand still weighted his shoulder, offering genuine comfort despite the disturbing images.

Sadly, he continued, "That nightgown is new. I took all the others . . . threw them all away. But Mom`ma—she went and bought another one. Why did she do that? Why would she do that when I begged her never to wear another black one? I took them all so this couldn't happen. So I wouldn't see her like that. Why didn't she listen to me, sir? She knows what I am."

"What are you, son?"

"You won't believe me . . . But others will. I think they know already . . . and they'll come for me next. But it doesn't matter . . . They can't kill me. I just wish they wouldn't try, but they will, you know? I think I've seen that too," he said as his gaze drifted to the curtain and his fingers clamped tighter on the pillow. "They will try . . ."

CHAPTER 3

With the Spencers traipsing around town, Ronnie pulled the pickup into the small gravel lot behind the Briggers' shop, relying on her intuition that she'd find a delivery entrance in the rear. And she wasn't disappointed. Like Olden Time, Finn's Corner butted an alley with a private entry to the back rooms. The Briggers, like Jade, undoubtedly spent hours sorting, cataloging, and repairing their wares despite the cluttered atmosphere in the public area of the store. Display room or showroom couldn't quite apply to the Briggers' crowded flea-market-style.

Rather than risk the Spencers driving by as she entered the front of the shop, Ronnie strode purposefully to the wide, swinging garage doors and found the bell to beckon one or another of the shopkeepers. Even as she awaited the dealers, she heard the engine vibration of the sedan echoing between the side of the nearest building and a garage crowded at the mouth of the alley. Tempted to climb into the pickup and back into her escorts' path to see how they'd handle that crisis; Ronnie already wore a wry smile when Lucy opened the door.

If the woman even questioned Ronnie arriving at the backdoor, no hint of it reached her delighted smile or livid eyes as she flung the door open wider. "Finn wondered if you might stop by again. Come on in . . . Where's that nice friend of yours today?"

"We decided we could cover more ground if we split up for a while," Ronnie commented, smiling. "And our tastes are a little different," she added while entering the dusky warehouse. Even with tracts of florescent light scattered over the open rafters, the atmosphere carried a perpetual shade that seemed reflective of antique dealers, and it was no wonder her husband found the business appealing. He might have walked into a stockroom like this years ago and formed an instant, intimate connection.

As Lucy closed and latched the door behind Ronnie, the shade thickened, and somewhere in the shop, a clock chimed a distinctly morose sound that sent a weird tingle over Ronnie's shoulders. Time. "Olden Time." Time to get moving. The time has come. Time to do something . . .

She muttered a curse aloud at the eccentric thoughts flashing through her mind.

"Just watch your step," Lucy coaxed while taking the lead through barely passable aisles. Old farm equipment, from rakes to scythes, scattered between wooden and cardboard boxes. "I keep threatening if he don't clear out some of this stuff, we won't even have room to breathe back here."

"I know the feeling," Ronnie admitted. "We have several rooms that look exactly like this."

"That's the price we pay for hooking up with junk dealers," Lucy said as if the entire idea were a burden, but the sparkle in her eyes betrayed her love of the same. "Somehow, I just don't think you two will ever let a place get this bad. Not 'til you're our age, anyway."

"How long have you had this shop, ma'am?" Ronnie asked as she stepped carefully over a stack of plastic-wrapped papers that had apparently suffered from a slight breeze recently. Belatedly, she identified the comic books, and with her sudden preoccupation, she missed whatever Lucy said. Stooped, she began gathering the books, recognizing enough of the covers to know these had been around for a while. And they were probably worth a great deal. Shaking her head, she collected the scatter, glancing over the top books. Her attention snagged on another small box as she replaced the magazines.

Baseball cards!

Wade Kreider sprung to mind. That youngster had already built a fortune in cards thanks to a certain wily antique dealer.

"We just got that lot in a couple hours ago," Lucy said while returning to hover over Ronnie's shoulder.

"Any chance you'd consider parting with it?" Ronnie asked as she pushed afoot, turning in the narrow space to find Lucy smiling with a wry grin.

"I hope you're not taking too many lessons from your husband, dear," she said and patted Ronnie's arm. With a vibration of laughter, she decided, "I'll let you talk to Finn about that lot, but for heaven's sake, don't let him think that he even has a slight chance of swindling you. The first time Zack came by here, he let Finn hoodwink him out of a small fortune." Conspiratorially, the woman leaned into Ronnie, nearly whispering, "Finn felt so danged guilty, he ended up sending Zack the latest edition of the Schroeder's Antiques Price Guide a couple weeks later. Just don't tell either one I told you. It's too much fun watching them dance around the issue of that book, both of them pretending they're dumb as dirt about pricing."

Laughing, Ronnie followed Lucy through the connecting door and spotted Finn bidding someone farewell at the main entrance. With only slight improvements in the lighting and walking space, the adjoining rooms could pass for one. The same comfortable clutter and weathered ambiance touched Ronnie, waking a weird homesickness within her. She needed to get home. Wanted to be home. And home was Olden Time. Even if they managed to find and buy property to build a house and haven in the woods, that old shop would be their first home . . . and why did that thought suddenly bring tears to her eyes? With an iron will, she blinked the tiny sting from the corner of her eyes, managing to recover before Finn spotted her and called a hearty welcome.

"I sort of thought I might see you again, gal," Finn said with a twitch of a smile on his day-stubbled lips. "Where's that pretty little thing you had with you yesterday?"

"In search of music boxes," Ronnie said honestly. "She'll probably stick around for another day or so, but I'm heading home in a little while. Just thought I'd stop back and see if there's anything I missed. Zack wasn't too specific about what I should look for."

"Knew that boy was scatterbrained the first time I laid eyes on him," Finn said with a wink and a smile. "And it sure ain't no surprise he didn't give you any help. The good lord knows, he don't even know what he's looking for half the time when he comes in here."

"She took an interest in that lot of books and cards you just bought, Finn," Lucy helped while sidling around the old bar-top counter to perch on a tattered bar stool. Glancing at Ronnie with a conspiratorial twinkle, she continued, "I told her she might be able to pick it up reasonable since your eyes ain't what they used to be."

"What's my eyes got to do with it?" Finn bought with a cagey grumble, a lifted gray brow that formed a perfect question mark above his twinkling eyes.

"Mighty hard looking up all those titles when you won't go and get your new glasses."

"My old glasses work just fine, don't you worry, gal."

Leaning on the bar, listening and enjoying the elder pair hashing it out, Ronnie waited for the argument to end, knowing the ruse. Behind the battle,

Finn had considered the business end of the transaction, and by no surprise, he forfeited his bantering to comment, “I could probably let you have that lot for a franklin, missus. There’s some pretty decent cards in that box—if you know anything about baseball card collecting. Me—I’d just as soon steer clear of that kind of trade anyway. We’d get too many kids running in and out of here, and we get our fair share now.”

“I’ll think about it, okay? I’d like to browse . . . Well, that’s not exactly true. I was thinking about that story you told us yesterday. About Ethel.”

Finn’s eyes lighted with mischief. “Fine lady, she sure was.”

“Oh, now you done it,” Lucy heaved in mocked exasperation. “You’ll have him started up again.”

“What’s on your mind?” Finn asked.

“This will probably sound just a little bit weird,” Ronnie said with her smile intact. “But I’d really love to have something from a genuine bordello. My uh . . .” Curiosity flickered in Finn’s shaded eyes. Ronnie continued, adopting a sheepish grin. “My husband and I have this running battle about the French, and I’d absolutely love to see his face if I could hand him something from an honest-to-God cathouse.” She refrained from mentioning that their bedroom—before her decorating skills demanded a change—had reflected the unmistakable flair of a French bordello. “Is there even a slight chance I could find something of Ethel’s anywhere in town?”

The atmosphere had changed suddenly, almost as if a cold wind had blown through dusty rafters, and both Briggers seemed to notice, exchanging glances that were not as comical as a few moments earlier. Something unspoken passed between them, making Ronnie extremely uncomfortable before Finn eyed her with a slightly troubled brow.

The difference was too large to ignore. “Uh . . . if I said something to offend you—“

“No, missus. Nothing like that,” Finn said hurriedly, his elbow hooked on the bar adopting the posture of a bent old man that defied his nature. “Just strikes me . . . was maybe a year or so ago, I had a conversation with the boy. Reminded me, that’s all.”

“I uh . . . hope you’ll explain, sir.”

“Ethel has a way of cropping up in conversations, now and again,” Finn said, attempting to smile, but the spark had faded. “She sure was something. A legend, if you know what I mean. Feistiest old dame you’d ever meet, and she sure had a way of getting around.”

This was leading somewhere; Ronnie was just not sure where exactly.

"Fact is, when she passed on, her stuff got auctioned off. Folks, they came from as far away as New York just to bid on some of the stuff that old girl collected. She had more genuine Tiffany lamps than you could shake a stick at and jewelry—by Christ, that old girl could have outfitted a whole company of Broadway dancers. And mind you, gal, it wasn't cheap imitation, either. When Ethel wore a pearl, you could be damned sure it came from the Orient. She used to wear this diamond brooch with a rock the size of my thumbnail until some scallywag tried to heist it right off her—"

"Finn."

"Well, you know what," he said while fleeting a more natural smirk toward his wife. His eyes lighting a sparkle, he continued, finding his rhythm. "After she danged near beat that boy to a pulp, the sheriff asked her to keep that brooch under lock and key for public safety. Truth be known, he threatened to arrest her if she wore it again, seeing as how it would be a public nuisance or some shit." He barely paused, "That brooch sold in the neighborhood of fifty grand at that auction, and that was more than twenty-five years ago. Don't know how much truth there was to it, but somebody said it was worn by that queen of France in the 1700s. Ya know, the one that got her head chopped off?"

"Marie Antoinette?" Ronnie guessed with a slight smile, considering the providence. French queen, French bordello. French psychic.

"That's the one," Finn said soberly and continued, "Couldn't prove it by me. I didn't have fifty bucks to waste on it back then, not that I got much more than that now. I was mostly just picking up scrap metal and iron around that time, seeing as how I was still working at the Foundry over in Johnstown.

"Anyway, like I was saying, folks came from all over to buy a little piece of Ethel, and if I remember right, the proceeds went to the orphans' home out on Bristol Lane. There, toward the end, I guess you'd say Ethel tried to make up for some of the unsavory things she'd done over the years. She had a hell of a lot to do with getting the college started here in town, but you won't find that in any history books. Any more than you'd see her name on that girls' home. Was more just us knowing that when a roof got fixed, the money come from somewhere. The same way it come when the college faculty decided they had to shitcan the addition of a library for lack of funds."

"Ethel didn't have any family of her own?" Ronnie guessed, once again enthralled by the story and rhythm.

"There's folks who will tell you one of the first infants out at the orphans' home was Ethel's, but don't you believe it. I know, for a fact, that first youngin' was born in one of the high society houses just out the road a piece. Fact is—if Ethel ever had a child, she didn't have it here."

"Then you think she did."

"She traveled a lot, honey," Lucy said lightly. "Sometimes she'd be gone for the better part of a year, and it's just speculation, but we all sort of figure she had a lot of relatives, probably in Europe. She always left with a steamer trunk."

"And usually came back with two or three," Finn mused, shaking his shock of gray hair. "If she had family—or kids—we suspect she left them on the far side of the Atlantic. There was something special about that lady. She had a certain kind of class that you can't buy in a bottle if you know what I mean. Sort of like yourself," he said, then nearly bit his tongue. "Now, don't you take that wrong. I'm not likening you to what Ethel did for a living."

Amused, Ronnie shook her head. "I didn't think you were."

"It's just that way of looking at the world. Maybe a worldly look," Finn pondered, spying her in soft speculation. "Your man has it, too. A way of looking eye to eye and not giving a damned what somebody else is thinking or saying. I'd bet dollars to donuts that you'd have given Ethel a run for her money if she crossed you, but I sort of doubt, you'd have looked down on her like some of the folks in town tried a few times. Lady or not, that dame wouldn't take no guff from man nor beast . . . nor Puritan," he added with a reflective twinkle that preceded another tale. "She laid the Lady Flanigan—and I'm not shitting you, gal, that's what Irma Flanigan liked to be called, The Lady Flanigan . . . right up until her bible-toting husband passed away and she became the Widow Flanigan. Anyway, Ethel laid her flat out in the center of town after a church social. One punch—that was all it took. Was one a the funniest damn things I ever had the pleasure to witness, and I couldn't have been more than ten or twelve at the time. Still funny . . . all those hoops and petticoats tumbling as the Widow Flanigan went ass over tin cups. Course, Ethel almost ended up in jail over it, but I'll tell you, it was worth the price of admission . . . ."

Even now, Ronnie guessed, noting the shine in both older pairs of eyes.

"Guess we sort of got off the track a little bit," Finn said with a slightly tainted shine, his gaze landing and focusing, less misty with nostalgia. "There's not much left of Ethel around here. The fellas in town who could afford it were too afraid to bid on any of that stuff lest their wives got wind of their interest.

Probably a bunch of sorry sons a bitches went to their graves wishing they had a little reminder of Ethel."

But Finn Briggers would never be one of them. Apparently, he'd purchased something at that auction, but his reaction to the thought of that artifact rang a sour note in Ronnie's mind. She could do without it. Only that thought held momentarily. Whatever it was, she wanted no part of it.

"Funny, you asking about Ethel," Finn said pensively. "I mean wanting something of hers to take to your man. I didn't even give it a thought when you were here yesterday. Been a hell of a long time since him and me talked about it."

"Mr. Briggers, I—"

"Just Finn, gal," he said and pushed off his elbow, fleeting a glance at Lucy. "Mind the store, Luce."

More positive that she wanted nothing to do with whatever created the tension in this elder pair, Ronnie accepted the hand signal to follow and trailed after Finn toward the backroom. Insanity. Certainly, some artifact from a bordello couldn't be that bad . . . Unless it was some kind of warped dildo, in which case, it was doubtful Lucy would allow her husband to show it off to an unsuspecting customer. Let alone a female customer.

"Back when I bought this here thing, I didn't know what the hell it was, but I figured it for around the WWII era," Finn said as he pushed and held the door for Ronnie to pass through. "Mind you, if I'd have known, there's no way I'd have bid on it. Can't imagine Ethel even having it if she knew what it was. Figure it was one of those things one of her customers give her, and she tucked it away in a back room, the same as I've done all these years. Sure ain't something I'd want sitting on an end table. The fact is, I damned near burnt it a long time ago. Never did figure out why I held onto it."

"Mr. Briggers . . . Finn—if you've kept it this long, I really don't think you should part with it—"

Leading her toward a corner of the room where metal shelves might have stood for the past twenty-five if not fifty years, Finn continued, "That's what's funny about this, Mrs. Bently."

"Please, just Ronnie," she offered rather than explain the name change her husband had undergone. Bad enough one of the shops she'd visited earlier had demanded to see her driver's license after reading the tax number. Olden Time and Jade Laquette were not related in this town. That only one dealer had questioned her authenticity was the only surprise.

Finn reached the corner, bending and dragging a stout dusty wine barrel closer to the shelf, then climbed up with the agility to betray his advancing years. Stretching toward a high shelf, he latched onto a large cardboard box coated in black dust and visibly aged.

"Really, Finn. This isn't necessary," Ronnie tried again, unnaturally tense as she stepped closer—either to keep the elder man from falling or dropping the box on his head as he wiggled it free of its perch. "I just thought a hairbrush or a vanity mirror—"

Grunting, he dragged the box from the shelf, stirring up enough dust for him to sneeze as he caught his balance. Before she could decline again, Finn lowered the box into Ronnie's hands and caught her eyes from his elevated position. Already, his beard stubble wore a haze of dust, and his brows arched in grayer points. "Your man said he wouldn't buy it from me but maybe someday somebody would give it to him as a gift," he said bluntly. "Me, I'm too damned old to think about how funny some things work out. You just take it off my hands and give it to that man of yours."

"I-I'm not sure I understand this, Finn," Ronnie admitted, uncomfortably tense as she felt the considerable weight of the box. "Maybe you better tell me what it is I'm buying."

"You're not buying it, gal," Finn said and nearly buckled to another sneeze as he grunted, stepping off the wine barrel. Across the top of the box, he caught her gaze again while bringing a handkerchief from his pocket, wiping his nose, and halting the sneeze. "I'm giving it to you to give to him. I've had that damned thing sitting on my shelf too damned long." As if belatedly sensing her distress, both with the size and the puzzle, he reached and took the box from her grasp. "Here, I'll put that in your truck. No use you getting all dirty."

"Finn," Ronnie stated as he brushed passed her. "I'm not sure this is something I'd like—"

Stopping, he looked over his shoulder with a shine of dismay in his eyes. "I was about three sheets to the wind when I bid on this thing twenty-five years ago. Took me a good long time to figure out what it was, but your man, he wasn't drunk when I let him have a look at it. Don't think he really liked it much, but it sure seemed like he'd be the one to take it off my hands. I wouldn't suggest you look at it. Just take it along. He can figure out what to do with it . . . unless you're really against having it, then I guess, I'll just shove it back up there."

A treasure hunt . . . and this was the treasure she'd been sent here to find. A quarter inch of dust—nearly soot—layered the overlapping flaps and disguised the frayed edges of the cardboard. The folds appeared undisturbed for two dozen years, countering any thought of Jade actually looking inside this ominous box. If he'd alluded to taking possession of it though . . .

The sense of following a plan, his plan, eliminated her doubts. Troubled, she nodded and looked at Finn. "All right. I'll give it to him."

And she would take the comic books and baseball cards as well she decided as she followed Finn through the shadows which seemed far more oppressive now. Stooping, she collected the smaller of the two boxes and returned to her feet, catching up to Finn outside. Not once since stepping out of the hotel this morning, had she truly taken a moment to appreciate the unseasonably warm weather or the sunlight streaming down through the buildings. Presently, nothing had struck her as more beautiful and welcome than the breath of clean air she drew while unlocking the passenger door. "I'll take the books and cards, too," she said offhandedly, glimpsing at Finn who stretched over the tailgate to position the box in a safe corner. Just the thought of it nearly countered the heated air flowing from the cab as she opened the door.

"I'll just go and get them then," he said and passed her in what appeared to be a hurry.

Uncomfortably, Ronnie stood alongside the truck, unconsciously drawn to spy the shabby box. On the surface, it appeared as harmless and natural as the truckload of other items, but somehow, she knew the illusion. Whatever that box contained, it wasn't pleasant, and decidedly, it could remain a mystery for a while longer. When she caught up with her wily husband, he better have a damn good reason for sending her on this blasted errand.

Finn arrived, his smiling natural self again, gingerly sliding the box of magazines onto the precarious mound in her front seat. "Looks like you been mighty busy for a gal without any clear directions."

"The price of such a venture, Finn," she said in a sighing tone. "After my dear husband sees what all I've bought, I doubt he'll leave this end of the business to me in the future."

Finn chuckled, waiting for her to lock the cab before starting them into the shop. "Think you're going to catch on just fine to this business . . . but I think I'm going to have to give you a few pointers like I did your man. It's a good rule of thumb, never jump at a fella's first offer. Like them comic books and cards . . . you can't just figure everybody in this business is going to be honest with you. If I was a shyster, I coulda told you there was just about anything in that lot and maybe the only good one was on top. You can't just trust every Tom, Dick, or Harry to come along, Miss Ronnie. You have to do a little haggling and really look at what you're buying."

"I assume you'll give me a fair deal, Finn, and I do know a little bit about cards—" At least what she'd learned from Wade over the past few months. "I don't trust everyone," she said and sent Finn a glance to suggest, he was exclusive.

By his frown, his attempt to teach her a lesson had backfired; a fact corrected when they stood at the counter and he handed her the sales ticket with his, "Figure seventy-five will cover it."

"We agreed on a hundred, Finn," Ronnie said with a slight smile. "I'll pay a hundred and if I lose a few dollars, I'll consider it the cost of an education." Paying in cash, she bid Finn a pleasant farewell and walked through the shop with Lucy leading the way.

Lucy had something on her mind, Ronnie knew, and she was only slightly surprised when the elder woman took her hand, smiling warmly as she offered, "Thank you." Nothing else, just 'thank you.' And Ronnie knew the woman referred to that damned box as if by taking it, she'd done them a tremendous favor. Unfortunately, as Ronnie backed away from the delivery entrance and flagged a wave through her open window, she suffered no such relief or gratitude for collecting that ominous cargo. More than a dozen times before ever reaching the end of Elmview, Ronnie considered pulling over, tugging the lid open, and spying the contents. The dark ill-omen shrouding that damned box hung like a cloud at the edges of her mind, and it wasn't a feeling she could shake, any more than she could calm the quiet wiggling in her gut.

Once on the main highway, her sights set toward home, she continued to contemplate the simplicity of pulling over, and more than once, glanced in the rearview mirror, equally disturbed by a sense of something left undone.

Possibly, a lingering effect of leaving Donna and Tim in Elmview, a reactionary sense of abandoning them . . . or being abandoned by them. They had their life. They deserved a couple of nights together without two kids underfoot and a third . . . a third on the way. Donna would probably tell Tim about their new addition, and Ronnie smiled as she considered his reaction. Tim would probably undergo the full gambit from shock to dread to joy. Without a doubt, he would be surprised when not long ago, he'd mentioned a few more kids, and Donna had read him the riot act. He would be surprised.

Jade never was. He'd known before Ronnie ever breathed the words aloud, and she supposed she'd known by the furtive glances he'd sent her at least a few times before her announcement. Oh, he'd pretended to be surprised, had even attempted to appear stunned and overwhelmed—the shit. He'd known before she had.

Her thoughts turning at lightspeed to offer the truck tires a fair race, she remembered his gentle smile, the quick acceptance and joy . . . and the almost painful sadness that flickered briefly behind his proud pappa smile. Sadness . . . the same sadness she'd seen in the hotel mirror only yesterday morning. A hallucination, she'd believed then, but even in hindsight, she couldn't convince herself of that possibility.

She'd seen him there, lying in a pool of blood . . . and from that pool, he had risen and stepped into the silver, merely looking at her with the warmth in his hazel eyes, the sadness curving his walnut mustache into a dim smile. He'd worn a suit, one of his Italian-cut black suits as if dressed for a ball . . . or a funeral.

A shiver slid down her spine, gripping her hands tighter to the wheel. The man might possess a few weird quirks and unnatural talents, but he wasn't God. He couldn't propose to know all there was to know . . . and with an iron will, she clamped down the fleeting image of that black box in the distant corner of her truck.

CHAPTER 4

Lifelike, he found himself standing in the shade behind the wall of climbing ivy and solid black iron rails of his balcony . . . a child then, no more than eight or nine . . . A man, now, to stand in the shadows, watching, listening . . . Voices were rising from the patio below . . .

Only a moment ago, he'd rested at his desk in his room, lost in his latest mediocre pastime of clay modeling, but the sun streams coming through his French doors had distracted him. He stood in the sunlight, now, a brilliant spring sunlight that should be heating him through his sweatshirt, but nothing of warmth penetrated. In fact, he felt chilled. He'd chilled the moment he'd stepped onto his little window to the world as his mother referred to his private balcony.

Not much of the world could be seen from his balcony unless one considered tree branches a world. The great oak to shade the backyard through three-quarters of the year had already budded like the vine. Sounds of street traffic mixed with whistling birds and the Eldersons' dogs, three little Scotties that his mother threatened to have impounded or something. Dogs were a nuisance, a noisy nuisance, according to Madame Laquette, who thought nothing of housing six cats. Jade liked the cats, but he would have preferred owning a dog. It wasn't as if a guy could teach a cat to fetch or wrestle with one, the way Ernie Carver wrestled with his sheepdog. Jade had decided long ago, when he got older, he would buy a big dog, maybe a Doberman Pincher. Now, *that* was a dog—

"That's nonsense, of course, Miss Laquette," the unfamiliar soft voice lifted on a note of agitation. "You and I both know you're preying on my mother's vulnerability, and I want it stopped," the stranger continued.

“Do not be ridicu`lous, mon chérie,” his mother’s silky voice countered, her lyrical notes lifting over the balcony. “I provide a ser`vous. A very legal, and helpful ser`vous—“

“You’re nothing but a two-bit scam artist—you French slut,” the visitor snapped. “And I’m going to put this simply—either make some excuse to drop my mother as a client, or by God, I’ll have you investigated, and I doubt this little scam of yours will hold up to the scrutiny. I’ll sue you for every nickel my mother’s spent on you and retribution for mental anguish. Is that plain enough—“

“I soog`jest you consid`air those actions carefully, Matilda,” Mother said in a slightly brittle tone. “First of all, ma chérie, your moth`air is a healthy, ma`shure adult, quite capable of making her own decisions, despite her var`ious analysts in the past. Surely, you would not woont this little blemish on your family’s impeccable reputa`tion, nor I am sure, would you enjoy besmir`shing your fath`air’s campaign . . . as I hov told your moth`air, mon amie, he will maintain the senate posi`tion, providing extenuating circum`stanzes do not interfere with this elec`tion. The stars are in his fa`vor, mademoiselle, unless of course, something should transpire to offset—“

“Is this the kind of shit you feed my mother? Making threats? Is this what you’ve already done to destroy my family?”

“Mademoiselle, I und`airstand your skepticism,” his mother said with a placating lyrical tone. “As I hov been expecting your vis`et, and anticipating your hostility, I have no inten`tion of off`airing you any of my prognostica`tions . . .”

Had he? Had he already seen this woman, Matilda, in his mother’s house, warned his mother of her visit?

In a flashing instant, the vision erupted, but not of this young woman. He saw a man, older, not old, sitting behind a pristine table . . . and others existed within this industrial room of slate-gray walls and gray tile floor. A half dozen men wearing suits and ties, impeccably dressed, adorned with ornate watches and signet rings. Decision makers, all of them, and each one studying a collection of documents.

‘What you are proposing, Matthew, could be dangerous for all of us, and I, personally, want nothing to do with it.’

‘It’s a little late to become Pontius Pilot, Rob. Dr. Schrieber is here, and whether we agree with his practices or not, we have a lot to learn.’

'He should never have been brought into this country,' another husky voice commented. 'That screening process should have weeded out this monster. He should have been hanged with the rest of them.'

'For doing what we've been doing in this country for years?'

'Matt—'

'Don't pretend you don't know what I'm talking about. The eugenics program has been in place for years.'

'A family competing in a blasted Fitter Family Contest at a state fair is a far cry from conducting experiments of this nature, Matthew. We're talking about torture and genuine acts against humanity. Even if I believed there was some benefit to these atrocities—which I flatly do not—I cannot condone turning this monster loose to continue this madness.'

'I'd have to agree,' another spoke, while the two others remained silent, merely flipping through the pages. 'If even half of what you've presented here is accurate, I think we'd be better off—as surely the American people would be—by sending Herr Schrieber back to Nuremberg to answer for his crimes, and make no mistake, these are crimes.'

'I don't think we should be too hasty to condemn this fellow, or the others for that matter,' another man spoke, his tone aloof. 'We've already seen what the dilution of the races can do . . . If this doctor can aid in our mission to see our lines pure . . ..'

In stopped time, a snapshot image caught for all eternity in his young mind. An emaciated male body splayed and strapped to a metal table . . . and to his instant horror, he realized the flesh being flayed from the bony arm. Clearly, he saw the gaping mouth trapped on a silent scream, eyes bulging, face twisted—

Not an experiment. Not this!

A hobby!

Whoever held this blade sought neither knowledge nor the betterment of mankind! A hobby! No more, no less! A madman to feed on the pain and suffering!

Stumbling back from the ivy and balcony rail, he swallowed his scream as the voices continued to volley inside his mind.

'Suit yourselves, gentlemen, but you need to understand. It's too late to claim innocence, and if anything we discussed here ever leaves this room, we would all be held to account.'

'Rest assured, Matthew, this is not a subject I would ever discuss as I am ashamed to have even heard it,' the man spoke while pushing away from the table. But part of that was a lie . . . *he would speak to another.*

'We're not finished here, Rob,' the spokesman stated.

'You know I have always been a staunch supporter of the cause, Matt, but this . . .? This is going too far and beyond. I won't be a party to it beyond this point. It's one thing, gentlemen, to seek the betterment of mankind, but genocide is, by no means, the answer. If you persist, you may consider my support withdrawn . . . .'

Below the balcony, the voices continued to volley, his mother's voice raising only slightly with her lofty, lyrical tone.

". . . nor am I inclined to attempt convincing you of my talents. I am merely pointing out that your par`ents as well—as your broth`air and sist`air—have far more to lose by your threat of legal act`ions. I will, how-ev`air, compromise with you, ma chérie. I will speak to Aga`tha about this vis`et and—"

"You'll not talk to my mother!"

"—if she feels for the sake of fam`ilee peace, she must forgo any further vis`ets, I will und`airstand—"

Heaving breaths, he stumbled into his bedroom, aware of an urgency driving him across the room, staggering him into the second-floor parlor. He needed to stop her! Nothing held more clearly in his mind as he stumbled, needing the banister rail to keep from falling. Trembling, he stepped off the staircase and halted, awake to an image on the floor. His breath caught in his throat. His mother! His mother lay sprawled within a cross current of lights from the doorways on either side of the main entry. His lips parted in a silent cry as the dark circle overflowed, fanning from beneath her wild array of black curls . . . Her big black eyes—gypsy eyes—widened as round as silver dollars . . . And Jade saw the ornate front door opening, knew at this second who would enter . . . knew he would stand in that doorway.

To the sudden burst of motion in the corner of his eye, Jade's dark emerald eyes pivoted toward the door to his mother's office. His focus locked on the lovely blond-haired young woman as she shock-stopped, startled by the sight of him. . . And his brow furrowed as he flashed mental images of her with a man, tangled in silky sheets. His head canted, his pale face drained as both sentences rushed, hushed off his lips, "They're gonna kill my mother. Your boyfriend's writing a story about you—"

"Oh, Christ," the woman hissed and shook her head as she continued toward the door. Her short, flowered skirt clung to her slender hips, pronouncing her every anxious step. "A madhouse."

The screen door slammed behind her. Jade's muscles jolted, and a cold chill spilled off his shoulders, trembling him, shaking him. Weak and dizzy suddenly, he clasped the knoll post and eased himself down on the bottom step. His elbows landed on his blue-jean-covered knees; his shaggy walnut curls sagged between his palms. . ..

A scam artist and an extortionist, his mom`ma, and he knew she would die too soon in his life. If he could stop her, warn her . . . but already the images were fading from his young mind. On the outside looking in, he saw himself huddled on the bottom step, shivering and alone; on the inside looking out, he suffered the certainty of his mother's early demise and the confusion over the same. Surely, not. Surely, this was a vision he could change! Not every image led to another . . . and already the images were fading. Like a retina stain, he saw the flowery, clingy skirt and knew the significance of the woman striding through the screen door, disappearing across the shrouded cove. She would speak to her father . . . and her father sat at that table.

Significant, this image swirling within his drugged mind. He knew himself then—nine or ten years old, sitting on the shined marble steps, and Nan Duncan coming hurriedly to his side. She settled on the step beside him, tugging him under her arm like a mother bird drawing its hatchling under its wing.

'What's happened, lil darlin'? What's this now?'

'I think they know, Nanna . . . I think she already told them.'

'What, darlin'? What did she tell them?'

'About the monst`air,' he uttered in a trembling soft voice. 'I think I told her about the monst`air . . . like Franken`stein . . . Like Doct`air Franken`stein in that book, Nanna,' he uttered and fisted the tears from his eyes. Withdrawing from under her arm, he looked up into her troubled, warm brown eyes. 'He is, Nanna . . . He is like the monst`air."

'Who, darlin'?'

'I . . . I hov to stop her, Nanna . . .'

He had tried to stop her . . . He'd known his curse would initiate his mother's death. He'd tried to stop her. He'd begged her to stop forcing him to touch things that ultimately connected him to wicked pictures and strange sights. So many things, he hadn't understood. And others, he'd understood too clearly. She was afraid of him. She'd feared the things she saw in his eyes when he looked at her or touched her . . . And she'd touched him only at the wrist, forever, it seemed now. To force his hand into other people's lives, to draw the weird words and visions from his mind . . . 'Pleeease no, Mom`ma . . ..'

His curse, he knew, was an addiction to anyone it touched. His mother could no more stop using him than Carson had been able to stop testing him . . . and something his father had told him once slid through his drugged mind.

'. . . You are to mortal man what the holy grail is to the lowly, my own bastard. A symbol to lust after and to fear, to seek and understand, to possess and abuse . . . and people have died for lesser quests, my son. Perhaps, when you are older, you will understand.'

He was older, and he understood, but no relief accompanied his insight. Whatever he touched, whoever he touched, would be destroyed. His wife, his child, included, regardless of his death. The quiet life, the normal life he'd sought with all the fervor of a quest for his own holy grail . . . a fantasy. Jade Laquette truly was dead. If, in fact, he'd ever existed. And the man who'd risen from the ashes wasn't a man to suffer illusions or fantasies.

"Doctor! Dr. Heinz! He's waking!"

No. No more fantasies. No more illusions. Jade Laquette was dead, but Dominique Jardonet was very much alive, and he was waking again, waking to realize he was once again the subject of interrogation and testing. And to know this time would be no more successful than the first. At eleven years, he'd outwitted another of this doctor's ilk.

Heinz. Did this Dr. Heinz truly believe he would be any more successful than his predecessor?

2,1,4 . . . a perfect seven.

That line returned like a holy mantra from the distant past.

2,1,4 . . . a perfect seven.

CHAPTER 5

Cy Trascar was the most unlikely candidate as a savior as he was a saint, but as Ronnie spotted him ambling up the sidewalk alongside Olden Time, she saw him as both. By his walk, a rolling gate which lent him a perpetual sway, he was currently on the wagon, and that too came as a relief as Ronnie waved out the driver's window, passing him and turning into the alley. She could probably just leave the truck parked and loaded, but she would rather not. Besides, Jade often found odd jobs for Cy when the fellow was sober. As if he'd answered a summons, Cy strolled around the corner just as Ronnie touched the electronic keypad to raise the garage doors.

"Looks like you got yourself a fine load, missus." He spoke in a reverent tone that he'd adopted from their first introduction. No matter how often Ronnie offered her first name, Cy continued to address her as 'missus,' perhaps, because of his confusion over Jade's given name. God knows, most people in Bentwood still called him Isaac or Mr. Bently and, in the same respect, addressed her as 'Mrs. Bently' like Finn.

"Any chance you're needing some help here?"

"Every chance, Cy," she said smoothly. "You're a godsend," she added, and his alcohol-flushed cheeks reddened a deeper shade before he ducked his head away.

Like Ethel in Elmview, Cy was one of Bentwood's more colorful characters, a fellow who spent nearly as much time in local lockup as he spent in his shack near Tucket's Creek. Not much past his middle age, he looked twenty years older with weathered lines in his lean face and silver streaks in his nearly blond, shaggy hair. Inevitably, he wore a pair of faded coveralls and a flannel shirt with the elbows worn thin, along with a pair of work boots that he'd once removed while sitting on a barstool, claiming the boots dragged him off the chair. Allegedly, Jonas Hickory, the bartender over at the Night Owl, retaliated by stashing Cy's boots behind the bar for a week while Cy spent the week walking in his stocking feet, hunting for his boots all over town. Not until Sam Hayward had received a few too many complaints about Cy entering public places like Meg's Diner in his bare feet had the chief of police ordered a manhunt for the missing boots. Someone had allegedly started a poll to buy Cy a new pair of boots, but Cy was too proud to accept the donation. The philanthropists donated the collected money to the Night Owl to keep Cy in beer for weeks.

According to local gossip, Cy Trascar wasn't destitute. His forefathers, a great or great-great grandfather had helped found Bender Falls, and unless the rumors were just that, the fellow had enough money to stay drunk as long as he lived. By Jade's reaction, however, Ronnie sensed the rumors were just that. Her husband was no fool nor a bleeding heart, and it wasn't a rumor that Cy's beer tabs had a way of getting paid right before Jonas or Ed Hammond over at Crowley's Inn threw the town drunk out on his ear.

Strangely enough, Cy had been on the wagon far more often than off over the past few months, and Ronnie wasn't the only one to notice. According to Amy Sue over at Cuts and Curls, it had to be a woman. So far, no one had discovered where or with whom old Cy spent his Friday and Saturday nights.

Parking the pickup in its usual spot, Ronnie climbed from the cab, remembering the clutter of Finn's Corner, and judging this warehouse *clean* by comparison. At least empty shelves existed, easily accessible. She barely lent Cy directions on where to unload and started away when she remembered her unwanted cargo. Uncomfortably, she spied the box, then looked at Cy as he lowered the tailgate. "Put that cardboard box aside, will you, Cy? Maybe over there against the wall," she commented, genuinely relieved that she could avoid touching it again. How long she would wait before she buckled to her curiosity would depend on when her wayward husband returned.

Only after Cy had followed her direction and started on the next box, she left him alone with a suggestion to come through the office entrance when he finished.

Home. This was home. Her clutter. Jade's clutter. The comfortable rhythm of a symphony echoed softly through the showroom doors. Whether Jade liked classical music or just enjoyed the clash of sounds of a full orchestra, Ronnie had never decided. He had collected a fine selection of classical records—most converted to cassette tapes—and almost as many cassettes of modern rock and jazz. The man was a contradiction waiting to happen.

Pausing outside the office door within the shadowy hallway, Ronnie nearly lost her keys with an uncanny prickle sliding down her spine. Fumbling, she unlocked the door, but even as she passed into the brighter light of the office, into the more audible melody and comfortable ambiance filtering from the shop, the sense of foreboding . . . and abandon continued. Short hairs lifted at the nape of her neck; her muscles gripped. Alone . . . she was alone. All alone. And that was ridiculous! Absurd! Through the slightly parted office door, she heard Elaine talking to someone and other voices transcending the distance.

Still, that sense prickled her, tensing her, overwhelming her.

Reacting uncontrollably to something internal, she stumbled as far as the desk and settled clumsily into the upholstered leather chair. High-backed and thick-cushioned, the chair had undoubtedly originated in a doctor's office, if not a bank. The smell of cigar smoke and lemon polish threatened to gag her despite the uncanny stillness in her gut. Quiet. For the first time in hours—if not days—Tad was quiet. Not even a flutter or quiver to his credit. But her muscles were not so well inclined. Something . . . something was terribly wrong!

Overwhelmingly wrong!

Her muscles cringed as if she feared the walls were about to collapse around her. Jade . . . that was her first thought. Her only thought. Something was wrong! Jade!

No! Not possible. He was well! He was all right!

Someone else! This feeling of panic—it had to come from someone else. Someone close to her. Her father . . . her mother . . . her brothers. *Someone!* The sense of death seemed suddenly palpable, a living, breathing entity within the confines of this office. Someone . . . the news was coming.

The news was coming!

Not in months had her instincts, her intuition struck with such overwhelming force or conviction. Electric, her nerves tingled, fingertips numbed. Death. She felt it. Heard it. The swelling that overwhelmed her and took control at the scene of a crime . . . the intuition that had driven her to become what she was, to do what she did . . . to touch and halt the madness which destroyed the lives of others. At this moment, she knew . . . she hadn't escaped or prevented the destruction. *Someone was dead* . . . And the abandonment that had threatened to overwhelm her time and again over the past twenty-four hours was here now.

Unescapable. Unavoidable.

She knew before she heard Sam Hayward's deep voice, knew what message he carried. Shaking her head, she heard him addressing Elaine, "I know she just pulled in . . . I just saw her truck go by."

"What's this about, Sam?"

"I'll talk to Ronnie first," Hayward stated. "How about getting your key for the inside door, Elaine? If she went upstairs—"

Ronnie was still shaking her head when the door opened, and she found the bleary silhouette in the doorway. "No," she uttered, lifting her hand and wiping her eyes clear, steeling her nerve and catching her breath. *No! She would not believe it! Refused!*

"Ronnie, uh . . . Hi," Sam started.

Pushing off the chair, she lifted her slightly manic gaze to lock onto Hayward's steady gaze, not truly seeing Elaine a half step behind. "Sam," she said in a slightly elevated voice, a pitch of hysteria barely controlled.

Coming partway into the room, Hayward closed the door behind him, blocking the glow from the shop. Far more clearly, his rugged features came into focus, his eyes tense and unfathomable. "We have to talk, Ronnie, and uh . . . it's—"

"No," she stated.

"It's about Jade," he said in a thick, low voice, continuing around the desk and arriving within arm's reach to collide with her. His head canted to look down at her, his expression grimmer than she'd ever seen, he spoke carefully, quietly, "And somehow I think you already know what I've come here to tell you."

She shook her head, feeling as if spiders crawled beneath the roots of her hair. "No! Do you hear me, Sam? Whatever you're about to say—no."

For a long moment, he studied her; his eyes betrayed nothing beyond the intensity of his gaze. "Dear God, you do know," he nearly uttered, his voice breaking slightly. "I'm sorry, Veronica," he said in a low, strained voice. "I wish to God there was some easier way of saying this, but I got the call about an hour ago . . . I tried reaching that hotel where you were staying, but you'd already checked out. I left a message for Tim to find you . . ." His hand clasped her arm as she started to sway, and he moved her, moving with her to sit her down, then stooping alongside her. His rugged face masked in torment, he clasped her numb hand while continuing, "Honey, if there was some easier way of saying this . . . If I could have put it off . . . But there's no way it'll get any easier."

"A—a lie . . . Sam, it c-can't be—"

"Honey, I don't know how the hell it happened or what the hell he was doing on a plane . . . But they have a positive ID. Sometime yesterday evening, a small twin engine with two passengers crashed down in Kentucky . . . From what they've been able to piece together, it took off out of a municipal airport near Cincinnati and was just over the Kentucky border when it ran into trouble. Neither passenger survived. They uh . . . they couldn't make a positive ID until this morning, and they're still sorting through the wreckage . . . I—I made them check, honey. I made them double-check and check again until that state policeman I talked to probably thought I had a few bats in the belfry . . . But there's no denying it. Some of uh . . . Some of Jade's stuff was found in the wreckage . . . I uh . . . I called that municipal airport in Cincinnati, and I made them get somebody on the phone who uh . . . They saw Jade get on the plane, honey. They described him right down to his boots. God almighty," Sam uttered, his deep voice strained, his hand gripping hers in a fierce hold. "You don't know how sorry I am, honey."

Her heart hammered a leaden beat, but a stillness swept over her. A quietus spiraled from the very depths of her soul as she shook her head, refusing to believe what her ears, her mind, and her heart attempted to tell her. Until she saw him with her own eyes, until she touched him, she would not believe this—could not believe it. "Where is he, Sam?" she asked in a voice that sounded almost reasonable to her own ears. "Where is Jade?"

"I m-made arrangements . . . He'll be . . . They'll be sending him home here, honey. His . . . the plane should get into our municipal airport around six. They have to get clearance—and there are some formalities . . . Honey, are you okay? Can I get you something? You want me to call someone for you?"

She shook her head, the stillness not letting up. As if she were wrapped in a warm cocoon, she felt the stillness. The words—Sam's words were not meant for her. He was speaking to someone else. No other explanation seemed more feasible. Whoever received this news would be devastated, and she wasn't devastated. Warm and safe, comfortable within the soft leather seat behind an immaculately neat desk. Jade never left his desk a mess. Organized clutter stood in neat piles at either corner, and a stout ceramic pen holder stood near the desk lamp that resembled an alien in an old science fiction movie, the head dangling on a flexible tube. Concentrated light would form a perfect circle on the clean felt mat . . . she just needed to lean and press the ignition switch. She remained calm, not bothering with the switch, the light. The stillness held her, halting even the start and thought of a shiver to find Sam Hayward poised at her side. Curiously, she studied the firm ridges in his face, the pain in his eyes, grasping his sorrow. She should comfort him. She'd comforted victims of violent crime before, the heartbroken and terrified alike. No words reached her lips.

"Sa-am?" a hesitant voice started.

Toward the familiar voice, Ronnie turned her attention and watched Elaine appear at the edge of the door.

Stout of heart and build, the rounded face seemed pale under the fluorescent light, the brown eyes squinted and furtive, darting from Sam to Ronnie, back to Sam. More hesitantly, more haltingly, Elaine moved into the room. "Sam?"

"Elaine . . . I'm sorry," Sam huffed softly.

"Wh-what is it, Sam?" she nearly begged, her voice rising an octave. Her eyes widened accordingly, her head shaking slightly.

"Laney, it's . . . it's Jade," Sam managed and seemed now to beg something of Elaine. "Do you . . . do you have the numbers to reach Ronnie's family?"

"Howww?" Elaine whined. "Sammm, howww?"

Rising, still clasping Ronnie's hand, Sam answered in a strained voice. "A plane crash . . . late yesterday afternoon."

Ronnie shook her head, denying, rejecting those words as she looked up at Sam's profile. He'd come here on official business, his uniform pressed and tucked on his wiry build. In full regalia, his badges and shields glowed under the soft light. Neatly cropped, his hair lay immovable, manikin-style . . .

But it was Jade's hair she saw suddenly, his unruly waves that nearly begged to be mussed in her fingers. His strength, she gleaned in his long-muscled length. Never more powerful, he seemed to her than at this moment, and he was looking at her, besieging her with his liquid green eyes. The sadness haunted the curve of his mustached lips; his dimple winked at the corner of his lips. *No.* She shook her head, felt the touch of his warm eyes . . . and heard his voice at the edges of her mind. 'Be strong, my love . . . Be strong for me. Keep the candle burning . . .'

The tears came then, trickling down her cheeks. Her eyes pleading, she shook her head slowly. *A dream . . . a nightmare.* She wanted to wake up. "I can't—" she uttered.

'For me . . . for our child, you must,' the words whispered, soft and silky, a balm on the start of panic threatening to break through the warm threads around her.

Shattering, Elaine's started, stifled cry.

Her heart hammering suddenly, Ronnie saw only the bleary image of the woman clasping a hand over her mouth, coming forward with an outstretched palm. As if propelled by an external force, floating within the safety of whatever tranquility had overtaken her, Ronnie rose and collided, welcoming the woman into her embrace, welcoming the strength of the arms to fold around her. Detached, Ronnie comforted the woman, feeling bad for her . . . And it wasn't the last time she would feel this futile sympathy. Ronnie knew about loss, understood the complexities of grief. Senseless to believe she might truly comfort anyone in a time of crises, but she'd always been a good listener . . . She could listen. Clinically. When all the facts were in, she could look at this crisis objectively after compiling the data . . . not becoming emotionally involved. That was how she worked, how she handled a case . . . detached.

The house was quiet, like a tomb. Not even the cats stirred. Within the small bay window, curled on the colorful cushion of the window seat, the largest of momma's cats, Merlin, curled as if asleep, but its green eyes glared from the black fir, watching as if imbibed with a mystical, scrying power. Merlin was just a cat, just an immense black cat with its weird eyes caught in a sliver of sunlight sneaking between the thick drapes.

In deference to his mother, Nanna Duncan kept the curtains closed, and sitting on the parlor chair, curled in the corner a lot like Merlin, Jade rested, staring at the cat as intently as the cat studied him. If he tried, he wondered if he could control the cat the way he sometimes directed other people's thoughts . . . and his lips curved in a slight smile with his thought. Perhaps, mind-bending a cat wouldn't be too awfully bad, not worthy of a spanking. That's what mom`ma called it—mind-bending. If he tried . . .

Across the slight space, Merlin blinked its huge, glistening eyes, and its black silk fir began to puff up like an inflating black balloon.

Jade withdrew his thought to call the cat to him. Mom`ma had threatened to spank him into the next life if he tried any more stunts. He hadn't deliberately asked the nice lady at the supermarket to buy him a candy bar; he'd merely seen the nice lady lifting his favorite kind and handing it to him.

Mom`ma had waited until they were home to spank him and shake him. 'Do you want people to know what you are? Is thot it? Do you want them to take you away? They will, you know. If they find out whot you are. . . .'

They were coming.

A chill crawled over his skin, lifting goose bumps under his thick sweater, a sweater he'd pulled on over his shirt when the chill had first started. Sometimes putting on extra clothes helped . . . but not today.

They were coming.

As if a window sprung open, he saw the gray-haired man sitting behind a wide desk, caught the scent of a tangy cigar, and tasted the beeswax emanating from the shined oak shelves. A bright room, this office where the elder man rested, holding a telephone to his ear.

'What time are you saying he left St. Augustine's . . .?'

To the glimpse of motion, he titled his head, fully grounded in the moment, awake to the shadows lingering inside the parlor. The scent of his mother's perfume overwhelmed the aroma of incense. No incense burned in the colorful urns on the ornate end tables. No soft clouds drifted from the open door of his momma's office as often happened between her readings. She wasn't here. Nothing of her essence lingered.

As if on tiptoe, Nan Duncan crossed the oriental carpet, barely brushing her soft soles to whisper a sound. A soft sigh slipped off her lips as she settled onto the cushion near his shins. Gently, her hand landed on his knee, and she tilted to meet his vacant gaze.

Far more critically, he studied her slender face, her soft brown eyes. She was older than his mother but not by too many years . . . But in an odd moment, he saw her older face, lined delicately about the corner of her eyes and smile. A touch of gray sprinkled at the edges of her short chestnut hair—shorter then than now. Shoulder length, the wispy hair fell over her troubled brow and brushed at the pale blue cashmere at her shoulders.

Sadly, she tried to smile, but her eyes moistened with tears. "I didn't hear you come down, darlin'. How about I make your breakfast? What say . . . French toast and sausage? Would you like that, sweetie?"

Nanna Duncan made the best French toast in the whole world, and usually, when she offered that fare, she added a wry smile with her words. Madame

Laquette preferred most things French; Jade preferred most things edible. But he wasn't hungry.

They were coming.

He shook his head against the armrest, drifting his gaze to the cat. "I'll wait . . ."

"Darlin', you haven't eaten much of anything in days," she said while brushing her palm over his knee. "I know this isn't easy, lil darlin', but starving yourself won't help a thing. Now, why don't you come help me in the kitchen . . .?"

"They're coming," he said quietly. In his mind's eye, he glimpsed the woman and two men pushing through the cast iron gates at the stone sidewalk. Dressed in a dark blue skirt and jacket, the woman led the procession, swinging a briefcase at her side. The men came empty-handed, wearing business suits to put him in mind of the small gathering at the graveside. The enhanced smell of flowers in the bright sunlight wavered the image of the visitors striding toward the front door. For an instant, Jade saw him there—the black-clad man standing in the shade of trees laden with autumn orange and red leaves. Beneath the brim of a black hat, the head canted at an angle as if to study him; the eyes remained shaded, but the curve in the mustache betrayed no hint of humor. A cold chill penetrated him, now, as it had then. A fear so intense as to hold him stricken and still.

"What is it, darlin'?" Nan barely finished the words when the doorbell chimed its oh-so-familiar melody akin to the gong of the grandfather clock chiming across the room.

Time. It was time. His life was about to change.

Had changed . . . with the arrival of three social-worker-impersonators, he knew at the deepest levels of consciousness. As clear as a shined crystal, he saw them. Stone-faced and austere, they presented the official papers to a distraught Nan Duncan.

'Until such time as we can find a relative . . . A ward of the state . . .'

More like 'the nation,' he corrected as he awoke within the familiar room. Even with his eyes closed, he recognized the brilliant light, the mechanical sounds. One machine drew attention as the tiny bleeps and pings sounded in erratic patterns. Behind closed eyes, the man, who had been the child Jade Laquette, amused himself by bouncing the needles and gauges from one side of the screens to the other, shooting the lines from the tops of the graphs to the bottoms.

"Something's happening, doctor! The monitors are off the charts!"

An understatement in his regard, Dominique might have mentioned, but his attention sailed in another direction. As if a window opened in his mind, he viewed his lady, his love, and suffered a wicked pang of guilt for her distress.

Letting the needle flatline, he wasn't amused as panic erupted in the room around him. That his captors feared they'd killed him might be slightly amusing considering his fully conscious mind and body . . .

If not for the heartache in that most vital of all organs.

CHAPTER 6

Cy Trascar ambled hesitantly through the back door, then hurried, more resolved and alarmed. "Sam?"

"Cy . . . there's been an accident . . . plane crash . . ."

How many more times would Ronnie hear those words? How many more times would the words 'plane crash' echo through the vacuum of her thoughts? A tragedy . . . a loss. A crime only in the ethereal sense. A mystery . . . *a lie.* To believe otherwise would be to lose whatever remained of her sanity, and never had she come this close to that fateful event.

"Ah . . . goddamn . . . goddamn," Cy uttered, and the strength of his grip, the low timbre of his voice, distracted Ronnie. "Come on, missus . . . there now," the deep voice chanted. "Laney . . . go an' lock up. Folks'll be flockin' here. Sam . . . call on over to the Diner and tell Meg we're needing her. Have her bring some coffee . . . Let's go, missus . . . We'll just g'on upstairs . . ."

How it happened, Ronnie had no quick grasp. Cy was there. Chanting his low assurances. Meg, teary-eyed, her voice quivering and uncertain, breaking on the brink of sobs, barely restrained. Elaine stayed, too, making coffee, taking phone calls. Doc Blackwell came, his chiseled features wracked with pain, his eyes haunted as he spoke in lulling tones to fall hollow against her ears. Only beginning, Ronnie knew as she lay staring at the ceiling of her living room. Only the beginning and the worst was yet to come.

The thought hung in the back of her mind, a whisper of sanity telling her the worst was yet to come; she would need to be strong. Take each moment as it came. Welcome the numbness to steel over her, the comfortably warm embrace which seemed to hold her on the brink of awareness while protecting her from the horror outside.

No escaping the weight of that horror. As if a thundercloud loomed above her haven, she suffered the relentless hammer blows of reality conveyed in the soft strained words and wet eyes. Jade was dead. Those were the words these visitors seemed to persist in citing. Her lover, her husband, her friend . . . gone. Stolen from her by a fireball that had been an airplane before its deadly descent.

Unable to sit, to lie idle and let the thundercloud pound her, Ronnie rejected the words and hands that tried to stop her and moved without direction, drawn to the nearest window where she stood, parting the sheer drapes, looking out on the dusk sky. Hours . . . how many minutes or hours had already passed? In haunting images, she remembered the day she'd thrown open these velvet drapes and let the sunlight pour into this darkness. Directly below the window, the dark gray awning over Olden Time's entrance prohibited her from seeing if a crowd had gathered.

Four months ago, a crowd had gathered . . . barring her entry, accusing her of destroying their friend, their neighbor . . . Isaac Bently.

Insanity, then. Or an omen? That she would destroy the serenity he'd known in this small town. Were they prophets, the lot of them? Rallying around a man whose charisma transcended the boundaries of gender, demanding and commanding, either loved or hated.

A lodestone, this man of hers. Attracting and repelling people at whim or whimsy with no rhyme or reason.

Distracted by the voices, and the arrival, Ronnie looked over as Donna and Tim came through the door, pausing to address Meg. Donna appeared wrecked, her lovely face washed of color, red pinpricks standing out on her cheeks, and her eyes blazing with blood streaks. Tim seemed likewise devastated, with his deep blue eyes ringed in red, his face a granite mask about to crumble. Tears streaming, Donna crossed the room, and like others, her arms opened, offering or demanding comfort. No longer able to decide, Ronnie accepted the embrace, hearing the murmured, cracked words against her ear. Detached.

"I'm s-so sorry . . . I'm so-so sorry . . ."

Tim's arms folded around them, offering his stability, his comfort. Forever it seemed, they stood, molded together, a single pillar of strength on the verge of collapse. When they parted, Donna's eyes conveyed the sorrow, a shared sorrow, and pain. Absently, she brushed at Ronnie's bangs, attempting to smile in the face of calamity, failing. "Are you a-all right, h-oney?"

"Do I have a choice?" Ronnie asked, and it seemed those were the first words she'd spoken in an eternity. Hollow to her own ears, those words echoed, and the answer remained in the shadows of her mind. No choice. She carried their child . . . their joint creation. Three hearts . . . beat as one. For Tad, she had no choice. She needed to carry the candle . . .

'Look for the letter, m' love,' the words scrolled across his mind before he drifted from the immediate realm, hearing the voices from a dozen planes. Like scrolling through old film strips, he sought the familiar and zoomed through the annals of past, present, and future events.

Not before this moment had he consciously traveled through the portals of time, but he had a sense of the concept. For every action, there was a reaction, and that theory could be no less true regarding time. Every instant was governed by the preceding moment and thus affected the next. Only the past remained unchangeable. He could no more thwart the crucifixion of Christ than he could resurrect his mother from the dead. At a single instant before 1:26 pm, October 9, 1971, something intangible—and yet unchangeable—had transpired to affect that specific moment in time.

Finding that moment had become paramount to all else.

Until he knew exactly how his mother had become a target and connected the dots to expose the threat, he couldn't alter the future.

The answers were in the past and those he needed to find before moving forward.

The past . . . back . . . back . . . back . . .

He stood pressed against his mother's desk, her five-sided table with inlaid tiles of abalone and mother of pearl . . . a wondrous pattern crafted by a master artisan. Five points, five colorful points, each outlined in black onyx . . . and a stark white-silk handkerchief fluttered on the colors in bold contrast. Beneath his palm, he felt the black threads rippling.

J.

The letter 'J.' The monogram wove through the white silk—black silk on white. Black and white . . . and as he stood within his child's trembling body, he grasped the simple truth behind that adage. Nothing was ever just black and white. So much gray. . . .

And he saw them then, the gray figures animating within a crackling film, his senses waking on every level to be one of the sheep herded in this ominous parade, to realize where this doomed crusade would lead. Child and man merged to know the significance, to realize he wore the Star of David on a band at his arm, so marked and destined to die . . . and he'd touched this young Jewish boy in whose footsteps he walked, touched him, or something of his essence.

Young and old, his mind shied from that knowledge, from the vision.

He'd seen this film, had sat for hours watching this march, had suffered the fear, the desperation, the resignation . . . as surely as he'd reveled in the conviction of the man behind the clattering film who believed himself righteous for chronicling an event of such magnitude. The photographer. Even as he recognized the essence of the photographer, he'd grasped his own witness, reveling in his reactions as he watched this wicked crusade . . . and the film blurred within his vision as well as his mind.

The Holocaust.

On his upper arm, he wore the band with the bold red symbol of the Third Reich. The swastika set him apart, stood him on a pedestal . . . and he knew himself growling, near to screaming on a dozen planes as the film continued to scroll in the past, into the present.

The answers were there, somewhere in these archives.

'. . . the hand of the devil . . .'

She'd touched the hand of the devil . . . his mother . . .

The answers were here, in the past, in this place, and even knowing he would find those answers before moving forward toward his own certain doom, he couldn't simply step over the abyss. He'd needed to be in this place, to feel, to see, to understand, and even in his drugged mind, he knew he drew closer to the answers he sought.

In wicked rapid freeze-frames, he saw himself strapped into a semi-reclined chair, his wasted body writhing within the straps as others had surely twisted, screaming as the pain ripped through his flesh and bones . . .

'Painless,' a low soothing voice chanted. 'Nothing to fear . . . I don't want to hurt you, really.'

He'd heard those words before. Someone in this wicked place had spoken those words. To him and to another . . . another born in this place, and in a stopped instant, he saw the face hovering above him, stifling his breath, halting his thought.

Santa Claus . . . Jade David Laquette had never believed in Santa Claus, not even in his earliest memories, but he hadn't minded pretending to believe and sitting on the old man's lap at the mall, smiling for his mom`ma to take his picture . . . only until the man behind the beard had changed and the new pretender had given him wicked visions. A pedophile, he knew now; he'd understood only the oily sense of the man behind the mask then . . . and this image staring down at him within a halo of white light was the same, and yet different. A monster.

Latex and glue held the raggedy gray beard and brows to the face, bulged the nose, and crinkled around the flared nostrils. Excitement glowed behind the round, windowpane reflections covering the eyes. The color of the eyes was lost as surely as the much younger face hidden behind the latex, but there was something familiar in this image.

Past, recent past, and . . . was this image from the future then? This image of a deranged Santa looking down at him no differently than the mad doctor who looked down at him in the present?

Heinz. The man's name was Heinz. Dr. Heinz. And the fellow was as obsessed as his predecessor, determined to discover secrets far and beyond his grasp. Far more naturally, this Dr. Heinz resembled Santa Claus with his shock of white hair in a rendition of Einstein. Ah, and there was a fellow worthy of distinction . . . Once, not all that long ago, Isaac Bently had acquired a set of pens that had passed through the hands of that notable fellow, and his mental scrying had nearly landed him in a coma. This Dr. Heinz was no comparison. Intelligent, yes, but more fanatic than brilliant.

'. . . the holy grail to the lowly . . .'

Proof of psychic phenomena.

Heinz wanted proof, but whether he sought to be heralded for the discovery, or like others in the past, sought to manipulate and capitalize on that discovery was yet undetermined. Others . . . others existed who would like nothing better than to harness the power of the mind, perhaps, to use those traits or recreate them in a superior race.

Ground zero. He rested at ground zero with technicians following orders whether in loyalty to Heinz and his cause or in allegiance to a greater tenet . . . the eugenics program. An even mix, he knew. Without ever seeing their faces, he knew these technicians following Heinz's direction, answered to another higher power, prepared, as it were, to eliminate the test subject at the first order, and that order would come. The powers behind this operation that had nearly taken his life already merely awaited a sign, and they were already anxious . . . or nervous.

Shouted voices and anxious demands resounded through the heavy door. Hands and fists banged the thick mahogany wood. Inside the room, the faint trace of cordite mixed with the cigar smoke rising from the stout Columbian smoldering in the crystal tray. With the dull lamplight circling the pristine felt mat, the elder remained in shadows, but the cessation of life remained clear.

"Matthew! Matthew, please! Open this door!"

Now, or later? Still to come or already gone? A possibility or a given?

Had he fully considered the effects of heavy sedation, he might have chosen a different route to his destination.

Even in his drugged state, something of the curse uttered off his mustached lips, drawing the attention of at least one of his captors . . . the same young fellow who'd hovered over him inside a helicopter. Forward or back, he heard the propellers whirling overhead and saw the intensity in the dark brown eyes. This one had meant to take his life—or the life of Jade Laquette and the fellow waited on standby now, prepared to take the life of his captive regardless of who rested before him. In the name of national security . . . or so he was programmed to believe. Whether he was a true believer in the cause or just another expendable pawn—the result was the same. If given the order, this intense young man would load the syringe and plunge the needle into the IV line without a first or second moral thought . . . or at least he would try.

As if a window burst open, his attention riveted on the most stunning image . . . an image he might have seen a thousand times in the past, in the present, and . . . the future? Aglow within a brilliant sun stream, black waves tumbled, shimmering over her shoulder, falling in the most carefree style to set him ablaze as quick as mesquite to a bonfire. Pensive, her lovely full lips carried only a hint of the smile that always warmed him, and her diamond blue eyes glistened with a whisper of tears on her lashes as she gazed at a sunbeam. Shadows. No matter the sunlight glowing on her long sleek image, a pall of shadows surrounded her—the darkness threatened to engulf her.

At the lowest realm, something stirred inside him, and a near-feral sound slipped off his lips. For her, for the precious cargo she carried for both of them . . . he needed to continue on this desperate path.

'. . . candle in my darkness . . . Be strong, m' love . . . find the letter . . .'

CHAPTER 7

Ronnie stood at the window looking down on Maine St. beyond the gray canopy when she heard Robert Bryson Sr. arrive. As if he belonged wherever his shined Oxfords landed, he entered the apartment, overwhelming the others in his tow, including Fiona, who broke from his escort and hurried, falling on Ronnie like a bird of prey about to swallow its meal. Over her mother's quaking shoulder, Ronnie watched her father approach, the strangeness of his arrival, his appearance, touching her deeply. This wasn't his environment. He'd never entered this apartment—not even when he'd come to walk her down the aisle. He'd booked a block of rooms at the Bentwood House Inn and only ventured as far as the showroom on the first floor of Olden Time. He'd never once climbed the stairwell to see where his daughter dwelt.

Out of his element, he scanned the austerity of the room as if judging the integrity of the furnishings. This wasn't the ramshackle, dilapidated apartment he'd undoubtedly imagined. Every bit as elegant and stately as the Bryson mansion, this apartment, consisting of more than a dozen rooms, reflected the man who'd dwelt within, a king in his own castle.

Ronnie had entered his life and parted the curtains to his world, letting in the light, but the apartment was Jade's. And these people . . . even the Spencers were intruders here. This was her husband's haven. A place he'd kept to himself, inviting only a select few as far as his den . . . but they were everywhere now. In his kitchen, in his living room, camped and murmuring sounds in the front parlor, on his phone . . ..

An arm's reach away, her father stood, looking down at her, meeting her eyes with a mirrored blue reflection. Troubled . . . not devastated or grief-stricken. His sculpted features remained pensive. His raven black hair barely touched with gray as if brushed at his temples for effect. He was too set in his ways to even attempt a smile of reassurance or comfort. He appeared grim as if his stocks had plummeted or one of his refineries had been ambushed. No emotional investment in this event . . . troubled.

"You have my sympathies," he said in a low voice, as hollow as all others, more feigned than some. "Are you all right?"

A pillar of strength, this intruder, Ronnie considered as she eased from the manic embrace, tipping her attention to find her mother's soulful wet eyes. Death . . . any death would have reduced her mother to tears, but the wife of Robert Bryson would persevere. They were not allowed to grieve like others. Never fall apart in front of a camera. In a heartbeat pause, Ronnie remembered the chaos of her grandfather's funeral . . . Reporters and photographers had bombarded her family from the funeral home to the church to the gravesite, chronicling the life of Robert L Bryson, one of DC's elite. The public has a right to know.

Why? What gave the public that right? What unwritten or written law defined what one person needed to know about another's personal grief or tragedy? What gave the public the right to intrude and invade? Why did the Brysons need to wrap their grief into a tiny knot inside themselves to protect that most private of all emotions from the public?

Not all right. At this moment, Ronnie knew she wasn't *all right*, and the appearance and warm embraces of her brothers and sister-in-law offered no comfort. Only James, her younger brother by three years, appeared genuinely affected by this tragedy. Unlike Robert Jr. and Linc, when James held her and spoke, his words reeked of pain for her, pain for himself that he shared her loss. He and Jade had become friends . . . These others had merely tolerated the marriage and might have prevented it if they could. The distance that had begun between her and Bobby four months earlier widened considerably, noticeably, as he offered his heartfelt sympathies. For her, he felt sorrow, but he'd never trusted her husband. Hook, line, and sinker, he'd swallowed the picture Agent Mark Jarvins—his old college buddy—had painted four months earlier. He probably still believed Jade had murdered those farmers.

Hypocrisy, this collection of solemn-faced visitors. Only a scant dozen others in this gathering conveyed the depth of genuine sorrow that she must surely be feeling.

Words reached her—hushed, masculine voices turned low. She found her father and older brother in a huddle with Tim Spencer and Sam Hayward . . . "Sax drew up a Will . . . We're going to have to talk to Ronnie . . . Blake's sending out a-a car to meet the plane . . . He prepaid his fucking funeral . . . Tim, why don't you go on and sit down . . . N-no, I'm all right . . . Mr. Spencer, you have my sympathies. I know you and my son-in-law were friends . . . This isn't right. It just doesn't seem possible . . ." The words, the voices ran together. Fr. Groggan joined the huddle at Robert Bryson's signal.

Ronnie couldn't even recall when Fr. Paul had arrived, and somehow his appearance, his black-clad body joining that odd collection, drove the reality deeper. Trembling internally, she withdrew her gaze, moving absently from the close-knit group of women who'd gathered around her in a basket weave. In the kitchen, Ronnie stopped. Elaine stood at the sink; Mrs. Handler, their debilitated octogenarian neighbor, leaned at the table, arranging covered dishes. Food had begun to arrive in abundance. More food than she and Jade could eat in a month. The table was covered with aluminum foiled plates, glass-topped dishes, and steaming pans. Absently, Ronnie sought the trivets beneath the heated dishes—heat on old wood could leave permanent scars, damage the wood . . . Pristine, that claw-foot table and baker's cabinet where more plates and bowls rested.

"Honey, why don't you sit down?" Fiona intruded, clasping Ronnie's arm.

Jolted from her reverie, Ronnie barely glanced off her mother, knowing what she needed to do. 'Be strong, my love . . . Find the letter . . .' The words echoed in her mind as she slid her arm from her mother's encompassing hold and turned.

Purposely, she strode from the kitchen, aware of voices attempting to stop her and other faces turning to watch her hasty departure. Just inside the den, she shoved the door closed, blocking whoever had attempted to follow. At the landscape painting against the inside wall, she halted. The man had his quirks. So much secrecy in his life. A mystery, this fellow who had stolen her heart.

For the first time since their marriage, she pushed the painting aside and used the numbers he forced her to memorize to unlock the safe. A single leather pouch occupied the narrow bottom slot. On the higher shelf, a half dozen velvet boxes stood in a neat stack. Absently, she lifted a royal blue box from the nearest shelf, lifting the lid and trembling slightly with the sparks igniting in hundreds of tiny prisms. Diamonds. Blue diamonds . . . No more than a quarter karat each, the cut stones glistened on a mat of black velvet, laced together on a thread of soft old gold. She'd never seen this piece of jewelry before . . . But she knew it was hers. Ever since that wonderous day when he'd slipped the blue diamond engagement ring on her finger, he'd adorned her in diamonds. No more than a week ago, he'd slid a pair of diamond earrings under her pillow for her to find following a wicked bout of morning sickness. That every box in the neat stacks held a gift for her, she didn't doubt.

Tears stinging her eyes, she replaced the box and reached for the leather pouch. Organized clutter . . . nothing to chance. Legal issues would never be left to chance.

Outside the door, she heard the low cadence of words, understood the concern clustered just beyond her sight. With the pouch in hand, she moved behind the desk and settled into the soft leather chair. The scent of him from an imported cologne to the wild fragrance that was all his own, touched her nearly as overpowering as the feeling of his presence at her side—hovering at her shoulder. As if his hands guided her, she unfolded the leather and drew out the contents.

The flutter of stationary caught her eye. Her gaze lowered to the single fold of paper that had slipped from the stack. Trembling, she set the others aside and lifted the folded page, knowing before she ever read the first word . . . This was to her and to her alone.

My dearest, Veronique`,

At this moment, I have only a sense of clouds on the horizon, but I fear that storm will be upon us soon. As I once sensed a storm advancing on you and was powerless to prevent, so I am blind again. A tragedy, I think, but I cannot know. That, I also fear, will change, and from that change, I will protect you. You are the light, my love, and I am the darkness. That you shined in me—even for a short time—was more than I ever had a right to embrace. I cannot take you with me. Physically, we will be parted. If you are reading this, I will know the accuracy of that prophecy. As will you, my lady, my love. I am still fool enough to hope but do not take that to mean that hope is for fools. Carry that candle for me, my love. Where I fear I must go, I can't keep it burning. A strangeness, this, to feel such conviction and pray I am wrong. If you judged me a madman, I wouldn't blame you. Know, my love, I have lived a life of madness, and you are my only sanity. Weep not over this parting. I will be with you, whether I walk at your side or in your shadow. Not even God could prevent that.

Take care of that I have given you, and be strong for me, my lady, my love.

Eternally yours,

Jade Laquette was dead, but Dominique Jardonet was very much alive. And very much aware of himself being ignored by his white-frocked companions, who wheeled him headfirst toward a destination that he'd anticipated. A helicopter . . . He'd glimpsed the flanks and open doors, heard the whizzing blades bisecting the darkness overhead, and too soon, the ceiling turned gray above him.

At the outer edges of his vision, others moved, moving with him, crowding around him. His head rolled; his eyes barely opened enough to identify images veiled by his thick eyelashes that wouldn't entirely lift. Wrong . . . something was wrong. Nothing moved on his own power. And he grasped the panic belying the urgency around him. What should have been a mild sedative had become a nearly lethal dose of curare—the same drug the Taxidermist had used to subdue his victims . . .

Ah, the puppet masters had struck again. The same men who had deemed Felicity Laquette expendable a lifetime ago had decided the son was likewise a threat . . . if not more so than his mother.

Were he a lesser man, or even the same man collected from Chateau Laquette a single day past, they might have succeeded.

Even in his dull senses, he grasped the images transforming around him. Near death, he'd been delivered and received.

Savior or executioner, one of his captors hovered over him, looking down into him, head canted. If Dominique had ever seen this man before now, the memory eluded him, but a sense of familiarity touched him. As if gazing at a double-exposed picture, he saw another masked face, glasses reflecting the light. The Taxidermist . . . the fellow wore blue hospital scrubs, surgical scrubs. Rather than the sober intense young face above him, Dominique suffered the certainty of the Taxidermist within the hospital attire, knew the twisted excitement hidden behind the mask . . . 'Alas, you are mine.'

"Just relax, Mr. Laquette," the low voice at closer range cut through the monotonous sounds. "You're in good hands . . . We'll be moving you to another room soon . . . nothing to worry about . . .."

A lie, he sensed it, felt it. A great deal to worry about, but the thought slipped away as the sturdy face tipped away, addressing another.

"How's his vitals?"

"Still low but steady," a crisp voice answered.

They weren't moving him far, not far at all. Only in his mind's eye, he recognized the increase in engine sound within the fog, more muffled now, but the noise remained overpowering. Numb, drifting, Dominique knew when the craft lifted, sensed vibrations of motion and the significance of sounds changing tempo around him. Whether he dreamed of flying or flew now, he lost thought to wonder. Fading in and out, the images of strangers and the sounds fleeted through his consciousness. Nothing remained long. Sleep . . . he knew the sleep he needed. In fluting rhythm, he heard his mother's voice whispering at the edges of his mind, telling him to sleep now. *Recover.* Mesmerizing, that distant voice, but even now, the fear lingered at the edges of his consciousness. Dying . . . he'd always felt himself dying, the numbing death in the wake of his curse. Nothing moved. Whether he struggled against the sleep of the dead or against the drugs mainlining in his system, he retained no clear grasp. Against his mother's chanting rhythm and the vibrations, he was no match. Sleep . . . he needed to sleep to recover. Still, he battled . . .

Fear. He knew the fear at his lowest level of awareness, knew what she asked of him, demanded of him was dangerous . . . for him, for her. Other boys . . . he wanted to be like other boys. Not a monster! . . . Nanna understood. She treated him like other boys . . . and he wanted her now. He wanted her to come and wake him like she'd awoken him so many other times before. She knew how this frightened him, knew he feared the sleep of the dead would take him one day and not let him go . . .

Re'd for me, bab`be boy . . .

Nooo! Pleeease nooo. . . not again, Mom`ma . . . pleeease not again . . . But she'd forced him to read again. No playing ball like other boys . . . no walking to the park with Nanna now . . . different. He was different . . . she knew it. Nanna knew it. He was a warlock . . . like his Pappa. 'A warlock . . . like your pap'pa,' that's what mom`ma told him. Not like other boys. Things he touched . . . talked to him. He had to read . . . learn to read. *A monster . . .*

". . . He's getting restless . . . Due for meds . . ."

"How the fuck did this happen? . . . That wasn't supposed to be a goddamn lethal dose!"

. . . A monster . . . to be feared . . . to be afraid. And he was afraid . . . more afraid of living . . . than of dying. What they could do to him . . . would do to him. Had already done to him?

'Do you want them to take youuu, bab'be boy? Isss thot what you want? . . . If theeey knew whot you were . . .'

"Blood pressure's climbing . . . pulse . . . He's waking up, Conners . . ."

A warlock . . . and he could call others to him . . . mind-bending . . .

"Calm down," the husky voice demanded. "We'll have you down in a few minutes. Just relax . . ."

Not relaxed. Numb. And waking. The voices had become more real. The sounds louder, offensive. Struggling on the edges of consciousness, he dragged his eyelids open to spy the faces above him, to remember the helicopter. Nothing moved, but his entire body vibrated, numb and tingling against the thin cushion under him. Around him, the portable medical equipment hummed in tune with the propeller blades and engine roar still echoing in his mind . . .

'Mayday! Mayday! . . . we're going down!'

A trip . . . a little trip. A little chat . . . trip to a hospital . . . another hospital.

His head shook. His liquid gaze drifted, searching the faces. Strangers, again. Those within his view were strangers. The one who'd spoken to him earlier, dark-haired, crisp blue suit . . . not a doctor. The man no longer wore the white smock in reflection of a medical technician. Within his chest, Dominique recognized the leaden beat of his heart as he studied this stranger who watched him with equal intensity. Not right . . . a lie. He knew the lie, knew at this moment, they had taken him to a hospital and administered the antidote to counter a near-lethal injection . . . A pity he needed to endure this ordeal to reach his destination. He might just as easily have walked into this facility. Que sera, sera. One minute into the next . . . sequence.

He doesn't look so tough. Surely not a threat to national security, the young man considered silently.

Americans, the son of Jean-Pierre Jardonet trusted them no more than he trusted the French, but Jean-Pierre had spared his son this final odyssey.

His head shook. His gaze held steady. Anger and frustration vied for attention within his throbbing leaden mind. Nothing moved . . . straps on his wrists, his ankles, across his chest and thighs. Immobilized. His muscles wasted within the effects of whatever medication flowed through his veins. Whether physical exhaustion or the drugs held him immobile, he remained limp. His fingertips tingled, numb from vibrations. With an effort, he formed fists, and for a moment, he believed his hands wrapped around a steering wheel, flying . . . racing. Loved to drive . . . fast. Needed to drive fast . . . The devil raced at his heels. Forever. Chased, hounded by the devil, and the faces never mattered. These were just more of the same entity.

Aware, but paralyzed, Dominique listened and watched, understanding the activity around him as surely as he recognized the slate-gray walls to pass. . . blue diamonds. Like tiny diamonds on black velvet, he glimpsed the stars . . . soft blue diamonds.

All too swiftly, the comfort of those sparkles abandoned him, lost in a wash of blinding fluorescent light. Suffering blindness, his stomach rolled with the change in motion—a downward motion. An elevator . . . he remembered the elevator . . .

Hazy, the faces came from the past. Faces of nurses of doctors . . . Dr. Carson traveled at his side, careful not to look into his eyes. He'd told them about mind-bending . . . Mom`ma had spanked him for mind-bending the nice lady . . . but he hadn't done it on purpose. Fear gripped him when he tried promising to behave, pleading not to be hurt anymore. He'd promised mom`ma, he would never . . . but he had. And he would again . . . And Dr. Carson would take him for more tests. . . They would hurt him, make him watch, feel.

Black and white, gray and darker gray, the bodies tread in the broken animation of an old film. The clatter of a movie projector remained as vivid as the faces turning away and ducking in shame and fear of the spotlight. Huddled, men and women marched, clasping youngsters to their hips and shoulders. Their tattered coats and brimmed hats suggested a chill in the air around them. White spots and spider-webbed lines cluttered the film, blotching and spotting the broken animation. Still, the barbed wires and enclosures, the smoke of steam engines and trains, the walls of a factory . . . a barracks . . . chambers . . ..

So, it had begun, the film reel clattering in the background.

CHAPTER 8

As still as the casket hovering on wide straps above the open grave, Ronnie stood gazing at the mounds of flowers. Fall flowers, roses, an orchid . . . all colors and varieties mounded on the emerald hood of the casket which presumed to carry her husband, her lover, to the life after. She hadn't seen the remains. Tim Spencer had spared her from that horror, and he'd suffered dearly for his compassion. Haunted, he'd stood by her as often as her brothers, attempting to offer strength and comfort. The loss wasn't hers alone to bear.

With the interment service ended, the last prayers and testaments to a life concluded, sobs broke in the ranks. Not alone, but as still as a stone monument, Ronnie stood, listening to the snivels and sniffs, the broken sounds as the collection of friends and neighbors began to disperse. A closed service . . . a private ceremony. Only the nearest and dearest of Jade Laquette/Isaac Bently's friends had gained access to this remote section of the cemetery. He'd chosen this place. He'd sought it out as much as four years ago, according to Charlie Blake who'd orchestrated the event with a solemn precision that he hadn't needed to fake. For five years, Jade had lived in this town, conducting his affairs and developing friendships that would have endured a lifetime even if he'd lived to be a hundred.

Her gaze lifting, Ronnie scanned the trees, aware of the gray haze lingering as if a pall had fallen over the land. The temperature had dropped considerably lower than two days ago when she'd stepped out of the sunlight and into this nightmare. Crisp, the chilly breeze rustled the drying leaves and branches, the taste of winter as palpable as the scent of death.

Shivering internally, unaccountably numb, Ronnie turned under the propulsion of dark-clad bodies, moving in automation within the soft, sullen voices and sounds. For two days, she'd heard these voices, these consoling words, desolate sounds. For two days, someone had hovered nearby waiting, anticipating a need to catch her from collapsing. No collapse. The calm to enfold her hadn't abandoned her. In whispered words, one or another had mentioned 'shock,' while others believed she was drugged, and still, others considered her 'cold' and 'unfeeling.' Even in death, she sensed the jealousy swirling around her. Old faces . . . old hostilities.

For five years, Jade had lived in Bentwood, an eligible bachelor for whom as many single as married and divorced women had pined. Rumors were vicious and never more than at a time of tragedy. Even understanding that fact, Ronnie suffered the effects, remembering a moment outside Blake's Funeral Home when Jen Andover and Frank Engler had stood side-by-side, arms crossed, and lips twisted in a snarling smile.

Numb, Ronnie accepted the murmured voices, letting one or another clasp her hand, kiss her cheek. Not much longer now. She could put this behind her. And maybe now, she would sleep soundly. The nightmares that had jolted her awake for two days enhanced the haunted shadows beneath her eyes. Nightmares, ugly nightmares where she saw Jade, the child Jade, strapped to a bed beneath a brilliant light, twisting and turning, growling, and screaming curses as if the light burned him . . . the darkness. She was the light . . . he was the darkness. Three hearts together—

The sudden break in the chain of bodies, the hushed voices, the stopped silence in her immediate vicinity—all of it combined couldn't compete with the sudden chill wrapping around her, alarming and alerting her. Before her gaze ever landed, she knew who she would see.

Only once—very briefly—she had met Jade's father, but she would have recognized him even without an introduction. From Jean-Pierre Jardonet, Jade had inherited his unnatural shade of green eyes, but while her husband's eyes were filled with warmth and life, this fellow's orbs glittered nearer to emerald, colder than any jewel, colder than death.

Standing apart from the cluster of mourners, apart from the ceremony, he poised in position to force others to lend him a wide berth en route to their cars strung along the hillside. Hands in his coat pockets, a brimmed hat casting a shadow over his features, he braced against the breeze with the long black coat pressed at his shins. From head to heel, he wore black . . . no differently than he'd worn at their wedding reception. Now, as then, he traveled in the company of other men who scattered at his flanks, watching the crowd as if anticipating an action. That they might face off against the secret servicemen who stood about, likewise poised to act on Robert Bryson's behalf, Ronnie had only a moment to wonder before the power of Jardonet's silent presence drew her from her startled pose.

He'd lost a son . . . What she would say to him, what she could say . . .? The thoughts slipped away as she stopped before him, looking into his emerald eyes. A strangeness spilled over her—a strangeness to know he suffered no grief over a loss. His gloved hand slipped from his pocket, offered and commanded her response. "Madame," he said in a low voice.

As Ronnie accepted his hand, he dipped, and his chilled mustache brushed her cheek. Chilly, that kiss, as if a winter wind touched her. "Sir," she said, again catching his eyes, noting the curve of his lips twitching under the mustache in reflection of Jade's natural smirk.

"You hov mon sympathies," he said in a heavily accented low voice. "I apolo`gize for not coming soon`air to share in this tra`jedy."

"If I'd known you were coming, we would have waited, sir," she said in a hollow voice, a shallow consolation. "I am sorry."

"Will you walk with me, madame?" he asked with a quick glance toward the casket. His eyes betrayed nothing of pain or grief. "I will pay my re`spects now, *s`il vous plait?*"

"Oui, monsieur," she said and let him guide her hand about his arm, turning with him. No one intruded; no one followed. She felt others watching as she accepted the strength of the presence at her side and fell into stride. In her gut, Tad quivered, his presence and motion more a comfort than a disturbance or distraction.

When they stood alongside the casket, Jardonet spoke. "My son . . . for however short his stay, was a lucky man, Veronique. This . . . c`est a tra`jedy, but you are a . . . sar`vivor. You will sar`vive this loss."

Momentarily, Ronnie gazed at the flowers, then tipped her head and looked up into Jardonet's emerald eyes. "You've taken him from me, haven't you, sir?"

His brow arched, an oh-so-familiar expression reeking of bewilderment and surprise, but his eyes darkened a shade in the hazy light. "Why would I do sush a thing to you? To him? He wos my son, Veronique."

"You have other sons, damn you," she hissed softly, holding his arm with a force to quiver her muscles. "Why did you take my husband from me?"

"I am given sush cred`et," Jardonet said in a sighing tone. His gaze shifted, drifted toward the casket. He shook his head almost sadly. "If only I had sush power."

"He's alive, isn't he?" she asked, her voice calm but firm.

The emerald eyes slipped to her, dark with thought and speculation. "Why would you be`lieve sush a thing, ma chérie?"

"Because I know the man I married," she said smoothly, her words firming her conviction as she gazed up into the emerald eyes, unwavering. "He wouldn't walk onto a plane that was about to crash . . . Any more than he'd walk away from me and his child unless he thought he must. My husband's alive, and I think you know it, sir. I think . . . I believe you helped him arrange this departure from my life, and I want to know why."

"Ma chérie, there are things not even I can control," he said quietly. "Your hus`band, mon fils, es one of those things."

Nothing he could have said would have rung truer in her mind. Nothing. "You know he's alive," she said, searching the handsome face, the sparking eyes which slid toward the flowered mound.

After a moment, his dark eyes sparked, and a smile haunted the corner of his mustached lips. "You know . . . as do I, that his re`mains are not in this vessel . . . Why, ma chérie, did you keep sush to yourself so long?"

A fair question, a reasonable question considering the exhaustion and pain of the past two days. So much grief, so much tragedy. She felt the loss, but not of life . . . not the cessation of life. Her focus drifting toward the mound of flowers, she realized, "Because I trust him. Because—" She lifted her gaze to Jardonet, "He wouldn't do this to me unless he had no other choice. Whatever he's done, whatever he's doing, I do trust him."

"He hos shosen well, ma chérie," Jardonet said in a low voice. "And so, I will warn you, madame, the man you mar`ried? The man you tru`sted? He may`be does not ex`ist any long`air, and thot, I fear, c`est not in my con`trol. If I could con`trol him, I would know where he is—whish I do not. Now, you understand my ah . . . predica`ment?"

In an odd moment, she believed him and sensed his shared distress. "He told me he had a mystery to solve. What do you know about that?"

With an offhanded gesture, he answered, "Like yourself, I think, I be`lieved he was in Cleveland to solve a murd`air." His gaze held hers intently. "Et would not be the first time he has de`fied me and shosen that course. I hov," he smirked and shrugged. "Forfeited any attempt to stop him."

"He . . . you're saying he used his . . . gifts to solve crimes elsewhere? That four months ago wasn't the first time?"

"Ah, to admit sush would be a lie," Jardonet said with a note of disgust, His eyes sparkling as he looked at her, a dark amusement surfaced. "His gifts used him, ma chérie. It has been that way since I first took him in . . . but whot's inside of him could not be con`cealed or ah . . . con`trolled by a shild. He wos always afraid to use his gifts. He wos a phantom in all of France, striking and disappearing, running from himself." Amusement danced in his eyes. "Sush a wonder, this son of mine. If he wasn't sush a bastard, I would love him less for the trouble he has been."

With that title slipping so easily off the mustached lips, Ronnie's temper flared. "I don't appreciate that address, Mr. Jardonet."

Jardonet's smile enhanced as he commented, "You would be offended by the truth? He is my bastard. He knows as much." He lifted his free hand, slipping his index finger along Ronnie's jawline, which might have been viewed as an endearment. "Not unlike the shild you carry, ma chérie. In the literal sense, yes? You are carrying my bastard's—"

Her hand lifted, not quick enough to avoid being caught and held in a quick vice. Her eyes sparked with fury. "Don't you ever call my child—"

"Would you hov the shild better than his pap`pa?" Jardonet interrupted, appearing only more amused beneath his hooded lashes. "This shild—il es lucky per`haps to have his pappa's name at his birth, but who knows how many oth`airs there could be, eh? My son . . . he wos not a priest. Ah, and now I hov upset you again," he said smoothly, his gaze reflecting a brooding light. "But per`haps, you will take comfort as I know, he has created no oth`airs in love—if any oth`airs exist. You are to him, whot his moth`air was to me, if only for a short time. Judge me not too harshly, ma chérie, even the dev`il hos his favorites."

A shiver skittered down her spine with the simplicity of those words and the glitter of light behind the emerald gems. Her husband was, indeed, this man's favorite, but that was no blessing for Jade. The amusement behind that slight smile couldn't be mistaken for humor or jest. At this moment, she could believe—incontestably—that this man had walked upright from the gates of hell. If he offered her a deal, her husband for her soul, she wouldn't be surprised, and she shivered more with the question hovering at the edge of her mind . . . and the answer too close to the surface. "You came here to find him, didn't you?"

"I came here to pay my re`spects to the widow of my lost son," he said smoothly, and without visibly moving his hand, he produced a glossy-black business card which he slipped into her palm before releasing her hand. "If there is anything I can do for you, madame, reash me. C`est not easy for a woman alone to raise a shild, and I would not like to be a strang`air to my grand`shild."

Before she could raise the protest and denial to her lips, he turned them both smoothly, looking down into her fierce, angry eyes and smiling crookedly. "Sush fire in your eyes, ma fille. I am glad to see thot you are feeling better."

"You're not getting him, monsieur," she said in a soft angry tone. "I will find him, and you're not getting him."

"Madame, he is al`ready mine," her father-in-law spoke in a low silky tone, and she might have protested again if not for his eyes turning, the emerald shade darkening and smile transforming, chilling.

Turning to see what held his gaze, her heart hammered a quick angry beat. Jean-Pierre wasn't the only one who'd arrived late. Special Agent Mark Jarvins had joined the crowd waiting at the limousine. Presently, he stared in her direction, but apparently, he was more interested in the man escorting her across the lawn. Without a doubt, Mark recognized Jardonet. Whether they'd ever met, Ronnie had no idea, but judging by Jardonet's expression, he was well informed. How much the man knew about the events in Bentwood, about the trouble Mark had attempted to cause for his favored, wayward son, she couldn't imagine, but apparently enough. Without a change in pace, Jardonet led her to the gathering, and with every step, the walls of that warm cocoon wrapped tighter about her. Not even the anger lasted as she glimpsed the red-blotched faces and grim expressions. Loss. The grief of so many. Was this safe mask of indifference a weapon? A shield against the pain she would be forced to endure?

"Jean-Pierre," her father spoke in a low cadence, offering his hand to her escort. "You have my sympathies, monsieur."

Breaking a hand away, Jardonet accepted the handshake and reverent acceptance which began a new series of condolences and started more tears flowing. That Jardonet could pull it off, becoming glassy-eyed as though battling his grief with a firm resolve, Ronnie had only sense enough to notice. When she might have been shuffled aside, her father-in-law held her close, keeping her arm and somehow holding the onslaught of well-meaning women from falling on her. And in an odd moment, she was nearly grateful for the reprieve.

Too soon, the procession was moving, and again, Jean-Pierre stayed with her, ushering her into the limousine where he leaned and brushed a kiss on her cheek . . . flashing a smile and a wink which nearly started her blood pumping in outrage. Preoccupied, she listened as he exchanged more words with her father, apologizing in advance that he couldn't accept the invitation to join them at the church hall, suggesting he might see them again before he returned to France.

When they were inside the car, her parents, her brothers, and Vicky, Linc's wife, Fiona spoke offhandedly, "I do wish Mr. Jardonet would change his mind. At a time like this, he shouldn't be alone. This must be hard on him."

"I'm sure he'll cope in his own way, dear," Robert said in a preoccupied tone.

"I've heard he's one of the richest men in France, Dad," Bobby said carefully. "Do you know if that's true?"

"I would imagine there's some truth to it," her father answered.

"You've met him before. I mean you knew him before Ronnie and—" *Jade met.*

"I've heard of him, as I'm sure he's heard of me, but no, I don't recall meeting him personally before this summer," Robert answered with his natural diplomacy.

"Did uh . . . does he have a lot of family?"

"Bobby, I don't think we need to discuss this right now," Fiona said quietly.

"You're probably right, I'm sorry," Bobby said quietly. "How you holding up, sis? You all right?"

"Fine," she said in a hollow tone.

"Sweetie, I know this is hard, but you'll get through it," her mother said gently, squeezing her hand. "We won't stay long at the hall . . . We'll just make an appearance. I'm sure everyone will understand."

How many lives had he touched? How many people, like the Spencers and Meg Price, and Cy Bender and young Wade . . .?

Wade had come after school two days ago and banged on the side door until someone had let him in. For just a second, he'd met Ronnie's eyes, seeking, receiving confirmation, then turned and fled. With his mother, he'd come to the funeral home last evening. Lynn Kreider hadn't held a grudge over the Laquettes' marriage; she'd visited the shop and chatted with Ronnie for hours, only pleased that her son chose to emulate a man of Jade's character. For the first time since kindergarten, Wade had begun bringing home A's and B's, studying on his own even before Lynn came home from work in the evening. Jade Laquette was the reason. 'I want to be as smart as him,' Wade had confided to his mother weeks ago. And so many others.

For such a small town . . . or possibly because it was such a small town, he'd touched the lives of so many people that Ronnie couldn't begin to recollect them all. But she'd heard the epitaphs in words and tones, had felt the shared sorrow in the embraces, seen the grief in the eyes of near strangers who'd held her hand a few seconds longer. Deedee Spencer was devastated . . . She'd stood near the casket, touching the rail, her eyes as murky as blue marbles until Tim had scooped her away and delivered her into the hands of his mother and father.

Even with the privacy insured by local police and secret service, a line of cars formed a train behind the limousine . . . And in an odd moment, Ronnie remembered thinking of that old wives' tale about counting cars in a funeral possession. Bad luck. Allegedly. She hadn't counted cars four days ago. She'd merely rested behind the pickup's steering wheel and watched the procession trailing behind Jack Trumble's hearse. Following her intuition, she'd fallen into line and arrived at the cemetery, halting a reasonable distance away and watching the mourners striding toward the mausoleum.

A fresh grave, a mound of flowers . . . She'd been drawn to read the inscription of the recently deceased Emmet Duncan outside her window, and again, when spotting the ornamental tomb of Ethel Savrel. Had those images carried a message? Had Jade sent her to Elmview to prepare her for this event? Had he lent her an omen to sense what lay ahead for her. A widow . . . at twenty-six. That stigma would remain. He could never return to her. Not as the man he had been. However it had been arranged, no doubts remained. His clothes . . . his wallet . . . a body had been found on that plane, and she shuddered with a thought of what nameless entity would now lie forever in the earth beneath her husband's tombstone.

For the losses, the severance of friendships, the crushed dreams they could never share from the house in the woods to the thriving business he'd built—the tears lifted in her eyes. What could have driven him to this? What could have been so important that he would forfeit their life and go to such extremes to be certain they would never recover?

CHAPTER 9

Relaxed, sprawled in the single recliner to occupy the room, Dominique affected a doze, his thoughts turning far more rapidly than his posture suggested. Time had passed, a great deal of time since he had entered this private room where the locks engaged silently after every visitor and remained locked. If only by the changing light through the curtains, the depth of shadows, he sensed the clock ticking. No television or radio. No clock or watch. Nothing to verify how long he'd spent in this container under critical observation. The apartment ambiance of the room lacked the amenities to attach him to the world beyond these walls. But he certainly possessed other means to meter events . . . and he'd given himself license to exercise his ability.

Jade Laquette had been laid to rest.

Whether the room where Dr. Heinz and Asst. Director Lakeland argued their culpability rested above or below him, Dominique had no desire to learn. In his way, he knew they'd argued often over the past few days and engaged several others in their discourse. This moment—not the exception.

'. . . He's not Jade Laquette. Your people screwed up.'

'You don't have the option to play Pontius Pilot, doctor. I think I should remind you—Laquette wasn't coming in on his own . . .'

'National security . . . Aren't those the words I've heard more often than I care to count? And as I recall, I voiced my objections several times . . .'

'Don't hand me that. You wanted a crack at Laquette, and I don't give a damn if you hide behind the sanctimonious babble of science until the sun comes up. The means to the end wasn't as important to you as the end to the means.'

'Arguing over the semantics will not improve our situation, gentlemen . . .' Another man—Chalmers, Ben Chalmers, a member of the President's cabinet, another bureaucrat had joined the caucus. 'The fact remains, we have the wrong man, and the problem remains, how do we handle this situation without creating an international incident? Your orders, as I recall, were to persuade Jade Laquette to come in for questioning, not to blasted abduct him.'

'If my men weren't already in place to extract him, chances are Laquette would be dead. That dose could have killed him—'

'Oh, and there's an irony if I've ever heard one under the circumstances. Need I remind you, we may be currently holding a French citizen against his will, and if I'm to understand this, he's more than aware of that situation.'

'That's really the issue here, Mr. Chalmers,' Heinz interrupted. 'He does know. And if you've seen those tapes, you will note, he has an uncanny ability to collect those very details from us. The longer we attempt to deceive him, the harder that's going to become . . . no matter who we have now, he's gifted.'

'What are you suggesting, doctor? That we simply walk in and apologize for the mistake and the inconvenience? Possibly appeal to his sympathies and pledge him to silence while we enlist his help to find out whatever Laquette knew?'

'That might have been far easier than you make it sound if not for the fact that Jade Laquette was on that plane three days ago and God pity you, Mr. Lakeland, if you had anything to do with that man's death. As I understand it, they may not have shared any close personal relationship, but in this case, I'd wonder about that maxim—blood is thicker than water . . .'

Not easily, the combined forces had reached a tentative decision, and by no surprise, Dominique sensed the anticipation behind the cameras.

Yawning, stretching, he feigned a natural awakening, then jolted abruptly, darting his gaze about the room as if disoriented. Letting a curse slip off his lips, he pulled the lever to retract the footrest and pushed to his feet. A thermal coffeepot, compliments of the house, rested on the small table, along with his cigarettes, a silver engraved lighter, a coffee cup, and an ashtray.

This wasn't his first awakening in this room, merely the first that he was fully awake and shaking off the lingering effects of a drug-induced fog.

As if undecided, he fumbled with the coffeepot momentarily then uttered another curse and filled the cup, lighted a cigarette, and moved with both to the window. Parting the slatted louver blinds, he portrayed the image of a man judging the time of day by the platinum depths of the sky though there wasn't much to see.

Early morning. If the sun had risen at all, it had remained hidden behind clouds, adding little to the shadowy landscape beyond the glass, and suddenly, he wondered if it was truly sunrise or sunset. Night could be descending. He felt the pull of the moon, and in a sudden epiphany, knew he had always suffered an affinity to the night though he'd never truly looked forward to the darkness. A necessary evil, he supposed.

Where would the devil reign, if not in the quick of night? The darkness cloaked a world of sins, even for the righteous, he mused. How else would the population rise to explosive proportions? The good wholesome, God-fearing righteous wouldn't shed their frocks in the quick of day and propagate in wanton bliss. No, certainly not. And where would the sanctimonious find fuel for their fire and brimstone speeches? If not for the existence of evil, how would the world accommodate the evangelists, the journalists, and the talk show hosts who thrived on the condemnation and moral decline of man? The night served its purpose, raping the innocents, freezing the homeless, battering the unsuspecting, starving the poor. What would the world do without victims to raise the moral consciousness of the victors? A boring world that would be, to have all men sated, all men standing on pedestals directing a flock of likewise bejeweled orators.

'Man is Good.' 'Man is Merciful.' 'Extra! Extra! Read all about it! . . . God is Laid Off, Folks!!!'

Subtitle: Lack of work.

End of story. . . Armageddon. The end of mankind.

The yin to Hitler's yang.

"Utopia, my ass," he muttered under his breath and turned as the door opened. The smile playing at the corner of his lips unsettled his austere visitors.

Two, he had seen on prior visits. Heinz and Lakeland. The third man, Dominique studied momentarily before grasping details . . . Ben Chalmers truly was just another bureaucrat, enlisted for the sole purpose of damage control, a spokesman on international relations. Unfortunately, just another expendable pawn in this cat-mouse intelligence game. The real players . . . whoever had begun this game more than eighteen years ago remained well behind these gentlemen, and in a moment of crystal clarity, Dominique felt slightly bad for them. They had even less of an idea of what they were doing in this room than he did. On a scale of three to one, Dr. Heinz had the most integrity. The fellow had been sucked into this through his genuine volition to improve the conditions of mankind, or at least, reach a base understanding. Eugenics, in that single word, he'd found a bone to sink his teeth into. The others were following orders, blindly, and apparently, interested in saving someone's ass, their own included. Of those two, Lakeland carried the weight as well as wisdom.

Amused in the space of thirty seconds or less, Dominique moved to the table, fleeting a glance at his guests between crushing out his cigarette. Landing his gaze on Lakeland, he commented, "Decide to come clean, have you?"

"Mr. Jardonet—"

"Hmm, an improvement," Dominique commented and focused on Chalmers. "And you, sir, ah . . . Chalmers, is it?"

Younger than both others by at least ten years, this sharp-dressed fellow wore the first signs of aging via hair loss and an expanding middle. Furtively, he darted a glance between his comrades as if he questioned their concerns.

More amused, Dominique tilted his gaze to Heinz. "You did warn him, yes? By no fault of yours, he failed to realize the accuracy of your consensus. Cannot fault him either though, can we, doctor? He has no idea what he is up against, but you do. Why do you persist in buckling to these bureaucrats? You could work wonders in the private sector and have far more rein to conduct your archaic experiments."

"Mr. Jardonet, if you are finished," Lakeland stated crisply, his French precise. "Possibly, we could sit down and discuss a few details."

"You already know what we are about to discuss. Is that right, Mr. Jardonet?" Heinz asked while taking the lead, coming toward the table.

"Maybe yes. Maybe no," Dominique mused and pulled out the nearest chair, motioning to the other for Heinz. "Please, join me?" he said and bounced a glance off the single remaining chair, then looked to the others. "Perhaps you should have preempted your numbers and brought an extra chair, or would you prefer I sit in the recliner, and you can rearrange these three—inquisition-style—in front of me?"

"Mr. Jardonet," Chalmers said placatingly, likewise speaking textbook French. "I understand your anger at the moment, but if you will bear with us, I am certain you will understand."

"I am sure I will," Dominique said in a slightly darker tone, sliding into the chair he'd pulled out. "Forgive me if I do not wait for you to join me. I seem to be suffering from a recent malady that has left me slightly weak in the knees."

"Then you do know what we are here to discuss," Chalmers said as if pleased with an inadequate student. A teacher in another life, a prior occupation.

Even with his tailored pinstriped and bold-patterned tie reflecting flair, he epitomized a grade-school academic. Reaching the chair ahead of Lakeland, possibly engaged in a child's game of musical chairs, he slid a briefcase onto the table, skidding the coffeepot aside although it wasn't in his path. "I understand you feel someone in the United States government is responsible for that recent malady, Mr. Jardonet," the man said as he settled into the chair, getting down to business and oblivious of the tension in Heinz's gaze that might have forewarned him.

Affecting an expression of serious interest, Dominique softened his gaze considerably—all ears and intrigue. "I am under that impression, yes," Dominique said carefully, subtly implying he might be willing to hear otherwise. If this fellow had listened to the tapes that Heinz had suggested, he wouldn't be making this mistake. "Please. Continue if you will?"

Catching, folding his pudgy hands on his closed briefcase, Chalmers postured an intimacy and honesty, his smooth rounded face shining brilliantly under the fluorescent light from the panel directly over his head.

Despite the shine, the fellow wasn't sweating, Dominique noted. Chalmers merely possessed the smooth, overexposed skin to reflect light and lend him the wet look. If he wondered why Dominique's smile twitched, he chose not to ponder too deeply.

"Dominique . . . do you mind if I call you Dominique? I am Ben, by the way, Ben Chalmers," he said and freed his hands, stretching one across the table. When Dominique reached for his cigarettes instead, Chalmers lowered his hand slightly and continued earnestly. "I am acting on behalf of the United States government to investigate your situation, Dominique. You've . . . pardon me for saying so," he said while retracting his hand, wrinkling his brow. "You have made some serious accusations during your recovery. Accusations which could present serious ah . . . let us say repercussions if you believe them. If I understand this, you believe that someone in our government conspired to kidnap you and bring you here. Do you have a reason for believing that, Dominique? Is there . . . something you have not said to justify why the United States government would take that action against you—an apparently well-known French citizen?"

"Am I a spy, do you mean to ask?" Dominique asked with a feigned reluctance.

"Well . . . Oversimplified. But I would imagine I am. Were you in this country for reasons other than those cited on your passport?"

"I am certain you could answer that question better than I, Mr. Chalmers," Dominique said, sparking anger. "I have only impressions of the time I spent strapped to a table in your lower chambers, where you, I am sure, have the transcripts from the same."

"Dominque," Chalmers started to lean back, almost sighing his displeasure.

"You asked, Mr. Chalmers, but I do not recall agreeing to the informality you persist in using. Forgive me if I take offense to your liberties, but I would prefer we refrain from addressing one another by first name, as such implies that we are friends. I am Inspector Dominique Jardonet," he barely paused to add, "I also take offense to lies and deceit, but—" He shrugged, making a dismissive sound. "*C'est la vie.* Continue if you feel the need. Such things are beyond the power of men to control. Part of their nature, I have come to realize."

"Mr. Jardonet, I am not here in an attempt to deceive you—"

"Ah, let me guess," Dominique said with a fleeting glance at the briefcase, a smile playing at the corner of his mustache. "You have brought physical evidence . . . in the form of statements from the operatives who responded to the action taken against me in the rear of my hotel Wednesday evening. You will . . . show me further evidence from doctors who attempted to treat me as I lay in a coma in an emergency room. You will produce transcripts to certain parties in the government documenting the calls placed on my behalf to enlist a helicopter to collect me from the rooftop of said hospital? I am exceptionally good at guesswork," he said with a dark shine in his eyes. "And I am guessing further that you will produce these compiled facts and present them to any interested parties in my government, including Ambassador Andre` LeLonet, to clarify any misrepresentation of your facts that I could offer those same parties."

"Mr. Jardonet—"

"Please, refrain from further attempts to qualify your actions or intentions. I accept your proposal."

Silence dropped. All three men looked at him as if he were mad, each one speculating in varied degrees about what he might intend to do. Lakeland trusted him far less than either of the others and rightfully so. He'd spent several years in the field. Knew enough about the working operations of the intelligence community to justify his distrust. Chalmers, a bureaucrat, wondered if the situation had truly warranted his attention, and if so, why did this seem far too quick and easy? Heinz wondered what motivated Dominique to accept the lies, or was that too simple? If he believed his life was in jeopardy, he would have no choice but to accept the only means of escape available. No one was about to let him out of here with the power to incite an international incident.

"Mr. Jardonet, I'm afraid there's one more situation we need to discuss," Chalmers said gravely, his pudgy features drawn with an expression of dread. "I understand there were questions raised earlier about your half-brother, American citizen Jade Laquette," he said carefully. "I'm sorry to say, sir . . . Mr. Laquette was in an accident. We're still attempting to piece together the facts, but it appears he was in Cleveland, Ohio, around the same time as you. It's true, in fact, that a few of our federal agents attempted to enlist his help to solve the crimes in that city. We're not exactly sure how he managed it, but we've been able to learn that he, in fact, rented a vehicle that was delivered to a restaurant. From there, we learned that he arranged to board a private craft registered to an overseas company at a municipal airport in Cleveland's suburbs. The plane landed at another municipal airport near Cincinnati, Ohio, and after a brief layover, departed for Tennessee. From what we have learned from the pilot's radio transmissions, the craft underwent an engine malfunction. I am sorry to say, Mr. Jardonet, your brother didn't survive the crash."

Head tilted at an angle to suggest he sought either lie or truth, he spoke almost indifferently. "He was my half-brother."

"I know you expressed concern in a few of your more lucid moments recently."

"He took the precautions of a man on the run," Dominique said thoughtfully, halfheartedly wondering what else he might have said in those semi-lucid moments. Eventually, he would recall every second if it ever became necessary. Currently, he couldn't care less. His unreadable gaze shifted to Heinz, then lifted to Lakeland. "There, the mystery arises, sir. Will you explain how I was mistaken for my bastard brother when I had numerous communications and affiliations with your agents in Cleveland? Or should I guess there is more than meets the eye to all of this? I do recall an incident in the morgue, a heated discussion with one of your agents who seemed ah . . . adamant that I was Laquette? Now, I need wonder . . . do you know who wanted to kill my half-brother? And why, perhaps?"

"I don't think I quite understand the question, Mr. Jardonet?" Lakeland said though he understood perfectly. He wanted a more defined clarification of what Dominique might already know.

"Let us say, between ourselves, naturally, that what you insist on presenting as the truth is the truth—that your agents rescued me. From whom, sir? If I were who you believed—Laquette—why would someone have assaulted him? Attempted to kill him? And further, a curiosity, that he should die in a plane crash . . . and I should be assaulted? Which event preceded the other?"

"His plane went down late in the afternoon."

"Ah, and I was ab—" *—ducted.* "Rescued," he corrected with a wry smirk and a glance at Chalmers. "Later in the evening," he continued. "So, and I wonder, did he have an entire hit squad chasing him, my friend?" Dominique asked with a slight smile. "Or were his enemies as confused as you appeared to be upon my awakening? Were they not convinced they killed Laquette and assaulted me as well? You understand my concern to reach the truth, I am sure. If I was abducted either by your agency or another, my life could remain in jeopardy. Why would someone want to kill my half-brother? What has Cleveland to do with that situation? Why did someone in your government enlist my services if my half-brother was already enlisted? Too many unanswered questions, Mr. Lakeland."

"We haven't been able to determine if the plane malfunctioned by accident, but we are considering the possibility of foul play, Mr. Jardonet," Lakeland spoke warily, carefully, not entirely comfortable with the language or the subject. "Why exactly you were administered a nearly lethal injection, we haven't learned, but we have an investigation underway."

"Ah, I'm sure you do," Dominique said as he continued to scry Lakeland, understanding the man's genuine conflict. What had begun as an almost simple directive to enlist an American citizen to assist in a murder investigation in Cleveland had become a debacle. And Lakeland wasn't the brains behind this operation. Like Chalmers, he was a pawn, with at least one of his agents insisting that they were holding Jade Laquette, that the man couldn't have slipped away from them in Cleveland. Evidence to the contrary had arrived via other operatives, with eyewitness accounts positively identifying Jade Laquette boarding planes, accepting the keys to rental cars . . . And to make matters worse, Lakeland did know the partial truth that Laquette's abduction was a strategic operation designed to bring the man in quietly for questioning. Somewhere during that day, Jardonet had usurped his half-brother. . . and that was neither coincidence nor accident.

The evidence that Laquette had held a secret detrimental to National Security had only enhanced; unfortunately, the man was now dead. Whether by accident or through someone in the government, who wanted those secrets to remain hidden, was yet to be decided.

None of which could be discussed openly with the Frenchman who had apparently been used by the same people who might have wanted Laquette silenced.

Complicating the entire issue was Heinz's unfounded belief—almost absurd belief—that Laquette and now this half-brother possessed a psychic power. And therein certainly lay the irony. Laquette had been enlisted under the pretense of psychic ability . . . and he was no more psychic than the man on the moon. Someone had tipped him off, and considering his marriage to Robert Bryson's daughter, it wasn't a stretch to assume from where that information had come.

Was Bryson acting for or against his son-in-law? That question burned in Lakeland's mind. *And who tipped off Bryson to this operation? Or was Bryson behind the operation? Maybe the old man held a grudge against the marriage. Rumors were circulating the capitol hill set to suggest Bryson possessed good reason to neutralize his son-in-law. And if not Bryson, who? Who and why?*

"Very good questions," Dominique said quietly, his gaze still steady on Lakeland, whose eyes flickered and shaded considerably. Shrugging, Dominique continued quietly, "Perhaps you should ask your comrades to step out of this room and disengage those cameras. I do not think what we are about to discuss should be ah . . . of interest to either a direct representative of your president's cabinet or the half dozen security guards who maintain the system. If you and I are to reach an understanding, it will be between us."

"I'm afraid I have to object," Chalmers stated. "If there's to be any discussion of these matters which could reflect—"

Lakeland flashed a heated glance to Chalmers, addressing him in French. "You did your job, Mr. Chalmers. You presented Mr. Jardonet with the facts of his ordeal, and he has accepted them. The issue of his half-brother is more of a personal interest." His gaze shifted to Dominique. "Correct me if I'm wrong."

"I would," Dominique answered with a twitch of a smile which annoyed Lakeland even as he turned his gaze to Chalmers.

"I doubt anything we say beyond this point would be of interest to either a National Security Council or the President. It's a domestic situation."

Dominique looked to Heinz, who studied him intently. "I think you should join your comrade, doctor, and step out of the room. As much as I know you find me as intriguing as a white mouse under glass, I tend to become irritated under such duress. Do see that Mr. Lakeland's orders are obeyed despite your desire to the contrary."

Heinz considered arguing, but on a scale of three to one, his voice carried the least weight within this room, and his belief in Dominique's ability overwhelmed his desire to object. Resigning, he pushed off the chair and looked to Lakeland. "I'll see that the monitors are disengaged, Mr. Lakeland," he commented in English and started toward the door.

CHAPTER 10

"If you're about ready to go, Sweetie, we could go pick up a few of your things. Your father has the plane standing by, and I really think we should get you home where you can rest."

Those were the first words to truly register since Ronnie had entered the crowded church hall. Drawing her gaze from the barely touched portion of roast beef and potatoes, she found her mother's soulful gaze. As always, Fiona Bryson appeared as finely sculpted and painted as a porcelain doll. Her auburn hair swept into a classic style to enhance her slender face, no hint of gray or visible age-line detracting from the image. Timeless, this delicate vision of southern gentility with whom Ronnie had never shared an intimate relationship. They were mother and daughter, as different as night and day, and in a stopped instant, Ronnie regretted that detail if only for her mother's sake. "I will be going home soon, Mother, but I won't need a plane to get there," she said quietly.

Concern whipped across her mother's brow, there and gone, as her mother decided the words were an attempted jest and tried to smile. Her hand found Ronnie's on the table, squeezing gently, as she had a million times in the past two days. "I checked with Dr. Amhurst, sweetie. There's no danger for you to fly at this stage, and I really don't think it's a good idea to drive all that way."

"I'm just going down the block, Mother," Ronnie said and decided now was a good time to depart. She needed the walk. Needed the quiet of a short walk. Setting the fork aside, she barely started to scoot the chair backward when her mother clasped her hand, and heads turned.

Directly across from Fiona, Bobby's attention riveted, but Ronnie determined not to notice. The chasm had widened considerably after she'd spotted him huddled with Mark Jarvins a short time ago.

"Honey, we agreed, you shouldn't be alone right now. Coming home is the best thing for you and the baby. Bobby can take care of whatever legal issues come up. You needn't worry about making any decisions right now."

"What's going on, Mother?" Bobby asked, drawing their father's attention from a discussion with Al Spencer, Tim's older brother, and the newly elected State Senator.

"Your sister seems to be changing her mind about coming home," Fiona started.

"On the contrary, Mother," Ronnie stated and caught her mother's mildly confused eyes. "I am going home. To my own home," she clarified and looked past Fiona to Robert Sr., who studied her as if she had just spouted a curse at the national anthem. "I do appreciate the offer, Father, but I'm afraid I must decline. Forgive me if I've delayed your departure."

"Veronica," he started but stopped, seeming to already know what her mother had yet to fathom—his daughter was just like him. Too headstrong, too temperamental, and far too independent to be led around on a shoestring. His hand slipped off the back of Fiona's chair to her shoulder as if he meant to protect his wife from the discovery, and to Ronnie's slight surprise, he pushed off his chair. "I understand, dear. If you're ready to leave, we can have our driver take you."

"Dad?" Bobby started, obviously surprised by their father's capitulation.

"Robert," Fiona started in bewilderment. "She can't—"

The mere squeeze on her shoulder halted Fiona's words, accompanied by a flashing glance. As Ronnie rose, his attention returned, resolved. "We can't force you to come home, dear, but I trust if you need us, you'll call."

"I will," she said smoothly and accepted the hand he offered. Rather than hit and run like most of their physical encounters over the years, he held her fingers as gently as he had on her wedding day when he'd placed her hand in Jade's. More than anything he could have said or done, that slight gesture touched her deeply, lifting the prickling tears to her eyes. "Please," she said softly. "Make my apologies, and don't ask your driver to take me. I think I need the walk."

An oddly gentle, disheartened smile touched his lips, and he'd never appeared more human, more real to her than at this moment. "You always did find that mode of travel more appealing than a chauffeured car." Shaking his head as if the thought eluded him, he leaned and brushed a kiss on her cheek. "Take care of yourself, dear, and do call if you need anything. Anything at all."

"I will, Father. Thank you," she said and turned, gratefully close enough to the door to avoid the main flow of the gathering. Fighting the innate desire to burst into tears, she managed several offhanded farewells and received countless quick hugs, not excluding Max Hagen, who appeared slightly older than any moment past. A few seconds longer, he embraced her, sharing her sorrow rather than conveying his own. Such a tangled web. Her, Max, Jade . . . Eighteen years ago, Max had answered that police call to arrive at the Laquette home . . . and that memory had never stopped haunting him. In his expression, the sadness lingered, his features drawn to mask the smile he'd worn even in the most troubling times.

"If you need anything, don't hesitate to call me, baby doll," he offered with his disheartened smile.

"I will, Max. Thanks," she said and spared a quick embrace with Jesse, Max's daughter, her childhood friend. "I'm glad you came," Ronnie admitted, seeing and feeling the dismay in Jesse's blue eyes. They hadn't remained close, not since parting for separate colleges.

"If there's anything I can do," Jesse strained softly, honestly. Despite living at the opposite end of the country, pursuing her lifelong ambition to become an actress, Jesse would drop everything and come to her aid. Perhaps the years hadn't changed them. In fleeting seconds, they were the same two renegade girls who'd hung around Max's precinct more often than a mall. By the time they'd turned twelve, Jesse had perfected the expressions and emotions to mime a mugger as perfectly as a hooker, and Ronnie had begun sensing the madness behind violent crimes, empathizing with the victims and residual victims.

Haunted by the nostalgia, Ronnie reached the door, needing a breath of fresh air, unaware of her father following until he caught the door at her back.

With an expression of apology, rare but real, in his blue eyes, he commented, "You may still need an escort, dear."

Why . . . why had she even considered the possibility of walking alone? A mere glance at the collection of men outside the door and a fleeting glimpse at the reporters gathered on the sidewalk evidenced the futility. As if she'd swallowed lead, she felt the weight in her gut as heads turned, and bodies started toward her. Reporters . . . her own associates . . . and they would hound her, as they had hounded her family, as they had hounded and persecuted Jade Laquette eighteen years earlier. Even in death, they refused to let him rest.

Already she'd heard inklings of the tabloid sensationalism hitting the news wire only beginning with one headline, reading . . .

'Psychic Dies in Fiery Crash.'

"It might be safer to ride, dear," her father said, and again the apology fleeted in his eyes and knitted his brow as the secret service men closed the loop to halt the reporters from a full-frontal assault. If Robert Bryson could forfeit his fortune and fame to free her from this mayhem, she had no doubts at this moment, he would do so gladly.

Tired, just too tired, and heartsick to care, Ronnie barely started to agree when the hand touched her back.

"If she's ready to leave, Mr. Bryson. We can—"

Pivoting her gaze, she locked on Mark Jarvins, remembering his belated appearance at the cemetery and his heart-wrenching condolence offered as she'd sat at the table inside. That she'd once believed herself in love with this man was nearly too much to fathom. Never had he seemed more like a weasel, showing up now, feigning the knight in shining armor routine as if he would, or could rescue her from her grief. He wasn't half the man Jade was, and somewhere behind his mocked, sorrowful gaze, he knew it.

"We'll give you a ride home, Ronnie. I have my car."

A half-step away, respecting her personal space, Len Devinio stood, braced against the assault of cameras that would be snapping if not for his broad shoulders. He'd come last evening. He'd arrived in the crush of bodies flocking into the apartment. As out of sorts as all others, he'd held her briefly and kissed her cheek. If Len was alone and offering his escort, she would accept the ride.

"Len, why don't you go bring my car?" Jarvins stated as if Devinio were his personal chauffeur.

Ronnie flashed her gaze to her father, catching a hint of his peculiar speculation directed at Jarvins before he looked at her. "If your driver's still an option, Father, I'd appreciate it."

"Of course, dear," he said and needed only a glance and a nod to the man who had followed them from the hall.

"Ron," Len started. "We could give you a lift. It's no trouble."

Stepping from under Mark's touch, Ronnie barely started to decline before she glimpsed Meg holding the door for Hazel Handler. Without a thought, Ronnie stepped to catch the door from the outside, freeing Meg on the inside. Hazel relied on a cane, her legs swollen often and painful beyond measure, but she hadn't missed a visitation nor an opportunity to offer her comfort or assistance over the past two days. This wasn't the exception. Between these two women, they missed nothing. Whether they believed Ronnie was on the verge of collapse or meant to offer support against the power of her prestigious father, Ronnie couldn't decide, but their appearance offered inspiration.

"Are you all right, honey?" Hazel asked as she cleared the threshold.

"I'm just a little tired. I think I need to get home. Could I offer you both a lift? My father's lent us his car."

The decision was made, and Ronnie thought she might have glimpsed just a tiny flicker of an appreciative smile in her father's eyes before his security men offered a human shield for her to reach the waiting car. In the backseat of the Lincoln, Hazel muttered choice words for the familiar faces in the plethora of reporters who tried to shout through the glass. The race to reach Olden Time was won, hands down, and gratefully, Ronnie slid through the side entrance, thanking Meg and Hazel, promising to speak with them after she rested for a little while.

For the first time in three days, Ronnie stood alone within the matrix of hallways and doors that combined to become Olden Time Antiques and Collectibles. Exhausted suddenly, she rested against the wall in the shadowy first-floor hallway. Chateau Laquette had never felt more empty, more dark . . . And for a long moment, she listened to the preternatural silence while staring at the dull lightbulb overhead. Anywhere else, a 75-watt bulb would probably offer sufficient light. Here, in this hallway, she'd be lucky to read the time on her indigo watch . . . and she remembered the first time Jade had escorted her into this narrow walkway. Even in the dull light, the discomfort had haunted his hazel eyes—compounded when he led her into his shadowed apartment on the second floor. Darkness. He'd lived in darkness, preferring the dim-lighted hallways and heavily curtained windows to the light of day. Whether he'd meant to keep out the light or merely intruders and sightseers, she'd never ascertained.

She was the light . . . he was the darkness.

What had those words meant to him? Was she the symbol of exposure in his mind? Had she somehow destroyed him by recognizing him at the onset? She had promised never to divulge his identity. She'd understood his need for secrecy, if only to avoid the publicity which would have—and had—erupted in the wake of his announcement. By his own decision, he'd reclaimed his given name, determined to marry her and give her his name, to grant their child that name regardless of the consequences.

They had made the tabloids . . ..

'Psychic Returns After Eighteen Years.' . . . He had laughed a little over that heading, and she remembered his offhanded comment. 'I wonder if they consider me a ghost? Or better still, the savior personified? Will we hear next, Washington Socialite Marries A Resurrected Psychic? Ah, I have it! Sensational Journalist Marries Suspected Psychic Serial Killer! We haven't heard that one yet. Has a certain sibilance relative to the snakes that would fabricate such a story . . ..'

A ghost of a smile slid into her lips. The man could be downright nasty when referring to her colleagues and he got away with it every time, winking that dimple and flashing those pearly whites. A menace . . . her menace. She wanted him back more than ever, at least long enough to hurt him real bad—after smothering him in a few zillion kisses. And even as she considered all the nasty things that she would do to him for putting her through this hell, she prayed for the opportunity to implement every single one. Living a life without him, without hearing his voice in her ear, feeling his touch in the quick of night, seeing that devil-be-damned smile . . . life without the man she married would be a life not worth living.

Paradox. She'd never loved and hated the same man as deeply as she loved and hated Jade Laquette at this moment. But that wasn't exactly true. This devil possessed an uncanny ability to stir those emotions in her without half trying, and he'd been managing it since their eyes had first met outside of Meg's Diner. The shit. The whole time she'd been hiding behind dark mirror sunglasses—sizing him up as a centerfold for Playgirl— he'd been catching her every thought and sucking it all in. For that alone, she should have whacked him in the jaw a few times. Instead—damned fool that she was—she'd fallen in love with him a measly ten minutes later. Well, and the damage was done. She'd married the devil for better or worse, and the worse was over—for the moment.

Finding him . . . Finding him held priority. After that, she could decide what recourse to take against him. And God help him if his reason for all of this was anything less than the crises she suspected. Even as she mustered her mad and pushed off the wall, she knew nothing short of disaster would have led him to these lengths.

Reflecting uncomfortably on her father-in-law's words, she shivered as she ascended the steps. Technically, legally, Jean-Pierre Jardonet wasn't her father-in-law, but no relief accompanied that thought.

'. . . He's already mine.'

Like hell, she nearly said aloud before the image of Jardonet's smile slid through her mind, along with the irony of her words. Like *hell* was already Jardonet's domain—his territory, at the least.

"Bullshit," she muttered, wading in her coat pocket for her keys. She couldn't remember locking the apartment before leaving hours ago, any more than she recalled pocketing her keys. She found them, though, and unlocked the door.

What did she think, anyway? That her father-in-law was a minion of the devil? That he was on a first-name basis with the big S? "Bullshit," she muttered again, stripping off the heavy coat and tossing it on a chair in passing. Nervous tension kept her moving, but no relief came as she entered her kitchen to find the table crowded with covered dishes and plastic-wrapped chunks of cakes, cookies, and brownies with enough calories per bite to send her off the scales within the week . . . and probably enough sugar to turn Tad into an Olympic swimmer by his sixth month.

How dare Jean-Pierre Jardonet even suggest that . . .

"Damn him," she uttered irritably. The nerve of that man to say enough to make her mad, then gauge his words to suggest he meant no blasted offense by referring to her child—and his own child—as a bastard. Then he had the gall—the gall-blasted-*gall*—to suggest he would like to know his grandchild? "Bullshit!" Not if she had any say . . .

What did she really think of her father-in-law?

Jade never talked about him. Not one way or the other. Even after they were married and she'd broached the subject, he'd circumvented the conversation with his natural subversive tactics. She knew Jardonet was wealthy, as Bobby had apparently discovered. She knew Jade had lived with his father for a few years . . . possibly eight years.

Jade had disappeared from the public eye within weeks after his mother's death. He'd once admitted to departing his father's house on his eighteenth birthday and swearing never to return. And Jardonet's words about Jade striking and disappearing regarding crime-solving made a certain odd sense. Her husband had changed his name several times over the past ten years . . . but he'd never offered her a reason for that enterprise. Avoiding his powerful father . . . or himself, as Jardonet professed?

She found herself at the wall safe in the den, spinning the combination and retrieving the letter Jade had written to her.

Two days ago, she'd returned that note to the safe, removing only the leather pouch to confirm a few suspicions that her husband had left her an extremely wealthy widow. Even Bobby had whistled softly when looking over the Will that Jade had written and filed three months ago. Incontestably, he'd bequeathed most of his worldly assets to her . . . His sports cars, the pickup, Olden Time, and all the material assets therein, and a sizeable portfolio of stocks, bonds, and certificates worth well over ten million dollars, along with a not-inconsiderable bank account. Obviously, to avoid paying inheritance tax, he'd assigned most of his assets to joint ownership, attaching her name to his holdings. In the event of an heir, he'd requested that she open a trust in his name to mature when the child turned twenty-one. And as a final request, he'd willed certificates to friends—one of which would become available about the time Wade Kreider reached college age and would undoubtedly, cover the boy's tuition and living expenses at the college of his choice—with a few dollars to spare.

He'd known—the shit had known as much as three months ago that he wouldn't be here to see his child mature to twenty-one, or to see Wade Kreider enter college, or to see the Spencer children grow up.

And the finality of those bequeaths, the sizeable amount of his estate which now fell on her shoulders, brought tears to her eyes before she ever unfolded the note. Finality. Leaving her a wealthy widow. Walking away from his cars, his business, his life . . . everything he'd accumulated in the past five or six years. Like an albatross, those things hung about her neck, and for the briefest instant, she wondered if she would have the courage to walk away from so much. Could she truly just walk away from Chateau Laquette and leave the entire fortune to the government? Could she walk away from her family, friends—new and old?

If it meant living with the man she loved?

Yes. Unquestionably.

But what kind of life could she give Tad in exchange? A life of running, hiding, secrecy, and deceit . . .? Forever looking over her shoulder for fear someone would recognize her, her husband. What kind of life was that for a child?

And that answer was undeniable as well.

No life for a child.

"What have you done to us, Jade?" she uttered as she opened the page, again reading his words through a wall of tears. The question . . . the curiosity which had brought her into the den to reread the message, leaped off the page. '. . . A tragedy, I think, but I cannot know. That, I also fear, will change, and from that change, I will protect you. . . .' Not the tragedy . . . He hadn't feared the tragedy. Himself. '. . . I think, but I cannot know. That, I also fear . . . From that change, I will protect you.' He feared himself, and from himself—from what he could know—he would protect her.

Prophecy . . . from his ability to foresee the future, he would protect her, and as she read through the letter again, the words continued to leap out at her. '. . . Physically, we will be parted. . . .' Already, his prophecies had begun taking control. '. . . If you are reading this, I will know . . . as will you. . . .' Know the accuracy of his visions? Know he had no choice in whatever had driven him from their hearth and home? And hope. '. . . carry the candle for me . . . can't keep it burning. . . .' But he'd given her the candle. He'd given her hope to carry. '. . . Whether I walk at your side or in your shadow. . . .'

Not a prophecy of conviction. Not a statement of fact. An option.

He might as easily have written, 'Either I will be with you, or I won't.' And at this moment, she knew he hadn't deliberately deceived her with that option. Whether he'd written those words with the last of his hope or in genuine confusion toward his own demise, she couldn't decide, but one thought held supreme—she needed to find him.

The battle lines were drawn. Jean-Pierre Jardonet, for whatever reason, had sanctioned her husband's permanent withdrawal from her life and assisted in that event. And maybe that son-of-gun enjoyed a good fight. He'd certainly not denied his knowledge, hadn't doubted her grasp of the facts . . . and he'd given her a springboard.

Cleveland, Ohio.

CHAPTER II

Chalmers attempted objections, but Lakeland fielded those with the smooth efficiency of a top-notch attorney. Escorting both men from the room, Lakeland sent an order to his escorts directly outside the door, then returned to the table, sitting down with all the feigned nonchalance of a supreme court judge. Kicking his chair back, he hooked one shined Oxford over his knee and lifted his lapel, studying Dominique while drawing a pack of cigars from his jacket.

Equally relaxed, Dominique held the man's gaze, reading the speculation and curiosity behind the intelligent brown eyes. When he felt the cameras disengage, he commented, "I wasn't sure if I could trust you, Mr. Lakeland. I'm not usually so lax, but I'd imagine that's only natural after intense interrogation."

"I think we've agreed, you were not interrogated—intensely or—"

"If we intend to reach an understanding," Dominique interrupted quietly. "We will do so with the base understanding that I am fully aware of the situation regarding my half-brother's abduction. You sanctioned that event by no fault of your own other than trust in supreme orders mandated by your office."

Lakeland started to move his foot, a prelude to rising. "I think this discussion—"

"I would like to know who initiated that order and why, as much as you would," Dominique continued, his gaze holding Lakeland. "We can discuss this, or I can resort to alternative means of investigation. I am, you will note, not accusing you of foul play, nor do I have any interest in becoming involved in a scandal, international, national, or otherwise. Frankly, I have agreed to accept the lies, and if questioned by my government, I would be forced to consider your agency exemplary. Although I will mention, the packet of documentation in your associate's briefcase would not discredit me in the least. I am regarded rather ah . . . highly in the circles I travel. I know it, you know it, and my half-brother knew it before he dragged me into this conspiracy."

Lakeland's attention riveted. "You're saying you and he were working together?"

"Nothing can be quite that simple, Mr. Lakeland. My half-brother and I have not stood on the same soil in more years than I care to consider. Unfortunately, the connection we share cannot be ah . . . disconnected by space. Nor phone wires, I'll mention. I do not make a habit of visiting the United States. I came on what I would consider a whim if I were to be as clever a liar as your associates. To be clear, I sensed a need to be here. Now, let us continue with what else I have been able to discover. . .

"First, foremost, the contact you traced to Robert Bryson initiating my enlistment in Cleveland's murder investigation. Privy to this information as only I can be, I know Robert Bryson acted on the request of my dearly departed brother. Let's assume then, Laquette knew something about what awaited him in Cleveland. Namely, that your agency intended to abduct him. Knowing as I do, that he was rather content and madly in love with his new bride—and expecting his first child, so I've heard—I do think he would attempt to subvert your mission . . .

"You are following me so far, yes?"

"I'm listening."

"Hmm, so you are," Dominique mused. "Which leads us to . . . what did my half-brother possess that you wanted to either take from him or conceal permanently?"

"Excuse me?"

"Mr. Lakeland, deny this as I know you must, but the fact remains, you did make a mistake when you abducted me rather than my half-brother . . . and that was a planned mission. Your agent ah . . . Jarvins, is it? Initiated that abduction maneuver, but the order came through you. Now here we are, faced with the problem that I am aware of your conspiracy. The problem for me is this, you believed that operation was paramount to either the safety of Jade Laquette or the country. So, the question remains, what did he have that you wanted? What were your ultimate orders, and why was I subjected to interrogation?"

For a moment, Lakeland wrestled his thoughts before realizing the futility of further lies and deceit. "Unfortunately, you've reached the heart of this situation," he said bluntly. "I was asked to enlist Laquette's services. The premise for that operation was that he possesses certain powers of observation which could have assisted in the swift apprehension of a psychopath. Ultimately, in the event of his success, he was to be brought to this facility for extensive questioning into the nature of that ability. Our Dr. Heinz, as you probably realize, is an advocate of psychic phenomenon. Initially, the interrogation—as you seem fond of calling it—was designed to discredit his abilities and debunk the theories Dr. Heinz is attempting to promote and advance. For the record, Mr. Jardonet, I didn't anticipate or issue any directive that would have brought your half-brother to physical harm. At no time would he have been in danger."

"Hmm, I would believe that more if he were alive," Dominique said quietly, his gaze steady on Lakeland. "And it seems odd that someone would want to kill him over a theory, do you agree?"

"We do not have evidence that his death was anything other than an accident."

"Whether you have evidence or not, I am in a position to know my half-brother would not have initiated the actions he took if he hadn't sensed the danger to himself—or more precisely, to his family. First and foremost, to be clear, he despised me nearly as much as I hold him in contempt. We do not—have never—worked in tandem toward any goal. The mystery is this—that he would put me in a position to land in the thick of things, as you Americans say. And now, let us reflect a moment . . .

"Are you aware that he spent time in this facility many years ago?"

"As a matter of fact, I am. In fact, I understand that he departed from this facility under slightly questionable circumstances. That was, however, a very long time ago, and if you're suggesting any correlation between then and—"

"Let us attempt a different approach," Dominique smirked. "Honesty . . .? My half-brother escaped from this facility to the chagrin of certain doctors who would have—like Dr. Heinz—enjoyed studying him for a very long time. Not that I can blame them. The fellow should have been held under lock and key for the rest of his life. But that's my opinion based on familial knowledge. Returning to the issue at hand—and conveying knowledge that you would rather neither possess nor believe—the fact remains, someone knew his potential. Meaning not to boast, Mr. Lakeland, but I share a similar affliction, and I'm not of a moral fiber to refrain from putting my ah . . . talents to use. Good, bad, or otherwise."

"If you're suggesting—"

"I am not suggesting, my friend. Merely stating a fact, and I could qualify that statement or debunk it at will. Consider this, Mr. Lakeland, we've been speaking for more than five minutes about information that should be privileged. And the signal you intended to await should erupt right . . . about . . . now."

The electronic monitor across the room emitted a beep, and a husky voice announced, "All clear, Mr. Lakeland."

"Goddamn it," Lakeland uttered, his gaze riveted toward the door, lifting to the monitors.

"Have no fear. I didn't begin this conversation until I knew the system was off. Nothing we've said so far has been captured on film or tape."

Far more critically, the brown eyes fixed, the brows knitted. "If you're attempting to verify—"

"If I meant to verify, I would inform you of the status of your surveillance of a certain questionable doctor in Cleveland." Dominique shrugged. "What I am capable of is not a talent I would discuss—either to disclaim or prove. I am what I am and do what I do. Obviously, to my half-brother's misfortune, he was similarly gifted despite his vigilance to the contrary. Now, that said, is it possible that someone directly relative to the past felt either threatened or ah . . . obsessed by Laquette? And take into consideration that his mother's murder was never solved. Would it be reasonable to wonder if, perhaps, whoever sanctioned her murder might want the same end for the son? And bear in mind—somewhere in this facility, the transcripts evidencing his talent could be concealed?"

Lakeland's attention held even as he sucked on his cigar, holding the butt between his middle and ring finger like a common thug. Contemplation and consideration reigned in his deep-set eyes. "Are you guessing there's a connection, or ah . . . using your talents, Mr. Jardonet?" he asked after a moment, not quite concealing the subtle sarcasm.

"Both and neither, Mr. Lakeland," Dominique answered as his eyes darkened a shade close to emerald. "There is a connection between his mother's murder and these recent developments. What that connection is, I can only guess. But I do believe, with the conflicting sources of ah . . . concern you are receiving, I would wonder at what they knew to have them both assassinated."

"Any chance you want to guess?"

"I don't need to guess," Dominique said quietly, refusing to be offended even as he held the intense brown eyes. "It is something of significance that someone, perhaps, many in your government would consider threatening. And there is an irony here, sir. Make no mistake, an irony which supersedes my ah . . . guesswork?"

"I'm still listening," Lakeland said.

"Two of them, actually," Dominique said indifferently. "First that my half-brother's mother wasn't psychically endowed. Second, Laquette was so terrified of the curse upon him in that field that he would not have remembered a secret if one had been revealed to him. You cannot appreciate that irony, but I certainly can. The wealth of information at my fingertips is mind-boggling, even for someone of ah . . . my aptitude. Now, then. Knowing what we do, what course of action would you presume we take?"

"I'm not sure that we know anything more than we did before we began this asinine discussion, Mr. Jardonet," Lakeland stated.

"Then you are a fool, and I've wasted my time," Dominique said and leaned, clasping the coffeepot and refilling his cup, glancing over. "Just bear in mind, if I find the person or persons responsible for my brother's mishap, I may be honor-bound to act on his behalf."

"I think you better bear in mind, Mr. Jardonet, this is definitely not your jurisdiction."

"Do you really think I give a tinker's damn?" Dominique asked in a chilly tone. "Whether you initiated my brother's abduction or his murder, the culpability falls in your domain. He would have been killed in this facility or locked up indefinitely as your Dr. Heinz would like to do with me. The scientific discovery of a man capable of looking into the past, present, and future on any continent would rock the foundations of the intelligence community and possibly shift the political trends of several countries. And such a man does exist, Mr. Lakeland. He did not board a plane destined to crash. Do you understand what I'm saying to you?"

The cigar butt pinched between the stout fingers; the hand nearly gripped in a fist on the crossed knee. Momentarily silent, Lakeland studied him before asking in a low, angry tone, "Who the fuck are you?"

"The man who will either assist you in sorting out the conspiracy which began eighteen years ago or destroy whoever steps in his path toward that same goal. And do not threaten me with further incarceration. I am here because I allowed myself to be brought here. I do not walk into situations from which I cannot walk away." *Unless I choose to,* he might have added as a prickle slid down his spine.

"You do realize that with every word you just spoke, you countered the possibility of you walking out of this facility any time soon, right?"

Slowly, sedately, Dominique leaned back, smiling just a little. "Did I really, Mr. Lakeland?"

"You wouldn't get far, and you certainly wouldn't leave this country."

"You're no longer even certain when I entered this country if you'll pardon me for noticing," Dominique said with a spark of amusement in his eyes. "Am I Dominique Jardonet pretending to be Jade Laquette? Or am I Jade Laquette pretending to be Dominique Jardonet? Which of us—do either of us—really lie in a casket? Either way, when I decide to leave, I will leave, but you need ask yourself, what will I have taken with me? Because, truthfully, Mr. Lakeland, I will have the answers to my questions before I depart. Whether or not I share that information will depend upon the next moments of our friendly discourse. The choice is yours. Do you stand behind whatever oaths you took to fulfill the position you hold, or do you follow commands blindly and protect whatever secrets have justified the murders of the Laquettes . . .?"

"What exactly are you proposing, Mr. Jardonet?"

"How long has Dr. Heinz worked here?"

"Fifteen years."

"Then he arrived within a few years after my half-brother's departure," Dominique said absently, pausing to light a cigarette, holding the smoke as he considered his proposition. His gaze leveling on Lakeland, he continued, "He would have heard enough about those events to become ah . . . obsessed, yes? To the point where he might have become well acquainted with the information compiled."

"I'll grant you, he may be obsessed, but I wouldn't consider him a serious candidate for an attempted assassination for the obvious reason. He would rather study and authenticate the subject of psychic ability than destroy the missing link."

"He wasn't against the abduction of Laquette. In fact, I would venture to say, he cooperated to the fullest, even providing the technicians to see that ah . . . the lethal injection wasn't as lethal as it appeared?"

"We're treading delicate ground, Mr. Jardonet."

"Ah, yes, but of course, you cannot admit such details," he smiled and shrugged. "The point is, he has information that perhaps, you and I do not. Information, as I mentioned earlier, contained within this facility and regarded as ah . . . top secret?"

"I've seen some of that information, and I will tell you, nothing I viewed suggested the boy should be considered either a threat to national security or a personal threat to anyone."

"You saw what you were allowed to see, Mr. Lakeland, and by your own admission, did it warrant the frenzy of your Dr. Heinz to risk the oaths and integrity of his post here? I would ask myself, what did he see that I did not? If for no other reason than because he is a medical practitioner versus your clandestine nature. To me, those two practices are not generally in full agreement, much less partnered, unless bound by joint allegiance. What was your alliance? Has he often assisted in extracting information from otherwise uncooperative witnesses?" Not awaiting a response, Dominique tipped his head. "No, I didn't believe so. Now, I ask again, does it not seem curious that he would willingly agree to a venture slightly outside his normal code of ethics over information that you believe irrelevant?"

"Based on the probability of him receiving the same directive I received, it could be argued that he complied out of duty."

"Argued, yes. Accurate, no. He is ah . . . straining at his tethers for a crack at me, Mr. Lakeland. He has no doubts about my capabilities, and therein, I find another curiosity. I am not generally wildly accepted and believed. Though I cannot imagine why," he said with a wry smile which triggered a reflexive action in Lakeland's bristled lips. Shrugging, Dominique continued, "He already knows what you are still attempting to discover and believe, Mr. Lakeland. Simply, I am psychic. Quite like, and yet different from my half-brother. What I propose is simple. Let me see these archives where my half-brother's documentation exists. Let us look at them together and decide what is relevant and what is not."

"Even if I considered agreeing to that, which I won't for obvious reasons, I'd need slightly more clearance."

"I am tempted to consider you a fool, but I'll refrain for another moment," Dominique said quietly. "You will not seek clearance, for the same reason I would not, in your shoes. You are faced with an unknown entity in the hierarchy, and this entity has the influence to muddy the waters within your ranks."

"I'm not sure I believe that at all, Mr. Jardonet."

"Then you are a fool," Dominique said without effect, his gaze steady. "And you are unwittingly participating in a plot for another murder. Deny the facts, as you will, but you know the accuracy. You have a traitor in your field. And that traitor has a separate agenda from the one you have acted upon. Whatever this secret revealed by the boy—it is important enough to demand the death of the man and any others who could be too close. And let us be clear, Mr. Lakeland, as long as I am in this facility with Dr. Heinz shouting his conviction of my talents, I am marked for extinction."

"If what you're saying even carries a grain of truth, why is Dr. Heinz still alive, Mr. Jardonet? I would imagine he has read the information, and if secrets were revealed—"

"That's why you and I need to view these archives in tandem, Mr. Lakeland. Whatever exists, whatever prophecies my half-brother offered, they were not crystal clear. What you hear and what I see will be two very different things. And if you doubt, perhaps, I should mention the name . . . Whitman James Reddinger. It means something to you, yes?"

Lakeland's eyes reacted if nothing else startled a half second before narrowing. "What does that name mean to you?"

"It means that you believe you have found the psychopath stalking innocent victims in Cleveland. I hope you are keeping a wall of surveillance around this fellow. I have a sense that we have not seen the last of this Taxidermist." Which wasn't entirely a lie.

"What does that mean, exactly?"

"You should warn your men, he is more and less than he seems."

"If you know something about this maniac that my men should—"

"The future is ah . . . flexible? Perhaps, I have impressions, glimpses of a dozen possible scenarios. Perhaps, he is not your man, but who is to say? If I were to shout a name to the heavens, you would be in a quandary, searching for the means to the end you seek—thus, immobilized by doubts. When—if—I grasp the moment to act in advance to reach the end you desire, I'll let you know. I have given you a warning. What it means, and how it relates to your case is for you to decide or ignore. Be sure your men do not ah . . . become bored or fooled by his ah . . . normalcy? If they become too complacent, this maniac will act accordingly. Little else can I tell you now. Prophecy, by Dominique Jardonet," he said with a smile and a cant of his head to affect a bow. "Now, my proposal?"

Lakeland hesitated before deciding, "I'll take it under consideration."

Tilting his head more, Dominique drew the last drag off his cigarette and leaned to crush the butt, catching Lakeland's eye. "Don't wait too long, my friend, or one of us may attend his own funeral in the not-too-distant future."

CHAPTER 12

Escaping Chateau Laquette without alerting a string of reporters or announcing her departure to the entire town posed the single remaining obstacle. Once outside, Ronnie knew she could avoid notice. Ten minutes in one of the storage rooms had provided everything a lady needed to become invisible in a crowd, from a weathered hat and granny glasses to a pair of ungainly shoes tucked at the bottom of an auction box full of antique linen.

Sitting behind the desk in the den, her hand still on the receiver, Ronnie considered her options, searching her mental banks for who she might enlist to aid in her escape. She'd placed the mandatory calls. She'd talked to Meg and Hazel, bowing gracefully from both invitations for either dinner or company. Knowing how Donna and Tim worried, she'd phoned Donna and suggested she wouldn't mind meeting for lunch or dinner tomorrow. If any others phoned, they could leave a message and wait for a return call. Considering the score of reporters camped outside her door, no one should be surprised or overly concerned by her decision to steal a page from Jade's book and become a hermit for one evening. As an added touch—before placing any calls—she'd ignited nearly every lamp in the apartment, a sure sign of her occupancy if not her neurosis.

Now, she needed to focus on how to escape—

The buzzer erupted from the wall speaker in the living room, announcing a visitor at the side door entrance. Mechanically, Ronnie pushed off the leather chair. In lieu of her condition, Jade had installed an intercom—the alternative to her navigating the stairwell to receive either visitors or deliveries at the warehouse doors. At the apartment door, she hesitated, reconsidering her decision to acknowledge an intruder. If she meant to leave an impression of occupancy . . .? She pressed the button on the state-of-the-art control panel. "Yes?"

"Uh, Mrs. L . . .? I ahh . . . This is Wade."

"Quick, Hon—when you hear the buzzer—come in." Lending him ten seconds to ready his hand, she depressed the button on the control panel. A distant buzzing sound announced the door lock disengaged on the first floor as she opened the apartment door. Shouted voices echoed up the stairwell for an instant before the door banged shut below and muffled the words.

Heart hammering, the odd coincidence flashed neon in her mind. Forever, it seemed, Wade arrived whenever her wily husband needed assistance—rather like Cy Bender's arrival three days earlier. Coincidentally, in time to unload the pickup. Once—if not a hundred times—she'd reaped the reward of Jade's weird talent to send a silent summons . . . and it truly was another of Jade's talents—this summoning.

And if she allowed herself to buy into that belief—that he possessed the ability to call others to him like a blasted wizard or warlock of folklore and legend summoning his followers . . .? She might go stark raving mad, and her husband, rather than their creation, would be the cause.

Suffering a chill, she reached the top of the steps just as Wade appeared below.

Golden brown, his hair caught the dull light, but he moved with the slow, hindered gate of an ancient, his upturned face a ghostly-pale echo of the handsome boy of a week earlier. Her heart banged another leaden beat as she considered how deeply the loss had affected this youngster. Landing one good solid punch to her husband's jaw might justify the effort to find him.

How could he have done this . . .? Not just to her but to all of them? This was their home! These were their friends! This teary-eyed child had loved him like an older brother, if not a father.

"Hiya, Hon . . . what's—"

"I uh . . . I didn't mean ta bother you, Mrs. L," he said with a hint of genuine anxiety, his eyes searching and confused. "It's just . . . that I . . . I don't know," he muttered, resigned. Dipping his head to avoid her gaze, he shrugged while ascending the last steps. "I just felt like I had to come over." His gaze lifted, begging for either understanding or explanation. "Is everything okay? Are you okay? You're not . . . You're not feelin' sick again or nothing, are you? It's prob'bly not my business, but I just started thinking and worrying, like maybe you needed me."

"Oh, honey," she said and wrapped her arm around his shoulder, barely starting to offer reassurance when his words registered. The revelation detonated in her mind like a fireworks display. The summoning! Whether she or her husband had called him, she did need him! And the plan tumbled through her mind with a speed to leave her speechless as she led Wade into her apartment. "There . . . there really is something . . . There's something very important that you could do for me . . ."

In less time than it took to outline her need, Wade improved upon it, relying on a natural resilience and imagination that had always made him shine. Ten minutes later, they stood looking at the saddest rendition of a human being that either one had ever seen, and Ronnie almost managed the first genuine smile in two days. If nothing else, she could use this pitiful construct as another Halloween prop to decorate the front windows of Olden Time. God knows, the thing looked like an extremely lame stage prop. The long platinum wig, teased to affect curls, hung over the Styrofoam head, making the blank white face appear even more ghastly. The long sleeve shirt stuffed adequately with newspapers at chest height would probably start half the males in Bentwood gawking at her to judge the telltale signs of her advancing pregnancy. With her thought, she punched the paper down, taking at least an inch off the boobs before noting Wade's slightly amused eyes. Winking, she decided, "Think that's just a little better."

"Yes, ma'am," he said reverently, too polite to offer further critique; after all, he'd tightened the belt to lend their stick figure form.

"As long as you don't take it too close to the curtains, or the head doesn't fall off, we'll be in good shape," she said while considering the probable failure of their plan. With her luck of late, the head would fall off the broomstick as Wade carried it close to the windows, and a passer-by would call an ambulance. She could just imagine that headline. 'Distraught Widow Loses Her Head!'

"How long you figure on being gone, ma'am?" Wade interrupted in natural concern.

"Maybe just a day or two, hon," she said honestly, looking into his haunted eyes and attempting a smile. "If you'll stick around until about eight . . . You can leave the kitchen light on, and I'll leave the light on in the den. If anybody asks you directly, hon, don't lie for me. Just tell them I needed time alone, and you can tell them how you helped me avoid the reporters."

"You won't tell me where you're going, huh?"

She shook her head, touching his shoulder. "I really don't want you to lie for me, hon, and I'd rather not have anybody looking for me. I need . . . I do need a little time alone, and I'd rather not try explaining that to anyone."

"You're gonna do something dangerous, huh?" he asked with the intuition born of brilliance and a child's perception.

"I . . . not intentionally," she said, refusing to lie to this wide-eyed wonder.

He dipped his hand into his jeans and looked down as he brought something from his pocket. Lifting his steady gaze, he handed her a pearl-white stone almost as large as a marble. "Know this is probably dumb, but . . . well, that's my lucky stone. I used to have a whole collection before I started collecting cards." His gaze shadowed, and he averted his eyes, his sadness rising anew. "I . . ." He looked up as she closed her hand around the stone. "The first card I ever bought, Mr. L. traded me even for a lucky stone. I was just a dumb little kid then, ya know?" he said with a shadow of a grin to suggest he was years older and wiser now. "I really thought I got took 'til Mom helped me look up the card in a book she bought me. I still have that card, ya know? It's worth about fifty bucks now."

"I . . . I think that lucky stone was probably worth a great more than fifty bucks to Mr. L," she said quietly.

Wade nodded gravely, "Me too, ma'am. He used to keep that rock on his cash register, and I saw him pick it up once or twice and put it in his pocket when he and Mr. S were gonna play poker. I don't think he ever lost."

Did this boy know . . .? Did he somehow suspect the truth and understand at a base level that her husband was gambling with something far more important than money? The question haunted her as he walked with her, carrying her overnight bag to the warehouse.

Not until he put the bag in the passenger seat of the Maserati—the quietest engine in the fleet—did he speak again. And only then to say, "Take care a yourself, 'kay? And don't you worry about a thing, here. I'll make sure nobody suspects anything, and I'll lock up when I leave."

If Wade Kreider said he'd see to things, she could count on at least a few blissful hours of anonymity . . . and probably at least a day. As the youngster trotted to the garage doors, her attention wavered, an unnatural inkling of something touching the edges of her mind. Not in two days—not since entering this warehouse—had she thought about that filthy box. Her gaze found it now, tucked down in the shadows against the wall beyond the pickup's bumper. The auxiliary night lights barely lent it shape . . . like a black cat hunkered down under a bush, ready to leap. Shivering, she started the engine, grateful for the crowded aisles and shelves that muffled the sound. . . and again, she looked over at that box. What drove her? What logic or omen touched her? She knew only the impulse that forced her from the car.

Without conscious thought, she grabbed an old packing pad off a shelf and strode to the box, covering it before lifting it. Even through the cloth, she suffered the prickling of evil portent emanating from the contents, but it was too damned late to back out now. For whatever madness drove her, she wasted no time wrestling the trunk lid open and stuffing the box into the compact compartment. Logically, whatever this damned thing was, she wanted no part of it, and disposing of it alongside a dark highway might be the safest means to the end. Maybe she would pull over somewhere and pitch it into a ravine, or lake, or snake pit . . .

Wade opened the door manually, only high enough for the car hood to clear the bottom, and Ronnie thanked him as she crept into the alley. Keeping the engine idling low, the headlights off, she navigated the hedge-lined shadows toward the streetlamp on the next block. No cars or bodies raced into the alley in her wake; no headlights blinded, or shouts echoed. She glimpsed the garage door closing as she crept away, smiling over the conspiracy and talent of her husband's prodigy. In the future, she vowed—if a future existed—she would take care in what endeavors she coerced Wade into. He was far too bright and willing to oblige without any clear grasp of the consequences.

It was true what someone had once told her about Bentwood. A person could drive from one end to the other via alleyways, and if she chose the correct side street, she could reach Interstate 79. She chose the side streets, avoiding the Maine where Jade's Maserati might be recognized. Apparently, Wade's lucky stone was working. Despite the darkness distorting the houses and lawns, she recognized the intersection and Interstate ramp. Igniting the headlights for the first time, she sailed onto the four-lane, barely twitching her toes to reach a sweet fifty-five.

It was certainly no wonder that he loved these little gems in his fleet. According to the Atlas, it was two and a half to three hours to Cleveland. In this car . . . in her present mind? Two . . . maybe one-hour max. And in the pit of her stomach, her tiny little captive cargo squirmed as if delighted.

"Boy, are you in trouble, kid," she uttered while testing the response of the steering wheel, zipping past a semi-trailer. "Big trouble. Not a sane parent to your credit. I don't think we'll even worry about proper diet or sugar control . . . Heck, we might as well toss morals and principals and responsibility right out with the trash. I feel bad for you, Tad, m' love. Freedom of choice—that's something you won't get for a long time to come. So, you're stuck with us. A menace and a maniac . . . That's not a pleasant outlook for you, I know, but don't even think about sticking around in that fishbowl any longer than five more months. And don't get any ideas about disowning your parents either, kiddo. That only happens in the movies . . . And why do I have the feeling, you'll be just like your father? Why am I positive, that I'll vote for the first law to raise the legal driving age to twenty-one? You really are enjoying this, you little shit . . .

"You should know, Tad, I really don't think the good Lord did you any favors by making you ours, but just for the record . . .? I'm not giving you back. Sooo . . . hang on. E.T.A. Cleveland uh . . . 7:32, give or take thirty seconds."

Dominique knew when his private nurse, Carol, succeeded in her clandestine mission, and the smile slid into his mustached lips as the pressure of the cameras slipped away. By midnight, when the two guards were found snoring over their disengaged control panels, Dominique Jardonet would be departed. The gloved hands changed inside his mind. Behind his closed lids, he saw his orders fulfilled. Like an automaton, Carol obeyed the silent commands; her long, lovely fingers broke open the capsules and stirred the contents into the coffeemaker where the guards routinely refueled.

With the first phase complete, Dominique pushed off the bed and strode to the door, reaching it in time to coincide with Carol's arrival. As she moved inside, her lashes fluttered, confusion lighting a half second before he locked his gaze, freezing her thought. In a far more natural low voice, he spoke conversationally. "You will bring a wheelchair, Carole`. You have orders from Dr. Heinz to take me downstairs for another CAT scan. I am not happy, but I have agreed to the tests. Go, now. Bring the chair," he commanded softly and released her.

For a half second, her brow knitted before she commented, "I'll be right back with your ride."

Within moments, Carol wheeled him passed the nurses' station. Offhanded, she spoke to her comrade, affecting dismay over Dr. Heinz's order for another series of tests. With a soft smile to offset Dominique's frown of displeasure, she reassured him, "It's not that bad, sir. I promise it won't hurt a bit."

Mechanically, she used her keys and card, passing them through the locked doors and into the elevator. Clasping her fingers as they descended, Dominique caught her eye and instructed. "When we stop, you will leave the wheelchair in the access room outside the doors, then you will program the elevator to take us to ground zero, Carole`."

"I'm not authorized to enter that level," she said with a troubled frown.

Dominique smiled as he pushed from the wheelchair. "You will let me worry about that, my dear."

As commanded, Carol rolled the empty chair into the hall, positioned it neatly against the wall, then stepped back into the elevator and followed his order to descend them another three levels. Like every other floor, the elevator shaft remained separate from the main body of the complex, and Carol possessed only the clearance to open the door into the connecting hallway. Planting a suggestion for her to return in an hour, he passed through the door alone. Wire-reinforced windows and thick iron mesh formed an effective blockade, but the human factor built into the security system was—as always—the weak link. In natural curiosity, the uniformed man behind the glass lifted his gaze, and Dominique needed only a glance to capture his eyes, halting whatever alarm he might have triggered.

Automated, the man rose from his chair, jangling his keys as he sidled to the door. Without a need for words or explanations, Dominique entered the secure area, supplanting suggestions and asking directions.

What he sought occupied the older section of the archives, segregated from the modern, fully automated system which recorded the daily advancements in hundreds of current experiments.

The heart of the monster, Dominique considered as the guard led him through the narrower corridor. Recorded behind the locked doors, undoubtedly, some of the most fascinating, possibly horrifying discoveries in the past several decades resided. Setbacks and advancements, studies citing all aspects of mental degeneration, testing and torturing toward psychological updates, profiles, breakthroughs in treatment . . .

The institution touched all bases, conducting studies and experiments into the function and capacity of the human brain.

Whether the treatment of Jade Laquette was the exception or the rule by which these studies progressed, Dominique had never discerned. Eighteen years ago, he'd been brought into this institution against his will, legally, and studied extensively. He knew what the data contained. Physically, he'd undergone every test available, from blood tests to X-rays. He'd received drugs to sleep and to remain awake, drugs to raise and lower his normal body functions . . . He'd sat for hours in a windowless room, subjected to lights and sounds, to silence, to pain. The memories were vague, lost forever in a distorted haze, but he remembered enough.

What had become of Dr. Carson?

Clearly, that face loomed large at the surface of his mind. Deep crevices winged the eyes and cut from the nostrils to define the corners of the mouth, slicing through the planes of his cheeks and jowl as if carved by a chisel and hammer. On a younger man, on a thinner face, those lines might have defined character . . . Dominique remembered only the fear which had never ebbed under Carson's attempt to smile and reassure him. In a classic case of Stockholm Syndrome, Jade Laquette had warmed to his tormentor, needing him at a primal level that Dominique couldn't fathom even now. He'd certainly never loved Carson, but in fleeting images, he remembered begging others to call Dr. Carson, to have the doctor present whenever a test began. He remembered once . . . only once he'd broken. He'd wanted to please Carson, either to gain his mercy or his favor. Perhaps on some childish level, he'd believed if he gave Carson what he wanted, the man would order the madness stopped. Whatever his reason, he'd tried to 'read' the objects placed in his hands, had tried drawing his talents to him . . . but his was a wily curse, refusing to bend to a child. Whatever that granite-encased man had learned, he'd learned in those moments that Jade Laquette would never willingly remember.

Relieving the guard to return to his post, Dominique entered the expansive room the fellow had opened for him. Floor-to-ceiling, the banks of knowledge stood on metal shelves, in bins, and in metal file cabinets reflective of a doctor's office on an industrial scale. A long metal table and a dozen chairs provided a workspace for industrious scholars or students. Overhead, tract lighting provided a soft glow and created a low-wattage hum amplified in the quiet hiss from air ducts. Without a doubt, the temperatures were monitored in these rooms, and the gun-metal gray floor and walls formed a barrier against moisture. How much of the documentation in this room had already been transferred to the banks of computers he'd passed en route? Quite a lot, Dominique imagined, but doubted any of the original data was destroyed.

Meandering, as if he had all night, he moved along the front of the aisles, acclimating to the filing system and ambiance. The answers were here. That knowledge held dominion in his mind as he moved more deliberately, rounding a corner and continuing deeper into one of the long aisles. By years, by subject, the various tests and results appeared in a convoluted order of precedence, but he found what he sought. Tucked between two safe-like vaults, the door on the file cabinet read simply, "Laquette, J.D. . . . W. m. 1/8/1960. Parapsychology." White, male, date of birth . . .

It was only two-thirds accurate, Dominique mused and touched the crank handle to open the vault.

Too late . . . far too late, he knew his mistake. His hand clasped the lever with a force to mold the lead to his flesh, his fingernails driving spikes into the soft tissue of his thumb muscle.

An impression of Dr. Heinz flashed neon in his mind, but there were others. Faces and sensations exploded one after the other, taking his breath away. Impressions, sensations . . . white hot spirals of excitement, confusion, brooding, anger, desire, hatred and frustration, fear . . . horror. Panic. Outrage . . .

Every hand to have touched this vault left its imprint, slamming one against the other, assailing him as if he'd fallen off a cliff into raging white water. Hammered against reefs, he had no clear grasp of the histories or ideals or names of those who had come here before him. But like glimpses of bedrock behind the swirl, he understood the flashing images which stirred such violent emotions in each one . . .

And those deeper volitions were clearing. As if he were sinking beneath the swirl, below the tide, the images were clearing . . . His own face., pale and gaunt . . . his eyes haunted in stop-action frames captured from the endless reels of film . . . Twisting, turning beneath the cotton bands, he writhed and screamed when the torment and pain became unbearable to his wasted young body . . . Dreams within dreams, nightmares within a nightmare . . . but so few were illusions. None imagination. From the outside looking in, through the eyes of those who had come before him, studying this vile collection, learning, brooding, collecting data . . . He saw the wicked data contained behind this vault. On dual planes he hovered . . . on the outside looking in, on the inside looking out . . .

In his mind, he heard the click of the projector, saw the black and white images, their animation broken like marionettes if only by the time-worn quality of the film. White spots, black streaks of imperfection, but the images were clear . . . heads lowered, hats, scarves, heavy coats, and long skirts. The beat of a train engine thundered at the edges of his mind, and he heard himself moaning as he tried pulling his focus away.

He was here, now, strapped to the leather chair, vibrating with the horror of an adult, the terror of a child. Above him, the carrion face of Dr. Carson was illuminated in a hazy shadow within the brilliant light. Fear emanated from the elder, as much fear as excitement and determination. Carson knew . . . he knew what lay before him. Dozens of reels of filmstrips had documented the facts, and even now, the clips raced behind his intense pale eyes, verifying every belief . . . psychic phenomenon existed. Inside this wasted young body, the ability to see the future, to step back in time, to alter events . . .

Oh, but they needed to be careful! . . . Even with the black mask covering the odd green eyes, Carson felt the boy's probe, the mental touch. The boy called it 'mind-bending'—a term his ill-fated mother had coined to describe how her child could manipulate others to his bid. They had learned early on, Carson recalled. He had seen the proof at the onset and taken precautions to blindfold the boy for every session. Still, there were moments, like now, when Carson could feel the mentalism attempting to break through almost as if . . . *as if the iron mask was no more than an inconvenience.*

Conversationally, though his young voice vibrated, the words escaped, 'You hov off'aired them the proof to seal my fate, doctor . . . They will come for me . . . They will come for my wife . . . My child.'

Carson jolted and gripped. His attention riveted with the certain knowledge that this wasn't a child's voice emanating from the parched lips. Against his own ethics, the doctor had buckled to the orders from on high, the orders from his benefactors. Half-starved, and dehydrated, the child appeared little different from the test subjects on those films, and Carson shuddered with his revulsion to having viewed those wicked films. Not like them—this child wasn't being tortured like them! He—Dr. John Carson—wouldn't compare his own humane tests to that monster who'd brought those wretched films to this country—

'But you are, doctor,' the soft voice confirmed almost sadly. 'They have made you the monster now . . .'

'English, Jade-David . . . speak English, now.'

'Ah, anglaise . . . oui,' he obliged. 'You are the monst`air now, doctor . . . I will not survive much more of these tests . . .'

This wasn't possible! Neon, those words ignited in Carson's mind as he considered the injection that he'd personally administered only a short time ago. The child should be sedated, should be resting comfortably and oblivious by now, not speaking with the clarity of an adult.

'We are both dead men, doctor,' he spoke softly. 'You have given them what they want . . . You have given them proof.'

'They won't hurt you, son, not either of us in fact,' Carson said in quiet reassurance. 'We have too much to learn, and these tests . . . they don't need to be so difficult. You'll see. We just needed to verify your gifts. If you behave now, we can continue—'

'They are afraid, doctor . . . Afraid of what I know, afraid of exposure. It will begin in Cleveland . . . the birth of a madman . . .'

Drifting, he watched the images swirling through his mind, felt the burn of the liquid through his veins . . . death. An end. His end . . . Carson's end.

A ball of flame blasting into the afternoon sky held him rapt, his focus following the wonder of vivid colors igniting and dousing. Death. Again, death . . . and his attention riveted yet again.

He had seen these images, hazy images, gray on gray, marching in a bedraggled line . . . and the crackle of old film clattering from the movie reel, broken images flickering on the white screen.

Every limp muscle attempted to cramp, collapsing as he found himself strapped into a stiff leather chair. The film scrolled through his mind's eye more clearly than on the wide screen directly in front of him. Puny, his body vibrated, jostling the thin wires attached to his skull, chest, his arms, and legs. Caught as if in a spider's web, he rested helpless, watching the endless procession of hazy gaunt faces, male and female, young and old. They clung to one another in their bulky coats and sweaters, and he understood the significance. The beginning of his own end. These were the pictures and the knowledge behind them, and only in his mind, he shook his head, denying, rejecting . . . *elating?*

Nooo, he nearly moaned aloud. How was that possible?

But in the next instant, he knew, he understood. Even as his young mind recoiled, repulsed, another young body had rested in this chair, reveling in the images, anticipating more of the gruesome film. The monster grew, more enthralled each time he viewed this wicked film, and they knew it. Intrigued, they had fostered and fed his growing obsession, testing, retesting, and permitting him to recreate the scenes on the tapes. On corpses at first, they had granted him access to flay the dead flesh. A necrophiliac they had believed at first . . . Oh, but he wasn't content to handle only the dead . . . and they had shown him other films, fueling his fire, adding a face to focus his obsession.

Two birds with one stone . . . create one to destroy the other.

And Dominique knew himself splayed upon a metal table . . . a deranged Santa Claus hovering over him.

'I will meet him in the city by the lake,' his own young voice transcended time.

'What city, child? When? Do you know?'

'Cleveland . . . He will begin in Cleveland. We will meet in Cleveland,' he heaved softly, eager to please before the pain could strike again. No lights now. No film. Behind the thick black mask, he saw only the mind pictures as Dr. Carson prodded in gentle tones.

'When, child? Do you know the year?'

'1989.'

Neither panic nor fear touched his mind as the pictures continued to scroll across his mind's eye. Curiosity, though, that he should see Agent Leonardo Devinio, suddenly. Ah, and he was a handsome fellow, this tall brawny Italian. 'Flawless . . . at the onset, he'd recognized the flawless texture of this young agent's face . . . and the other was gone. Fate had robbed him of that one's flesh . . . destroyed in a fire . . .'

Only in his mind, Dominique heard the rage beneath the monster's surface even as the fellow strode from the familiar entrance of the Cleveland courthouse . . . a member . . . not a member of the task force. In tempered strides, the monster descended the steps, following the agent at a safe distance. He'd taken a chance, parking his van so close to the courthouse, but he needed to be ready. That's what the others had told him. Be ready. And he was ready, more than ready. He followed the agent, who followed the others . . . a parade, the monster considered wryly. Quite a grim parade . . .

He was alive . . . barely . . . but not meant to be alive, he understood. Someone wanted him dead . . . wanted them both dead.

Confusion spilled through his senses, his attention keening. *The past?*

The image erupted, neon in his mind's eye, a black-winged angel spread within the points of a star. He'd seen this image—past or future. The black angel sprawled to greet him, and his breath turned leaden in his breast as he stared at the image, as uncertain as ever another moment in his life. Past or future . . . would this moment come, or had it gone? Like the ghosts of Christmas in Dickens' novel, would it come, or had it passed?

The stillness suddenly floating in his mind created another quandary and abstracted the fear threatening to explode inside him.

On a slow tide, the images continued to glide, rippling in spirals outwards where every image created another, overlapping, replaying in new dimensions.

People were dying, had already died, would die . . . but some could be saved, surely.

A single gunshot echoed, lost in the rush of the wind surfing across the choppy black water. The wood planks vibrated underfoot, barely visible with the illumination of a single bulb at the entrance of the boat ramp. Even in the dim light, the muzzle flash was blinding, a bright white flash, a circle of death on an alabaster forehead . . .

But this wasn't his mother's face. The face of an angel, his angel, his guardian angel.

2,1,4 . . . a perfect seven.

The birth of a madman . . . Cleveland.

"Forgivvve meee . . . I haaad nooo chroooice . . ." a voice cried out in the night. If she was here, then she knew far more than she should. She knew. And she would never stop digging, not now, not with her husband gone. She would need answers . . . and she could destroy them. Everything they had worked for would be lost.

If not him, then someone else. Someone must stop her . . .

'. . . touched the hand of the devil . . .' Those words startled Dominique even now, but he couldn't pull away. His mother clasped his hand, forcing his fingers to touch the hand of the devil. And the devil was alive . . . protected . . . sanctioned. *'Here, momma . . . He is here . . . She knows him . . . So many dead . . . blood on his hands . . . She's holding the devil's hand . . . They're protecting him . . . He murdered hundreds . . . thousands . . . and they let him come here . . . to this country. . .'*

Whether the image of his mother sprawled on the marble entry floor, or something deeper affected him, he knew only his terror as he had fled from the conscious realm.

No closer. He hadn't wanted to get any closer to that horror or the images flashing in his child's mind. But he wasn't a child now. He stood, grasping the handle to the vault where his life had shattered, and he wasn't a child now. Not a frightened traumatized child to shy away from madness or death, from the force of adults who demanded his obedience. His hand clasped upon the door. His anger rising, ascending, he scrolled through the sequence of events, knowing, now, why he had been brought to this institution, knowing what had been done to him, here. His own reaction . . . the day of his mother's murder . . .

'What time are you saying he left St. Augustine's . . .?'

'. . . Sir, he's not Laquette . . . I've seen some of these new tapes. He's not Laquette, but he's of similar talents . . . I think he knows what's on those tapes . . . He sent Dr. Heinz and Ben Chalmers from his room and met privately with Dir. Lakeland.'

'Then we don't really have a choice. He is not to leave that facility under any circumstances. You know what you have to do . . .'

'. . . *This didn't have to happen. Why didn't she listen to me, sir? She knows what I am . . .*'

'What are you, son?'

'You won't believe me . . . But others will. I think they know already . . . and they'll come after me next. But it doesn't matter . . . They can't kill me. I just wish they wouldn't try, but they will, you know? I think I've seen that too,' he said as his gaze drifted to the curtain and his fingers clamped tighter on the pillow. 'They will try . . .'

CHAPTER 13

Two choices, Ronnie considered as she zipped the little car through city traffic. She had only two choices. Either find a sleazy hotel where credit cards were the furthest thing from a requirement or check into an expensive hotel where the color of a credit card bought anonymity and loyalty. With the classy sports car wrapped around her like a warm glove, she chose the latter.

Listed in a brochure that she'd picked up en route, she located the Lakefront Inn without much trouble and rolled smoothly under the elaborate carport entrance. Parking at the curb, she slipped from the car, spotting the valet attendant. Lively, the uniformed fellow stepped from the etched glass doors, reaching her as she reached the passenger door.

"Ma'am, if you'll pull forward," he started, apparently accustomed to making that request a million times every day.

Tossing him the keys, Ronnie leaned and brought her overnight bag from the front seat, catching his startled eyes as she straightened. "Park it for me, will you, hon? I'm a born optimist, and if I'm wrong, you'll make twice the tip when I need it returned." From her jacket pocket, she brought a wad of bills, managed to leaf off a fifty, and handed it to him with an engaging smile. "Do be careful with it, will you, dear? It's a classic."

By whatever signal valets and bellhops communicated the young man tipped off the uniformed gentlemen inside the door. Before Ronnie took more than three steps, another pleasant young man offered to carry her bags.

If she'd intended to draw attention to herself, she'd succeeded.

Without a need to feign either arrogance or sophistication, she sped through the glass doors, aloof and confident. Hustling, the bellhop remained a half-step ahead to clear her path. By the time she reached the registration desk, the bellhop communicated with the woman behind the counter. In record time, Mrs. L. received the keys and a zealous escort to a suite on the eighth floor—along with an assurance that guest lists were confidential. As her tour guide pointed out the finer amenities within the four-room suite, Ronnie plotted her course of action and tipped the fellow considerably.

"If there's anything I can do for you, ma'am, just ask for Ken," he said smoothly. "And enjoy your stay."

He barely started to turn when Ronnie halted him, speaking hesitantly. "Ken, there is . . . Well, I wondered if you could tell me. What's all this I'm hearing about well . . . murders and riots?" With an appropriate touch of worry in her eyes and a slight tension in her voice, she continued, "I haven't had much chance to watch the news lately, but I caught something on the radio as I drove in. I need to go out this evening, but I started thinking . . . I mean, is it safe? You don't have some lunatic—just snatching people off the streets here, do you?"

Uncomfortably, he wrestled his conscience versus the first rules of his employment that dictated—one should never say anything to upset the guests. His conscience won, citing the second rule that guests should be accommodated and protected. She was a lone woman, after all, and he'd apparently seen the picture of the last victim—dark hair and pretty, about the same age. "I'm not sure what all I can tell you, ma'am. The papers really aren't giving a lot of details, but there was uh . . . uh, at least one woman was found, and from what I've heard, she might not have been the only one. So far, the ah . . . the killer's still at large, and it might not be a good idea to go out by yourself. I mean, if you stay in crowded places, you should be fine, and I think they said something about the killer knowing his victims or something."

"My goodness," she said warily.

"Really, ma'am, I didn't mean to scare you or anything. You'll probably be just fine. The mayor has a special task force set up, and the Feds are working on it. Heck, they even had some guy from France working on it. And I know the police are working a lot of overtime—patrolling, and stuff."

Some guy from France? "They . . .? They have someone from France?" she said, affecting her curiosity and surprise, neither of which she needed to feign.

He looked as if he wanted to bite his tongue, and his eyes conveyed his second thoughts. Far more carefully, as if he knew he'd already said too much, he nodded and continued, "They said something about it in the papers the day before yesterday. The mayor was talking about all of their efforts, and he said something about a guy from the French Embassy assisting in the case. Anyway,

I don't know if that part's true. There's been a lot of talk along those lines. The point is—there's probably nothing for you to worry about."

"Do they have any suspects?" she asked as if hoping, her thoughts still spinning. She knew how to read people, had been reading people forever. This one knew something more than he was saying. His relief with the subject change came too quickly, too visibly.

"They had a couple guys in custody. A couple of those white supremacists, but I think they had to let them go. Might not be a good idea to go anywhere near the courthouse. Seems like everybody and his uncle's over there protesting and rallying. The uh . . . the situation around here is pretty tense. If you have to go anywhere by yourself, it might be a good idea if you let us check it out for you. I mean, if you check at the desk, we could probably steer you clear of any potential danger."

"The man from France, Ken," she said hesitantly, knowing if only by the lack of a reaction downstairs, the name wasn't Laquette. "Do you happen to remember his name?"

His eyes carried the discomfort and wariness. "I don't think it was ever ah . . . mentioned, ma'am."

Time for a judgment call . . . and looking into the slightly tense brown eyes, she reached a decision while pulling out her wad of bills. Glancing down, she peeled off another fifty and handed it to him, meeting his more tense gaze. "I'd really like to know whatever you can tell me about this Frenchman, hon."

He looked at her, at the hundred dollars in his hand. "I uh . . . I don't understand, ma'am. Are you uh . . . ? Are you from the Embassy, too? I mean, you don't look like a federal agent, but . . .?"

Her ears perked at the word 'too,' and a thought of Jean-Pierre's frustration flashed neon in her mind. If her father-in-law had lost her husband, it was a fair bet, he'd used a little of his influence to recover his loss. At the same time, she realized the Frenchman had been in this hotel and that Frenchman was her husband. "Do you know his name, hon?"

"Ma'am, I really don't think—"

"Ken, I've had an extremely bad week," she said without a need to fake her weariness. "I believe this Frenchman—whose presence I was led to believe was to be held in confidence—is my husband's cousin. In which case, he's the man I'm supposed to be meeting at this hotel. If you could tell me his name, I would greatly appreciate it."

"Ah . . . we're not supposed to give out names. I mean if someone were to ask—"

"Ken, I'm not with the Enquirer, for God's sake. I assume his name was Jardonet. If I'm wrong, then he's not the man I'm supposed to be meeting."

"Uh . . . you're not wrong," he said hesitantly. "But you missed him. He checked out the same day he checked in. You might want to check with the FBI or the French Embassy. They could probably tell you where he is."

"I'll do that, thank you," she said simply and peeled off another fifty to hand to him.

Waving off the bill, anxious to escape, he again started out the door.

"Ken?"

Dreading, he halted and looked at her, albeit pleading to depart.

"Don't mention to anyone that we've had this chat, and please, don't mention my name to anyone. I do value my privacy."

"Not a word, ma'am, I promise," he said smoothly and slipped out the door.

How long before someone from the Enquirer appeared in the lobby? If the fellow names dropped under such slight pressure . . .

Jardonet. Jean-Pierre had said it earlier . . . 'I already have him.'

Her husband had recovered the name his father had given him, and knowing how Jade felt about that man, that name, she wondered at his frame of mind.

The weariness that had tugged at her for the past dozen hours swept through her once again, threatening to collapse her in her tracks. He truly had tossed it all away. Their life, their home, their child. He'd come here as Jardonet and somehow arranged to have Jade Laquette extinguished in a plane crash. *Why?* That was the single question she would ask him . . . right before she walked away. That really was the only question remaining in her mind. Why. Not how. She knew him well enough to know how. She knew him well enough to know he could manage this without a stitch of trouble.

Isaac Bently. That name hadn't worn well on him, but he'd lived with that name for five years, meeting people, laughing and joking, building friendships and business associations. In Elmview, he was "Zack." To the Spencers . . . "Sax," a nickname derived from Deedee's speech impediment at the age of two. "Uncle Isaac" reduced to "Unc' Sax." And Deedee might mourn for her Uncle Sax for the next few decades.

Jean-Pierre was right . . . so damned right. The man she'd married was gone. Jade Laquette, the man who had held her and whispered to her, the man who had written a note claiming their love could last forever . . . gone. she'd fallen in love with a lie. A fantasy. A phantom. And the illusion was shattered. If he'd taken any other name, anything other than Jardonet—a name he claimed to despise. Any other name than the one that bound him to a life for which he had professed only contempt. The tears came, spilling down her cheeks. Hissing a curse, she flopped down on the small couch. Jardonet . . . what could have possessed him? And therein lay the final stroke. *Possession*. His father had held dominion.

No. Whatever else her husband was, he wasn't a man to be controlled. Even Jean-Pierre had admitted that detail, and doubtful, he'd faked his annoyance. Whatever had possessed the man she loved to ditch her, it had nothing to do with Jean-Pierre or someone else controlling his actions. He was in control. Consciously, he'd walked away from her and returned to a name that offered him the freedom to move mountains.

She would find him. If for no other reason than for her own peace of mind. Whatever he was now, she knew who he had been, and had loved who he had been. She needed to see that man once more, and she held only one question for him. Why? Why had he thrown their life away? And God help him if he attempted even a half second of subterfuge. She'd buried him once, and she wouldn't be obligated to attend the funeral of a cousin or . . . a brother.

The son of a bitch was too arrogant not to turn himself into a legitimate heir to the Jardonet dynasty! And Jean-Pierre had known it. She'd lost a husband, and he'd gained a son. Was it any wonder he expressed no damned regrets over the loss?

Anger helped. When all else failed, Ron Bryson could always count on anger to pull herself through, and by God, she just might ditch the Laquette name, too. Maybe she'd reclaim her maiden name. Veronica "Ron" Bryson had worn well enough for twenty-six years. According to Jardonet, she was having an illegitimate child anyway. If she was forced to raise this child alone, then by God, she would raise him with a name he could be proud to wear. Obviously, the Laquette name meant nothing to the man who'd given it to her. Divorced women reverted to their maiden names—a widow probably could. If this son of a bitch could walk away from her, his life, his child, his name . . . then by God, she would follow suit!

First, however, she needed to find him and kick his ass just once!

Hurt him. Oh, she would hurt him all right! She might just land that fateful blow Donna had mentioned avoiding. At least, she'd make sure no other

Jardonet heirs cropped up out of the woodwork twenty or thirty years down the road.

How dare he take the Jardonet name and leave her stranded with a dead husband, a pall of sadness, and a child to raise alone after all their hopes and plans! How dare he just take off, sending her on a wild goose chase, not even offering her an inkling that he was about to crash and burn. Did he foresee this, too? Did he know just how mad she would become? Just how much of this nightmare had he foreseen?

Did it matter?

Not to him, obviously.

'. . . you have one mystery to solve . . . I another.'

Yea, well, if he was in Cleveland solving this mystery, he had a few surprises. Only starting with the fact that Ron Bryson, investigative journalist, was now on the same case—his case. And she knew just where to start.

Barely needing to move, she reached to the end table and lifted the receiver, punching the long series of numbers. A half dozen rings later, a breathless voice huffed, "Saunders! Hello?"

"Hiya, Pete. How's everything?"

"Uh . . . Ronnie?"

Considering the immense flower arrangement delivered by her lasting friends from the paper, she understood his hesitation. What does one say to a woman who buried her husband less than ten hours earlier? "I need to ask a favor, Pete," she said quietly.

"Uh . . . yea, sure, Ron. Name it," he said with an echo of dread. Undoubtedly, he anticipated a request for whatever information had come over the wire service concerning a plane crash in Kentucky.

She probably should have taken a moment to lose the crisp edge of anger in her voice, but he should be accustomed to that tone even under duress. "Who's covering the Cleveland affair?"

"Cleveland . . .? Oh, you mean, the Taxidermist thing?"

"Excuse me?"

"That's the handle they're putting on this wacko," Pete said, almost sounding like his old self before he took pause. "Uh . . . how are you, Ronnie? Is everything okay?"

"What do you know about this Taxidermist?" she asked bluntly. If anyone in the office knew more about the mechanics and day-to-day affairs passing from layout to print, no one more than Pete Saunders, the office goffer. Years ago, when she'd worked at the paper, she'd learned more about publishing from Pete than she had learned in four years of college.

"What do you want to know?" he asked.

"Start at the beginning. When did he first strike? Where . . .?" As she spoke, she leaned and grabbed her purse, dragging it close enough to begin scrounging for her notebook.

"First strike—unofficially, mind you—August 30th. A college kid by the name of Abraham Lowenstein . . ."

Sitting on the gray floor, knees drawn, elbows propped, Dominique held his thudding head between his chilled hands. Mental overload. Exhausted, he leaned against the bank of cabinets opposite the vault where a brief segment of his life remained forever captured. The memories hadn't let him go.

He rested, scrolling through the past, sorting, sifting, and cutting, locking onto isolated fragments of film as efficiently as a Hollywood producer. By what method he'd segregated himself to look objectively at this wicked collection, he couldn't decide nor dwell too deeply. He'd seen his mother's death. Regardless of how well he portrayed the entity of a half-brother, he couldn't deceive himself. In the main entrance of the Victorian house in Arlington, he'd found his mother's corpse. Shot twice. Once through the chest, once through the forehead, and in his way, he knew she'd been alive when that second bullet had shut down her mental processes. Standing over her, the gunman had spoken, and her final vision in life was that of a small black circle, like the pupil of an eye within the broad crystal circle above her. The horror of that thought no longer affected him. Objectively, he simply knew the terror she'd felt while facing her executioner. Curiously, he suffered an equal indifference to the vision of himself trapped within a small theater, forced to watch the scenes of the Holocaust unfolding on an original raw production of the worst horror in modern history.

A test . . . possibly one of the cruelest tests he'd undergone within this facility, he considered with the heaviness pulsating in his skull. He'd viewed other scripts, excerpts from history caught on tape, from the famous footage of President J. F. Kennedy's final ride through the streets of Dallas to the attempted assassination of George McGovern. Under the auspices of "Behavioral Analysis," Carson and his cohorts had filmed ten-year-old Jade Laquette watching the films, but none of those had affected him as that film of Auschwitz—not one of them. And the reason came to him, now, as it had then. Where the dozens of other film clips had been captured by non-biased, innocent photographers and most of those he'd watched were reproductions of the originals, that film of Auschwitz had been captured by a genuine participant in that gruesome affair . . . and it was an original.

Lambs to slaughter, those animated figures trudging toward their doom, most oblivious until the final throes of death blinked the light from their eyes. And on a dual plane, he experienced the blind fervor of the followers who had implemented those wicked orders, marching thousands through the doors of the gas chamber, only to carry the corpses to furnaces minutes or hours later. Film. It was the most gruesome footage ever caught on film, and in a private viewing room, ten-year-old Jade Laquette had been forced to watch it in the name of science.

An experiment. Behavioral analysis. Given his 'sensitivities and extra-sensory perception,' how would the child protege react to this footage? By the time he'd endured that phase of the tests, Carson had become ninety-nine percent positive of Jade Laquette's authenticity. Miles of taped sessions had confirmed his belief. Hour upon hours of physical and mental tests under extreme conditions with endless questions and reactions recorded. Microscopically, Carson had dissected the mind of a child, breaking down whatever conscious resolve might have safeguarded his subject under less grueling conditions. A genuine psychic. The real thing—not an elaborate hoax or an ultra-intelligent child with natural gifts to read body language or facial expressions. With every test imaginable, from Zener cards to electrical pulses, Carson had confirmed the existence of psychic phenomena and validated the *'modern-day Solomon'* as he'd written in one of his notes. *'Merlin,'* he'd scrolled in the margins of another, *'This boy can look inside a crystal ball and spy the secrets of the universe . . .'*

But Carson wasn't the only one viewing that plethora of documentation. Another faction existed with access to those films and political influence . . . The same political influence to initiate those tests, to institutionalize and analyze Jade Laquette in the name of science. The masterminds behind that conspiracy had followed those test results with far more interest and understanding than Carson. Where the doctor had sought a breakthrough in the known sciences and reveled in the unimaginable benefit of such a new science—'. . . *similar to the diagnostic writings of Edgar Casey,'* he'd written—another faction altogether had kept watch, aware of the potential danger of such an anomaly.

And a reason existed, Dominique knew at this moment, the same reason belying the murder of Felicity Laquette and would have resulted in her son's execution within this facility eighteen years ago. The original wicked films. His knowledge and his reaction to those original wretched films of mass murder had sealed his fate then. Within a week after watching those films, reacting to those films, and proving the existence of psychic phenomena, he'd been marked for extinction. If not for his father . . .

His father had rescued him . . . As surely as he had tracked down the hired gunman who had taken Felicity's life. An eye for an eye . . . Jean Pierre had caught up to that fellow in a flophouse in Florida, and a bullet had found a home in the assassin's frontal lobe.

By the same respect, Dominique knew what had become of Dr. Carson. He knew at this moment, Carson had disappeared and suffered tremendously after assisting in the rescue of a small boy. Unwittingly, Carson had carried that emaciated child from this institution—had smuggled him out and delivered him into the hands of strangers without ever consciously knowing his participation. And Carson had died under interrogation by the very faction that had manipulated him into conducting those wicked tests.

Because of that tape . . . an original tape from the very depths of hell.

What was one more death when stacked against that reel of macabre film? A reel of film captured by madmen and delivered into the hands of the United States government . . . by an original participant in that madness.

Amnesty. Sanction. Sanctuary . . . They'd offered Herr Schrieber a home sparing him from the noose he'd deserved in Nuremberg. Madmen. American-born madmen who believed in the omnipotent collection of scientific knowledge, placing value on that knowledge rather than human life and a vile contradiction in itself.

All of it—the torture, the tests, the continuation of inhumane experiments—all toward the alleged betterment of mankind.

Eugenics. The belief in a superior race. A pure white race. For the sake of eugenics . . . and the secret society within the United States government still existed. Its mission—to improve society. Obsessed with that single premise. As much as eighteen years past, men and women deemed unfit for society were still being sterilized in prisons and mental institutions without their consent . . . and the process continued even now.

"Damn her," Dominique uttered, understanding at last, why he'd carried the burden of guilt for his mother's murder. She'd used him. Time and again, she'd used him, forcing him to touch the personal items that she demanded of her 'clients' and 'potential clients.' If a greater scam artist had existed, none more than Felicity Laquette. She'd accumulated a fortune, playing on the nature of the wealthy, promising health, happiness, and further financial gain through her astrology charts.

Clearly, he recalled the endless stream of clients who passed through the front entry, ever eager to pay Felicity Laquette her outlandish fees if only she could tell them whether they should attend *this* political party or donate to *that* worthy cause. She had a gift—the gift to spot a mark at twenty paces and a seductive charm which could draw them in and sucker them for life . . . And she'd used her bastard son to enhance her charisma. Through him, she'd strengthened her hold, telling her clients things about their past—sometimes their future—which had gained her the reputation as a 'psychic wonder' as well as an avid astrologer.

Right up until she'd informed one of her clients about her husband's affiliation with a Nazi doctor and the probability of public outrage if that information ever came to light.

Blackmail. His mother had walked a fine line toward extorting one of the most powerful men in DC . . . and unwittingly threatened to expose the secret society. With the insight he'd given her, she'd sealed her fate—and his own . . .

'You're nothing but a two-bit scam artist, you French slut . . . Either make some excuse to drop my mother as a client or by God, I'll have you investigated . . .'

'I soog`jest you consid`air those actions carefully, Matilda . . . Surely, you would not wont this little blemish on your family's impeccable reputa`tion, nor I am sure, would you enjoy besmir`shing your fath`air's campaign . . . I have no inten`tion of off`airing you any of my prognostica`tions nor am I inclined to attempt convincing you of my talents. I am merely pointing out that your par`ents—as well as your broth`air and sist`air—have far more to lose by your threat of legal act`ions. I will, howev`air, compromise with you, ma chérie. I will speak to your moth`air about this vis`et . . .'

'. . . They're gonna kill my mother. Your boyfriend's writing a story about you—' the child had spouted while clinging to the knoll post in the grand foyer.

The story had made the tabloids . . . Even tucked down between the sensational articles about Watergate, the scandal had made headlines. The unscrupulous reporter had slept with a senator's daughter to write an exposé about the amoral conduct and promiscuity of Washington's young socialites . . . And the young woman had enlightened her prestigious father of a certain scam artist's child who had tried to warn her. Unwittingly, that young lady had suggested that Felicity Laquette had orchestrated the scandal to ruin her in retaliation for her visit . . ..

CHAPTER 14

As Dominique had suggested, Carol arrived on schedule, opening the door into the elevator hallway just as he emerged from the secure area. An expression of doubt creased her brow; confusion and uncertainty haunted her blue eyes as she held the door for him. Not unnatural, this conflicting preoccupation in the wake of his tampering. Touching her arm, he escorted her back into the elevator and designated the required floor. Later, perhaps, in the quick of night, she would suffer a few weird dreams involving Dominique Jardonet, but none of those would follow her into consciousness. At the ground-floor level, he planted a suggestion for her to report to Dr. Heinz as instructed and verify that her patient had taken his prescribed medication without protest. After which, she was to depart from the facility at her appointed hour.

Needing her assistance only once more, Dominique passed through the security area checkpoint and strode into the more natural lobby atmosphere as if he were an authorized visitor to the research facility. At the reception desk, he locked gazes with the woman who considered questioning him, smiled, and continued through the glass doors that she was kind enough to release for him.

Mowed lawns, tended hedges, and paved walkways concealed a world of sins to the untrained eye. Dominique suffered no illusions as he passed from the neon-bright entry into the more subdued fluorescent glow of vapor lights and ground-level spotlights. Within the trees crowded near the building in park-like precision, the lighted upper floor windows offered the illusion of a hospital or office facility, enhanced by the neon marque designating the facility as a research laboratory which had the gall to quote a line from Hippocrates. *"primum non nocere"*... First, do no harm.

Amused, Dominique continued his stride as a dark sedan skidded and halted less than twenty paces in front of him, and Milton Lakeland climbed quickly from the driver's seat. By no mental tampering, this fellow had arrived on schedule, and only more amused, Dominique watched him stalk around the car, already searching the facility entrance as if he searched for someone to provide an explanation. No hint of a disturbance, no alarms sounding, or security guards racing through the doors to halt a loose patient.

"Who authorized—"

"Mon ami, if I had waited for you, I would be dead," Dominique said and continued the last few paces as Lakeland rocked on his heels. "And I am truly not the most patient man about town. Shall we go?"

"Go where?" Lakeland stated, contemplating the gun under his jacket.

"If I did not agree to be poisoned, I doubt I will agree to be shot. Do leave your weapon holstered. We can talk while you drive."

"You haven't said where we're going," Lakeland noted, holding his steady pose and posture.

"Nor will I until we are inside the car leaving this facility. We can work together or apart—the choice is yours—but do not take long to decide."

Lakeland needed only a second and backed off, motioning to the car as he turned and started around the sedan's front bumper, sparing another curious glance to the entrance.

"You came alone," Dominique commented as the assistant director started the engine. "Am I to understand you took my words and cautions to heart and realized the potential danger in seeking assistance within your company?"

"Let's just say quite a few questions remain to be answered," Lakeland answered offhandedly, concentrating on his driving only long enough to navigate the turns through the parking lot. At the main entrance, a guard booth and wire mesh gates prohibited any unexpected guests and thwarted intruders. Lakeland passed through without more than a fleeting glance and wave to the attendant. "Now," he said while pulling onto the highway. "I think you better tell me exactly where you intend to go and why."

"Where I'm going is not as important as where you are going," Dominique said offhandedly. "You do realize a separate entity's working through your esteemed company toward an end that is not entirely in line with your own."

"Try that again in English," Lakeland stated.

Amused, Dominique obliged, literally. "You hov someone working against you from the inside, Mr. Lakeland."

The headlights veered off the highway. Lakeland recovered the wheel and pivoted his gaze between the strip of blacktop to Dominique and back. A half dozen times, his attention ricocheted, searching the man who rested, watching him work out the initial surprise. English. Even under extreme interrogation, Dominique Jardonet had proven his ignorance of the English language, and Lakeland had heard those tapes and seen the video portions to verify his belief. To have the English words spoken with the faintest trace of an accent . . . "Who the hell are you?"

"Who I am is not as important as what I can tell you, or it shouldn't be," Dominique commented. "Your ranks have been penetrated. Your operation was manipulated, and your goals were compromised. I suspected as much when I arrived in Cleveland. It was uh . . . obvious, to me, that someone with a great deal of influence tampered with that affair. Perhaps, even ah . . . initiated it."

"The situation in Cleveland is well under control, Mr. Jardonet."

"If you believe that, you are a fool, and you've proven you're not that. If I had been allowed to continue on my given course, I would have eliminated the threat with ah . . . how's it said? Extreme prejudice?" he asked with a smile which the dashboard lights enhanced. He shrugged indifference. "Fate took ets course. Now we are left with a maniac still on the loose, and he has ah . . . friends in high places as well as his own agenda. He is mad, you know? If your office had received all of the information—which, I fear, it did—then you knew as much as three months ago that he was only a fledgling in his art of madness. If the chain of command hadn't been altered, you, personally, would have ordered your primo agents to that front. Everything about Abraham Lowenstein's death suggested the signature of a serial killer, and yet . . .? You tell me, sir, how does the case only take precedence after the fourth victim? Why was he allowed to continue his mad quest?"

"We had agents on that case nearly from the onset," Lakeland stated.

"If the maniac committed fraud or embezzlement, they would have caught him. You had a signature killer. Not a white-collar criminal, and yet, your profilers were busy elsewhere? Your chief forensic specialist—elsewhere. There are no coincidences in life, just manipulations, mistakes, and oversights which lead to calamity."

"Mistakes, I'll grant you," Lakeland said grimly. "I wasn't kept abreast of the situation as I should have been. That doesn't necessarily mean that I was deliberately misled."

"You were coerced into an operation to abduct an American citizen," Dominique countered.

"We've covered that ground, Mr. Jardonet," Lakeland stated, glancing over. "I've already compromised what should have been classified material. Yes, I gave an order which would have resulted in Mr. Laquette's apprehension. Under the National Security Act, I was within my jurisdiction."

"My comrade, Paul Lejeune nearly died, Mr. Lakeland," Dominique said quietly and studied the man's grim expression in the gauge light. "Did your order include murder?"

"You're obviously aware of the attempted assassination. And you do know if not for my agents, it would have succeeded."

"And you're aware of a breach in your security measures. Someone knew what your operation entailed and acted accordingly. Is your security so lax that anyone could have monitored a frequency and collected that information?"

"I admitted I have a few questions."

"You consider this ah . . . assassination attempt a mistake, monsieur, because you would rather not believe that someone possessed the ability to switch the intended medication given to your agents. What should have been a staged performance, nearly cost a life and you would rather believe that was an accident. I understand your predicament, mon ami, but that does not erase the fact that someone in your command took orders from another or that a French citizen remains in critical condition within that research center."

Lakeland was silent for a long moment before commenting, "Lejeune will be all right."

"Oui, monsieur, he was caught in time. But I believe it was ah . . . decided that I wasn't the man they were ordered to kill. A simple communication may have saved my life, along with Lejeune's. Jade Laquette, after all, was already dead."

"We didn't have that information until the next morning," Lakeland pointed out.

"I lost more than twenty-four hours of my life, monsieur. Who de`cided to lower the injections and allow me to awaken?" The order had bypassed Lakeland, Dominique knew before turning his gaze through the window. "So," he said absently. "You are beginning to realize the accuracy of my concern."

"You do realize I came this evening to look at the Laquette files personally."

"I work much faster with fewer reservations," Dominique commented. "My half-brother was abducted by your government eighteen years ago. He was subjected to tests for more than eighteen months, and I have reason to believe, he would not have lived much long`air if my father had not intervened through Dr. Carson—the doctor who headed the investigation of Laquette's talents. The same people who initiated his mother's murd`air arranged for that study, and I have further reason to believe, were instrumental in the activity this week, resulting in his death. Bluntly," Dominique glimpsed the dark eyes flashing off him to the highway. "The same people who worried about what he knew then were worried about what he knew now. Perhaps, they feared that with his talents, he would uncov`air them and their secret."

"What kind of secret? Any idea?"

"A very good idea, monsieur, and it is ah . . . may be worth killing for even after all these years. Perhaps, even worth the wasted lives of a few innocents in Cleveland, and knowing what they do about Jade Laquette, they would not doubt he would be drawn toward that madman since he admitted that detail on film nearly eighteen years ago. He told them when, and where to find him." Dominique shrugged, indifferent and slightly amused. "The problem we face, mon ami, is that a half-brother with Laquette's talents has surfaced. Now, I am also marked as a lamb for slaughter. Fortunately, for myself, I am more like a wolf, eh?"

Lakeland glanced over, not appreciating Dominique's slight smile. "You said you knew this secret. I think it's a good time to mention it."

"Suppose I better, since our joint enemy will learn soon enough that the lamb's not lying on a slab in the research morgue," he said lightly. "Et is simply this, mon ami. About uh . . . thirty years ago, highly regarded officials in your government sanctioned the safe passage and eventual citizenship of a doctor of ah . . . questionable ethics?" His voice rang with dark amusement. "More clearly, monsieur, he was one of those who served under Hitler's command, instrumental in the slaughter and making use of the abundance of human subjects for the advancement of science and ah . . . fun. A cabinet or ah . . . council of medical practitioners welcomed this maniac into the United States and accepted his consultation? After all, it wasn't unheard of even in this country, to sanction human experimentation from physical to mental. Rather than condemn the man for his practices, they did indeed welcome him. Unfortunately, for my half-brother and his mother, someone in liaison with that fellow, was ah . . . a client? And Jade Laquette, even as a child, was highly sensitive to touch. More unfortunately, his mother was something of an extortion`ist. Obviously, he said enough for her to gather a partial picture, and wittingly or unwittingly, she attempted to use that knowledge."

"I'm not sure I'm buying any of this," Lakeland stated with an edge. "You're telling me that some nut out of WWII made a home . . . what? Here in Washington? And because of that, we have another maniac in Cleveland? Along with the unvalidated murder of Laquette—"

"Two Laquettes, monsieur. And I would not make the mistake of simplifying what I am telling you. What would happen if, say . . . the press learned of this digression? Bear in mind, we are discussing the moral creed governing the AMA and NIMH. Even the sugges`tion that an authentic Nazi murderer served on that most prestigious collection of highly regarded professionals would create a public outcry to make Cleveland's recent decline look like a rally in a kindergarten playground. You may reject that theory, but those who have acted to conceal this secret suffer no delusions in that respect. They know what they did, and they know the poten`tial danger of enlightenment . . .

"If you think bigotry and racism are a problem, now, my friend, consider the compounded moral, ethnic, and religious battles that would ripple across the nation. Hospitals, mon ami . . . whether they had a Jew or a German on the board of directors, would become the focus of riots and protests. Jewish communities and supporters would rise in indignation as surely as the supremacists would shout with triumph and glee. The stamp of the American Medical Association would become a symbol of distrust. Government buildings and facilities would be bombarded with radicals. Hell, you would see enough of a decline in doctor's visits alone to account for an economic recession, not to mention the death toll when patient-doctor trust deteriorates, and treatments are rejected and ignored. Would you want a Nazi operating on your gallbladder, mon ami?"

"You've made your point," Lakeland stated.

"I'm not sure I have, monsieur," Dominique said quietly. "Because to be honest, I believe our madman in Cleveland is only the tip of the iceberg. A trial run, so to speak."

"What the hell's that supposed to mean?"

"As I said, they have killed to keep this secret, and they know the consequences of exposure. What is to say that we face only one faction? Only one enigma? We are dealing with men, mon ami. Wealthy, well-educated men who have sanctioned the practices of the greatest tragedy in history—supported it in a small way. Why would they do sush?"

"Oh, Christ. You think they have an alternative . . . a long-range plan . . . to expose themselves and bring on this catastrophe you're predicting?"

"Themselves, no," Dominique said as he gazed through the side window, remembering. "I walked in the mind of a madman. I've seen what he's seen and spoken words from the depths of his conscious and subconscious thoughts." Bringing his gaze to connect briefly with Lakeland, he commented, "You heard the tape from the morgue in Cleveland, Mr. Lakeland. That wasn't a hoax, not a trick I planned, or a fabrication. The words you heard were his words . . . and unless I am wrong, he referred to others . . . to world dominion. A new order rising. He sees himself as an artist, not a politician, and yet he believes he will lead a new world. If I may ask . . .? Where did Monsieur Reddinger receive his schooling?"

"John Hopkins, goddamn it . . ."

"His schooling may have come from that revered institution, monsieur, but his indoctrination transpired elsewhere."

"You realize Reddinger has an entire string of letters behind his name and has prestigious awards coming out the wazoo. He's been recognized by the AMA for his exceptional skill, and he's currently employed at one of the most highly regarded research hospitals in the country. You do know all of that, right?"

"A policeman in Cleveland . . . he said something to lend me pause, monsieur. It amounted to this . . . if you cannot trust your doctor, who can you trust? He further consid'aired the thought of going under the knife, so to speak, with this maniac holding it."

"Uncomfortable thought, I'll grant you, Mr. Jardonet, but Reddinger wouldn't be the first doctor to become a serial killer. The profession's not exempt, and I doubt we'll see your chaos theory when we bring him in."

"Meaning not to destroy your confidence, Mr. Lakeland, but if the wrong person wins in this game of deceit when you bring Reddinger in, it will tip the precarious balance known as law and order. We are not merely shedding light on the antics of a single maniac, Mr. Lakeland. If he is part of a conspiracy within the ranks and files of the major medical fraternity in the country . . . voila! Chaos. And it will take only his one moment in the spotlight to create that domino effect."

Traffic had increased considerably, forcing Lakeland to pay closer attention to the highway, but it amounted to lip service. His thoughts lingered far more deeply, and rapidly as the silence dragged between them. More than five miles passed before he glanced over and commented, "You haven't told me where you intend to go, Mr. Jardonet."

"I have an appointment to keep," he answered honestly. "And you have a conspirator to find within your ranks. I would suggest you begin by speaking with your colleague, Leonardo Devinio. I have a thought he has information that could assist in discovering your nemesis. After that, mon ami, I trust you'll know how to handle the situation."

"If you know so much, Mr. Jardonet, why not just drop me a few names?" Lakeland said with subtle sarcasm. "Or is that what you've just done by qualifying Dr. Whitman Reddinger as our maniac?"

"All things have a moment, and that moment has not come, monsieur. Even if I could be certain of the names or name you seek, even if I confirmed this doctor as your madman—whish I will not—to simply spout an accusation before a proper progression of events could be to alter the outcome. A contradiction, yes, but fate is the true master in this game. A fateful mistake could be fatal."

"How does this work, Mr. Jardonet? If you know the outcome . . .?"

"Think of the future as a magic puzzle where all the pieces must be placed in sequence, one piece fitting against the next to form the picture. A piece at a time, the puzzle unfolds, but if the right piece falls into place in the wrong sequence—voila! All other pieces will change shape and color. You and I talking, now? It leads to the next piece, but if we try finishing the puzzle with the last piece . . .? Do you understand?"

"You give me the names, and we end up with a slew of loose pieces and a whole new puzzle," Lakeland said thoughtfully. "But what happens if this piece doesn't fit, Mr. Jardonet? Let's say, we skip a few steps, you give me the names, and I go after our nemesis? What happens then?"

"Do you have evidence to accuse and arrest a few of the most prestigious gentlemen in the capital, Mr. Lakeland? If you knocked on a door at this instant, could you stop the chaos? Or would you end up dismissed from the ranks and files?"

"Good point," Lakeland commented.

"It's already taken me too long to trust you. Finding a replacement and ally could take more time than I'd care to waste. You use your talents, mon ami, and I'll use mine. Hopefully, between us, we can alter the outcomes before too many more lives are lost or destroyed. Drop me off at a conven`ienze store, will you?"

"I'd still like to know where you're going and who you're meeting."

"You could hand over my wallet and passport, Mr. Lakeland. And the next corner will do fine."

"I think you and I have a few other things to discuss, Mr. Jardonet. Only beginning with the diplomatic relationships between our countries."

"I have already accepted the overwhelming tactics enlisted by your Mr. Chalmers," Dominique said with a slight smile. "I'm sure my understanding of my experience was nothing more than a grand hallucination brought on by the effects of the drugs my would-be assailants administered. We will leave it at that, shall we?"

Lakeland considered momentarily, then agreed by action, wading into his suit jacket and extracting Dominique's credentials from an inside pocket. "I wouldn't advise leaving the country just yet, Mr. Jardonet. And I'd appreciate it if you'd keep in touch."

Too easy, this agreement, and in a stopped instant, Dominique understood—his father was in the country. Possibly, in DC. And Lakeland assumed Dominique intended to seek refuge in the French Embassy. Getting dropped off at the front door by an assistant director of the FBI might support Chalmers' official statement, but too many questions would be asked. In his own way, Lakeland was leaving the explanations to Dominique and was fully prepared to accept the consequences. Lakeland hadn't risen in the ranks on the coattails of others; his base instincts supported the wild claims and innuendos. Something was wrong, and he was willing to take risks to find the answers.

At the corner, Dominique stepped out, then leaned and looked over at Lakeland, who suffered second thoughts behind his grim expression. "Bypass Mr. Chalmers when you speak to someone on the President's cabinet, Mr. Lakeland. I've described a conspiracy theory that might be better handled by the State Department but do be careful with whom you speak. This may be coming out of the AMA, but I sense our Nazi friend may have gained supporters in other ranks. Your CIA has never lacked creativity in covert ops, and several of the experiments in your archives bear a striking resemblance to the mind games conducted in the 50s. Our Nazi visitor did not arrive on American soil via U.S. Post. He had a great deal of help, and as the saying goes, a single man might move the world with a large enough fulcrum—but he would need a great deal of help to lift a lever of that size."

"I'd imagine so," Lakeland commented with a tight smile. "Take care of yourself."

"Always," Dominique said with a smile and snapped the door shut before stepping onto the curb.

CHAPTER 15

What she would give for ten minutes with Amy Sue Bradway was almost immoral. That lovely local hairdresser in Bentwood could create a masterpiece with a ball of twine, while Ronnie could barely manage a decent ponytail, much less a French braid. Disgusted, she studied her accomplishment in the vanity mirror. Her black locks twisted more like a French knot than ever a braid.

Muttering a curse, she yanked the folds and stood looking at her scattered black waves. How could a woman who had grown up under the wing of one of the most fashionable women in D.C. lack even the basic concept of hairstyle? A Freudian thing? Had she rebelled so fiercely against her mother's lifestyle and occupation that she had refused to master even the most mundane skills?

More probably, she'd never felt any great desire to impress anyone. The one time she'd tried—the very first time she'd sat through Amy's ministrations, she'd meant to knock the socks off an arrogant, drop-dead gorgeous antique dealer, and she'd fallen flat on her butt. Not only had he failed to appear impressed with her new do, but he'd also picked a fight with her. Well . . . that wasn't entirely true. His lofty indifference had struck a raw chord in her nature, and she'd forfeited the interview with something slightly less than cordial aplomb. In fact, she was sure she'd insulted him first.

Oil and water . . . more like fire and smoke, she considered as she stepped back from the mirror and leaned at the wall, her gaze still on her reflection. She was fire, damned ready to ignite with a bit of hot Irish temper . . . and he was smoke. A damned illusionist. Ready to vanish under a soft breeze.

"Well," she muttered, her cool blue eyes sparking back at her. "Where there's smoke, there's fire, bub, and you can bet your ass, the California blazes will look like a damned campfire when I catch up to you."

Uncomfortably, Tad squirmed, apparently not in agreement with her present fit of rage.

Scanning her reflection, half expecting to see the ripple in the mirror, Ronnie shook her head, lowering her eyes toward her waistline. "Tad, dear, your father and I have been colliding like this since we first laid eyes on each other. Don't let it bother you. God knows, maybe we are the light and the darkness. I'd certainly like to pound him into a shadow of his former self at the moment. Unfortunately, we must find him first." Her gaze lifted to the rat tangle of black waves that she'd created in an attempt to alter her appearance. "More unfortunately, I never paid attention in the haute couture class offered daily in Chateau Bryson."

Why worry about it? With her thought, she gathered her hair at the back of her head, twisted it into a spiral, and used a dozen plastic combs to hold the wad in place. If she lost the hat, the gig was up anyway, and she was certainly not dressed to impress. In fact, once she pulled the somewhat baggy wool coat over the tattered jeans and blouse and donned the glasses and hat, she looked like the kind of unsavory character who might visit a dead guy after dark, the kind who might take refuge in the doorway of a family crypt to escape nasty weather.

Forcing a scowl, she studied her features again and shook her head. No one would mistake her for Mrs. J. Laquette. Not in this garb.

Her scowl ebbed slowly into a more natural frown.

This was not how Ron Bryson investigated a murder. She flashed a press card, used appropriate sources, talked to the victim's family, friends, and neighbors, and scoured through information that could be found in the public domain. To get a feel for a place, to collect the ambiance, she generally spent hours driving its streets, visiting crime scenes, looking into the political conditions, and gathering names from the local law enforcement agencies. She did not—had never donned a disguise and hung out on the sidelines of a gathering of her colleagues, hoping for whatever tidbit of information the legal establishment tossed out like scraps of meat to hungry wolves.

Muttering a curse, she tore off the hat and slapped it on the dresser. Still cursing, she ripped the combs from her hair and yanked off the wool coat. By God, she was Veronica Bryson-Laquette, and someone would talk to her! Someone would talk to her, indeed!

Stalking to the living room, she yanked the telephone receiver to her ear and jabbed the long series of numbers She should have made this call hours ago.

She should have tracked this fellow down and demanded answers or cornered him when he offered to drive her home.

Three minutes later, Devinio growled, “Yes?”

“Are you in Cleveland?” she asked directly.

“Ah . . . Ronnie, are you all—“

“Don’t even think about trying that tact with me, Len,” she stated. “Are you in Cleveland at this moment?”

“Yes,” he answered, his tone guarded.

Without pause, she continued, “The badge issued to me four months ago, compliments of our mutual acquaintance, was never rescinded, and if you even think about correcting that oversight, this will be the last time you and I will talk. That said, you can either accept my status as ‘Special Consultant’ and assist me in getting from my current location to your own—which I’m assuming is somewhere within the Cuyahoga County Courthouse—or I can bring an entirely new string of chaos to the madness already gathered on the courthouse lawn.” She paused, then, only to add, “I want in on this Taxidermist case, Len, and it’s in your best interest to oblige.”

“Ronnie, considering what you’ve been through—“

“We may discuss that as well, Len, very shortly. Right now, you have two choices. Help me or await my arrival. I’m sure you’ll recognize when the pitch of shouts reaches whatever window you’re standing near. Question, Len—can you really afford any more publicity regarding a maniac who is not only stalking his victims but skinning and deboning them like a hunk of chicken? Considering the Lowensteins’ influence, along with the moral outrage of a public which the local officials—at the suggestion of the FBI—kept in the dark, I really don’t think you’d want me working against you, would you, Len?”

“Honey, you’re walking a fine line.”

“It’s a line you and your associate laid before me,” she snapped. “Do you bring me in willingly, or do I make a few more phone calls before blowing this case to kingdom come?

“I really wish you’d reconsider, honey. I know you’re not thinking clearly, or you wouldn’t be making that threat with the potential danger. This one’s bad, honey. If for no other reason, think about the words you just said and ask yourself if you really want this guy to pull stakes and crop up in another city a year from now.”

“He’s in too deep, dear. He couldn’t walk away from this now . . . any more than I can,” she said absently. “My question again. Would you like to send a car around for me, or do I drive my pretty little black Maserati right up to the courthouse steps and ah . . .? Possibly connect the death of a well-known antique dealer to this case via the Federal Bureau?"

"Where are you?"

"Far closer than you may care to know, mon ami," she said bluntly, hearing the catch of silence at the echo of her husband's favorite address.

"Damn it, you're in Cleveland."

"Touché, Len. Should I drive over and visit? Or would you prefer a more subtle approach?"

Len needed only a second to realize she never bluffed, then muttered a curse. "Where are you, Ronnie?"

"Are you coming personally and alone?"

"Where do you want to meet?"

"My question, Len. Are you coming alone? And don't misunderstand me. I don't want to see Mark Jarvins in front of or behind you."

"I'll be alone," he said in a low voice.

"I'm assuming this hotel has a rear entrance. I'll send a bellhop to let you in and direct you. And, Len . . .? If you even think about being clever and sending someone to put me on ice in a safe house, you'll have to kill me to shut me up before it's all said and done. I'm at the Lakefront . . ." That she meant every word occurred to her only as she replaced the receiver without awaiting Devinio's reply. As much as she loved Len—as much as she respected and admired his competence, she wouldn't hesitate to use every ounce of her talent and ability to destroy him, along with his revered agency. J. Edgar Hoover would be turning in his grave by the time Ron Bryson ran out of ink and voice, but whether that old warhorse would be twisting in admiration or horror was yet to be decided. She had influence. She knew politics. She knew how to dig for the corruption which belied the system. If it took a lifetime, she would uncover enough dirt to send shockwaves rocking the foundations of the White House.

And the reason slipped through her mind as she rested, staring at the varnished table in front of her . . . Something far more dangerous than a serial killer belied this case. Her husband wouldn't have thrown their life away without a damned good reason, any more than he would have boarded a plane destined to crash. A reason existed. And knowing his distrust of the government and his cynical nature, she sensed a far more sinister plot behind his actions.

She might be angry with him, she might even hate him as fiercely as she once loved him, but she still trusted him. Whatever he was doing or had done, he possessed a reason, and she and Tad were part of that reason. To believe anything else would be to deny what they had shared, to deny the love she'd felt in his arms and seen in his eyes. To believe anything else would be hell.

Only once since leaving the country sixteen years ago, Jade Laquette had traveled in the Nation's Capital, and with his thought, the heartache that Dominique had successfully ignored since waking in the institution surfaced. All too swiftly, he remembered racing toward D.C., resigning to the course set before him. He'd cut those five hours to four, fleeing like a demon from hell, determined to find his only love and start a life, despite the fear that had nearly paralyzed him. Something on the horizon. Something lurking just outside the proverbial door. Even without the full use of his curse, Dominique had sensed a catastrophe lying in wait. And he'd been a damned fool to believe it could revolve around the potential threat of a psychotic killer in Bentwood—or one in Cleveland, for that matter.

Veronica's life could be forfeit—that much he had known, and that alone had nearly altered his course. If he'd seen clearly—if he'd known he would be allowed only four blissful months with her . . . would he have spared them both the pain? Four months . . . It wasn't a lifetime. Not the lifetime he'd promised when standing in front of a holy alter and vowing his love and loyalty . . . *'until death, do us part.'*

Death had parted them, but what he felt for her would never be destroyed by a physical severance. By comparison, the vow spoken in an unholy cathedral held more integrity. Those moments, too, fleeted in his mind. Neon, he remembered the wind and darkness descending over that wooded black shrine and his own words, so simple and more honest than ever he had spoken . . . *Heart and soul . . .*

Forever, he might have added then, feeling the emptiness like a vacuum within his chest. What he'd given freely to that wondrous of all women, he would never reclaim.

Only the emptiness kept him walking, oblivious of the bodies he passed, indifferent to the sounds of shouting voices or radios blaring from car windows. That he felt nothing, not remorse when passing a terminally ill man on the street, not the joy shining in a young woman's aura as she strode past on her lover's arm, not the hostility of a man with a pocketful of cocaine to pawn . . . nothing. Detached from the bond which had forever held him chained by his passions, he realized an odd sense of freedom . . . as if he were as immaterial as air, as inconsequential as an automobile. If he suffered a head-on collision, doubtful it would matter. When a man has nothing left to lose—why worry over a loss?

Whether the image of the grim reaper draped behind the glass, or his growing addiction attracted him, Dominique strode into the convenience store. Halloween paraphernalia hung from the ceiling, from streamers of ghostly design to pumpkin faces designed to give children the willies.

His birthday, he considered. The devil's night.

Smiling slightly to the store clerk who sported a lock of purple hair in a punk-rocker style—not disguised for the season—he bought a pack of cigarettes and received enough change to use the payphone that hung outside the glass doors. In heavily accented English, Dominique spoke with the manservant, not surprised when Robert Bryson accepted his call. No father-in-law, now. As estranged as his name, Dominique spoke in French, "Forgive me for troubling you at such an hour, but I believe it is important that you and I should meet. Perhaps, my ah . . . half-brother mentioned me to you? I am Dominique Jardonet."

"Where are you?"

"Where I am, now, is of no consequence. Where I will be in a half hour depends upon you. Meet me at ah . . . the Cafe LaRosa. It is not far from you, yes?"

"I'll be there," Robert Bryson stated.

"Be alone, monsieur."

CHAPTER 16

Waiting, resting at the dining table, Ronnie jotted notes in her old familiar leather notebook, but more often, her mind wandered over the past few days. The images drifted, images of the faces swimming past her in the receiving line, arms enveloping her with heartfelt sympathy. Max had been too choked to speak at the onset. In all the years she'd known him, she'd never seen him so close to tears, so near sobbing. Forever, he had been her mentor, the epitome of male strength and charisma, a figurehead to admire and respect. For that glimpse of Max nearly crumbling, she would like to slap Jade at least once. How could he do it? How could he have been so cruel to so many? Surely, he knew how people reacted to him? For eighteen years, Max had carried a special place in his heart for a little boy whom he had met only once. When they'd come face-to-face months ago, Max had maintained his composure, but their instant rapport had been as visible as a sunbeam.

She knew the story. Even without listening to them, she knew that Max had answered the police call and arrived within minutes after the first officers had arrived on the scene. 'He was something . . .' Max had told her years ago when she had interviewed him for her college thesis. That unsolved murder and the indiscriminate mismanagement of facts in the press had become the bases of her paper. Her own personal interest had added to her intrigue. With a wan smile, she remembered pining for the handsome upperclassman who had tragically lost his mother and disappeared from her life. Funny how some memories remained front and center from those early years. She couldn't even remember the face of the first boy she'd ever kissed, but she remembered Jade Laquette standing in a playground, leaning against a swing set. Briefly, their eyes had met . . . and their fate sealed.

'I guess what struck me most,' Max had said all those years later. *'He never cried . . . He was just sitting on the couch as if he were waiting for me, and when I took him to his room . . .? Kids have a strange way of coping with things. Then too, maybe he was in shock . . . but there was a strength about him . . .'*

Preoccupied, Ronnie strode to the door, answering the knock. Not truly seeing Len, she sidestepped and motioned him inside. The gravity of his expression sliced through her reflections. Too clearly, she recalled her threat and ultimatum. Glancing into the hallway, anticipating the presence of Mark Jarvins, she caught Len studying her more intently as she nudged the door shut. "I'm glad you didn't test me, Len."

"I took into consideration that you've probably just lived through the worst couple days of your life and decided not to take offense, Ron," he said quietly. "I hope you have a pot of coffee in this dive."

"We can call room service."

"Have you eaten?"

If not for the subtle note of hope, she might have believed him attempting another big-brother routine. "Apparently, you haven't."

"I could use a burger," he said and continued into the room, zeroing in on the leather menu and settling onto the couch. Leaning back, with the book in hand, he couldn't appear more relaxed if he lifted his feet and crossed his ankles on the coffee table. Rather than the customary black suit and tie, he wore black slacks, a thick black sweater, and a windbreaker minus the official lettering or FBI insignia. Only the grim set of his black mustache betrayed his attempt to appear casual. Tossing the book aside, he looked over as she settled into a chair across from him. "You want a look at the menu, or do you trust my taste?"

"A burger sounds fine," she decided, uncertain what to make of his attitude. He should be furious with her if nothing else. In the few years she'd known him, she had never offered him greater reason to consider her a typical rich bitch than she had a half hour ago. Still, she wasn't apologizing. Leaning back, crossing her knee, she watched him place the order and put a rush on it.

With the first order of business obviously tended to, he tilted his attention directly. "I'm not putting you on the billing," he said directly. "If you're consulting, you're doing so in gratia."

"That's fair," she agreed.

"And if you're on this case, anything you hear henceforward is confidential information. If I even think it hits print, I'll nail your ass for interfering in an official investigation."

"If it hits print, you better make damn sure I'm guilty before even attempting to nail my ass," she countered, her eyes sparking anger.

"That said," he hesitated, studying her intently. "Why do you want on this case?"

"I want to know what happened to my husband," she said honestly.

No visible reaction surfaced in Devinio's dark eyes. "That makes two of us," he said in a low voice. "But I'm not sure this case can provide that answer."

"Two mornings ago, you and Mark came to see Jade in Meg's," she said and gleaned his confirmation by the absence of denial. "Shortly after that, he canceled his prior engagement to accompany me on a brief trip. Why was he allegedly on a plane from Cincinnati to Nashville?"

"Your guess is as good as mine, Ron," he said in a deadpan tone. "If you have a theory, I'd be glad to hear it."

If he was patronizing her, he covered it well. Studying the absence of expression on his rugged features, the calculated blank gaze, she commented, "I don't think he was, Len."

His head canted a fraction, indicating she held his attention. "I'm listening," he conceded.

"I think he was—and still is—in Cleveland, Lenny, and if anyone knows that, I think you do. Now, I'd like to know why."

"I don't think I'm following you, mia amica," he said too carefully. "You're saying you believe he's alive?"

"A Frenchman was assisting you on this case two days ago. His name was Jardonet. What was his first name?"

"Dominique," Devinio answered without hesitation.

She studied him. "I was tempted to believe you'd deny that."

"There's no reason to," he said smoothly. "You obviously have your facts in order, and it's become rather common knowledge that we had a visitor from France assisting in this investigation. Before you ask, hon, yes, he was the son of Jean-Pierre Jardonet, who I understand is your father-in-law. I didn't need that information to recognize him, however. If you see him, Ron, you'll know his heredity. He bears an uncanny resemblance to ah . . . Jade," he said carefully. "I have a feeling—that likeness is only skin deep, though."

The likeness went a great deal deeper, she considered shouting but held silent, studying the intense dark eyes for a hint of the lie. "Do you believe in coincidences, Len?" she asked quietly.

"I'm finding I believe in a lot of things I never considered believing in, Ron."

"Why are you lying to me?"

"Excuse me?"

"You and I both know that Dominique Jardonet is—or was—Jade Laquette before three days ago. Why are you lying? It's a simple question. And after you answer that one, you can tell me where to find him."

"I'm going to tell you this because maybe you can shed some light on it," he decided. "Three days ago, I did stop into Meg's and invited Jade to join me in Cleveland. He wasn't thrilled, but he agreed. A short time later, we picked him up behind the shop and drove to Cleveland. We checked into a motel, and Mark spent about an hour on the phone. After that, things get a little screwy, honey. We collected a man we believed to be Jade, intending to take him into our confidence. I should mention, he asked us to call him Jardonet, and at this point, I'm at a loss to decide exactly who we recovered from that hotel room. There is evidence to confirm that Jade left that establishment, took a taxi to the municipal airport, and flew to Cincinnati. The rest, I believe you already know."

"You have doubts," she said bluntly, studying him and attempting to rein her hammering heart. Lenny was the one man she trusted to level with her. The only man, other than Jean-Pierre, who might fully understand and offer an explanation. He appeared genuinely disturbed, and that expression didn't wear well on his Sicilian features.

"Did Jade ever mention his half-brother, Dominique Jardonet?"

"He rarely, if ever, mentioned his family, Len," she said honestly, an inkling of doubt touching the edges of her mind. "He never considered the Jardonets family. I know that much."

"But you knew he had a half-brother?"

"He mentioned having at least two of them," she said with a dark shadow creeping over her thoughts. No. She could not—would not even consider the possibility. Jean-Pierre hadn't denied her words; he had agreed with her . . . But could she trust him? A legitimate heir with similar weird talents . . . when Jade had admitted refusing to use the gifts he possessed? What had Jade told her . . .? That he'd changed his name at eighteen to be free of Jean-Pierre? He hadn't granted his father the satisfaction to wear the name . . . And suddenly, Dominique Jardonet is in the United States, a legitimate son . . . who resembles her husband enough to give Len Devinio pause?

Troubled suddenly, she pushed off the chair, pacing away. What if . . . what if Jardonet wanted her to believe this imposter was her husband? Jade had said Jean-Pierre had only adopted him because neither of his legitimate heirs carried the curse. Jardonet had tried to force Jade into using his gifts . . .

And she was carrying Jade's child. A child who almost assuredly would inherit something of his father's considerable talents, not to mention a few of her own. Was it possible . . . was it even remotely possible that she'd been manipulated into believing that her husband was alive, only to be faced eventually with the arrival of Dominique Jardonet?

Turning on Devinio, far more troubled than she cared to consider, she asked, "Where is Dominique Jardonet, Lenny?"

"Another great question I'd love to have answered," he said with a mildly annoyed note. "He managed to disappear as easily as he appeared, and I haven't heard from him since."

Obviously, her father-in-law hadn't lied about his son's disappearance. "Could he have left the country?"

"Sure, if he snapped his fingers," Devinio said without a twitch of a smile. "Otherwise, I'd have to say, no. He booked reservations on a flight to New York, but we haven't confirmed he was on the plane. And by the reaction of the French Embassy, I'd have to say he's unavailable for consultation."

"When was the last time you saw him?"

"Two nights ago, ironically, a few floors higher in this dive," he said with an indifferent scan of the room. His gaze returned. "You should have asked for the penthouse. It has a fully stocked bar, a couple extra rooms, and the furniture is a little plusher. Great view of the lake, too. Now, you want to tell me your theory, Ron?"

Somehow, she wasn't as convinced of her earlier belief, and the revelation slammed the pain a little deeper. Was it possible . . . was it even remotely possible that she truly had buried the man she loved? Could she have been ranting and raving, threatening bodily harm to a man who would never walk through another door to hold her, or smile, or shake his head and besiege God to grant him the strength to endure her rages? Would she raise Tad alone? Was the albatross of his wealth and the pain of his departing the only legacy left to her?

She turned away before the tears lifted, walking heavily to the window to view the lake . . . not a good view. Darkness. And suddenly, she felt wrapped in that darkness like never before. "I . . . I can't believe he's gone," she heaved softly. "I can't let myself believe that . . . I couldn't handle it." And yet, she believed it now, more than any moment past.

The Cafe LaRosa on Arlington's east side wasn't a place where one might expect to find a gourmet meal or one of the most influential men in Washington. At ground level within a brownstone house, the cafe resided behind smoke glass windows of French design with frilly checkered curtains offsetting the typical barroom ambiance. High booths provided privacy for quiet conversations. Tables were scattered at random rather than lined up military style, each decked with ruby glass candleholders and leather tablecloths. Segregated, a small dining room boasted a wide selection of decent meals, sufficiently priced to accommodate the wealthy stepping down or the middle class stepping out.

Waiting at a corner of the bar where enough shadows offered him a slight advantage, Dominique Jardonet rested in a position to watch the door, idly sipping cognac and ignoring the flirtatious glances of a young woman seated several chairs away. It was a tossup as to which event would transpire first. He knew she contemplated rising and closing the distance, knew she would slip off her stool in fact . . . and at the same instant, Robert Bryson opened the door and entered somewhat reluctantly. In natural-good form, Bryson doffed his brimmed hat, his gaze darting and landing even as Dominique stepped off his chair.

Wearing a baseball cap, clear pane wire-rimmed glasses, and a second-hand sports jacket, Dominique wasn't, at first glance, the man who had married Bryson's daughter. At second glance, Bryson wondered and suffered the strangeness of his uncertainty. He had, after all, seen the official documents to verify his son-in-law's demise. Official papers, charred clothing, coroner's reports . . . They had buried Jade Laquette a dozen hours earlier, and Robert Bryson carried part of the guilt for that event.

Bypassing the slight redhead who hoped he was heading her way, Dominique reached Bryson as the man loosened the buttons of his black cashmere coat. "Monsieur Bryson?" Dominique offered his words quietly, speaking in French while proffering his hand. "Dominique Jardonet. I am glad you agreed to see me on such short notice."

Undecided, Bryson studied him intently while nodding, accepting the quick handshake. "Mr. Jardonet."

"We would be more comfortable in the dining room, perhaps?" Dominique suggested and motioned toward the arch.

No hostess stood to seat them. Dominique accepted the older man's gesture and led them to one of the booths toward the corner, deliberately positioning himself again to watch the entrance. The waitress caught up as they settled into opposing benches. She took their drink orders and delivered a laminated menu that they both ignored. Under the critical blue gaze, Dominique donned a sobering intensity, his head tipping slightly. "You have my condolences, Mr. Bryson. I understand the funeral for your son-in-law was held this morning."

"You bear a striking resemblance," Bryson said critically.

"A fact I could not change even to lessen the burden of your loss. He and I were ah . . . never close beyond the physical likeness." Dominique paused to light a cigarette, consciously or unconsciously canting his head and granting Bryson a glimpse of his eyes in the firelight. The color might be the same . . . the intensity was different, and Bryson recognized that difference. Blowing an exhale, Dominique commented, "The sooner you satisfy your doubts, the sooner we can discuss the details to elude me. I understand your ah . . . confusion at the moment. I have been mistaken for Mr. Laquette often over the past several days. An ocean between us always served us both in the past."

"What exactly would you like to discuss, Mr. . . .Jardonet?"

"I think you know," he said smoothly, his gaze intent. "I understand it was through you that my ah . . . half-brother enlisted my services. Considering our differences and his opinion of ah . . . my skills, I was surprised, to say the least. He was ah . . . desperate, yes?"

"Mr. Jardonet—"

"Please . . . just Dominique. And there is no reason to deny my words. Present circumstances, withstanding, we both understand his desperation . . . And I should admit, I spoke to him before his . . . unfortunate accident. Something troubled him deeply. As it now troubles me."

"Have you spoken with anyone in the French Embassy?"

"You refer to the search for me, yes?"

"Where have you been for the past two days?"

"Seeking answers to questions no one thought to ask," he said bluntly. "Some of those I have, now, but I think you have others for me."

"I don't appreciate whatever innuendo you're attempting to make, young man."

"Forgive me, then. I am not accusing you of orchestrating or initiating my half-brother's demise. As I understand, he and your daughter were very much in love. I doubt you would have made her a widow. I have heard she is a remarkable young woman."

"Yes, she is," Bryson said in a low voice, his gaze listing toward the flickering red sconce. Troubled lines touched his brow, his tension apparent at the corner of his lips. His eyes conveyed his anger as he looked over at Dominique. "For her sake, Mr. Jardonet, you can rest assured, I'll find out what happened to Jade Laquette and who's responsible."

"You already know, Mr. Bryson," Dominique said as he held the man's angry gaze, his own, indifferent. "The same people responsible for his mother's death eighteen years ago initiated the events which led to his demise."

"Even if that were true—"

"Oh, there is no question of truth here, I assure you," Dominique said quietly and paused as the waitress advanced. His words hanging in the air, he watched Bryson's distracted gaze as he moved his arm to accept the drink in front of him. To the question of dinner, he waved his hand dismissively without more than a glance.

Dominique smiled as he shook his head, not quite as rude when offering a similar dismissal to the waitress. Lifting his fresh drink, he gestured in the sign of a toast, catching the preoccupied gaze. "The only question remains—do you intend to wash your hands of another murder and continue to cover the secrets of the past . . . knowing that your daughter and grandchild could be in danger?"

"If you're even implying—"

"Eighteen years ago, Madame Laquette offered a service to some of the most influential citizens in this country. Wives and daughters, generally, but on occasion, she serviced male clients. She was ah . . . a con artist, yes?"

"I wouldn't know about that."

"Ah, I think you would, Mr. Bryson. But the fact remains, not all of her ah . . . information was a fabrication or clever guesswork. She possessed a remarkable talent that gained her a small, respectable circle of followers, as well as a reputation for authenticity. At times, her predictions startled even the husbands of her clients, one or two of whom had belief enough to avoid such calamities as Watergate well before it struck the news." And Robert Bryson Jr.

was the recipient of that goodwill, thanks to Fiona Bryson's one and only visit to the local guru.

"Incredible, this woman's talent," Dominique continued. "I am to believe, she assisted on occasion to change the course of history, applying pressure through wives to steer political trends. For those manipulations alone, she might have been in constant danger, but she was careful, yes? She had a talent for remaining on the edge, never delving too deeply into political issues. More content and accurately, she offered day-to-day advice . . . while charging outlandish fees. I understand—she once placed such negative emphasis on the color of a gown to be worn by the First Lady that the color wasn't worn by another woman for months." A flicker of a smile affected his mustache, and he shrugged indifference. "Harmless scams. The woman might have lived to be a hundred if not for a slip of the tongue."

"You seem to know more about that than I do," Bryson said, but he was listening.

"That I do, Mr. Bryson. She was my father's mistress before she became Washington's guru. The fact remains—she made a mistake. In the course of her ah . . . craft, she discovered something which, to her, seemed harmless, or perhaps, obscure enough to appear harmless. Wives talk to other wives, and wives speak to husbands. Husbands with things to hide," he said indifferently, still watching Bryson. "What Madame Laquette spoke in ignorant bliss was heard and understood by someone with a great deal to hide."

"As I recall, that theory was once speculated on—rather thoroughly—by the press and debunked," Bryson said carefully.

"It was," Dominique said quietly. "And shortly thereafter, my half-brother became the focus of a great deal of press coverage and speculation. During that same time, a few rather curious details concerning my half-brother reached the public domain—beginning with the fact that he ran from his elementary school, dripping blood from his forehead and mouth. A pity so many saw him. Doubtful, a coincidence of such extremes could be ignored. Taking into consideration that he was ah . . . phenomenal, the same man, or men, saw him as a threat as well. Using the press coverage to mask their motives, they brought him under their umbrella, so to speak. In the guise of protecting him, they took him to a secure environment."

"As much as I find this intriguing, Mr. Jardonet, I'm not sure there's a point."

"Mr. Bryson, Laquette was an extraordinary child," Dominique commented and sipped his drink, holding the man's stopped gaze. "I may not have enjoyed his company, but I admired his talents far more than he did. More so, now, as I look back on this situation," he said with a smile and a shrug. "Eighteen years after the death of his mother destroyed his life, he finds himself married to the daughter of a man directly related—if somewhat innocently—to the murder. Such a man seems to possess ah . . . sixth sense?" he smirked.

Bryson started to protest, parted his lips, then seemed to tabulate the details in time to counter his words. He reached for his drink, buying time. A splendid negotiator and an exceptional businessman. The facts were in order, and he knew the truth of the spoken words, speculating now on the coincidence that his daughter had, in fact, married Laquette . . . after a more coincidental meeting over a murder case.

"Mr. Bryson, your daughter was his catalyst. As I understand, they knew each other as children. If not as friends, certainly as passing acquaintances. Love is a strange concept, like a seed to be planted, grow, and later, bloom. That he loved her, I have no doubts. But I do need to wonder at his ulterior motives." Gravely, he studied Bryson. "You, I do believe, were one of those motives. You were not involved directly with the plot to murder Madame Laquette, but you knew of it . . . belatedly, yes?"

"There was a great deal of speculation over that murder, Mr. Jardonet," Bryson spoke aloud even as the image flashed in his mind. All too clearly, he recalled the gaunt face of his father—an old man surrounded by silk and struggling to speak with every breath. '. . . I withdrew, Robert . . . I withdrew, but that . . . did not stop them . . . They brought him here . . . and the boy knows . . . I think he knows they killed his mother . . . and the other . . . They will turn him loose . . .'

'What are you saying, father? Who was brought here—?'

"You are an influential man, Mr. Bryson," Dominique interrupted quietly, head canted and searching, seeing and hearing clearly, a dying man's declaration. "You have connections—had connections as much as eighteen years ago to such infrastructures as the State Department and Department of Defense. You were not directly involved in WWII, but your father was ah . . . instrumental in supplying government contracts. Your family's fortunes survived the Great Depression through the foresight and fortitude of your father, and he wasn't the sole survivor of that economic crisis. His friends and allies became yours, and you have them still. So it is, you became privy to ah . . . certain events which you are not proud to acknowledge. I am tempted to believe that your father washed his hands of those events long before Madame Laquette paid the price of her ignorance and greed."

Despite the absence of a reaction, Robert Bryson volleyed between a lingering sadness of his father's memory, anger over the details he had later uncovered through various sources, and discomfort that this young Frenchman—who too closely resembled his daughter's husband—possessed similar, if not the same weird talents. And those talents were real, Robert had discovered belatedly.

The image of that wasted young body flashed in his mind. He'd seen the films, the emaciated boy strapped to a leather chair. The memory both sickened and outraged him, but he'd scored through those chronicles to decipher his father's final words. If his father had known at the time what was being done to that child, undoubtedly, he would have intervened.

Quietly, Dominique interrupted. "You do know the faces behind the curtain of deceit, monsieur." *Not by choice, but Robert feared that might be true.* "Three days ago, those same men who plotted against the mother plotted against the son. One or another contacted you, perhaps, to ah . . . make certain of your position? It would seem, Mr. Bryson, someone intended to ascertain your participation in these events."

"If you talked to Jade, you know I wasn't in favor of his involvement in any of this, and I most assuredly didn't condone what you are implying."

"Perhaps, he was aware of your predicament, Mr. Bryson. It seems he provided you with an alibi," Dominique commented. "Your call to the embassy was recorded. You requested my services in place of your son-in-law while others in your government pursued him. And he was pursued. Whether he boarded a plane destined to crash or was abducted by another faction of your government, he would be dead now. And the tragedy buried beneath a cloak of secrecy no differently than his mother's demise." *Or so these fanatics chose to believe.*

In a fleeting instant, Bryson grasped the simple truth—both the plane crash and the abduction had occurred, but whether Jade Laquette had succumbed to either remained a question. The young man across from him, posing as a Frenchman, could be Jade . . . as the fellow had been Isaac Bently four months ago. Robert had never met the man in that guise. He'd known him only as Jade Laquette and that name had rocked his foundations the moment he'd heard it.

"The problem is this," Dominique continued quietly. "If the mother and son can be killed for what others believe they could see and know, what is to stop these same men from removing his wife and the child they'd created? Your influence could not protect your daughter from becoming a widow. Can it protect her when these same desperate men realize the child will possess the potential of his father?"

Even with the note of indifference, his quiet words carried an impact to have Bryson studying him far more critically. Not for an instant had Robert considered that possibility, had chosen not to fully buy into the psychic jargon. In rapid sequence, he remembered viewing the tape—a tape, wherein a young Jade Laquette had mentioned Cleveland, Ohio, nearly eighteen years earlier. Under heavy sedation, the child had described those events which had already come to pass . . . and predicted that another would come to take his place. As much as four days past, Robert had recalled reviewing that film and had unwittingly suffered the relief that Jade had asked him to phone the French Embassy and request Inspector Dominique Jardonet to assist in the Cleveland investigation. Too clearly, Robert remembered the child's voice citing a plane crash that would take his life and . . . and the other might be in danger as well if Robert remembered that prognostication. A shiver slid down Bryson's spine.

"Your daughter and the child will remain in danger so long as this secret remains, Mr. Bryson," Dominique confided as a statement of fact as he continued to study the intent blue gaze. "So it is—what means more to you? The reputation and continued corruption of your comrades and colleagues, or the life of your daughter and grandchild?"

"I think you know the answer to that, Mr. Jardonet."

"Yes," Dominique said quietly, a touch of a smile on his lips. "I believe I do, and I trust you will do, now, what you should have done when my father's mistress was killed. She wasn't anything to you, I understand. A name you heard mentioned after the fact, a woman whose life was forfeit, and without proof, you could not go forward to accuse those in your circle. Having the son resurface and to find your daughter already involved with him . . . it must have been a tremendous temptation to remove him when the opportunity presented itself."

"If you're about to accuse me of having him taken into Federal custody—"

"On the contrary," Dominique said smoothly. "You were manipulated even then . . . And it leads me to wonder," he said and canted his head to study

Bryson. "Is it possible that an agent Jarvins is one of the followers of this new order? This secret sect which you have unwittingly conspired to conceal?"

"Now, you're truly stretching," Bryson stated, but in his mind, as brilliant as a sunrise, he saw the elder face—a lean, sculpted face scored with age lines most often ascribed to wisdom. And his father's heaved words. 'Matthew . . . Matthew believes, Rob. Be careful. . .' Recovering his fumbled thought, Robert started, "I'll admit there's more than meets the eye to these events."

"Sir," Dominique said quietly. "All due respect . . . Do you truly believe your associates would go to these lengths to conceal the mere sanction of a Nazi-sympathizer . . .? Or to murder four innocents to conceal an act of madness from forty years ago on the outside chance that psychic phenomenon is real?"

Stopped, Bryson studied him momentarily. In rapid sequence, he saw his father's failing image and listened to the dying declarations that he'd attempted to dismiss as the ramblings of dementia or senility. The year was 1979 . . . and his father, Robert Sr., rested on his death bed, speaking of Nazis and Hitler modeling his ideals after the eugenic movement in the United States . . . And a Nazi doctor had been brought into the States. 1979—four years after the last Nuremberg trial, and Robert Bryson Sr. had wept with the grief of washing his hands of that atrocity rather than thwarting it . . . And as much as ten years ago, those fanatics had still been active.

"Consider this, Mr. Bryson, eighteen years ago, Madame Laquette—in her desire to appear authentic and omnipotent—repeated a few loose words about something she allegedly saw in the past of a woman she hardly knew. A woman by the name of Agatha—"

Jarvins.

Agatha Jarvins . . . Mark Jarvins' mother. And Matilda? Matilda Jarvins . . . Mark's sister. Matthew Jarvins . . . junior and senior. The head of the snake and the successor to this madness.

How many more? How many others were recruited and acting on the authority of these madmen? Men who even now plotted an insurrection to assist in cleansing what they considered their pure white race. For the good of mankind, they meant to eradicate the poor, the mentally or physically feeble, the criminal elements that could propagate, and the people of color deemed unfit or uneducated. They truly believed that women were nothing more than breeders, chosen by class and intelligence to further the cause, and the plans were in place. As the child, Jade Laquette had prognosticated years past, it would begin in Cleveland.

The Taxidermist . . . but even as the name ignited in his mind's eye, Dominique suffered the shiver down his spine. Whitman Reddinger . . . wasn't the Taxidermist. No matter what fabrications Dir. Lakeland might choose to believe.

"Dominique?"

Collecting his thought on the instant, Dominique fleeted his glance to Bryson, picking up his own thought through the intense gaze.

"Fact, Mr. Bryson, it wasn't words to set these wicked wheels in motion," he continued without more than a second's pause. "Madame Laquette merely provided a rough sketch to Agatha, and she, in turn, was so distressed by the thought of Nazis and communism that she showed the drawing to her husband. That she feared Madame Laquette might be warning her of an invasion, I do not doubt. Days or weeks later, however, Madame Laquette was murdered, and her son is ah . . . made a scapegoat then abducted, for lack of a better term, by men in your government."

Before Bryson could confirm or deny his knowledge, as neither was necessary, Dominique continued, "I assume, you know, or heard mention of a German doctor brought into this country under curious circumstances. I further assume you are aware that this doctor was enlisted by well-educated men in your circle of acquaintances. What you may not know, is that his wicked experiments were not merely studied for procedural benefit despite what this new order professed although, I'm certain, others of your ilk were coerced into this conspiracy, convinced the studies worthwhile.

"A study of those atrocities in Germany could reap more benefits, yes? But a scant few truly believed in those rewards. Your father—he washed his hands of this conclave of madmen as well as their twisted ideals . . ."

In vivid color, Dominique flashed a glimpse into the past . . . Bryson's past. He couldn't have been more than nine or ten when his parents had stopped entertaining in the same circles as the Jarvins. Before that, he and his siblings had often played in the same parks and visited the same beaches at Martha's Vineyard alongside Matt Jr. and the other Jarvins children. Until his father's dying declarations in 1979, a full eight years after Felicity Laquette's murder, Robert hadn't understood the severance of family associations. 1948. That was the last year that he and Matt Jr. had 'hung out together' as the teenagers would say now, and by the time Matt joined him at Harvard, their friendship had deteriorated.

In retrospect, Robert remembered Matt Jr as an intense young man . . . who had already set his sights on politics. By 1979 when Robert had sat listening to the ramblings of a dying old man, Matt Jr. had already held a seat in the Senate . . . and he still held a seat. Eighteen years . . . and his father, Matthew Sr., still carried political weight in DC.

"Your father," Dominique continued. "Perhaps, even though he believed the study of Schreiber's methods might benefit your country's quest for medical knowledge . . . On principle alone, he refused to be a party to sanctioning that madman's inception into American life, and I think he believed the others would come to their senses. He stood against this faction of fanatics and spared you. For that, I think you should be proud of him and grateful that you were not drawn into events that will likely create a wretched scandal and meet with public outrage.

"Unfortunately, others did not follow his lead, and I fear he learned too late about those who continued to support and protect Herr Schrieber. Given a new identity and alias name, that monster was permitted to preach his doctrine and spread his disease of madness. Your government went so far as to enlist military men as guinea pigs for some of his less-than-moral psychological experiments. Only a select few of his followers knew about his hobby of torture and his fetish for human skin, masked of course, as actual medical studies."

"If any of this is true," Bryson began quietly, merely holding his near-empty drink as if he might lift and swig the contents to wash away a bitter taste rising in his mouth. "And mind you, young man, I'm not certain—"

"More than twenty years after Herr Schrieber was welcomed into this country, his original materials brought from Germany were still handled by men who held direct access to his ah . . . documentation?"

"If those materials exist—"

"They exist, monsieur," Dominique interrupted quietly. "Those materials—including an original tape of the procedures which Herr Schrieber conducted in one of the concentration camps—are the reason the Laquettes have suffered their tragedies. Eighteen years ago, the taint and touch of those tapes carried a message that Jade Laquette was sensitive enough to receive. For that, his mother was killed. For that, he has met his fate. And for that, his wife and son will continue to hang in jeopardy. Those tapes and any of the madmen who view them under the guise of medical science, are part of a conspiracy that you, unwittingly, have assisted in concealing."

"You may be right to that extent, Mr. Jardonet, but I don't see that as a threat to what you're implying is National Security."

"At this very moment, a madman in Cleveland, Ohio, is flaying human flesh and harvesting bones toward a belief that he will rise above the common throng. It is my belief, he was deliberately manipulated, if not ordered, to begin his maniacal killing spree. In part, to trap Jade Laquette, whose psychic ability was once documented and deemed authentic, and in part, to evaluate the theory of an ultimate plan. These men whom you are protecting, my friend, they have created an army of madmen. They have infiltrated your Federal Bureau, and I fully believe they have allies in your Oval Office as I have met such a one recently. Consider me mad, Mr. Bryson, but when a French citizen can be abducted by your Bureau—even in a case of mistaken identity—I believe you have a serious problem developing. Now, I ask again. Would the life of a psychic be so important to a select group in your government unless there was an ultimate need to remove him? It is not just the past to which my half-brother was privy, Mr. Bryson. Your daughter's union is proof of his ability. He saw the future, understood the conspiracy, and for that knowledge, he would have been murdered more than once in the past."

"I think I should point out, Mr. Jardonet, there's no proof that he was murdered."

"Nor will there ever be, Mr. Bryson. It is my belief that he forfeited his life so that I might survive to sit where I am now to protect his wife and child. If others in your government knew me as he did—which they do now, make no mistake—they might have tried harder to murder me two days ago." With barely a pause, Dominique shrugged, admitting, "I am not Jade Laquette's equal in integrity or compassion. If you do not stop these madmen in your ranks, my friend, I will. And make no mistake, I don't give a damn who gets caught in the crossfire. Your son-in-law offered you a way out of this, believing you a man of integrity. As I agree, and as a courtesy to him, I am speaking to you . . . but I will mention, in the course of this conversation, you've given me the information I sought."

With a slow donning smile under Bryson's scrutiny, Dominique commented, "I don't have my half-brother's discretion. I tend to read minds as clearly as he once read books. And on that note, Mr. Bryson, I'll further mention, whatever your decision when you leave here, I'll know it. If you take appropriate steps to begin removing your madmen, I will stand down. If you don't, God be merciful on them, for I won't. Blood truly is thicker than water, and they've killed their last Laquette."

CHAPTER 17

The hand barely touched Ronnie's shoulder but seemed to collapse whatever resolve remained in her mind. Without thinking, she turned, needing to hold onto something, someone. Tears slipped down her cheeks; swallowed sobs lodged in her throat as she clung to the solid form. Not uttering a word, Len wrapped his arms about her, offering his silent strength, knowing he could do nothing more than hold her as the pain wreaked havoc in her head and body. Minutes or hours passed as she struggled to recover. Never in her life had she broken down, not like this. Rant, rave, spin out of control in fits of silent hostility, but never like this as if the walls were collapsing, her legs crumbling. "Wh-why," she cried softly. "Why'd this haa-appen to usss?"

"Ronnie," Len heaved softly, needing to swallow. His husky voice strained, "There's something . . . Something he made me promise him . . . and something I think he meant for me to give you . . ."

More minutes passed before the words registered in her spiraling senses. Clumsily, she accepted the handkerchief Len directed into her hands, clearing her eyes, swallowing, heaving breaths, and muttering apologies that he dismissed in low husky words. When her eyes were clear, if not just a little raw, she found his haunted dark eyes and read the troubled lines across his high intelligent forehead. Never had he appeared more miserable or more human. "Wh-what, Lenny . . . what is it?"

"I'm not even sure how to say this . . . God knows, I've played it back a hundred times, but those moments never seem to add up," he spoke with unnatural confusion. Leading her unconsciously, he carried them both to the couch and sat her down, settling next to her. His focus strayed off her hand to her searching eyes, then panned the room. Slowly, he landed his full attention on her. "This is hard, honey, and uh . . . it's going to sound as if I knew what was coming down. The fact is, I didn't. And that bothers me more than I can admit. I know Jade didn't want to come with us. Something was disturbing him over and beyond our request. He didn't say much on the drive, and he drove, so it was a short trip," he said with a disheartened attempt to smile. "What he did say offered more questions than answers. Later—and that's where this gets screwy, mia amica—later, he said it was already too late to back out. He uh . . . he already told me to call him Dominique Jardonet, and he was talking French as if it were his first language. So, I can't even be sure who I was talking to. The only thing I really know is that he was sincere and a little desperate when he made me promise to tell you something if he couldn't. And that was simply—he loved you. More in a single day than anybody could love another if they had a lifetime . . . Those were his words, honey, and he wanted me to make sure you understood how much he loved you."

His gaze shifted, as much to cover his swift shine as to avoid meeting her rising tide. He continued quietly, "I wish then I'd have had a little of his talent. I was ah . . . I tried to pull the plug on his involvement a few times, but he wouldn't let me. I know . . . in retrospect, I know he really didn't expect to walk out of this. I think . . ." He looked over with a wave of guilt shining in his dark eyes. "I think he knew, when Mark and I showed up that morning, he wouldn't walk away from this. It was almost as if he was waiting for us to show up . . . and something happened to him, Ronnie. It was . . . it was almost as if he became someone else right before my eyes, and I really don't know when he switched places with his half-brother. There were moments—very weird moments—when I was talking to Dominique Jardonet that I believed I was talking to Jade. But I can't even be certain of those now. . . And the fact that Jardonet just disappeared on us that same evening . . .? I don't know what to think, honey. That's as honest as I can be, and there really is something I have to give you." He shifted his free hand, dipping it into his jacket pocket.

Unconsciously, Ronnie shook her head, denying the words, rejecting the possibility and the evidence. Confusion spiraled in her eyes and mind as the fisted hand emerged, but she knew what he held.

"He uh . . . he didn't exactly ask me to give these to you, mia amica," he said in a low, strained voice and lifted his dark eyes. "But when he handed them to me . . . there was something in his eyes telling me—like he was saying goodbye, and that fucking scares the shit out of me, honey, because uh . . . At nearly the same moment he handed me these, the uh . . . the plane went down in

Kentucky. I only saw Dominique Jardonet once more after that, and he wasn't Jade Laquette when he clipped me in the jaw."

Numb . . . numb again, she accepted the offering on her palm and looked down at the glittering stones. His wedding ring . . . and the cross that he'd worn since their wedding day. Shaking her head, refusing to believe the words, the symbols, she looked up at Len, searching for the lie or an explanation. Searching for some semblance of reality in his words. If Len Devinio couldn't tell who stood before him . . . impossible! Or was it?

Who was he? What was he really? Jade Laquette . . . or Isaac Bently . . . or Dominique Jardonet? Was everything she had ever believed about him, every shared moment and every spoken word, a lie? Was he truly the little boy she'd fallen in love with nearly twenty years ago . . .? When she'd met him in Bentwood, he'd posed as an antique dealer. A good old boy . . . living a lie as an antique dealer. She . . . she had been the one to say his name, to discover his identity . . . They had been standing in Tim Spencer's backyard. He'd been furious with her . . . and she'd looked into his intense green eyes and seen the child she remembered. She hadn't voiced his name . . . she hadn't spoken his given name, and vowed, silently, never to speak it aloud or divulge his secret. He'd removed the burden of that vow, identifying himself as Jade Laquette and nearly daring Mark Jarvins to investigate him . . .

To her, he had been Jade Laquette . . . but was he truly Jade, or had she married a man posing to be someone he had never been?

"I . . . I never really knew him," she said absently and closed her fist around the symbols of their union. "I never really knew him at all . . . did I?"

"I think you knew him," Lenny said quietly. "And he wanted you to know that he loved you, too . . . He made me promise if he couldn't tell you himself—if something happened to him—I'd carry that message to you. Maybe it doesn't help. Maybe it hurts like hell, honey, but he wasn't lying. He didn't walk into this because he wanted to. It was more like he . . . like he didn't have a choice. That maybe something was happening that he couldn't control. Maybe he uh . . . maybe he knew the plane crash was coming, and he really didn't have a choice. Or maybe he didn't see it, just sensed it coming. He said he relied on impressions . . . All I really know is that he was covering a lot of bases. And you were foremost in his mind."

In a lingering moment, Ronnie considered the words, knowing Lenny meant to console and comfort, but the words had little effect. If her husband loved her—truly loved her—he would have spoken to her and offered her a forewarning. At least she might have gotten a chance to fight back. This . . . to be left angry and bereft, exhausted . . .? It was like railing curses at a thunderstorm. Futile.

The arrival of room service interrupted, and Lenny pushed off the couch, leaving her alone with her thoughts. No longer hungry, she automated at Len's request and settled into one of the two chairs at the small table. Eating took too much energy, too much effort. Barely touching the stacked burger, she shoved it aside and reached for her coffee.

Sitting around, waiting for something else to happen, tangled up with anger and frustration . . . and a pang of sadness she refused to acknowledge? This wasn't her nature. She needed to move, to act even if the goal no longer mattered. Whoever Dominique Jardonet was, he wasn't her husband. Not the man who had ushered her into the alley behind Olden Time, concerned that she would breathe too many fumes. Not the man who had held her and smiled, sending her off on a shopping spree as if she might be jaunting down the block. How could he have done that to her? How could a man, who claimed to love her, put her through this hell without a hint of warning? No, this man, Dominique Jardonet . . . he wasn't her husband. That man, she feared, she truly had buried, and she wondered if she would ever truly forgive him. Husbands and wives shared a lifetime. Not four lousy months.

"That burger's not bad, Ron. You really ought to try a bite before you shove it—"

"I can't keep doing this," she said absently and found Lenny's dark, troubled gaze. "I can't keep thinking about this—about him. I really will go crazy, and I vowed to Tad, I wouldn't become a statistic. So . . . so we're going to discuss this case, Len. Whatever his reason for coming here . . .? I'm going to finish it."

"Honey, as much as I appreciate the offer . . . I think we have this one in hand."

"Jardonet helped you, didn't he?"

Lenny considered his words before nodding, answering, "For all the longer he was here? Yea, he lent a hand and offered us a definite direction."

"You have a suspect?"

"Classified, Ron, but yes. We believe we have this guy. It's just a matter of keeping him under surveillance and waiting for him to make a move."

"You can't just get a search warrant?" she asked, considering the details that Pete Saunders had offered. None of those words touched her deeply. In fact, she felt nothing for the victims or this maniac.

"How much do you already know about this case, Ron?"

"I know he's stalking his victims. Two males and two females that you're aware of. Ages range from nineteen to twenty-seven. Does he know them in advance, or is he snatching them at random?"

"We think he might have known the first. If not him personally, a family member."

"The skin and bone . . .? Are those his souvenirs?"

"This guy's like a modern-day Dr. Frankenstein, Ron," he said while lifting his sandwich. Reconsidering, he put it down and leaned back, looking at her with a faintly disgusted smile. "Eating and discussing this maniac isn't a great combination. I'm thinking about changing professions, maybe transferring to the bomb squad. Maybe just retiring altogether and doing something exciting like building barns."

"Rachel will be happy," she said offhandedly, her thoughts listing to all the mediocre details of life that no longer mattered one way or another. Her life was in ruin. She had a child to raise and an antique business to either sell or perpetuate. Life would go on, but, at this moment, she doubted she would be a part of it. Maybe she'd shuck everything and move nearer to the Capital where she could at least make certain Tad received a decent education. Right. And become another Felicity Laquette . . .? Raising a child alone, depending on a governess, dying young?

Bullshit!

Shaking the angry thought aside, Ronnie firmed her gaze on Lenny. "You didn't answer. The souvenirs? Dr. Frankenstein?"

"We think he's creating something with what he's collecting from the bodies. It's only a theory, but there's a precision in his work to suggest he has a purpose for what he's gathering. As far as the souvenirs . . .? Each of our victims had a birthmark, and this last one was carefully extracted from outside his previous butchery. We think he's fixating on those for his keepsake."

"He's a doctor," she said thoughtfully.

Len nodded. "A plastic surgeon," he offered. "There's a loose connection to place him in the same vicinity as our first victim a few weeks before the murder. We think while stalking Lowenstein, he spotted Demarco. She worked at a grocery store, and we have a confirmed set of circumstances to land our third victim within Demarco's territory. The problem is—it's all circumstantial. And what's worse? There's not a lot of physical evidence to work with, not on the bodies or crime scenes. Even if we secured a search warrant and found his tools lying on his kitchen table, we couldn't move on him.

"His profession has us fucked. The only place we found a shred of evidence—and I'm talking threads—was in the backseat of Lowenstein's car, and the kid worked at a hospital, not to mention—his parents are both doctors. Chances are, the fibers matching the color of surgical scrubs belonged to the kid or his parents, and if they belonged to our perp, they've probably been cleaned a dozen times. Still, I have agents looking into the hospital's laundry service, but even if the numbers don't jive on the days after each murder, it's still circumstantial evidence."

"You have him under surveillance. Anything promising?"

"Not even slightly," Len said disgustedly. "He's been following his schedule for the past two days. Surgery, follow-up visits, consultations . . . He's on call five of seven days, and according to his colleagues, he's the best they've ever seen. He's patched up accident victims so well that—if you can believe this—one of them actually won a beauty pageant. A real artist," he said with a low growl.

"That bothers you?"

"Yea, because it fits. In fact, this guy wears our profile as if it was tailored to him, and the problem is, it's not out of character in his field. He's a renowned, respected professional in a line of work that justifies his arrogance and aloofness. I'm betting we won't find a single colleague who takes exception to this guy's behavior. Already, in our subtle inquiries, we found several keywords—admire him, respect his talent, and precision. One surgical nurse deems him a symphony in motion and looks forward to being on his team. He runs the show like a military commando, snapping orders and demanding excellence. You'd think that was a strike against him, right? . . . Nope. According to our lady, he asks no more than he's willing to give of himself. A hundred and fifty percent, whether he's working on a government-assisted accident victim or a privately insured puff getting a facelift. A real hero, this nut."

"What are the chances he has his trophies in his private residence?"

"Good, but not great," Len stated. "I'd believe he's working at home if we weren't ninety-nine percent sure he's butchering his victims in the dregs where we're finding them. It would be more likely if we were finding the bodies in trash bins or plastic bags at the city dump. Whatever his madness, he wants us to find his victims, and he's not taking anything home."

"Moral codes of ethics," Ronnie said absently, her gaze listing toward the window. "He knows what he's doing is wrong . . . Possibly, he can't bring himself to strip them of all dignity and toss them out like the trash."

"He believes himself superior," Len said evenly. "Maybe he has his wires crossed, but I don't think he's leaving them to be found through any sense of moral consciousness or respect. It's more like he's making a statement with these shrines."

She looked over at him. "The Nazi angle? You found evidence to support that?"

"I think it's a pet peeve. A little like some nut drawing a cross on the wall and claiming to be doing God's work while carving up a hooker. Fanatical, yes. Obsessed and profoundly aware of the preaching of God, sure. But the kind of guy who joins hands in the front church pew and lifts his voice to the heavens in harmony with others? Nope. This guy might see Hitler as a god, might even think he's carrying out his god's mission, but he doesn't understand the principles of his mentor. Ergo, he's interpreting them his way. Exploiting the premise. I doubt we'll find Dr. Frank attends public rallies or private sessions with others of his creed. If he's a true believer, it's a private obsession."

"I caught a news broadcast with the faces of two suspects. What's going on there?"

"A police chief with a bone to pick," Devinio said with a note of weariness. "Apparently, one of his daughters joined the cause and fell hard for one of the followers. Two months later, she was pregnant and claimed she was a breeder for the Movement. A couple weeks after that, she broke up with her boyfriend and had an abortion that nearly killed her. The police chief took one look at the crime scene and came out loading both barrels. Unfortunately, in his public debut, the Chief blasted the lid off the quiet investigation that I don't need to expand upon."

"The suspects were released," she commented.

"They were eliminated from the suspect list two months ago, Ron," he said with a touch of disgust. "Along with other known members of that faction. This investigation didn't just start a few days ago. The mayor set up a special task force after the second victim."

"Any serious suspects before a few days ago?"

"They were looking in the wrong place."

"Come again?"

"They were concentrating on the visuals . . . the symbol," he clarified, reaching for his coffee and taking several swallows, buying time to think. His gaze returned. "All the resources the Bureau has to offer, and the two agents working with this task force concentrated on the Nazis, looking for a connection in the group. Somehow, they decided to ignore the Chief ME's report that the weapon was a surgical instrument and cited a specific reference to medical expertise. My colleagues decided that meant they were looking for someone with experience handling a knife. Ergo, the 'Taxidermist' thing. Apparently, one of the Nazis has a grandfather in the trade. For the past month, the task force focused on the follower. Unfortunately, he was under surveillance the night Frances Cummings disappeared and was nowhere near the crime scene. Surprise, surprise."

"How could such an oversight happen, Len?" she asked, truly curious.

"All the proper procedures were followed," he said, sighing and losing a little of his disgust, realizing the futility of hindsight. "Crime techs were brought in, evidence gathered, and sent to the labs. Maybe it was as simple as too much information and too many hands stirring the soup. The Chief ME had a heart attack right after the first body was found, and he's still out on medical leave. His assistant, Dr. Rhoades, is running the show, and he doesn't have his Chief's age or experience. Add in the fact that our agents, Tagger and Springer, aren't specialists on serial killers, more like white-collar investigators. They were up here to investigate an embezzling scam when they were dragged into this mess. It was an oversight and one hell of a mistake," he said simply.

"If Mark or I had been here three months ago, we would have known what we were looking at. As it was, out of the dozen or so men on the task force, half of them tried pursuing the professional angle. Several admit knowing this guy wouldn't stop at one or two. Unfortunately, they were kept busy tracking down various criminal types that didn't quite meet the criteria—but came close.

"Truthfully," he said with another blatant ring of disgust. "They couldn't decide whether to focus on sex offenders, neo-Nazis, or just any convicted felon with a history of violent behavior. We had a kid working in a hospital, a scalpel, a coroner's report suggesting a professional hand, and a toxicology report suggesting a working knowledge of medicine not normally found on the streets. We had a crime scene that was way too neat to suggest an act of unrestrained fury . . . Christ, it couldn't have pointed more blatantly to premeditation and ritualistic precision if this lunatic had scrolled a number one with a lot of blank spaces behind it . . . And despite all that, it took three fucking months and four bodies." He shook his head, his gaze more weary than hostile. "I'm telling you, Ron, early retirement's looking really good. In fact, I might go see my godfather and take another look at the family business."

Ronnie smiled faintly, appreciating the attempted jest regarding the Mafia. "You wouldn't be happy sitting behind a desk and writing insurance premiums."

His mustache quirked. "As long as it was just property insurance, I might be content. Everybody needs a house, right? And someone needs to provide the security behind that American institution. I think . . . I really think I might consider it."

"Ten minutes ago, you were building barns."

"Yea," he smirked. "Did I ever mention my uncle owns a construction company?"

Too cute. She shook her head. "No, and I don't think I want to know."

"Seriously, honey. Uncle Salva," he said with a deadpan expression. "I often considered asking him what happened to Jimmy Hoffa, but I think I'm better off not knowing. It might be seen as a conflict of interest, me carrying an official badge and all."

Again, she shook her head, refusing to bite.

"Do you know . . .? I actually received a personal call from the local don. How the fuck he even got my name, I don't have a clue, but this character wants to make sure I'm doing everything within my power to catch the *bastardo* who killed Erin Demarco. He didn't ask if I had a suspect. Didn't ask me anything . . . He tells me either I find this *figlio di puttana* or else."

Worried, realizing the sincerity behind Len's dark eyes, she asked, "Or else what?"

"Yea, that was my question, but he wasn't specific. It was your basic courtesy call, letting me know the FBI isn't the only one looking for this killer. What bothers me, slightly more than the fact that my name wasn't listed in the public domain, is the possibility that my friendly compadre might believe we're dealing with an ethnic dispute. My guess is—my pal's been watching this case from the sidelines and keeping abreast of the situation since Demarco's death. If he believes our Neos were guilty and turned loose, we could have another fucking situation on our hands very soon."

"I . . . knew the situation was tense, Len. I didn't quite anticipate that angle."

"We're sitting on a powder keg, Ron," he said quietly. "It's only a matter of time before this city turns into a war zone. Generally, it's bad enough to have some lunatic stalking a certain type of victim. This guy's stirring up racial hostilities. He started with a Jewish boy, swung over to an Italian girl, snatched a Polish man, and swung over to an Irish girl dating a Jewish boy, and something I heard bothers the shit out of me, honey. There's a slight possibility that his next victim will bring in the Afro-American faction."

"I don't see the connection," she said honestly.

"It's a hunch, Ron, but one I can't ignore or overlook. I have guys working overtime to trace Francis Cummings footsteps over the last week of her life, but the chances of us spotting the next target are about a million to one."

"Do you think he's actually plotting ethnic and racial disparity?"

"I'm more inclined to believe it's a side benefit. Maybe not the basic requirement, but definitely a consideration behind this lunatic's madness."

"Are there physical characteristics he's targeting?"

"Only one trait we can actually confirm," Len said tiredly, his gaze listing toward his half-eaten burger with an almost wistful shine. "Flawless skin," he said absently. "You won't find our victims' names on a dermatologist's client list. If they were ever cut or suffered a case of acne, the marks were there and gone long before now. Not so much as nick or a blackhead. I had a chat with a cosmetologist who tells me these people were apparently extremely lucky . . . like yours truly," he said with a smug, slightly sheepish smile. "At least according to a lady I talked to," he added with a mocked arrogance, then lost his dramatic flair with a sigh. "Anyway, bottom line, skin, as a rule, has flaws. Weather, diet, hygiene habits . . . dozens of factors fall into play to trash the skin daily. Nobody's flawless, but these four people came pretty close. We have one whose driver's license photo looks like it was taken in a studio."

"Is there . . . could they have used a plastic surgeon?"

"Nope, and they didn't use the same hygiene products," he said with a slight smile. "I was hoping we'd get lucky and find out they all used the same Avon Lady as Dr. Frank. No such luck. They didn't even use the same body or hand soap. Different brands, different makers," he shrugged. "Talk about thin leads, huh?"

"So . . . you're saying he just picks these people because he likes their skin?"

"He has a trained eye, Ron, and an apparent mission in life. You and I would probably pass these folks on the street and not think twice. Apparently, this guy can pick them out of a crowd at twenty paces, and we think that's exactly how he's selecting them. How many others he's seen and rejected, we can't even begin to guess."

"Process of elimination. That's where the ethnic angle comes into play."

"Along with the supremacist angle," he agreed. "We're fairly sure he came across Cummings while she was visiting her slightly Jewish boyfriend at work. The timeframe works, placing our third victim, Labinski, in the same area at least once when Cummings could have been at the post office with her boyfriend. It's also possible that Dr. Frank's first choice was the boyfriend. Clean cut, handsome, decent skin . . . and Jewish heredity. I think the only thing to save Jordan's life was his gender. I think Dr. Frank's an equal opportunist, or he likes symmetry."

"I hope you have someone watching Jordan," she commented.

"You're one smart lady, Ron," he said lightly. "And I do," he said. "Despite a few groans, I put a team on him just in case we're wrong about the next target."

"You took me to visit a crime scene once before, Len. I'm not sure I offered anything of significance, but . . . I'd like to see where Dr. Frank lives."

"Honey, if—"

"We don't have to stop, Len. I'd just like to see his neighborhood and maybe get a glimpse of his home. Maybe I can help—maybe I can't. We won't know until you let me try."

Silently, Len debated the potential danger, both personal and a threat to the surveillance, then decided, "I can get you into the neighborhood—" His cellular phone interrupted with a distinctive ring. Muttering a curse, he reached automatically into his jacket pocket. "Excuse me," he said as he lifted the bulky contraption to his ear and offered a simple, "Yes?"

Pushing off her chair, Ronnie offered him a degree of privacy. If they were leaving, she'd need a jacket and purse, along with her notebook from alongside the phone. As she collected her jacket, she heard Len's slightly peculiar note.

"I'm not sure I know what you mean." A long pause then, "Yes . . . hold on just a second." Pushing away from the table, he caught Ronnie's eye while rising. "Mind if I use the next room?"

"Feel free," she said lightly. If it involved the case, she'd undoubtedly hear soon enough.

CHAPTER 18

Departing Cafe LaRosa via the kitchen entrance, Dominique strode through the alley, comfortable in the shadows and chilly night air. The meeting had gone well. Robert Bryson had made the right decision at the table. Discreetly, several influential characters in the Nation's Capital would retire early, and a handful of professors in prestigious universities would lose tenure and face criminal charges. Like dominos, the kingpins would fall, and the walls of secrecy would crumble.

Unfortunately, Dominique felt neither satisfaction nor relief in manipulating the events to shatter the walls around his mother's murderers. Perhaps, if he'd rung their doorbells and held a .45 to their heads, as a hired gunman had done with his mother, he could feel some relief. His father had taken care of that assassin by no ordinary means. Fleeting, Dominique recalled the flashing insight his father had given him on his wedding day—on Jade Laquette's wedding day, he corrected silently and gripped in anger.

There should be some relief . . . some fitting justice against the madmen who had sanctioned the death of far more than Felicity Laquette. He knew their faces now, their names. He had grasped them clearly through the eyes of Robert Bryson, who had begun his own quiet investigations nearly ten years earlier.

Bryson had needed to know if there was any truth to his father's ramblings. A Nazi war criminal, a murder, an abduction . . .? The ramblings had sounded preposterous, but not long later, Bryson had sat in a private room ten years earlier. As shocked and disgusted as any decent man could be, he had listened to other prestigious elderly men relating the tales.

Through his father, Bryson had joined the circle of power which belied the elected government officials, and he'd used that clout to uncover that wicked plot. Quietly, he'd begun an investigation into the murder of Felicity Laquette and the disappearance of her son, but eight years had passed. The cases had both gone cold.

Throughout his investigation, however, he'd discovered more than a dozen names with possible connections to that forty-year-old plot.

Supreme court judges, state department officials, appointed position holders who could influence the political parties as effectively as such factions as the EPA and Steel Workers Union . . . Those were the names and faces driving the machine that determined the course of the nation.

If he put his mind to it, Dominique could bring those old gentlemen to their knees and leave them gripping their chests in dire agony before they drew their final breath. He was his father's son and not much different from his mother; he could waltz on the edge of the political machine and toss a cog in the works now and again. Where his mother had strived for financial independence, he need only work toward revenge.

His thoughts turning in ever darker circles, Dominique strode through the shadows beneath a shroud of tree bows and tall hedges. En route to LaRosa, he'd spotted the payphone clinging to the wall outside the corner deli's front door, and toward that instrument, he was destined. A sense of urgency niggled at his mind, but he maintained a steady pace, offhandedly recording the sights and sounds, from cars passing to dogs barking and children laughing. Like Bentwood, he considered, and his anger enhanced tenfold before he ever began depositing the change, dialing.

Barely, he offered his name when a heavily accented voice spoke in rapid-fire French, redirecting his call. Only seconds passed the familiar low voice erupted.

"You have become slightly more adept at vanishing, Dominique," Jean-Pierre commented. "Is it possible you are prepared to come home, now?"

"You are a long way from home. As I recall, you never acquired a taste for American cuisine—or culture. Any particular reason why you have come?"

"I've lost one son this week. I preferred not to lose another," Jardonet said lightly.

"You have sons to spare if memory serves, Father. Be more specific, will you?"

A silence lingered at the other end of the line momentarily before Jardonet commented, "I had a few unsettling insights, Dominique. One revolved around a lethal injection and the possibility that you wouldn't fare as well as your half-brother in a plane crash."

"Odd, I should suffer the same dream," Dominique said lightly, his smile masked in the shadows alongside the building. "So, it seems one brother is more proficient at avoiding catastrophe than another. Perhaps, you should not trouble yourself further, Father."

"Dominique, I have never doubted your survival. You are a Jardonet, after all, but I wonder, is the sacrifice you have made worth the return on your investment? This woman you chose, by whatever means to your own end, my own . . . have you protected her? Or will the past repeat itself? His name will be Laquette . . . as was yours . . . as was my own."

Sober abruptly, his attention riveted, Dominique gripped the receiver at his ear. "You will repeat that, yes?"

"The name Laquette . . . it is as old as Jardonet, my own," Jean-Pierre said quietly. "Your mother knew that. When she took you away from France, she took that name with her and lent it to you as my mother lent it to me upon a time. Perhaps, it is a curse, that none of the males of our family should wear that name beyond our youth. You are my bastard, just as I was another's, and so too, your prodigy, regardless of how swiftly you repaired that misconception and lent him a name."

"I don't appreciate that address, sir," Dominique stated. "However, premature, there was no mistake in the conception or the union to bear fruit."

"You seduced her," Jardonet said simply.

"I was already in love with her," Dominique defended.

"Ah, such a word. Love. What do you know about that emotion or intimacy? No more than myself. Such a fanciful term. A quest, perhaps, and part of our curse that we should seek beautiful women in search of such a divine concept. Hah! You deceived yourself, and you deceived her, my own. Such is your nature—to deceive and manipulate. To allow yourself the ignorance of youth to cover your sins. A paradox, son. As much as eighteen years ago, you knew where the future would lead, and you led another into the madness of your existence that she would find you upon a time."

"Coincidence," Dominique snapped, but before the word fully lifted off his lips, he grasped the partial lie. He had apparently known something of the future, and—if not eighteen years ago—he'd fallen in love with Veronica Bryson four months ago.

"Damned fool," Jardonet said with a low deep laugh vibrating his voice. "Believe your lies if that will ease your conscience and suffer no regrets. You chose well. Even now, I believe your lover strikes out in the face of adversity and deems to finish what you began so foolishly. She will raise my grandchild without your help, have no fear. She possesses a power of her own and a fine instinct to survive. Perhaps, not all of history will repeat itself, but I do wonder . . .? Fact, my son, you have no paternal grandmother. Died young, so she did. A pity. I might have benefitted from her charm and sensitivities in my early years. As I have heard, she was quite the witch in her own right. A white witch, no doubt. Ah, but hindsight is such a clever deception in itself. We might will ourselves better and see ourselves as something more than the sum of what we have become . . . if only."

Tense, Dominique registered the cynicism in the voice, but the words . . .? Veronica striking out alone to finish what he'd begun? His grandmother a white witch . . .? In a letter months ago, Jean-Pierre had written those words. '. . . Your white witch has survived and thus, my own, you owe me one . . .' "Where is she, Father? What do you know?"

"Ah, so my clever son fails to see beyond his dark passions, does he?" Jardonet taunted. "And no surprise, with revenge circling in your mind and in your heart."

"What the hell have you seen?" Dominique asked tensely.

"A man's passions may run deep, but a woman's run true whether toward love or hate, joy or bitterness, grief or fury. If you've finished terrorizing this Nation's capital, I would suggest jaunting north . . . Toward Cleveland would be my guess. I sense she is not as willing to forsake you as you are to betray her."

"I haven't—" He started and declined the opportunity to defend himself to this perplexing man. "I need either a fast car or a small jet. If you can assist without initiating my untimely demise—on air or land—I'd appreciate it."

"Ah, coming to your senses. A trifle late, I think," Jardonet sniped smoothly. "Lucky for you, I think ahead. A result of advancing age," he paused a heartbeat. "If you can deliver yourself to the municipal airport, I have a small jet standing by. Do not even consider exploding another of my craft, or you truly shall owe me, and I'll collect from you in hell . . ."

Not since leaving the Lakeview's rear lot had Lenny uttered more than two words, and the silence had reached a painful level within the confines of the front seat. Uncomfortably aware of his pensive mood, Ronnie studied his profile within the dashboard lights. Just a few weeks ago, they'd met out at Crowley's Pub, the less rowdy of Bentwood's duo of bars—she and Jade, Lenny and Rachel, who had fallen head over heels for the big lug. Beneath the subdued raucous of the early evening crowd, they'd been discussing marital bliss and their anticipation over their new arrival. Shamelessly, Rachel had flirted, tossing playful hints of matrimony in Lenny's direction, and the spark in the dark eyes had verified his perception.

Presently, Devinio appeared as grim and sober as Ronnie had ever seen him, and she wondered absently, "Am I the cause?"

As if startled, he glanced over, then recovered his concentration on the traffic ahead. "The cause?"

"That phone call in my room . . .? Was it about me? Or this case? Are you having second thoughts about this drive?"

"Multiple choice," Len stated with a stab at humor. "I like that. Makes it easier to avoid admitting anything."

"Len?" Ronnie said haltingly.

"Actually, it did—and didn't—have something to do with you," Len said bluntly. "You remember when you asked me to run those plate numbers?"

"Seems like a decade ago, but I'm not senile yet," she said lightly. "You finally figured out who was behind the wheel and why?"

"Not necessarily," he answered, sounding more pensive. "But I know who issued the surveillance on you."

"Should I be worried?" she wondered, remembering the car had been waiting for her in the Inn parking lot in Elmview . . . and whoever had issued that surveillance had known where to find her. Doubtful Elaine had offered that information to anyone other than Jade, and he'd called before Ronnie had called the store. Her heart pounded a dull beat of pain . . . the intrusion of his name in her thoughts was a distraction she could do without. Would she spend the rest of her life like this? Thinking about him, remembering the stupid little things . . .

Like watching him drive with the skill of a concert pianist? God, she'd loved to see him behind the wheel of his sports cars. His fingertips barely brushed the steering wheels to slither around bends—or other vehicles in his path. Often, he clasped her fingers, carrying her along to feel the power through the gearshift as he slammed the gears on the console between them.

Lenny had said something. Distracted, Ronnie looked over, "Pardon me?"

"I uh . . . I said I don't think you need to worry," he answered with a darting glance. "Are you all right? You looked a little lost for a minute."

"I'm fine."

"Ronnie, I uh . . . I really don't like getting you this close to the action. We'll take a pass through the neighborhood, but we can't get close without jeopardizing the surveillance team. This isn't like a city stakeout. This guy lives in a nice upper-class neighborhood where the same car only passes once or twice if it belongs down the block. We had a bitch of a time setting up surveillance."

"How'd you manage it?"

"We got lucky. A couple of Florida snowbirds got a late start flying south, and we're house-sitting. We're still more than two-tenths of a mile from his driveway, but there hasn't been much to see this far."

She paused, considering everything Len had said in the hotel. '. . . Just a matter of time,' he'd mentioned, and he hadn't exaggerated. Time was a factor, and someone's clock could be running out. Until this nutcase moved on to another victim, however, they couldn't move on him. The only assistance she might offer by visiting his neighborhood was a confirmation of sorts . . . and she couldn't even guarantee that service in her present mindset.

The muffled ring of the telephone in Len's pocket offered a welcome interruption to her declining mood. Muttering curses, Devinio fumbled in his pocket, lifted the unwieldy device to his ear, and pushed the appropriate button. "Yes?"

Ronnie grasped only the faintest trace of a human voice, her attention turning through the side window toward a housing project butting the highway. The styles, not the structures, changed. Like a cardboard Christmas village, currently bedecked in Halloween decor, single-story houses with two-car garages and paved driveways extended from one yard to another, all aglow under streetlamps or sporting orange porchlights. In fenced backyards, she glimpsed swing sets and plastic playhouses marking the homes with children like those fireman stickers in windows to designate a child's room.

Again, she caught herself thinking about Jade, remembering their plans. Not a farm, they had agreed. Neither she nor Jade would know what to do with a hundred acres of farmland, but they had likewise agreed their child would enjoy a safe backyard and space to grow in relative comfort. Eventually, he might want a pony and, most assuredly, a puppy if the Spencer children had any influence in his life—

"I'm on my way."

The tone of his voice, rather than his words, snapped Ronnie from her reverie in time to see Lenny slam the phone down on the seat next to him. Apparently, his rendition of hanging up mad. "A problem?"

"Naaa," he growled. "No problem. I'm fucking heading a task force of imbeciles. But hell, what's new, right?"

"Want to talk about it?" she asked lightly, sensing his restrained temper as clearly as the car's acceleration. Before that call, Len hadn't been anxious to reach their destination.

"Not a great deal to say, other than we're officially fucked," Len commented as if that explained all and should be taken as a matter of course. His gaze flashed over. "You know how I mentioned we had this case pretty much under control? Well, that's become null and void. The local commander in charge of the Mayor's task force decided to pull strings and found a judge willing to sign a search warrant for Dr. Reddinger's domicile. As we speak, Dr. Frank's getting served and taken downtown for questioning."

"There's not enough—" She stopped short. Lenny needed no fuel for his slow-burning fire, and he certainly didn't need told that the doctor would walk unless they found hard evidence in his house. "Maybe we'll get lucky," she said temperately. "Maybe he took the souvenirs home."

"Right. I believe in Santa Claus and the Tooth Fairy, too," Len growled. "But on the plus side, at least we can look at his bankbooks. Maybe he rented one of those storage sheds or a warehouse downtown . . . And there's always a chance he'll crack under questioning—not that I'd consider that a plus. Dollars to donuts, he'll have a kickass attorney glued to his hip within the hour, and at the first sign of a breakdown, we're fucked."

"He'll be off the streets," Ronnie pointed out.

"Yea, that's probably what Chief Dartworth thought too, but the problem with that theory is simple . . . We're dealing with an above-average income as well as intellect. If he brings in a hotshot attorney, he could be back on the street in twenty-four hours or less, and he'll have a whole new ball of tricks up his sleeve."

"That's a worst-case scenario," Ronnie said, trying to sound optimistic but failing drastically. All too well, she knew the accuracy of Len's words. Homicidal maniac or not, the law would remain in the doctor's favor. "Maybe we'll get lucky," she said again, without enthusiasm, and turned her attention to the houses and patches of thick woodland passing far more swiftly.

Within minutes, they were gliding off the exit ramp, dropping through a patch of woods that might have fully concealed the thoroughfare if the trees still wore leaves. Against a low-hanging mat of clouds, neon signs, marques, and highway traffic created a pale glow overhead. Not much passed nine o'clock, traffic maintained a steady flow, with fast-food restaurants and shopping plazas drawing the thickest crowds.

Stopped at a red light, dead center between two carloads of teenagers, the booming music and shouted voices breached the sedan's windows on either side. At a glance through the passenger window, Ronnie recognized the hand-rolled cigarette passed over the front seat. No big surprise there. The long-haired kid behind the wheel looked like a throwback from the 60s. She suffered an almost insatiable desire to ask Len for his badge and hold it up to the glass. She'd probably give the kid a heart attack or send him careening through the intersection . . . and doubtful either action would make her feel better. The light changed in time to spare her from further contemplation, and too soon, Len sped into the righthand turning lane, catching another light which the long-haired kid blew through with howls of laughter and hoots of approval echoing from his backseat.

"We're getting old, Len," she said offhandedly.

"Na," he said without enthusiasm. "Just feels that way."

Recalling Elmview and its youngsters of all ages, Ronnie commented, "I've been thinking about dying my hair blond. What do you think?"

"Won't work," Len offered with a glance and a slight smirk. "Your hair's too dark. You'll end up purple or some shit."

"Bull. If I had Amy Sue do it, she'd get it right. Maybe a golden blond or strawberry . . . I might look good as a strawberry blond."

"You'd go orange, then," Len commented offhandedly and punched the gas as the light changed. "You look just fine with black hair."

"Maybe brunette," she continued in a maudlin tone, her gaze trailing through the side glass again as they sped passed a mall entrance. "I never did that kind of thing as a child. Maybe I missed out on something . . . probably a lot of somethings. Maybe I'll pierce my ears a few more times or shave my head and go new wave."

"Yea, a half dozen earrings strung up the side of your earlobe . . .? That's sort of sexy," Len said thoughtfully. "Amy Sue could probably manage that, too. You could go butch and wear cut-off tops. Hell, burn your bra and toss your Gucci's. Maybe instead of blond—just get Amy Sue to put a white streak down the side and carve your initials on the back of your head."

"That's probably a little radical," Ronnie said, maintaining a sober tone as if she were lending serious consideration to Len's outrageous suggestions. "I don't think this is a good time to burn my bras, though. The Gucci's could go. I could wear sandals."

"Have you seen a northern winter lately, hon? Think you better plan on moccasins or those tall suede boots with lace and fringe," he suggested while slowing and engaging the turning signal.

Another housing plan. They passed through an elaborate sandstone entry that offered an air of private property and probably thwarted the average sightseer. A planned housing development was a far more accurate description with high hedges, an abundance of trees, stone pillars, gated driveways, and the houses tucked within trees on at least one-acre lots—probably more like five-acre lots. To her slight dismay, Ronnie felt right at home. The Bryson mansion rested within a similar plan although the houses had stood in place before the turn of the century, and most boasted carriage houses above renovated garages. These were new and probably ranged in the half-mil bracket. "Our doctor does very well," she commented.

"A real prince among men," Len growled and turned onto another tree-lined lane.

"How'd they manage a warrant on such shabby evidence?"

"We have a hot-to-trot assistant DA, and the head honcho was out to lunch—dinner actually. Toss in the fact that Agent Springer didn't appreciate having the case pulled out of his hands, and we had a ready-made recipe for disaster," he said disgustedly. "I'm tired of the politics," he commented.

The time for talking had passed. Ronnie knew the situation was out of control the instant they rounded a tree-and-wall-shrouded bend, and Len's string of low curses joined her silent retinue. Not only were a half dozen police cars lining the street, but at least one news station had caught wind of this affair. The van parked at an angle in the street, boasting a local Live Action news station in bright, bold lettering, and a crowd had already gathered outside a cast iron gate.

"I'd love to know how these sons a bitches do it," Len snapped as he rolled passed the van. "No offense, honey, but I'm beginning to despise these newshounds."

"No offense taken," Ronnie said with her anger ignited. "But it's really no big deal to catch a lead. Someone on your task force owed somebody a favor, or the relationship was cultivated in advance . . . Hell," she muttered. "It could be the mayor himself, hopping on a campaign trail for all we know."

Turning into the entrance, Lenny blasted his horn and parted the bodies, but strobe lights swung wide, and Ronnie ducked her head as at least one anchorwoman lunged toward the window for a closeup. One of the uniformed officers had apparently been alerted of Len's arrival and flagged him through as other uniforms crowded the car and evicted the camera crew.

"Great. If not on a two-minute newsbreak, we'll be on the eleven o'clock news," Len stated and scowled as he rolled forward and slammed the car into park behind another unmarked vehicle. "Stay here a minute. If the doctor's still in, I'd rather you not meet him."

"No problem," she said smoothly. A stone border edged the driveway with neatly trimmed hedges blocking the first floor of a sprawling mansion; the second floor remained in shadows despite the spotlights casting a daylight glow through the barren trees across the front lawn. Scrolled cast-iron benches littered the grounds; life-sized sculpts decorated a stone path leading from the driveway into what could only be a summer garden and suggested an extensive lawn. No Halloween décor cluttered the ambiance. Her attention riveted on the cluster of officials—plainclothesmen and uniformed officers—gathered at the main entrance. No gawking neighbors to worry about, she considered when her focus landed exclusively on the tall, lean man who strode rigidly between a stout, suited man and two patrolmen.

For the first time in his life, Dominique had consciously, willingly, physically boarded one of his father's aircrafts, and as he rested, staring at the blackness in the small portal, he found his own phantom image looking back at him. A smile curved the corner of his mustache. His facial features remained shaded beneath the bill of the baseball cap that he'd worn at the Café La Rosa. The same face and yet different.

Dominique Jardonet.

Perhaps he had truly needed to return to that persona, to distance himself and call upon all the bitterness he'd harbored throughout his life . . . but that revelation offered no genuine relief. He had meant to live a lifetime with that wondrous black-haired witch, had forced himself to believe that he'd spend a lifetime with her . . . but there had been moments, strange moments when he knew a black abyss yawning before him.

Darkness, always the darkness, lingering just over the horizon . . . and the cessation of his visions, where his wife and child should exist, only darkened his thoughts.

If he'd been meant to live a life with them, he should be able to see himself there in the future—

Instead, a window burst open, and as if he stepped through a looking glass, he stood within the soft glow of lamplight, breathing in the scent of beeswax and lemon, the tangy sweetness of an expensive cigar. Adding a soft blue haze to the lamplight, a thin trail of smoke rose from the smoldering butt wedged between two spindly fingers.

Kicked back within a plush leather wingback of 18th-century design, the elderly gentleman held a telephone receiver to his ear, his pale blue eyes glaring toward the closed drapes as his paper-thin flesh pulsed at his cheek. Well past his prime, his neatly cropped hair remained as faded gray as his eyes, but the intensity of his expression defied his age.

'. . . Sir, he's not Laquette . . . I've seen some of these new tapes. He's not Laquette, but he's of similar talents . . . I think he knows what's on those tapes . . . He sent Dr. Heinz and Ben Chalmers from his room and met privately with Dir. Lakeland.'

'Then we don't really have a choice, Roland. He's not to leave that facility under any circumstances. You know what you must do . . .'

Then . . .

"You need to calm down, Sam," the gravelly voice ordered, as strong now as ever a vision past. Aged, perhaps, but this was the same face that Dominique had seen years ago—forty years ago within a slate gray room. "Everything's under control . . . The other one's under lock and key and the boy was buried this morning . . . I rather thought you took care of that," the elder spoke with a wry smirk, his rasping voice carrying a musing note. "I resent that, Samuel, although I should be flattered, I suppose. As far as I've heard, there's still no evidence of sabotage. It's being listed as an engine malfunction . . . No, we haven't identified the overseas company yet, but I'm sure someone's bound to come forward sooner or later. We'll deal with them then . . .

"About Bryson, I wouldn't worry about him. If he truly possessed any evidence, I doubt very much he would have phoned you directly. . . . Don't be a fool. After everything we've endured to come this far only to buckle to an asinine threat . . .? Robert wouldn't dare report a thing and risk his father's reputation . . . Of course, we know that, but I don't think he'll be willing to call our bluff. Besides, if he becomes too much of a nuisance, we might just give him something else to fret about . . .

"Of course, I'm referring to his daughter. And it's a little late for this righteous indignation, Sam. It's probably only a matter of time before I'll need to issue that order anyway. If we could have converted that child as easily as we converted the other, we would be that much further ahead. Leaving that ordeal to Carson was a mistake we won't repeat, I assure you, and who's to say we're not receiving a second chance here? Managed correctly and at a far earlier age, this child could enhance our gene pool a hundredfold. If we lay the foundations, our successors might reap the reward with this prodigy. You and I might not be here to witness the culmination of our life's work, but we've nurtured enough others to continue in our footsteps. There will come a day . . ." As the fellow drew from his cigar, his face tipped.

For an instant or an hour, the pale blue eyes riveted, the brow furrowed in slow motion, the thin, lined lips parted . . .

A slight, wicked smile kinked Dominique's mustache, and his eyes still glittered with menace as he refocused on his own reflection in the black portal. Well, and he hadn't consciously stepped away from himself in quite some time, but it was certainly not his first out-of-body experience. Whether he gave the old bastard a coronary or merely loosened a few more screws, he couldn't care less. All too clearly, that old man had referred to Jade Laquette's wife and child . . . and the need to finish what he had begun increased tenfold. The threat to Veronica, as well as to their son, hadn't been removed just yet.

CHAPTER 19

No suit or tie adorned the tall, lithe figure. Still, the professional executive image blazed neon from Dr. Whitman Reddinger's short, stylish blond hair to his leisure slacks, pale shirt, and sports jacket. Not close enough to read the emblem on his jacket, she doubted it came off a department store rack, and even in silhouette, she recognized the arrogance in his profile and posture. With an air of detached superiority, he stood erect as one of the officers opened the backdoor of a patrol car, and by his pose, he might consider the officer granting him a privilege of his station—rather like a chauffeur holding a limousine door. At the nape of her neck, shorthairs lifted, and in the pit of her stomach, a tiny little tadpole squirmed uncomfortably. Only one thought held foremost in her mind . . . If this wasn't Dr. Frank, this fellow sure fit the bill. And on the heels of her revelation, she knew this maniac wouldn't simply crack and confess.

Her heart hammered a quick beat to realize the accuracy of Lenny's surmise. Reddinger would be back on the street tomorrow evening at the latest. *By noon*, a silent voice corrected. By noon tomorrow, he would walk out of whatever precinct held him with a score to settle.

Spellbound, she watched as he slipped smoothly into the caged backseat despite his hands secured at his back. Obviously tense, the officer snapped the door shut, and a dozen officials hustled to other cars. Skin crawling, Ronnie watched as blue lights ignited and the procession turned within a wide oval. The car transporting Reddinger slid into a central position, and Ronnie suffered a quickening chill as the procession passed, Uncontrollably, her attention fixed on the shadowy figure in the rear compartment. Only for an instant, the pale face turned in her direction, and she glimpsed the sculpted face, the angled, lofty features. Her skin prickled when she realized he'd likely seen her clearly within the spotlight glowing through the windshield. In the hollows of his safe cocoon, even Tad seemed to shiver with her revelation. Reddinger could identify her if he ever so chose.

Unconsciously gripping her purse tighter with a fleeting thought of her Midnight Special, Ronnie slid from the car as the third patrol car passed. The need to find evidence had just increased a hundredfold, and she wasted no time, rounding the car and advancing on the remaining uniformed officers who eyed her suspiciously. She barely reached for her wallet to produce her identification when Len passed through the open front door and spared her the need. Tense, she caught his dark eyes as he flagged the officers away, and no words needed speaking. She'd seen the face of this maniac, and if he wasn't the man they sought, he was a dead ringer.

Grimmer, Len motioned her inside. "Don't touch anything," he coached needlessly, speaking quietly. "But if you get any vibes, I'd like to hear them."

More than vibes. She barely passed through the arch into a spacious entry when the chill skittered down her spine. Like walking into a freezer. Shivering, she pulled her coat closer while scanning the entrance.

On the surface, nothing appeared out of place or warped. Rich-colored carpets sprawled over hardwood floors. Immaculate side tables stood at the walls decked with glittering silver candlesticks and pottery vases overflowing with silk flower arrangements. Paintings—undoubtedly oils—ranged from landscapes to one beautiful work of an oriental gazebo in dark frames to contrast tastefully against the beige walls. Just inside the double doors, a stunning mirror with etched glass flowers caught Ronnie's eye, along with the wall sconces that might have been purchased in a shop like Olden Time. Thanks to Jade, she knew far more about antiques than she'd known a few months ago. But even without his tutelage, she might have identified air pockets and flaws in the antique silver behind the glass. If the entry was any indication, the house carried all the classic ambiance of a successful doctor—one with either an eye for detail and taste or the resources to hire an exceptional interior designer.

Donna Spencer could have put this ensemble together.

Ambling, unable to offset the chill or the quiver in her gut, Ronnie moved toward one of the wide arches. At the living room entrance, she paused and noted the hints of oriental decor in the foyer became far more visible. Chinoiserie end stands and cloisonne vases decorated the teak furniture, and although she identified the reproduction status of the dark red wood, she couldn't fault the quality of the carvings or oriental tapestries. Across the room, a wide sandstone fireplace centered the wall; the brass and glass screen blended magnificently with the fans of dried flowers and tall sculpted urns to either side.

A pair of plainclothes detectives stood across the room, either admiring a collection of ancient weapons displayed on the wall or judging the possibility of evidence by the same. Shaking his shaggy blond hair, the man spoke at a low volume. “You know what I just remembered?”

“You missed lunch?” the young woman, who appeared more suited to be a Dallas Cheerleader than a policewoman, wondered.

“That comment our mutual friend made about checking out local antique dealers,” the man continued without a hitch. “He said something about our guy maybe studying the ancient arts or some shit.”

“And you doubted, right?” the woman said in mocked disgust. “How much you wanna bet we find a stash of catalogs selling Japanese swords?”

“He probably has a few subscriptions to martial arts magazines and a whole collection of Bruce Lee training tapes.”

“Probably belongs to one of those Survivalist groups, too. We’ll probably find a few books on guerrilla welfare,” the woman commented and turned in time to catch Ronnie’s eye. Suspicion dashed into her eyes, and her soft, lovely features hardened considerably. “I don’t believe we’ve met,” she said smoothly, and her partner turned as well, his young handsome features transformed equally fast before darting past Ronnie and back, tense.

“I’m with the FBI,” Ronnie said.

“We’ve been getting that a lot,” the woman said while rounding a low stand on which another collection of vases formed centerpieces. “What’s your forte? Psychology?”

“In a manner of speaking,” Ronnie said without a hitch and scanned the room, still hugging her coat to ward off the chill. Her attention returned as the young woman came closer. “Forgive me for eavesdropping, but I assume you were referring to Dominique Jardonet.” Her focus darted to the male who had spoken. “He mentioned antique dealers?”

“Something like that. Do you know him?” the man asked.

“Personally, no,” she answered honestly and again focused on the young woman. “You may be right about the survivalist theory, and on that note, I suggest we begin looking for trapdoors in the lower regions of the house. If not directly accessible through the basement, we may find the equivalent of a bomb shelter on the grounds.”

Not awaiting a response or comment, Ronnie turned and strode from the room, pausing in another open doorway to watch two detectives ransacking what could only be a home office. In classic elegance, the oriental theme continued with tall vases and wall art scattered between a desk, chairs, and cabinets. Voices echoed from every direction. A lingering scent of spices flavored with the more recognizable aroma of a recently grilled steak. Apparently, the doctor had prepared a late evening meal, and as Ronnie ventured to the vacuous kitchen and dining area, she confirmed her belief. A single plate, wine goblet, and a mug rested on the black marble-top counter in what was otherwise a pristine kitchen, presently being ransacked by another pair of plain clothes detectives.

On the surface, nothing pointed to a deranged psychopath in residence, but the crawlies hadn't lifted. In fact, as Ronnie passed through another arch, the discomfort increased to skid over her shoulders, down her spine, and she caught herself glancing over her shoulder, expecting to find a butcher knife poised to pierce her skull or slice her neck. Not good. Fleeting, she remembered every classic horror movie she'd ever seen—the old ones where tension developed in the lack of details with blood splatters on the walls, a shadow at a window, a ripple in a curtain . . . This house carried an aura of that same dark tension. Behind every door, she anticipated a body. Behind every vase, she expected to find a bloody knife or a bullet hole. Doubtful she would even be surprised if blood erupted in a spot on the smooth tiles overhead. Unfortunately, no such blatant trail would lead to this monster's hidey-hole.

Echoing, a murmur of voices followed Ronnie as she descended the stairwell, and pricklies shivered through her despite the bright light and carpeted steps of a finished basement. Pleasantly, wood-paneled walls wrapped around the family room—a room complete with a television and stereo system, thick padded leather chairs, and an abundance of bookshelves. As many record albums as cassette and video tapes occupied the lower shelves of a long bookcase. One of the detectives had already turned on the television and VCR. At a glance, Ronnie identified a scene from an action movie recently released on tape. No kung fu thriller—just the basic alien invasion.

"Maybe he thinks he's an alien and needs skin grafts to cover his scales," one of the detectives commented while pulling out the movies, checking boxes and titles.

The other laughed tensely, "Yea, that sounds fitting."

"Christ, he has all the latest hits."

A crypt could feel no cooler than this basement, but as Ronnie meandered from the game room to find a generic storage room, a laundry room, and a furnace room, nothing of significance jumped out at her. In fact, only the cold seemed consistent, and as she stood scanning the insulated paneling in the furnace room, the revelation struck her. Nothing of emotional input truly touched her. As if she stood in a freezer, nothing of human occupancy registered, and that wasn't natural. She should feel something. Even at her worst, she always sensed the occupation of a house and suffered the prickling intuition which enlightened her to either the hospitality or animosity of the dwellers. At a crime scene, those sensations quickened to offer impressions of motive or intentions. Here, she felt only the cold detachment that she'd viewed on the occupant as he had stood outside the patrol car.

"Any luck?" the young woman asked as she came hesitantly into the furnace room, a flashlight ignited in her hand.

Distracted, Ronnie looked at her, not needing a sixth sense to realize the curiosity behind the woman's eyes. "None so far. Have they found anything upstairs?"

"An entire library of medical journals, as if that should come as a surprise," the woman said in disgust and glanced about the finished room. Aside from a few extra furnace filters against one wall and a workbench where the doctor might keep a few rudimentary maintenance supplies, there was nothing to see. "Funny, if you moved out the furnace and carpeted the floor, this room would be nicer than my apartment." Her gaze shifted to Ronnie. "Seems a bit much for one guy, huh?"

"Does he have a maid service, do you know?" Ronnie asked.

"He has a cleaning lady who comes twice a week. Your partner didn't mention it?"

"We didn't have a great deal of time to talk, and I'm coming into this a bit late," Ronnie said as she scanned the room before again looking at the attractive young woman. "I understand Mr. Jardonet was instrumental in pinpointing this man. Would you mind telling me what other insights he offered?"

Her attention darted as if likewise seeking something, if not a diversion. Shrugging, she caught Ronnie's eyes. "Most of what he said can be found on one report or another."

"Did you have much association with him?"

Defensive suddenly, her pale blue eyes held steady. "I'm sure you know, me and my partner escorted him to a few of the crime scenes. Guess we had a little more association with him than any others. Are you here on a murder case or to find Mr. Jardonet?"

"What can you tell me about his disappearance?"

"Nothing more than we already admitted a few times to your associates," the detective said bluntly. "He gave us the impression he intended to leave, but he didn't say where he was going."

"What was he like?" Ronnie asked despite herself and the woman's head tipped in question.

"Not sure I know what you mean?"

Considering the possibility that she would rather not know—that any answer could only lead to more questions—Ronnie shrugged and dismissed the thought. "I'm interested in knowing if he offered any other suggestions . . . Maybe hinted at what sort of person we're dealing with here? Why did he mention the oriental arts?"

"We uh . . . it was more in the line of brainstorming. It had to do with how this guy knocks down his victims. We considered the possibility of blow darts, but there's evidence to suggest it was probably one of those lancet devices that diabetics use to draw blood. If you read the toxicology report, you know the victims were kept sedated, but that never explained the initial abduction."

"Mr. Jardonet assisted in solving that mystery?"

"We kicked around ideas, and your coroner found the evidence on Cummings."

"Did you look into the dealers in oriental arts as Mr. Jardonet suggested?"

"We didn't see the need. The guy didn't use a blow gun."

With a sudden pause in thought, recalling all the coincidences in Elmview, Ronnie turned and started from the room. "Sometimes the most obscure comments can lead to enlightenment."

"Do you study the ancient arts?" the detective asked, following.

"No, just people," Ronnie answered offhandedly and continued through the short hall, reaching the stairway in record time and stopping short of the first step. Turning, she judged the four doors in the corridor, mentally calculating the size of the rooms in conjunction with the walls overhead. Something . . . she sidestepped passed the detective and stopped again at the game room entrance. One of the detectives still fussed near the wall of books; the other had begun moving the furniture and had pulled up a corner of the thick rug. Scanning the room, she shook her head. The sizes were comparable to the rooms overhead.

Muttering a curse, she turned again, ignoring the curiosity in the detective's eyes as she returned to the steps and climbed. No bomb shelter unless it was installed beneath the lawn. Ancient arts . . . coincidence? The mention of an antique dealer upstairs . . . coincidence? Maybe her senses were way off base. Maybe she wanted to believe that Jardonet was Jade. That he possessed a sense of what lay ahead for her and laid a foundation to lead her with coincidences.

And maybe the art dealer who furnished Dr. Frank's abode had some connection to the murders . . .

Reaching the doctor's home office where the hub of activity had concentrated, Ronnie stood a moment watching Len sift through a folder taken from a hideaway cabinet. Several other detectives, and at least one federal agent, were busy within the room, rifling through the desk and scouring the bookshelves, seeking more hidden compartments. As if he possessed a sixth sense of his own—which he probably did—Len looked over, his curiosity as apparent as his subtle hope.

"Have you found any receipts from art dealers?" she asked, and his brow hiked a notch, his gaze more intent.

"Not yet," he answered.

"Then we need to find them," she said and glanced at two of the detectives looking toward her. On Lenny, she remained intent. "He's probably a regular customer with at least one shop carrying a lot of imports. The teak is reproduction, but I doubt it was done on American soil. I'd venture a few of the vases are at least a few hundred years old. Not Ming Dynasty, granted, but you won't find that quality at a flea market. He has a regular supplier . . ." And she was certain of the importance if only by Lenny's increased intensity.

"Art . . . damn it," Lenny snapped and looked at the agent nearest the desk. "Go through that stack again." His gaze shifted to another agent. "Go through that other cabinet and see if you can find his house insurance policy. Maybe we'll get lucky, and he'll have copies of receipts."

Leaning against the doorjamb, Ronnie watched as Lenny finished rifling through the folder in his hand and turned to the two-drawer cabinet. In contrast, the beige color of the cabinet offered a respite from the dark wood of the folding doors and shelves, but the metal clashed with the austere ambiance. Glancing about the room, she glimpsed the placards on a wall behind the desk, undoubtedly awards or honors. His medical credentials probably hung in an office, and with her thought, she realized how little she truly knew about this case, this criminal.

She knew the names of the victims, the ages, and the basics of what this maniac had done to them in those final hours. This wasn't how she'd intended to progress, not how she operated. After a glimpse of this abode to secure first impressions, she would have begun asking questions and gaining details. Presently, she had no idea where Reddinger practiced, whether he maintained an office in a hospital or followed the trend and shared a private practice with a few other doctors. Malpractice suits and high insurance premiums had probably assisted in that trend. Not many doctors like Doc Blackwell existed anymore, and even he considered finding a younger partner to share expenses. Did this Whitman Reddinger have a half dozen partners to share his financial burdens? Lenny hadn't offered that information other than to mention the fellow being 'on call.'

She was out of her depth in this case. And suddenly, she wasn't even certain why she had come here. To stop a killer? To finish what her husband had begun? To find him or at least find out what had happened to him? The man she'd known and loved, the father of her child, was gone. If nothing else, she should accept that fact and return to Bentwood . . . but there was something she needed to do first.

With exhaustion already tugging at her mind, Ronnie pushed off the doorjamb and turned from the entrance. Making her way to the front door, she stepped onto the portico, aware of the temperature rising despite the cool breeze. Her presence interrupted a quiet conversation between the two uniformed officers who looked toward her. "My partner's going to be a while. Possibly one of you could give me a lift as far as that shopping plaza?" Barely, she finished the words when she glimpsed at the new arrival, and her attention riveted. Blond hair catching and reflecting the simulated light, the last person she wanted to see strode up the driveway toward her without a visible hitch in his stride. Even in the simulated light, she read the surprise in his sculpted face and intense blue eyes. A mistake . . . a mistake she might not have made under other circumstances.

"Why I'm even slightly surprised, I can't imagine," Mark said in a low tone as he stepped onto the porch. His attention darted off the uniformed men through the open doors, then returned with a softer shine. "Let's step over there and talk for a minute."

She had no desire to speak to him, let alone to offer the explanation he would expect, but neither officer needed to be privy to that detail. Nodding, she accepted his gesture and walked off the porch with him.

Three years ago, he had asked her to marry him, but Ronnie had known something was missing between them. As much as she had enjoyed his company, it hadn't been enough. In a fit of anger, he had stalked from her apartment and out of her life. The friendship they'd shared had ended that eve. Not a phone call. Not a postcard. Not a telegram just to say 'hi.'

They weren't friends, might never have been friends. Like all others before him, he had sought only one goal—to be her first—even if he had forced himself to believe otherwise and showered her with love accolades. That he would've followed through and married her was of no consequence. A man could do worse than marry the only daughter of Robert Bryson. Add her background to complement his, her basic knowledge of politics and protocol, and he would have gained a dandy housewife to carry his children and run his house while he climbed the ranks in the FBI. She could picture it now as she had then, him running off on his missions and her at home, raising his children. No wife of Mark Jarvins would maintain a career, much less a career in conflict with his. Raised in the old school—the same old school her father had attempted to force her to attend—Mark would have dictated her life and swallowed her identity.

He had made one major mistake, she considered, as she stopped next to him, feeling only indifference to the intimate touch on her sleeve. He had mistaken her virgin status for naivety and innocence. He had failed to recall that she'd followed dozens of leads into dark alleys and kibitzed with the dregs of society. Well, and maybe two mistakes. He'd failed to believe in her innate ability to read people. And what she'd read behind his intense pale blue eyes and smiles, her subconscious had rejected.

"Ronnie, I probably don't need to ask what you're doing here," he began in a reasonably solemn tone. "I probably don't even need to ask how you managed it. The fact is—you shouldn't be here."

"Save your speech, Mark," she interrupted smoothly. "I was just leaving."

"Honey, I know why you made this trip," he said more solemnly, his expression conveying the sympathy that she'd endured too often over the past two days. On him, it was fake. "But you're in no condition, mentally or physically, to be here. We are looking into your uh . . . your husband's accident. We have a team working on it. You have my word—when I know something, I'll tell you. But, I can safely say, this murder investigation—it's not connected. And I don't want you involved in this case."

"Why did you involve him in this, Mark?" she asked simply. With her back to the blazing spotlights and his face angled into the light, she recognized the absence of a reaction and knew the expression well enough to judge him masking a more natural emotion. "Why did you come to Bentwood and ask for his assistance?"

"It wasn't my decision, honey," he said quietly, his eyes softening again. "I can only assume that someone higher up in the Bureau knew him, or they had access to my report from this past summer. I really don't know what happened to him, Ronnie. I don't know why or even how he slipped away and boarded that plane. I'm assuming you know about his half-brother, Dominique Jardonet? I uh . . . I'd like to ask you. Have you ever met him?"

She shook her head, her gaze trailing over the dark patches of lawn and shrubs. The streamers of white glowing light from the spots added a surrealistic touch and lent a weirdly sinister ambiance to the shadows. Uncontrollably, she shivered within her coat. "No," she answered absently. "Jade never talked about him." Her focus lifted, finding Mark's intent blue gaze—lighter in the white light. "There are too many questions, Mark, and maybe too many coincidences. I know you and Lenny asked him to come here . . . Then he just happens to switch places with a half-brother who just happens to be on American soil? Now, my husband's dead, and his half-brother's missing? I do want answers. I'm just not sure you're the person who could or would give them to me," she said honestly.

"I uh . . . I know this is the wrong time to tell you this, honey," he said quietly, clasping her sleeve as if to convey his sincerity. His tone softened with his disheartened smile. "But despite everything that's happened between us, I do still love you, and I'd like to help you get through this. That," he said with a self-deprecating little huff of disgust. "Includes tracking down the answers to your questions, and when I have, I'll tell you whatever I can. You have my word on that."

He sounded sincere, and she suspected, in his way, he was. The wording, though—whatever I *can,* not whatever I *find out*—sparked her doubts. Open-ended, he promised not to promise how much of the truth he would divulge. If she harbored any further suspicions about his knowledge, those vanished. He knew more than he was willing to admit. Might, at this moment, possess the answers to her questions. "Thank you," she said with a weariness she needn't feign. "I do appreciate that, Mark, and I apologize for coming here. I think I just needed to know that it wasn't all for nothing, that something good has come from this. The sooner you put this maniac behind bars for good, the better."

"Oh, we'll get him," Mark said with a glance toward the house, a troubled line across his brow. "Unfortunately, I don't believe we have him at the moment," he said quietly. "Off the record, honey, I don't think we have the right man. And that's the main reason, I don't want you poking around this city or getting involved in this case."

A touch of alarm niggling the edge of her mind, she studied him. "You profiled him, Mark. This character fits the bill. Why would you think . . .?"

"It wasn't my profile to nail this guy," he said soberly, his gaze fanning over the lawn and house, returning. "And it's too neat. Too pat. Honestly, I don't think our killer's a practicing physician. I'm more tempted to believe he was a med school dropout."

Should she admit her sensation when studying the physician? Could she even trust her initial impressions in her current frame of mind? She had believed she saw a maniac, but how much of her reaction was based on prior knowledge and public opinion? A doctor . . . a plastic surgeon . . . a skin fetish . . . medical knowledge. "Why a dropout?" she asked directly.

"I uh . . . I'm going out on a limb here," he said with a tense smile, his gaze haunted. "But uh . . . it's something your uh . . . your husband told me," he said carefully. "On the way here, he mentioned something about having a firsthand account—an opportunity to profile a killer with a genuine account of the maniac in action. The idea was intriguing. If that were possible, it would eliminate the guesswork in what I do. I'm a skeptic. Whether it's my nature or something I developed to stay reasonably healthy in this line of work, I don't know, but uh . . . well, to make a long story short—I'm not as skeptical as I was a few days ago. In fact, I'm pretty sure that I have a fairly accurate account of the killer in action, and based on that knowledge, the man we're looking for is not a practicing surgeon who showboats his talent in an operating room daily. I think our psycho's craving that audience. If he is a doctor, he's not one with a fantastic reputation, and he doesn't live in a half-million-dollar home. I think Reddinger's too high profile to be our psycho. That's the long and short of it."

"Do you have another suspect?" she asked. "And does Lenny know what you're thinking?"

"I've been running a search for the past few days," he said and shifted his gaze toward the house, his expression tense. "Truthfully, I have about two hundred possibilities," he said uncomfortably and appeared genuinely troubled.

"This city's crammed full of doctors and various other medical professionals who might or might not have started out with grand expectations. As for Len . . .? He and I haven't been seeing eye-to-eye in a while," he said, sounding even more troubled if not a little depressed. The expression aged him and added a weariness that appeared all too genuine.

Sighing, he met her gaze with a disheartened smile. "I can't deny how I felt about you, Ronnie, or how I reacted to your involvement with uh . . . with Jade. It's probably way too late for an apology, and for that, I really am sorry. I didn't know who he was when we ended up in that . . . in Bentwood, but I didn't trust him. I didn't know what he was hiding, but I knew he wasn't who or what he appeared to be. Maybe someday, you'll forgive me," he said with a resigned faint smile. "I just didn't want to see you hurt."

He sounded miserable and appeared more miserable than she had ever seen him. The old standby humor was gone. Not even an attempted joke. At another time, maybe in another place, she would forgive him readily. His jealousy . . .? How foolish even to cling to that anger, now. His jealousy had been a mere inconvenience in the broader scope of events. She was hurt . . . but not in a way Mark Jarvins might have anticipated months ago. Wearier than she cared to realize, she listed her gaze, scanning the shadowy front lawn of a possibly innocent surgeon.

Sighing, she found Mark's sorrowful gaze. "I think you better talk to Lenny, Mark. You have a good partnership, and you work better together than apart. I know he's not happy with whoever jumped the gun on this warrant, and if this guy really isn't the killer, you can't afford to postpone that chat."

"That's why I'm here," Mark said, and at least part of his equilibrium had returned. Bouncing a glance to the house and back, he held her gaze. "You said you were just leaving. Do you have a car here?"

"I'm hopping a ride to the plaza down the road and calling a cab from there."

"Where are you staying?"

"The Lakeview," she answered.

"How about giving me a few minutes with Len, then I'll drop you off," Mark decided and reached into his long coat pocket, bringing out the keys. "You may as well wait in the car. It's too chilly to stand around out here."

For a split second, she considered rejecting the offer, then accepted the keys. Why look a gift horse in the mouth? Returning Mark's grim smile, she started down the driveway as he headed across the pavement toward the porch. Dawdling as if admiring the garden, she watched him pass between the uniformed officers and into the house, then followed his footsteps. At the bottom step, she caught the eyes of the older officer. "Tell Agent Jarvins I'll leave his keys at the front desk, will you? And tell him thanks again for the loan."

"Will do, ma'am," the officer agreed.

It could be argued Mark owed her one, if for nothing else, for sounding as if he had a right to decide where she should be and with whom. Striding alongside the line of cars, she found the newest addition and slid behind the wheel. After adjusting the bucket seat to accommodate her legs, she started the car and orchestrated a smooth three-point turn, avoiding a pass of the front porch. The officers at the gate parted the crowd and sent her through the growing assembly. Another news station had arrived, along with a half dozen more cars which undoubtedly carried more of her former associates. She was no longer a journalist—investigative or otherwise. Nothing remained clearer in her mind as she sped through the shaded lanes passing the ornate driveway entrances and glimpsing tremendous houses set back within the trees. Just what she was, she had yet to decide. Despite the card in her pocket, a gift from Mark Jarvins when he had wanted her under his thumb in Bentwood, she wasn't a Special Consultant to the FBI. Nor the wife of an antique dealer . . . or psychic . . .

She was a mother-to-be, she concluded as she stopped at the mouth of the housing development, awaiting a half dozen cars to pass before pulling onto the highway. And a widow with more questions than answers concerning her husband's demise. If nothing else, she needed to retrace his footsteps. She needed to walk in his shoes and see the hotel where he'd walked away from her, from their life.

With a thought of Mark's reaction when he learned of her enterprise, she navigated the highway to the interstate and again headed for the city. Traffic had slowed considerably, with more headlights in the opposing lane than taillights in front of her. The downtown area would likely be crowded, especially if the uniforms had hauled Dr. Reddinger into a city building for questioning. If Mark was correct about the doctor's innocence, she felt bad for whoever had issued that warrant or participated in that issuance. Doubtful that arrogant surgeon would settle for an apology. She could imagine his recourse and she wouldn't blame him one iota. Once Reddinger's name hit the news, his reputation would suffer tremendously, regardless of his innocence . . . and maybe she was a journalist after all. In fact, she might enjoy an exclusive interview with the doctor, in which case, she would offer his reputation a boost. Time would tell. Maybe once he was fully exonerated with the actual psycho in custody, she would contact him.

An odd thought crossed her mind then, a thought of her caution which seemed genuinely strange. She'd never actually preempted a confrontation with a criminal, but she'd never consciously avoided the possibility. The reason, she knew, was the tiny little tadpole floating quietly in her gut. Taking him into that house, the lair of a possible psychopath . . .? If she had truly believed Reddinger was a deranged killer, could she have walked so smoothly into that house? Would she have risked subjecting her infant to such a vile atmosphere?

In retrospect, she considered her efforts in Elmview, belatedly realizing how her subconscious had exercised caution there. Neither had she visited the country lane where Jack Trumble had met his end nor scanned newspapers for snapshots of the accident. Undoubtedly, a photo had made the front page of the local paper, but she hadn't even asked Donna to search the recent issues. Not once, had Ronnie sought the realtor's address or sped past his real estate office. She hadn't spoken directly with anyone involved in that crime. Unnaturally, she had remained at the periphery of that investigation, as if to venture too close would, in some way, jeopardize Tad's health. If, as the latest study indicated, a fetus could be influenced by reading or listening to music, then it was a safe bet, that same mysterious detail could pertain to other aspects of life.

She hadn't asked Len for snapshots of these murders, had, in fact, failed even to ask for a detailed verbal analysis of the autopsies . . . and in that detail, she realized her subconscious decision concerning another recent death. Not once . . . not once had she asked to view the remains of her husband, or the autopsy, or any snapshots of the crash. Was that decision based on her inability to face those facts, or more basic . . .? A subconscious desire to protect her unborn child from a memory he might retain through her association?

In either case, she was no longer an investigative journalist . . . and recalling the chill in Reddinger's house, she wondered at her innate talents. Could she have blocked any impressions or sensations she might have received to protect Tad? Was it possible that her subconscious had shielded him deliberately?

Only more questions and doubtful she could discuss those curiosities with Dr. Blackwell to wonder if all pregnant women underwent such extraordinary experiences. She wasn't normal. Had never been normal. Forever she had suffered the influence of impressions and intuitions to steer her toward the heart of a story and generally trouble. Perhaps, those same intuitive senses were leading her in an opposite direction, now, if only to protect her infant. And she could just imagine trying to explain that curiosity to Blackwell. Bad enough, he had nearly insisted on administering a sedative a few days earlier. If she even mentioned Tad's timely discontent at curious moments, Blackwell might insist on more than a tranquilizer. The only one who might believe her, who would understand these weird epiphanies, had abandoned her.

By the time Ronnie rolled under the elaborate entrance to the Lakeview, her curiosity had melded into mild, unresolved anger. Handing the keys to the valet attendant, who eyed her with genuine curiosity, she commented, "Leave the keys at the front desk under the name of Mark Jarvins."

"Uh, yes, ma'am," he said and pocketed the twenty she palmed him as he slipped behind the wheel.

Striding through the glass doors, she passed through the lobby, hearing, and ignoring a cranky child whining to a man attempting to book a room despite the receptionist's insistence of no vacancies. Passing around the corner as the child started to cry, Ronnie ignored the elevators and continued walking down the hall toward the rear entrance.

Car keys already in hand, she passed through the rear exit door and continued off the sidewalk. The distinctive scent of fish and a distant lapping of waves hitting rock reached her senses as she scanned the lot, searching, locating the little black car beneath an arc light. Apparently, the attendant had given the car its due and offered a position of safety. Spotting Mark's car rolling into a more shaded spot across the lot, Ronnie considered offering the valet her appreciation, then thought better of it. She would rather not be seen departing. Sidling toward the shadow of bushes, Ronnie reconsidered her foolishness. If Mark wanted to know if she was in her room, he wouldn't ask a valet attendant; he'd simply flash his badge at the desk and demand her room number. When that failed to produce results, however, he might be inclined to ask questions.

Even as she stooped, welcoming the shadows, she wondered at her further foolishness and fleeted a thought of her similar venture in another parking lot not long ago. Maybe she should become a cat burglar or some such thing. God knows she was sneaking around more now than ever before—sneaking out of her own blasted apartment, navigating alleys with the headlights off, sneaking into hotels and parking lots. Doubtful, this could be considered a good influence on her unborn child. God forbid, he was paying attention at the moment, but even as she graced that thought, she felt him squirming just a tad. In fact, he had apparently decided to wake up with a vengeance, and she hoped this wasn't an indication of his desired schedule when he drew breath.

One hand over her waist, tucked under her coat, she watched the attendant stride past without a second glance and reconsidered the car's safety and hotel security. It shouldn't be this easy to walk around an allegedly secure lot. When the guard passed through the rear doors, she scanned the lot for signs of other occupants or security guards, then pushed to her feet, stepping from the shadows and continuing toward her car. Foolish. The attendant would see her drive past—

A sound, a movement, a breath. Alarmed, abruptly, her senses keened, and her attention darted, scanning the nearest cars, her own just ahead. She felt it . . . felt someone . . . him. Without a second or first thought, she pivoted, knowing she would face Dominique Jardonet. Still, she wasn't prepared for the man to halt three steps away. Her breath caught; her focus riveted. He stood as tall as Jade and wore the same physique, a body she'd come to know as intimately as her own. A mustache . . . wire-rim glasses . . . a baseball cap pulled low, matching the silky sports jacket.

"Please, mademoiselle, do not scream," he said in a voice an octave deeper but still too near the voice she longed to hear.

Her senses reeled with darkness closing around her mind. Swaying slightly, she managed a step to offset the collapse. A mistake . . . her knees buckled, and the world spun out of control.

CHAPTER 20

Without a thought, Dominique stepped smoothly and swept her feet off the pavement as her body collapsed limply within his arms. Heart hammering, he stooped and collected the Maserati keys, remembering . . . remembering the first time he'd scooped her off her feet. A parking lot behind an Inn then, too. She'd suffered a concussion, fainted, and awoken in his arms. He'd already loved her then, and he loved her still. Cradling her carefully, he moved to the Maserati and stooped at the passenger door, unlocking the car and sliding her smoothly into the passenger seat. How he had wanted to slay that maniac a lifetime ago. He remembered little of the beating he'd delivered in place of a lethal blow, remembered his heart hammering then as it was now with a thought of Veronica hurt at a madman's hands . . . But the hands to hurt her this time were his own.

Striding around the car, he slipped into the driver's seat, fumbled with the ignition against a tremor, and started the car. Where he would go, where he would take them, he had no clear vision. Somewhere away from this lot, away from the hotel, away from anyone who could harm his wife or child. He was Jade Laquette . . . and this woman was his wife, his love, his life . . .

And she'd probably want to kill him when she awoke. A wry smile twitched his lips as he glanced at the sleeping princess. Without a doubt, she'd want to kill him, and with his thought, he sped from the parking lot, barely slowing to launch past the entrance and onto the street seconds before the valet attendant reached his station. Not fully concentrating, his attention divided between glances at the woman next to him and the street ahead. On autopilot, he navigated through the city and onto State Rt. 20, heading east, paralleling the lake. Not many tourists visited Lake Erie's shore this late in the season. He found the entrance to Cleveland Lakefront Park that boasted swimming and boat docks and wound beneath the barren trees. Driving as close to the beach as he could, he found a secluded nook, buried the black car in shadows, and dispatched the engine.

Not since talking to his father had he succeeded in banishing this lovely image from his mind. Sitting within the shadows, he rested sideways, admiring the contours of her serene face, the stream of black silk spread about her shoulders. She slumped at an angle, and a natural smile curved a corner of her lips. A million times in hi mind, he'd lain awake at night, simply gazing at her in a similar pose. He remembered the first time he'd slept with her, although he hadn't slept a wink. For hours, he'd simply held her hand, admiring her features from her pixie nose to her long lashes to the curve of her lovely lips . . . lips that had driven him wild throughout those endlessly long hours. In all his life, he had never merely held a woman's hand, had never rested enthralled by the sight of a sleeping woman. With her, he'd kept his counsel, relying on his sixth sense rather than rousting her from a sound sleep. The bruises on her cheek and lips had nearly driven him to madness. If not for the subsequent arrest, her assailant would have died that night. Never had Jade Laquette come closer to killing another man . . . and over a woman he'd professed to despise.

Shaking his head, he cast his gaze toward the darkness ahead, panning his focus across the black horizon. Where lake water ended and night sky began, he couldn't judge, and the low-hanging clouds offered no indications, blocking even a hint of stars. What to do . . . what to do now that she was safe? She no longer knew him . . . That much was clear. In those seconds before her collapse, he'd sensed her estrangement. She believed her husband dead and buried by at least a dozen hours. And in his way, he knew the partial truth in her revelation. He wasn't the same man who had stood on a sidewalk and watched her drive away. Whether that man had ever truly lived, he couldn't be certain. For her, he had become Jade Laquette . . . For her, he had become Dominique Jardonet. Who was he now? A phantom thing, perhaps. A dark and dismal spirit to float from one identity to another, changing names as often as he changed his clothes. How could he expect her to love him still? He had betrayed her. He had, in fact, killed her husband and made her a widow at the age of twenty-six.

At the soft breath and groan, his attention riveted to watch her animating. A hand lifted, brushing at her face as she lifted her head. Not slow . . . never slow, she awoke fully, sitting up, darting her gaze through the glass and pivoting her attention on him with a short breath.

"Please, madame, do not hold your breath again," he suggested gently.

"Wh—" She blew her breath out, took another, and recovered her quick wit. Her voice adopted a sharp edge that he recognized all too swiftly. "Where the hell are we?"

"A place where we can speak without ah . . . an aud`ienze."

"I'm not sure that we have—" She stopped short. Her eyes sparked blue fire even in the dreary light touching them from a distant streetlight. "On second thought, maybe we do need to talk, Mr. Jardonet."

Anger didn't mask the pain in her voice, the grief in her mind. He felt them both, his heart aching. How he longed to reach over and clasp her hand, but he forced his restraint, knowing her well enough to judge his precarious position. Undoubtedly, she carried her gun in her purse, and he was nearly certain that she considered drawing it. That he could never fully ken the future in her regard fleeted in his mind as he asked, "You hov ques`tions?"

"Oh, there's an understatement if ever I've heard one," she said in a low volatile tone. "Why don't you start by telling me who the hell you are."

He hesitated, holding her gaze at an angle, and answered quietly, "I think you know."

"No," she said in a hollow tone. "I think maybe I knew who you were once . . . At least once a few million years ago," she stated. "And that's the only part I have right, isn't it? For a little while, you were a man I knew as Jade Laquette."

"I'm ah . . . I'm not sure I'm following you," he said honestly.

"Let's try something a little easier, then," she said as she pinned him in a shiny gaze. "Didn't you ever hear of the word *divorce?* Granted, it's not a pretty word, but it beats the fuck out of *deceased* and *widowed*."

She'd reached her own conclusions. Perhaps, semi-proper conclusions to his sudden dismay. His heart hammered a more leaden beat as he cast his gaze toward the water. The estrangement he'd grasped had nothing to do with a physical difference between himself and his former self. As he would know when he stood within sight of her, she'd known his physical self even before she'd turned and looked at him. That she would believe he'd done this to escape a life with her . . .? Whether it pained him or angered him, he couldn't decide. He wasn't Jade Laquette, not a man burdened by his past or his talents. Something had truly happened to the man she'd met and married. Who he was . . . It was far darker, and from that darker essence, he would protect her again and again. Even if it meant hurting her.

"Why, damn you?" she asked softly, angrily. "Why did you do this to us? To me? Was it . . . was it a joke from the start? Was it all a lie?"

His gaze turned slowly to find her still looking at him, the shallow light catching on the tears glistening on the surface of her eyes. “I am the lie, Veronique,” he said quietly.

For a moment, she glared at him through her tears, then turned toward the dark water ahead. “Damn you,” she said in a leaden tone.

“But what I feel for you is not a lie,” he continued quietly, watching her head turn further from him.

“I . . . I almost prayed I was wrong,” she said in a distracted, hollow tone. “I . . . I came here hoping I’d find answers . . . And hoping I wouldn’t. I wanted to . . . to walk in the footsteps of the man I lost. I—“ She hesitated, then huffed a soft, quivering laugh of disgust. “I managed to convince myself that my husband really was dead in the physical sense.” The pain echoed far louder than the strength in her voice as she continued. “It might have been easier to face that than to know what a fool I’ve been.” Her head turned; her eyes lanced him. Her lovely face wore the conflict. “You are the same man who walked me to the alter though. The same man who fathered the child I’m carrying.”

Her contempt spilled forth on the sheer detachment and scathing notes regarding their joint creation.

“Answer me, Mr. Jardonet. I want to hear you admit those words just once, then you’ll never need to acknowledge those details again.”

The finality of that promise held him silent momentarily, his gaze heating. “I am not the same man you married, madame—“

“You’re lying,” she snapped. “And if nothing else, Mr. Jardonet, you owe me that single truth.”

“I’ve given you the truth,” he answered in a descended tone. “The man you married is gone.”

She studied him for a long moment, then hissed softly, “Then I truly did bury my husband, and there’s nothing more we need to discuss. So . . . get the hell out of my car.”

“No,” he said simply, his gaze steady.

“Fine,” she snapped. “Then keep the fucking car, but I suggest you not drive it around too long. I will report it stolen.” She pivoted her attention and clasped the door handle.

His hand lashed out, clasping her wrist nearest him, drawing her angry gaze with the start of a curse on her lips. “You hov never walked away from a fight, Veronique. Do not walk away from this one.”

“I only fight battles that are worth winning.”

The sparks under his palm drew her focus, and if not before, she knew at this moment, he truly was the physical aspect of the man she'd married. His gaze lowered, feeling the warmth, the heat of her anger and pain, the rage wrapped in as much love as hatred for him at this moment. Finding her eyes, his glare softened. "Perhaps, this is the next lifetime, Veronique. Perhaps, in this lifetime, I will win an argument?"

Her gaze held him as the memory of her words regarding winning an argument sailed across her mind. '. . . Not in this lifetime, sire . . .' "Why, damn you?" she asked more quietly. "Why have you done this? Why are you doing this? How, for God's sake? How could you do this to me, to us? To your own child? How could you let me believe that you were dead? Didn't anything we share mean a damn thing to you? Was it all a fucking game?"

"There are reasons I cannot explain, Veronique."

"Then fuck you," she snapped, as hot as she was hurt an instant before. "I should have known. I should never have trusted . . ."

She had trusted . . . and as he looked into her eyes, he could nearly hear her thoughts spinning at light speed. In fleeting glimpses, he saw a flower-draped casket, saw his father, felt her pain and anger.

"Damn you," she said in more natural distress. "Why . . . why can't you just talk to me? Why am I still the one ranting and raving? Why is it so damned hard for you to trust me half as much as I trusted you? What was it you said . . .? When you can, you'll answer me? Those were your words when I asked you for your insight. You told me never to apologize for asking. You said we had a strange relationship . . . Well, I'm asking you now. Why? Why have you destroyed the life you seemed to want as much as me? Why are you making me feel like a fool for falling in love with you? Are those answers too much to ask?"

His gaze listed toward the water, his thoughts turning in slow circles. Unconsciously, he found his cigarettes and cranked the window open a crack before lighting up.

"I don't know if you owe me the answers, Mr. Jardonet, but I am asking."

"I . . . I am my father's son," he said as he blew an exhale of smoke toward the crack. "That's a fact I have attempted to deny for most of my natural years, Veronique, but one I can no longer avoid. Any more than I could avoid doing what I've done this week. Et's not much of an answer or an explanation, nor is et an excuse. Perhaps, et is a curse to see too many possibilities, to know too much in advance, and to make choices. That I have lost you because of it, I have no doubts. But I have regrets. If I had seen another way, I would have shosen et, and perhaps, therein lies the true curse upon the Jardonet males, to see only the bleakest course to follow, to destroy whatever good we manage to do. I don't have that answer, but I do have regrets. What I feel for you hasn't died with the name I gave you, but that name, the man who wore it . . . I don't think he ever truly existed. Maybe . . . maybe et is better if you hate me as much as you once loved me, mon amour. I fear I would only bring you greater heartache and pain, and et is not a thing I'd wish on an enemy, much less a woman I love."

"How? How can you even say that the man I married didn't exist?" she asked in a soft careful tone. "And then claim to love me?"

Holding her hurt gaze, he asked quietly, "Would the man you married hurt you as I have hurt you, Veronique? This image you have of him . . .? Would he have done what I've done?"

She looked at him for a moment before turning her gaze toward the water. "I should hate you, shouldn't I?" she asked toward the lake. "Regardless of who you are or what you were to me, or who you pretended to be . . . you knew all of this was coming. And you let me believe that we'd have a life together." Her gaze came with the pain again on the surface of her eyes. "Was it all a lie? Was everything I ever thought and felt with you based on a lie?"

"Perhaps, not, Veronique," he said quietly. "Perhaps, only in death could Jade Laquette truly be free to be with you."

"So, you killed him," she said in a hollow tone. "And everything decent and kind inside of you died with him, didn't it? Or maybe you weren't lying. He never really existed. It's been a lie and a game from the first time we met. You are Dominique Jardonet. You were Jardonet even then. The little boy I met on a playground years ago—? That was Jade Laquette, but he died long before now, didn't he? He died with his mother."

Not too long after her, he might have admitted but held silent, his gaze trailing away from the heat of her anger. He'd lost her. If nothing else, he knew she'd never love or trust the man he'd become. In her eyes her husband was dead, and with every word he'd spoken, he'd only convinced her more. No matter how badly he longed to reach over and draw her into his arms, to feel her warmth and recover what he felt missing between them, he sensed the futility. He'd betrayed her, murdered her husband, and destroyed the life he'd fully believed they would share. If only he could be as naive now as he had been days earlier, with only impressions to guide him. The spontaneity of life had abandoned him. With a mere fleeting glimpse, he knew he'd slide from this car, knew she'd drive away. Nothing resolved between them.

Sighing heavily, he met her still angry eyes. "Nothing I say will shange what I have done," he said quietly. "And there are no explanations good enough, Veronique. Perhaps, someday, you will forgive me, but that day has not come." He barely paused before commenting, "I'll ask only one favor of you, ma chérie. Seek no further answers here. When you get to your hotel, pack your bags, and return to your home. It is not safe in this city."

She studied him a moment, then commented, "You know they have the wrong man in custody."

He considered, then shrugged, "Possibly."

"You were helping with this case. Do you intend to finish it?"

"Sometimes we are not given a shoice," he said offhandedly and reached, twisting the ignition key and straightening in the seat.

"I'm not leaving," she said as he backed onto the lane.

His foot touched the brake, and he looked into her eyes. "Is that a fact?"

"Take it to the bank," she snapped.

"We will see," he said and touched the gas. The car jumped backward at his command. Spinning the wheel and slamming into gear, he sped beneath the trees, igniting the lights belatedly.

"Your driving hasn't changed," she said offhandedly, her gaze turned toward the side window. "Obviously, that was the real you."

Refraining from a comment, he continued in silence, taking the shortest route into the city and pulling to the curb a half block from the hotel. Looking over, he commented, "You brought something for me."

For a half second, she thought he referred to the ring and cross she gripped in her pocket, but the revelation slammed her as he removed the keys from the ignition. *The box . . . that stupid box in the trunk.*

"I'll take it now," he said and slipped smoothly from the car.

He wasn't the man she'd married. Not the same man she'd watched in her side view mirror several mornings ago when departing on her trip to Elmview. But Ronnie couldn't deny she felt something for him still.

Anger, she decided as she stepped from the passenger seat, glimpsing him striding smoothly toward the trunk. An almost uncontrollable urge to circle the car and slam him in the jaw started her moving toward the end of the

Maserati. Not the same man. This one was a stranger. His tone, his intensity, even the way he moved with the dangerous grace of a mountain lion—although she could find no immediate fault in any of those attributes. She should hate him. Maybe she did hate him. Whoever he was, whatever he had been or had become, he was responsible for the pain and turmoil in her mind.

As he ducked to collect the box from the trunk, her hand slid smoothly to the hood. Uncontrollably, she applied a quick pressure, and if he had hesitated even for an instant, he would be seeing stars. Wearing a less-than-pleasant smile, she snapped the trunk lid down, barely grazing his fingers. Catching the spark of fire behind the clear pane glasses, she glimpsed the shadow of a smirk twitch at the corner of his mustache. "Sorry," she said innocently.

"Because I was slightly faster, I wonder?" he asked with a hint of amusement.

"I can't say that it's been a pleasure meeting you, Mr. Jardonet," she said as she collected the keys from the trunk. Maintaining her indifference with iron resolve, she looked into his eyes. "But if you ever come within ten feet of me or mine again, I won't even think about it—I'll just give you a permanent limp to remember me."

"I'll take sush into consideration, madame," he said and backed a step, canting his head as if granting her dismissal.

She started around the bumper but hesitated and looked at him, holding his gaze as she stated, "Goodbye, Jade." Not *au revoir*, she might have added as she continued to the driver's door, fighting a sting of tears. This time, it was goodbye, and she wondered if she should be grateful? If all people should be so lucky to have one last word with a dearly departed? God, she hated him!

Jamming the key in the ignition, she ignited the engine, slammed the car in gear, and cursed herself as the car jumped forward. Had she been thinking clearly, she might have hit reverse and tried again. If she had ever wanted—needed—to hurt someone, none more than the man fading in her rearview mirror. Uncontrollably, the image blurred under a wash of tears, and she cursed again while sweeping angrily at her eyes and slamming another gear. If she could just drive—just keep on driving until she ran out of blacktop . . . But that would solve nothing.

Cursing yet again, she swung into the hotel parking lot entrance, avoiding the valet corral and rolling smoothly between the tree-shrouded gates. It was already too late by the time she spotted Len Devinio standing with one of the attendants—way too late when she spotted Mark striding behind a line of cars.

Wheeling into the empty space beneath the vapor lights, Ronnie switched off the ignition and climbed from the car as both federal agents converged from different directions.

"Where the hell were you?" Len asked.

"I think you owe me an explanation," Mark stated.

He'd chosen the wrong time, the wrong woman, with whom to pull that macho arrogant crap. Her eyes catching fire, she snapped, "I don't owe you a fucking thing, Mr. Jarvins. I borrowed your goddamn car, and the next goddamn time you tell me where to wait for you, you better make fucking sure I'm not carrying a gun. Or you won't need to worry about catching a lift with a pal!"

"Uhhh, Ron?" Len asked with alarm and curiosity rising. "Are you all right?"

"I'm fine," she snapped, leveling her still-heated gaze on the man who stood at least a full head taller. "I'm just sick to death of men! All men! But especially the arrogant bastards who run around thinking they can dole out orders to women like they're King-fucking-Tut. Well, screw that shit," she stated and looked at Mark, who eyed her as if she'd grown two heads. "And screw you, Mr. Jarvins. I didn't marry you three years ago because I didn't love you the way a woman should love a man with whom she plans to spend a lifetime. And frankly, I didn't care for your holier-than-thou attitude either. I am not—and never was—some sniveling little mouse to run and jump at anyone's command, and you better know, if you have any aspirations toward matrimony, you're wasting your time with me. Now, both of you, stay away from me," she finished and might have made a grand exit if not for Len stepping into her path and catching her arm. "What part didn't you understand—"

"Ron, we need to talk to you about something," Len said carefully, his voice low and dark eyes more dreading than wary.

Alarm niggled at the nape of her neck. "What?"

"We uh . . . Well, we found something at Reddinger's house," he said hesitantly. "And to be honest, I'm not sure what to make of it."

Alarm rising, muscles gripping, she asked, "If it concerns me, I suggest you spit it out."

"Well . . . Shit, I really don't know what it means, honey, but the fact is, we found some receipts . . . and it looks like quite a few of the antiques in that house were purchased at Olden Time. Most of it—from what we could determine—was bought via phone and shipped COD. Did uh . . . did Jade ever mention anything to you? Anything at all about Dr. Reddinger?"

She considered, then shook her head absently. "The name didn't ring a bell when you said it earlier, and it doesn't now, Len, We do a lot of mail-order business though. We have a list of people from all over the country. Periodically, if we find something they're looking for, we give them a call. I know Jade keeps a camera handy for just that reason. Sometimes he sends a couple pictures first. With some of his better customers, he ships COD. Otherwise, he waits for a check to clear. Apparently, if Reddinger was receiving the merchandise up front, he was one of the better customers . . ."

Was there a connection? Did Jade have a connection to Reddinger and these murders? Those were the thoughts ringing in her mind and undoubtedly, spinning behind Len's dark eyes.

"What made you think of the art angle, honey? What made you ask about the receipts? Did you recognize something you saw?"

Remembering the overheard conversation in Reddinger's living room and the subsequent chat with the woman downstairs, Ronnie commented, "Those aren't easy questions to answer, Len. I noticed the antiques scattered around, but I can't say I identified any specific piece. Chalk it up to coincidences . . ." Not unlike her trip through Elmview. And was it another coincidence that her deceased husband had just pilfered a box from the Maserati's trunk—a box she'd intended to discard en route to Cleveland?

Inexplicably, uncontrollably, she shivered with an epiphany striking lightning in her mind. "Oh-mi-god," she muttered and darted her gaze toward the street entrance, hoping—praying—to see a car pulling in.

"What?" Len asked sharply.

"He knows," she said absently and looked at Lenny. "He does know! And I think he intends to face this wacko alone!" *God! She wanted to hate him!*

"Maybe you better tell me who you're talking about."

Recovering a half second after parting her lips on the word 'Jade,' she snapped, "Jardonet! Dominique Jardonet!"

"He was here? You saw him?" Mark asked, stepping closer for the first time.

Ignoring him, she continued to look at Len as she stated, "The answers, Len! The answers are in Olden Time, but Jardonet is here, and I think he already knows the answers. I think he's on his way to meet this wacko! He . . . Goddamn it, he told me not to seek the answers here, and I thought he was talking about Jade's accident. He told me to pack my bags and go home, that this city isn't safe. I think . . . I think he's in trouble, Len, and . . ."

And it would be worse than a plane crash! Dominique Jardonet was on his way to become the evidence to put a maniac away! "Goddamn him," she breathed softly, and her eyes stung suddenly. "Find him, Lenny. Put out an APB or something. I think he's driving a rental—dark blue or green! And keep your phone on. I'm going upstairs and calling Elaine. I'll get her to search our want files and pull every address from the Cleveland area. The answers are there." Not awaiting another word, she pivoted from Len's hold and sprinted toward the lighted doorway across the lot. "I think it was a Chevy!" she threw over her shoulder.

Passing through the entrance, she barely slowed before reaching the bank of elevators and slamming the arrow button between the doors. Huffing angry breaths and bouncing on her heels to hurry the car, she barely awaited the doors to part and flew inside, dodging the bellhop who started out. Swinging inside, she mouthed an apology and jabbed the 7th-floor button. Maybe she should have taken the stairs. It might have been faster. Cursing and watching the floor buttons ignite, pleading with them to go faster, she huffed another curse while leaping through the parting doors. Fumbling with her key, she reached the suite and stifled a breath while jamming the key, twisting the nob. In three quick strides, she grasped the receiver and stabbed the numbers to reach Elaine, glancing at her watch and uttering a silent apology. At nearly midnight, Elaine would be asleep . . . and the groggy voice awakening on the line only verified that thought.

"Elaine! God, I'm sorry for waking you," she huffed. "But it's an emergency."

"Ronnie?" Elaine asked, fully alert and anxious now.

"I don't have time to explain, Elaine. Trust me! This is urgent! I need you to go to the shop right away. Do you have a piece of paper and a pencil? I'll give you the number to reach me! I need you to call me as soon as you get there."

"Ahh . . . Honey, are you hurt? Do you need an ambulance?"

Remembering her quiet departure, Ronnie drew breath. "I'm not at the shop, Elaine. And no, I don't need an ambulance. I need you to check something in our files. It's terribly important. I'll explain as soon as I can. Please, can you go right away?"

"Ahhh . . .? You said you have a number to call you?"

"Do you have a pencil and paper?" Ronnie huffed, and with Elaine's quick affirmation, Ronnie recited the numbers off the phone base. "Hurry, Laney. It's mega urgent," she said, and the line went dead on Elaine's response. Up and pacing, Ronnie watched the clock, already counting the seconds, imagining Elaine yanking on a pair of pants and a blouse—probably polyester. Elaine favored polyester— "Hurry," Ronnie huffed, estimating the ten-minute drive.

Damn him! Just damn the arrogance and audacity of this man to make her love him, then mourn him, then hate him, then . . . *damn it. Then love him all over again. Damn it!* She hadn't fallen in love with Jade Laquette, not just a name. She'd fallen in love with Isaac Bently nearly from the moment he'd touched her hand. She'd fallen in love with him again when he'd kissed her. By the time he'd arrived in the Bentwood Inn intending to seduce her, she'd been more than willing to cooperate. Not a name, damn it. She had fallen in love with the man, and regardless of what blasted name he wore, she would keep on loving him. *Didn't he know that! The big handsome jerk! What did he think he was doing?* Making it easier on her? *Dead was dead, damn him! Whether he died in a plane crash or let himself get butchered by a maniac made no difference!* Either way, once he drew his last breath, he wasn't coming back, and at this moment, she would probably take him back even if he sprouted horns to match the green fire in his eyes!

Angry and anxious, she paced, muttering curses that would probably put a sailor to shame, then cursing again for being a lousy influence as a mother. Tad would probably pop out hissing 'shit' and follow up with a few choice words to curl Dr. Blackwell's straight gray hair.

"Damn it!" What was taking so long? Elaine should be in the shop. More than ten minutes had passed . . . She would need only three minutes to shut off the alarms, unlock the door, and ignite the fluorescent tracks to light the shop. Mentally counting steps, judging the minutes, Ronnie watched and paced as five more minutes passed, then remembered the reporters and that team of gentlemen who, she suspected, were FBI watching the shop. "Damn it!" Elaine had run into trouble! Without another thought, Ronnie settled onto the couch and lifted the receiver intending to call the Spencer abode. No dial tone? "Hello?"

"Ronnie?" Tim Spencer asked with a note of surprise.

"Tim?" Ronnie asked, likewise confused.

"Where the hell are you?"

"You called me," she stated, already annoyed with the mild accusation in his tone. "Where's Elaine?"

"Standing right here wringing her hands. She called me after you talked to her. She asked me to meet her here. What the hell's going on? Why aren't you upstairs asleep in this monstrosity?"

"Because I had something else to do," she snapped. "Would you please hand Elaine the phone? And since you're awake, maybe you could give her a hand."

"A hand doing what? Do you have a sudden anxious client—"

"Tim, ask Elaine to pull the notebooks we keep—our Want File?"

"Your what?"

"Damn it, would you pay attention! This is urgent! If you won't hand Elaine the phone, then ask her to pull the damned Want Files! Do it! She'll know what they are." Apparently, something in her voice sobered him. She heard him repeat her request and Elaine's mild surprise in the background. "Now why would she want that file?"

"Beats me," Tim said. "Sounds important though. If you know what she's talking about . . .?" His voice returned to the line. "Okay, she's getting them. Now, how about telling me what's going on?"

"I need you to go through those files and pull any names and addresses you find from the Cleveland area. Check the yellow pages in the phone book—go by area codes or zip codes if you can. I'll hold the line." She held her notebook and pen at the ready, not even positive when she'd collected her leather binder. "I need you to give me those names."

"Ronnie, I don't like to break this to you, honey, but it's after midnight. I doubt your customers will appreciate—"

"Tim, I'll only say this once," Ronnie interrupted calmly. "I am not suffering a nervous breakdown. A man's life is in danger, and the means to save him may be in those damned files. Now, please, either help Elaine go through those books or get the hell out of my store."

Rather than comment, he turned his voice from the receiver and instructed Elaine to begin the search. "All right, she's looking," he said then. "Now, assuming you're in Cleveland, tell me what the hell you've gotten yourself into, and tell me exactly where you are."

"It's a long story, Tim."

"Start by telling me—what man? Is it Len?"

"No . . . damn it, it's J . . . Jade's half-brother."

"Christ," Tim hissed. "This Jardonet character? Len told me a little about him. So, where is he? How's his life in danger? And how the hell did you get caught up in this?"

"I came looking for answers. If I knew where he was, I wouldn't be on this damned phone, and if you accuse me of getting myself into something I can't handle—if you even allude to the fact that you consider me an incompetent, naive female—I really will need to unload a whole world of frustration on you, and it won't be pretty. Now, help Elaine, Tim, I need those names, and Len's expecting my call ASAP."

"Damn it," Tim huffed. "Then that really was you with Len. Donna thought it looked like you. We caught a segment on the eleven o'clock news, but from what we saw, it sounded like that lunatic was in custody. How did Jardonet get into the picture, and what do these names—"

"Tim, I think they have the wrong man, and I'm not the only one," she said bluntly, leaving him a moment to grasp her meaning. "We think . . . no, I know," she corrected. "The real maniac is somewhere in that file. It . . . I think it has something to do with—with what happened to Jade. Please, help her, now, and quit wasting time. I think Dominique Jardonet is in trouble."

"All right, hang on. I think she found one."

CHAPTER 21

As Tim began to cite the first name and address, Ronnie heard a raucous in the background and recognized the ping of the side-entrance doorbell.

Tim muttered a curse before commenting, "Sounds like we have company. Any chance Len sent us a little help?"

"Probably a good chance," Ronnie answered, thinking of the surveillance team outside of Olden Time. They'd followed her from Elmview three days ago, and apparently, they'd hung around, although she hadn't seen them after the funeral.

"Hold on," Tim stated, and covered the mouthpiece, muffling his words. "You can go let them in, Elaine."

At the same time, Ronnie heard a knock at her door. Either Len or Mark had probably followed her from the parking lot. "Hang on, Tim," she stated and set the receiver and notebook aside as she pushed off the couch. At the door, she hesitated by habit, asking, "Yes?"

"It's me, Ronnie. Open up."

Relieved, Ronnie spun the knob, barely sparing Mark a glance. "I think a few of your associates just arrived at Olden Time," she said as she pivoted, heading for the phone. "Tim's with Elaine. We only have one name so far, but with a little help, we should have the whole list pretty fast." As she lifted the receiver, Mark reached her side, and under the grip on her shoulder, slight pressure, she pivoted her gaze. An unnatural prickle touched the edges of her mind even before Mark clasped the receiver and slipped it from her grip.

"Maybe you better sit down, Ron," he said with a disheartened shine in his tense pale eyes. Rather than lift the receiver to his ear, he leaned and hung up while applying a quick pressure, tipping her off balance to land, a little clumsily, on the couch.

Startled, she collected into a more natural sitting position, watching him lift the phone base. Unlike her husband, who generally sported several archaic rings, Mark's fingers were bare, and his knuckles appeared oddly magnified as he inverted the cloddish base, and tugged the phone jack from the back. Another prickle lifted under her hairline and skittered down her spine. His eyes—something wrong. Distress? Resignation? What the hell . . .? She'd never seen him more troubled. More solemn. Her curiosity fled behind her rising annoyance as she considered the symbolism. Clearly, he intended to unplug her from any further investigation.

He put the phone aside and backed a step, darting his gaze about the room as if orienting himself, then looked down almost sadly. Despite the hour, he appeared unruffled. He wore the same dark suit and long cashmere coat that he'd worn when arriving at the cemetery; the material barely concealed the slight bulge of his semi-automatic Glock in its shoulder holster.

"Mark, we don't have time—"

"Everything's under control, Ronnie," he interrupted quietly, his gaze landing on her with a more dispirited expression haunting his lean, sculpted features. "I really wish you hadn't come here."

Something in his voice, in his eyes, triggered an alarm in her mind.

"Do you remember how we first met?" he asked quietly.

Chicago, she remembered and nodded. Her intuition had led her to the heart of an investigation involving rape and murder. She'd become a serial rapist's next target after stumbling a little too close to the criminal's lair . . . But that wasn't the first time they'd truly met. Mark was referring to an earlier time . . . She'd been around fourteen or fifteen when Bobby had graduated from Harvard and Mark had graduated in the same class. The thought dated them, and for the first time, she considered the seven years difference between them.

"I think I was in love with you long before we ever really met," he said candidly, a slightly weary smile tilting his lips. "Destiny," he said, tongue-in-cheek. "You showing up in Chicago . . .? It just confirmed what I already knew. Sooner or later, I'd have arranged for us to meet. Socially, I could have justified marrying you."

Another alarm chimed with the words. *Socially?* The quiet emphasis on that word, the subtle insinuation that other factors might not be so easily dismissed, started her thoughts turning. Just where was this conversation headed? And why did he appear so damned resigned when they should be seeking the identity of a killer? "Mark, we really don't have time to get into this," she said reasonably. "We should be—"

"I really do love you, Ronnie," he interrupted, and his hands moved, one sliding under his coat as the other touched the lapel. "Unfortunately, I can't afford to take any more chances. You're a little too smart for your own good."

"Mark?" she asked, dumbfounded as the gun slipped from under his jacket lapel. Uncontrollably, she flashed a thought of Mark in the darkness . . . in an alley in Chicago. The maniac was down, pulled away, and thrown to the ground. Under Mark's protective arm, she'd been shaken. She'd hung onto him, needing his sturdy frame to keep her knees from buckling. Chicago. The alley . . . In shadows, the fellow had groaned, pushing off the gravel, collecting himself. He'd lost his grip on the knife—*he never reached for his knife*. Resounding, the blasts of gunfire reverberated off the stone walls as her stalker launched, skidding gravel and grit before striking the wall. In spasms, his limbs unhinged as bullets ripped his face, riddled his chest. She hadn't seen any gun. Only the knife. But in the aftermath, she'd heard Mark's report of the killer reaching for a firearm, leaving him no choice but to open fire. At point-blank range, Mark had fired . . . And he was holding his gun leveled on her now, his eyes conveying nothing of whatever turmoil existed behind his gaze.

"I wish this could have been different, Ronnie," he said quietly. "But I knew when we talked earlier—you wouldn't let this rest. Eventually, you'd have begun asking too many questions."

"You uh . . . you had Jade . . .?" With her thoughts racing, heartbeat quickening, she grasped the possibility. "You had Jade killed," she said absently.

Far too calmly, Mark stood holding his weapon steady despite the torment in his taut handsome features.

"Is that what I would have learned?" she asked, fearing the answer.

His eyes flashed annoyance; his cheek muscle twitched. "No. I can honestly say—I had nothing to do with your husband's demise," he said irritably "As I told you earlier, I do intend to get to the bottom of that. I'm tempted to believe the French government—his half-brother, to be precise—arranged for that development."

Obviously, he'd struck upon a partial truth, but if his expression and tone were any indications, he truly believed that Jade Laquette and Dominique Jardonet were two separate entities. How had Jade managed that? How had he arranged all of this . . . and did it matter? All too clearly, Ronnie realized she'd stumbled into something far more threatening than a single homicidal maniac in Cleveland. Mark Jarvins, a bona fide agent, one of the most valuable profilers in the Bureau . . . holding a gun on her because of something she could learn? About a serial killer . . .? About a plot to kill her husband . . .? What the hell was she missing? Where the hell was her husband when she needed him?

"Why would he . . .? Why would the French government want to kill him, Mark?" she asked as her mind raced in eccentric circles. Her purse rested on the table five steps away; her Midnight Special remained Velcroed to the inner lining. If he truly meant her harm—

"It's almost funny how things work out," he said absently. "Four months ago, I was called into what I believed to be a routine investigation. I honestly believed it was a coincidence, everything that happened in Bentwood, but now, I'm not so sure. In fact, with my new appreciation of psychic phenomena, I think there was a hell of a lot more to your husband than met the eye, and believe it or not, I'm almost sorry he's gone."

"What's going on here, Mark?"

"I find it a little hard to believe that you don't know, Ronnie," he said quietly, his gaze more intent. "You've spent the past several months with Laquette, and the fact that you're here leads me to believe he confided in you to a degree."

If only he had, she considered. "I'm at a serious loss," she admitted.

"That would be even more unfortunate," he said lightly and darted a glance, spotting her coat at the end of the couch. Sidestepping, he leaned and caught the cloth, lifted it toward her while rising.

She alerted then—heard the shift of cloth, a footstep, and keened to a sense of motion.

The 9 mm swung, and Mark's attention sprinted past her.

"Drop it," the deep voice commanded.

Mark's fingers sprung open, jolted, and his startled gaze spun. His focus froze, locking.

Jade! Only that revelation surfaced as her entire body prickled as if standing too close to a live electric wire. The 9mm Glock bounced off the couch cushion and tangled in her falling coat. With a dull thud, both landed at Mark's feet. Without hesitation, Ronnie sprang off the couch, consciously steering clear of Jardonet's line of fire, assuming he held a weapon. Darting a glance at Mark's frozen face, she kicked the coat aside, skidding the Glock across the carpet. At a safe distance, she ducked and collected the gun, scrambling backward to keep Mark in her sights as she brandished the weapon. He hadn't moved, not even to twitch, she noticed, and for the first time, looked toward where Jardonet stood.

Leaned, she corrected, as she scanned the length of him resting casually in the doorjamb leading to the bedroom. His arms loosely folded at his chest, he might have been posing for a fashion magazine. He still wore the baseball hat, one boasting the New York Yankees, but he no longer wore the clear pane glasses. Without them, he was unmistakably her husband in physical appearance. No gun . . . he held no gun. A slight smile flickered at the corner of his mustached lips, but his dark emerald eyes continued to study Jarvins as if pinning him in a high-intensity spotlight.

In split seconds, Ronnie raced through a barrage of emotions from relief to find him standing here, rather than meeting a maniac, to anger over the same, to confusion that he stood—unarmed—and held Mark in a frozen pose. Her attention wavered toward Jarvins, no less stunned to realize he had become the equivalent of a breathing statue. When she looked toward Jardonet, he was looking toward her. "What . . .?" *Or how?*

His gaze turned toward Jarvins, and he spoke in an amicable tone. "You have handcuffs in your pocket, mon ami. Bring them out and fasten them on your wrists."

Dumbfounded, Ronnie watched as Jarvins animated, obeying, reaching into his inside pocket and producing his handcuffs. His head canted, he appeared to watch his hands obeying the command.

"Now, sit down in that single chair," Jardonet commanded, and Mark stepped backward, settling into the only single chair in the circle. From his lean against the wall, Jardonet lanced her, his gaze indifferent. "Are you all right, ma chérie?"

"What the hell have you done? How . . .?"

He smiled, the same smile he always wore when he meant to disarm her anger. With a glimpse of his dimple and flash of ivories, he commented, "Then you are fine, yes?"

She glanced at Mark. In a hypnotic stare, he studied his cuffed hands. Shaking her head, she found Jardonet still watching her with his dimple twitching the corner of his mustache. "My God, what have you . . .? How are you doing this?"

"I did mention, I am not the same man you married," he said with an offhanded shrug and pushed off the wall. Advancing, he glanced at Mark, barely parted his lips.

"You heard what Mark was saying," Ronnie interrupted. "What's this about? What do you know about this?"

"More than I'll tell you," he answered smoothly, his head canted at an angle, his gaze intent. "At this moment."

Confused, her Irish ire rising, she bounced a glance off Mark. "You have him hypnotized."

"Suppose I can't deny that," he said and continued to study her.

Why that should surprise her, she couldn't fathom. There were moments—very coincidental moments in the past—when people just arrived as if summoned to lend a welcome hand—like Cy Bender coming to unload the pickup and Wade showing up to close the warehouse doors not long ago. The last time they'd made love . . . Only five mornings past, but it felt like a lifetime already. Uncontrollably, Ronnie flashed the image of her husband wearing jeans and a flannel shirt, oddly in sharp contrast to the fellow standing before her now. Black jeans, soft gray sweater . . . her focus skimmed down his long, sleek physique from his walnut waves to his black boots, her heartbeat quickening. They'd been standing in the alley behind Olden Time, discussing their trip to Elmview. She'd already won the argument to investigate the sense of foul play surrounding Jack Trumble's accident, and Jade had agreed to join her . . . He'd seduced her with a kiss before sweeping her into his powerful arms, starting them toward their apartment with else than murder on their minds . . . and Wade had arrived in time to cap the paint remover can and lock the warehouse doors in their wake.

Had that kiss sealed their fate—?

No . . . she refused to think, to remember.

This turn . . . to see Mark Jarvins tranced should not be a huge surprise, nor even a stretch of her imagination. Her husband had tapped into the human psyche more often than she could count, although he'd never needed to enlist that talent to seduce her. Damn it, this was different! In a split second, he had rendered Mark powerless, disarming him, freezing him . . . and if she wasn't so blasted confounded, she might be impressed. Instead, her anger rose.

"What the hell's going on here? And don't tell me that you can't—or won't—tell me," she snapped as her eyes lighted a crystal blue. "This . . . I've known Mark for years! If you know why he was holding this gun on me . . ." She held the heavy Glock, but even if she thought it would help, she couldn't bring it to bear on the man standing across the room. She might still like to hurt him but shooting him wasn't even a remote possibility. Muttering a curse, she half turned and found the chair near the table, settling into it before again looking to the man who seemed only to await her mental recovery. In her gut, Tad squirmed as if maybe he, too, sensed his father's undeniable presence. "Damn it," she muttered and recognized the quivering smirk in his mustache. "Don't even think about smiling now, or by God, I just might shoot you," she warned benignly. "If you know what Mark assumes I know, I think I have a right to hear about it, Mr. Jardonet. I have a bad feeling that my husband knew something that could get me killed whether I know any details or not."

"Unfortunately, I believe you're absolutely right. Fortunately, I've taken the necessary steps to remove the threat. It's just a matter of tying up a few loose ends."

She turned the gun, glancing down at it to Mark, then to her former husband. "Just a few, huh?"

"You would have been safer in Bentwood, mon amour," he said lightly and continued around the end table and couch.

"Bentwood," she said absently, glancing at the phone. "Oh-mi-God, Tim and Elaine." She started to rise.

"They're fine," Jardonet said with such quiet conviction that she stopped rising and settled again on the chair, looking at him in an entirely new light.

From the jump, her husband had exuded a quiet strength and confidence in his every action, but those traits had enhanced tenfold with every passing instant. He was in control. In total control, she realized at this moment. The apprehension he had always suffered when his talents took hold had abandoned him. No hesitation now, not to admit the unbelievable effects of his eyes on Jarvins, not to suggest he used something other than a phone line to know their friends were safe in Olden Time.

Ronnie needed a moment to process that revelation before she stated, "I was talking to Tim before Mark . . ." Damn it. Jardonet had been in the next room, listening to her entire conversation. "How the hell did you get in here?" she asked in irritation, and he smiled wryly. *Stupid question!* She was talking to a man who had just hypnotized a federal agent and held him in stasis even now. Shaking her head, she muttered, "Never mind. Just . . . just tell me what the hell's going on," she decided and held his gaze firmly. "And don't even think about hypnotizing me to shut me up."

"Wouldn't dream of it, mon amour," he smirked and reached into his jacket pocket, collecting a pack of cigarettes. Settling on the arm of the couch, buying time, he shook out a cigarette and caught the butt under his mustache.

Although she'd seen that action hundreds of times, there seemed something different in that now . . . as if the tiny flame from his butane lit an inferno in his green eyes.

Months ago, she'd sensed something almost dangerous about him, something nearly as seductive as it was threatening, and as she watched him, now, she realized those traits had risen to the surface. He could be cruel. He could be violent. He could use all the unbelievable talents inside of him without remorse or regret. At this moment, Ronnie had no doubts, he contemplated death and destruction, but not his own. "Tell me what this is about," she said more carefully, watching as he blew a thin trail of smoke from under his mustache. His eyes shifted, more catlike and wary than any time past. "I need to know."

"About?" he considered and glanced at Mark, then back. No amusement or friendliness emanated from his smirk. His eyes darkened with an unmistakable anger or hatred that sent a prickle down Ronnie's spine. This wasn't the man she'd married. Something truly had happened to him. "Murder, mon amie," he said without lifting his gaze.

Whether he meant those words regarding her question or her thoughts, Ronnie couldn't decide.

"Mass murder. Assassination. Serial killing," he shrugged, and his deep voice carried a poetic rhythm. "Howev`air you shooze to interpret it, the results are the same. Someone is left to mourn and grieve, as you may well testify. Sometimes those emotions boil and fester until the cycle begins anew in the living victims. Personally, I'd have made a grand assassin." His smirk enhanced. "Ah, but so the future holds that secret still. Will it come to pass? Who knows?"

"I'd venture to say—you do," she said, and his eyes flashed wild amusement.

"Know me well, do you, mon amour?"

"What do you know about four months ago?" she asked, thinking about what Mark had said moments ago. *No coincidences.*

"Are you asking what I know, now? Or what I knew then? There's a difference."

"Either or," she answered, watching him closely.

"Perhaps, we should roust your besotted lover and let him answer that," he commented.

"I'd rather hear it from you," Ronnie said quietly, her heart breaking to realize just how different he was. The man whom she had loved, who had loved her, seemed truly gone. This man who walked in his shoes was a stranger. A dangerous stranger.

"Hmm, fair enough," he said lightly. "I knew months ago that you were my catalyst, but impotent fool that I was, I refused to look too far into either the past or the future. That's not to say I was totally blind. Merely ahh . . . misguided," he said with a smirk and shrug. "Suppose in my way, I knew the futility of fighting fate, and the fates shined on me for a time, mon amour. I lived in a vacuum for a very long time, Veronique. You gave me substance. To love you even for a day would have been worth a lifetime to me. Believe that as you will or will not. The truth is, I couldn't see what the future had in store for us, or perhaps, I would have spared you the pain I've caused you. The past is irreversible. To ponder ifs and would haves is useless. I can only admit—what I know of four months ago, now, leads me to believe that we truly had no shoice, neither of us."

He paused, dragged from his cigarette, and glanced at Mark. With an exhale of smoke, he continued, "Maybe as much as twenty years ago, our course was set. I know for a fact, belatedly, that I did see the future as much as two decades ago. I knew when I first saw you that we'd see each other again, our lives would twine. Days ago, I gained only impressions on which to rely—along with brief glimpses which—in my own impotent way—I attempted to reject and recant as imagination. To see too far ahead, to know too much in advance, it could drive a sane man mad . . . As surely as it could drive one mad to see every death at every instant. A safety device in my nature, perhaps. I am only half mad."

"Mad as in angry, I won't doubt," she said carefully, gaining a sense of speaking with the man behind the boy she had known as Jade Laquette. The man she had never been allowed to meet.

He smiled almost gently. "I do love you still," he said quietly. "But that won't be enough, Veronique, not enough to keep me from hurting you. When this began, I was a shild, literally and figuratively speaking. I had no clear grasp of what I saw or felt. My clarity of insight might be better explained like a shild viewing a flower blooming. Nothing of the mechanics or details reached me in those early years. I had visions, yes. But did I know that flowers pollinated other flowers? That bees used pollen to make honey? Did I even know the name of the flower I watched bloom? Nothing of the mechanics touched me, but in my case, it was somewhat more like watching a nightshade plant blossom. Deadly. I didn't understand death any more than the next shild. Complicate that with the fact that I could read a book before ever learning the alphabet," he shrugged and smiled. "Imagine my surprise to learn that Nostradamus was dead. I had a horribly confusing shildhood. It took forev`air for me to realize

I lived in the twentieth century. Sometimes, thanks to my mother's insatiable appetite for old relics, including old books, I had a difficult time distinguishing between light bulbs and oil lamps. To me, people never really died. They just disappeared for a time."

He glanced down her front, and warmth passed through his shaded eyes before he smiled. "Please, take care in what you ask our shild to touch in those delicate years. If you'd like the little one firmly rooted, make sure you buy everything straight from the manufacturer. Don't even take the little imp to a museum until he is old enough to understand the difˆferenze between now and then. Visions of the past can be as devastating as those of the future."

"How long have you known?" she asked quietly, and his head canted in curiosity. "How long have you known you'd have a son?"

"Hmm, suppose I cannot deny knowing it. A slip of the tongue. I am sorry, mon amour. If I have ruined . . .? You already knew as well," he countered.

"Intuition," she said quietly. "I don't have your insight, but I do have something."

"That you do, mon amour," he said in an equally quiet tone, and the fondness lingering in his eyes countered the catlike shine. "Something almost blinding in its whiteness," he said with a kink in his mustache. "That, unfortunately, is as much your curse as my own."

"You're avoiding my question," she said quietly. "It's the same method, a different tactic. What's going on at this moment, hon, and how does it relate to what happened last summer?"

"I do love your fortitude," he said as if sighing in resignation, but his smirk lingered in a half smile. "Relative . . . you were my catalyst. Relative . . . nearly twenty years ago, I offered insights within an environment that someone had enough sense to record. Frankly, m' love, someone with the wherewithal to believe in psychic predictions, knew exactly where to find me and when. Four months ago, I regressed to my early childhood. I knew Len Devinio and Tim Spencer as I viewed them through the eyes of a ten-year-old. At that age and for about eighteen months of my life, I resided under government observation. I can only imagine what I might have divulged under their various techniques. What remains tantamount is simply this . . . I said enough to worry the people who contained me. I was considered a threat and undoubtedly slated for early extinction. Bluntly, m' love, they tried to kill me then. My father intervened and removed me from harm's way, not that I loved him for that. Not a day passes that I fail to wonder why I bother breathing. Death and destruction can get along well without me.

"In any event, you would like to know why your besotted lover turned assassin, and the answer is simple. The people who directed him to capture me a few days ago . . . by the way," he said offhandedly, smirking as he glanced to Jarvins and back. "He is pissed because I beat him to the punch line. If he could have killed me, he would have. My execution was to be a quiet affair, with my body shipped off quietly for dissection. I rather liked the poetic justice of instant cremation. The audacity of most megalomaniacs never ceases to amaze me," he said with a smile. "Imagine, if you will, attempting to assassinate a man, who you fully believe could see the future? Equates nicely with a dog attempting to catch its own tail. The bottom line is—I do see enough of my future to avoid those ultimate blunders and twixt fate a bit to keep my heart beating. You would think they might have figured that out twenty years ago."

"Why . . . why would someone want to kill you? What made you a threat . . .? Your mother's death?"

"Tip of the iceberg, so to speak," he said with a far more sober gaze and expression. "My mother was murdered because of something they believed she knew. Something I told her, and she ultimately used it innocently. As I mentioned, Veronique, I had pictures, but I nev`air fully understood what I saw or what it signified. What it amounted to was a conspiracy within your government. One which would have carried an impact then and would carry more impact now. Your friend here," he said with a glance at Jarvins. "He is a part of it, as is his fath`air and grandfath`air."

"What sort of conspiracy?" she asked carefully, hinged on every word and seeking the understanding which seemed slightly beyond her reach.

"Forev`air the American government has prided itself on moral righteousness. The American people, collectively, tend to view themselves as saviors. Save the poor, save the whale, save the rainforests. Hell, save the planet," he said with a ring of disgust. "What do you think would happen to that image if the American people learned that influential members in the government sanctioned Hitler's prescribed method of mass extermination of lesser races?"

"You're not saying . . .? Good God, honey. You can't possibly mean . . .? Our government didn't sanction Hitler," she decided.

"Hmm, no. Not the man himself, m' love, but those are the words that would ring off the lips of the world in the aftermath of enlightenment. Hitler, as far as I know, and I shooze not to delve deeper, died in a bunker with

Ava Braun. His followers, however, ballooned outward into the world, and the United States wasn't exempt from offering sanctuary. Key personnel in this government went a step further, mon amour. They offered at least one such fellow employment and lent him free reign to continue his life's work. Whether a human rights movement would be as effective as an animal activist group, I'd have to wonder. One certainty remains, howev`air. The American people would not be pleased to learn that in this modern day of moral and social consciousness, their government sanctioned human experimentation on men, women, and children behind closed doors. Complicate that issue further with the probability of mass genocide, and you have a recipe for disaster. Still further, muddle the soup by mentioning that this maniac not only had access, but a voice in the very Association to govern the health codes in the general population . . .? And you have a bomb about to explode across the continent."

She studied him, grasping the implications despite the lyrical ring of his deep voice and the faintly amused dark shine in his eyes. He wasn't fabricating or guessing. The scenario he'd just outlined was based on fact. "My God," she uttered.

"Considering which side of the battle He'd be on, I wouldn't call Him down just yet, m' love," he mused. "If we were to pit all the civilians in the states against all the health professionals, most of whom would be considered the enemy—if only by association—we'd have one hell of a civil war in the states. Toss in the religious aspect, and we'd have another Germany in the making."

"Oh my God," she repeated, considering the situation in the city around her. Dr. Whitman Reddinger . . . a health professional presently suspected of murder . . . white supremacists. Jewish victims . . . the swastika at the scene. Facts began tumbling through her mind, and she was making connections . . . too many connections with a thought of the mob she'd glimpsed on the television a few days ago. "This . . . the maniac here in Cleveland? He's part of it? You're saying this conspiracy is about to become a reality? There are connections to this madman?"

"To be honest, I think he's being used in a twofold plan. But, yes, he is connected," he admitted offhandedly. "First and foremost, Cleveland has become a testing ground of sorts. On its own, it provides the perfect atmosphere. Research and health care are a large part of the city's commerce. Like all major cities, it has its ethnic groups. If someone wanted to test the water in creating a civil war, this is the perfect location."

"That sounds like . . . it sounds self-defeating," she said absently. "You said conspiracy . . . Why would they risk exposure by . . .? Oh my God, you're suggesting there's a long-range plan about to unfold. You believe they're going to expose themselves to what . . . to bring on a war?"

"Do you have any idea what would happen if the United States suddenly became the Divided States at this point in time?"

The possibilities and probabilities were endless!

"Exactly, but foremost, the States would be wide open for outside attack. America would be vulnerable."

"I don't like to break this to you, honey, but you're scaring the hell out of me," she said honestly, her attention riveted on the man who rested so casually on the arm of the couch six feet away. "You're discussing the possibility of a designed World War III with its roots firmly entrenched in American soil. Please, tell me that's not exactly what you're telling me. Convince me, here and now, that we don't have some megalomaniac sitting in our Nation's Capital, possibly conspiring with other foreign powers for the ultimate hostile takeover."

"I've been to WW II," he commented. "It was an ugly place, m' love. If I didn't like it in the past, what makes you think I'd let it become the future?"

She stared at him more openly, confused and tense.

"Really, mon amour, I'm a man of insight, whether I care for that detail or not. Wisdom, I can't claim to have in abundance, but listen carefully, now, and receive the answer to your questions and fears." He barely paused, donning another of his enigmatic smiles. "You asked why someone would consid`air me a threat. Bear in mind, they tried to kill me at eleven years old. Futile. I saw it coming. My father, likewise, glimpsed the possibility, and thus, I survived. Eighteen years later, they felt certain enough of something I said back then to strategically send one of their own to a location that I apparently mentioned. Obviously, they couldn't kill me outright without knowing what I might have conjured up in my long absence. The plan then was to lure me into their madness and assess my skills against their own. Imagine their surprise to learn that I'd been visiting close to their chosen one here in Cleveland? Boy, talk about paranoia," he said with a smirk. "They really couldn't decide whether to kill me or catch me. Complicate that detail with my marriage to the daughter of one of the most influential men in the Capital who just happens to be a real patriot . . .? My, my, my, but they did have a mess."

"Did. That's past tense. You . . . you said loose ends. You've . . .? Somehow, you've stopped this? You've stopped them?"

"Me, personally? Au contraire, mon amour. I've been too busy sorting out who and what I am, a futile exercise," he said with a smile. "I do have things I intend to oversee personally though," he said and looked toward Jarvins. Mark hadn't moved more than a twitch since this frightening enlightenment had begun. Almost in a friendly tone, Jardonet commented, "You are paralyzed from the neck down, Mr. Jarvins, but you are awake and clear-headed."

That he might have spoken aloud for her benefit, Ronnie had little doubt. Stunned, she watched Mark blink and jerk his head. On his lap, his caught hands sagged within the iron, and he trailed his focus downward. His face gripped in an expression of horror and confusion before he darted his pale blue eyes about and landed on Jardonet. "You," he heaved.

"Sadly, mon ami, you are correct to accuse me," Jardonet said with a mocked sorrow. "Feeling a bit limp, are you?"

Jarvins glared at him momentarily, then pivoted his gaze toward Ronnie, appearing somewhat desperate as he sagged deeper in the chair. "Ronnie . . . the gun! He's not your husband! He's Jardonet! Dominique Jardonet! He killed your husband!"

"Save your breath, Mark," she said absently, sensing where Mark's litany would lead.

"Ronnie, I can explain," Mark huffed. "I know how it looked when I pulled that gun on you, but I didn't think you'd cooperate if I just asked you. I know how you get when you're working on a story. I wanted to get you out of here. I knew he'd come back for you!"

"Interesting," Jardonet interrupted. "You've perfected the art of lying. Were I a lesser man like yourself, I'd almost believe your motives pure."

"I don't know what you've done to me, mister, but—"

"Something as effective as you did to me, without the need of a needle or chemical," Jardonet supplied.

"I don't know what you're talking about," Mark stated.

"Monsieur, you are a fine liar, and under other circumstances, I would appreciate your talent. Unfortunately, I am annoyed with you, mon ami. Not only have you assisted in attempting to kill me, but you came here to abduct and murder my half-brother's wife and shild—a woman you claimed to love."

Mark pivoted his gaze to Ronnie. "You know me better than that. You know I'd never hurt you. I came here to rescue you from this—"

"Mark," Ronnie said quietly while considering the integrity of her former husband's words. "You said earlier that I was too smart, but you're treating me like an idiot. A rescue attempt doesn't generally include holding a gun on the person to be rescued. I can understand if you're desperate and currently a bit worried, but don't take me for a fool."

"Ronnie, I'm a federal agent. This man is wanted for questioning. He is not your husband, honey. Unless you help me, now, you could be considered an accomplice in a federal—"

"Mr. Jarvins," Jardonet stated and drew Mark's focus.

Instantly, Jarvins' lips froze, his eyes glazed.

To the sound of a sigh, Ronnie looked to Jardonet and read the spark of anger in the emerald eyes.

"My tolerance isn't what it once was," he said offhandedly, appearing to apologize. "Have you heard enough lies, mon amour?"

"He did come here to murder me, didn't he?" she asked numbly.

"He had no shoice, mon amour. You are here. He could only assume you already knew too much. If you had waited for him in the car, I'm afraid you would be swimming in Lake Erie by now. He is not very industrious."

"He told me he came to Reddinger's house because he believed they had the wrong man," she remembered and studied the murky hazel eyes, the color of jade again. "When I mentioned my doubts about the doctor, you didn't disagree . . . Is he the killer?"

"Even if he were, the evidence against him would never hold up in court."

"Then he is guilty and . . . Mark intended to pull the heat off him? To help clear him?"

"A reasonable assumption," he said indifferently.

"Damn it, quit playing games, Mr. Jardonet," she snapped. "In case you haven't noticed, I'm already involved in this mess up to my eyeballs. I suggest you level with me. Is Reddinger the killer? And how do you intend to stop him?"

"You still don't trust me, Veronique," he said, donning a mocked pout in his expression. "Do you think me so incompetent that you would need to assist me to ensure your own safety?"

"Let's not get into trust, Mr. Jardonet," she said curtly.

"Obviously, a poor shoice of words. You are a wise woman, mon amour. So, let me be blunt. Do you believe I am so incapable of protecting you from a madman that you would insist on knowing all that I know?"

She parted her lips to fire another snappy comment but caught herself considering his words under his compelling gaze. This wasn't Jade. This wasn't the man who had promised to love and protect her in sickness and in health until death did they part. Dominique Jardonet had killed the sensitivities she'd loved in her husband, the vulnerabilities that had made him human despite his strange talents and insights. How or why no longer mattered. The facts rested before her. This wasn't Jade Laquette, and this man needed no one—least of all a wife and child to hold him down or stand in his way. Torn suddenly between her love for him, for the man he had been, and the reality that he rested across from her, she listed her gaze. He hadn't rushed headlong to face a killer and his own death. He wasn't a man to take risks, and with her thought, she realized the time they were wasting within this room as if he had all the time in the world to waste. Turning her gaze to find him still watching her, she thought she glimpsed an echo of her husband's warmth in his eyes but doubted it an instant later. "What do you intend to do, now, Mr. Jardonet?"

"Please, just Dom or Dominique?"

She shook her head, refusing to acknowledge an informality. If nothing else, an image of Jean-Pierre Jardonet halted even a thought to become friendly with this ghost of a man across from her. "What do you intend to do, now?" she asked again, refusing to be sidetracked.

"If I ask you, now, madame, will you return to your home and leave this investigation to me?"

She should give him credit for attempting to sound both reasonable and considerate. He could have just told her to butt out of his business, and clearly, this was his personal business. Her gaze trailed to Mark who rested in repose, staring at his knees. His head had fallen at an angle against the back cushion, and if not for his open eyes, he might appear asleep. Looking at Jardonet, she sensed him waiting. "What do you intend to do with Mark?"

"You are concerned on a personal level?"

Beyond the fact that he might or might not have meant to kill her . . .? She had known him for several years. And who should she trust? They were both strangers. Without a thought, she disengaged the weapon for the first time, laid it on the table, and pushed off the chair. Pausing momentarily, she gazed at Jarvins. She had believed herself in love with him once. They'd never become lovers. The intimacy she'd shared with Jade Laquette was a one-and-only event. Her gaze trailed to the man who rested in her husband's guise. One and only . . . and Jade was gone. This man who could walk away from her, who would walk away from her, who had destroyed everything they had shared . . . If this was the man she'd fallen in love with, love was more elusive and blind than she had ever imagined. To hell with him, too, she decided silently and turned away, walking heavily to the window. On a personal level, she was concerned for Mark Jarvins. But he'd walked out of her life, too. In fact, Mark had stormed out when she'd rejected his marriage proposal, along with his physical advances. That she had once believed herself in love with both men in the room behind her posed a wicked irony in her mind . . . And both of them might already be dead for as alone as she felt while parting the curtain and looking out at the black horizon.

Shivering internally, she wrapped her arms across her waist and hugged her elbows. She had Tad to think about, to worry about . . . and this wasn't the kind of life she intended to give him. In fact, she had already subjected him to too much violence and too many risks. Turning, she found Jardonet still gazing at her, his expression more pensive than any time past. "You don't have to ask again, Mr. Jardonet. I am leaving, but I suggest you leave Mr. Jarvins' fate in the hands of the proper authorities."

She glanced only once at Mark before she strode into the separate bedroom. She hadn't unpacked. In a few ticks, she gathered her bag, deciding the sooner she left Cleveland, the better. She could be back in Bentwood within two hours, or she could stop at a hotel en route.

Tired . . . she was so blasted tired all of a sudden. The bed seemed to swell in front of her, taking on the size and depth of a meadow. A warm breeze, scented with spring blossoms . . . The flowered quilt seemed to call to her, beckoning . . . .

CHAPTER 22

Dismayed, Dominique rested on the arm of the couch, staring at the paisley print on the cushion and cursing himself in several silent languages. He hadn't consciously decided to do what he'd just done. The thought of Veronique walking from this room, leaving him, the finality to wrap around her mind before she had decided to leave . . .? In split seconds, all the reasons he should let her go had flown by the wayside. He wanted her here, needed her here where he could see her and watch over her.

His mother should have beat him harder for mind-bending.

"Merde," he muttered.

A practical decision. A compassionate decision. After all, she had appeared exhausted, and he'd sensed her flagging energy. Allowing her to set out on a two-hour journey would have been dangerous. And he could justify his actions. After all, he hadn't glimpsed any accident on the highway. She wasn't about to fall asleep at the Maserati's wheel—not when she slept soundly in the next room.

"Damn it," he muttered and glanced at Jarvins. He'd seen this image of the federal agent in stasis before this moment, and he was just as certain suddenly that he would walk into the bedroom and gaze upon his sleeping wife. In her mind, he might be a *former* husband. In his own, she remained his wife, his lover, and the mother of his child. Damn her for coming to Cleveland! She'd never appeared in any of the images he'd glimpsed of Cleveland, but then, he rarely gleaned even flashing images of the future in her regard. Irritating, to say the least, when she and her cargo were the most important aspects of his life.

She'd attended his funeral. He'd glimpsed her sitting, standing, kneeling, in St. John's Catholic Church in Bentwood. Shedding silent tears, she'd endured Fr. Groggan eulogizing over Laquette's coffin. He'd seen her inside their apartment, ambling from room to room, listless and agitated, grief-stricken. Where she was concerned, his blasted visions were never clear, never set in stone. Even a lifetime ago, he'd known she'd be a part of his future, the most important part toward the end of his life . . .

Well, and that had certainly come to pass. His life as Jade Laquette had apparently ended, and what did that say about his full-proof prophecies? "Not jack shit," he uttered the American colloquialism in an angry breath.

In her eyes, he was dead, as he had envisioned, but the visions hadn't ended any more than his life. Ever since he had spoken with his father, the damned insights were changing, bursting, rearranging. A lifelong plan was blasting itself into eccentric directions. Damn her. If she'd just remained in Bentwood as he had believed she would . . . Or *had* he believed that? Damn it. She had carried that wretched box in the car's boot and delivered it to him as he'd known she would.

Accepting the visions by no means offered clarity into them. In a moment of crystal clarity, he knew his fallibility. He saw things in advance, yes. But the tiny details to weave one moment into another seemed far more crucial than he had ever imagined.

Was he the master, or just another puppet dangling in fate's nimble fingers . . .? Maybe a bug caught in fate's web, he corrected with an angry flash in his mind. Too clearly, he imagined an immense spider waiting to pounce and weave him into a cocoon. Fate. Obviously, fate intended to keep him guessing. Otherwise, he would be knocking on a door by now and possibly delivering a lethal dose of medication. The box would have gained him entry into the maniac's lair. The box and a name . . .

Jade Laquette.

His gaze listed again toward Mark Jarvins, another puppet. In another life, he might have felt sorry for Jarvins. At the moment, Dominique suffered only outrage. This lunatic had held a gun and plotted the death of the woman asleep in the next room. Oh, and there was fate again, intervening.

All too clearly, Dominique recalled driving past the hotel's entrance when the vision of Jarvins standing in this room had struck like lightning in his mind's eye. Acting on pure adrenalin, he'd wheeled into an alley and left the rental at a loading dock. In a madcap sprint, he'd returned to the hotel's service entrance, mind-bending the bellhop en route to unlock the security door and bring Veronique's room key. Barely, he'd stepped into the suite before he'd heard the elevator ding and sensed Veronique racing up the corridor.

He wasn't in control, and the reason was all too blasted simple. The woman in the next room was a witch and double-trouble with a little warlock in her womb. Had he conspired against his own father at such a tender age? Had he played similar tricks and foiled his father's plans, allowing his mother to escape to the Americas? Were the black spots in his visions of the future directly relative to the power he had already passed into the child she carried? And what did that tell him, then? That they were all—the Jardonet males—scattered pieces of a puzzle, each gifted with an ego the size of Mt. Everest from the moment of conception to believe himself more powerful and wily than his predecessor? Well, it would certainly seem that way. And did that mean his arrogance worked against him? Who was he, after all, to believe himself in control of the world spinning around him? A puppet. A blasted puppet on a string, acting and reacting on the instant, governed by a higher power while buckling to the weaknesses of any normal man. Vanity. Self-satisfaction. Arrogance. Man was a loathsome beast, and he wasn't the exception. If, as he suspected, he had subverted what might have become a cataclysm, he wasn't acting of his own volition.

"Shit," he muttered and looked at Jarvins. The fellow rested like an unstrung puppet, slumped in the cushion, his hands held on his lap merely by the chain between his wrists. A puppet, a pawn, one metaphor was as good as the other. Jarvins had been programmed from an early age, destined to rise within the Bureau and become one of the top guns in the new regime. Strategically, the madmen had positioned him to use the resources of the Bureau toward the common end. He was only one of the dozens who had infiltrated the ranks and files, his record, true blue, his background spotless. Behind that clean-cut facade, however, Jarvins wore the face of every zealot, prepared to shave his head and raise his hand in pledge to a new leader. He had intended to marry Veronica Bryson if only to solidify his position in the government. A marriage of convenience.

Studying the limp figure more closely, Dominique waded through the sludge of Jarvins' dormant psyche, clearly seeing the fantasy that had sustained this imbecile. Jarvins would have made love to Veronica and planted his seed . . . He'd meant to produce at least one grandchild to satisfy the elder Bryson and confirm his ties to the Bryson fortune. On a dual plane, Jarvins had become obsessed with the thought of loving Veronica, controlling her, claiming her as his own, and . . . holding her inquisitive nature in check. In his arrogance, he imagined her obedience and loyalty, saw himself as a king in his castle. The idiot. He was even more disillusioned by his fantasies than Dominique had first imagined. Veronica would have squashed him like a bug for attempting to rein her nature in the unlikely event that she'd fallen for his charm. The jerk believed himself irresistible, and Veronica's rejection had certainly not fared well on his ego—not three years past, not four months past.

The only surprise was that Jarvins hadn't opened fire a few months ago. Jealousy had nearly tipped him over the edge then . . . and in a blinding epiphany, Dominique realized Veronica had sent Jarvins over the edge hours ago outside the church in Bentwood. If she had turned to him then, he might have forgiven her past indiscretions and allowed her to live. Instead, she'd scorned him for the third and final time, and he'd enlisted his team—the same private team he'd ordered to watch her days ago in Elmview. They were in Olden Time now, awaiting orders, no differently than Jarvins' team months ago who'd spied on Veronica under the guise of catching a maniac. The idiot had known Jade Laquette wasn't the homicidal maniac, but his assembled fanatics had rested within a block of Olden Time, watching Veronica, waiting for a chance to capture her fiancé and accuse him of the crime.

Enter Jarvins' new plan and his obsession to picture himself as Veronica's savior, her knight in shining armor, when her husband died at the hands of another maniac.

"Asshole," Dominique said to the inanimate figure across from him, but on a dual plane, he viewed the two men inside the office at Olden Time. They had flashed badges and confiscated the books. One of them had intervened in Tim's attempt to redial the telephone when the line had gone dead in his ear. Subsequently, Tim rested on the small couch, tense and alarmed, merely watching as the agents appeared to pour over the books. Allegedly, they needed to keep the phone line free to await a call from their Cleveland office. Tim Spencer was no fool. He knew, by body language and action, something wasn't quite right about this pair, but they held federal badges.

An idea came to Tim as he contemplated how to reach Len Devinio. "I'll need to use that phone for a minute, gentlemen," he said smoothly. "I promised my wife I'd call her after I talked to Mrs. Laquette. If I don't make that call soon, she's likely to roust Chief Hayward from his bed to pay us a visit . . ."

"That call will have to wait a few more minutes," the man behind the desk commented. "We'll deal with your chief if he shows up."

They were waiting for Jarvins' orders, Dominique knew abruptly and focused on Mark. If things had gone according to Jarvins' plan, he'd have phoned Olden Time and ordered his men to confiscate the books and clear out. Eventually, Jarvins would deal with the locals in Bentwood; after all, Spencer and his ilk were a group of bungling country bumpkins, no match for Mark Jarvins' prowess.

Death was too kind for Mr. Mark Jarvins, but alternatives existed. With his thoughts, a smile crept into Dominique's lips. A pity his talents were governed by the natural laws of hypnosis. If any man could use a personality overhaul, Jarvins certainly qualified. Even now, however, Jarvins struggled to rise from the trance and break the restraints on his muscles. Holding him in a dream state indefinitely would be impossible as surely as changing his subconscious to any beneficial degree. Jarvins was warped. His self-image inflated. He believed himself not only superior to the common mass but separate from it, as his father, Matthew Jarvins had convinced him.

. . . A single gunshot echoed inside the room. Blood splattered the leather chair and the gold swag curtain. The body jerked and slumped, collapsing over the leather armrest. The weight of the small caliber handgun dragged the liver-splotched hand to land on the crisp black slacks. Meticulously, the elder had dressed for death as he had for life. Black suit, tie, starched shirt with gold and diamond links. A black tie held his clean-shaven chin from sagging and prevented his lined lips from gaping. Barely, his lips parted as if in a prelude to surprise, but a sliver of red snaked from a corner staining the white collar above the pressed black jacket. One arm dangled, the fingers nearly brushing the oriental carpet.

Shouted voices and anxious cries resounded through the heavy door. Hands and fists banged the heavy mahogany wood. Inside the room, the faint trace of cordite mixed with the cigar smoke rising from the stout Columbian smoldering in the crystal ashtray. With the dull lamplight circling the pristine felt mat, the elder remained in shadows, but the cessation of life remained clear.

"Matthew! Matthew, please! Open this door!"

Matthew . . . Mathew Jarvins, Dominique identified on the instant, his attention again riveted on the man across the room. If not for the knowledge of this fellow's intention to murder him several days earlier, Dominque might be tempted to feel sorrow for him. That news, news of his grandfather's demise, would reach him. If not already, then soon. . . that elderly gentleman would determine his own fate to avoid prosecution for his participation in the attempted insurrection in the Capital.

They had planned—Mathew Jarvins Sr. and his select group of fellow fanatics—to implement the techniques outlined by Herr Schreiber. Already, a facility existed . . . a house of horrors. Dominique flashed an image of a theatre room . . . an operating room. Clearly, far too clearly, a metal table glistened under brilliant white light, a table oddly reflective of a morgue. In sharp contrast, medical equipment designed to sustain life circled the room beneath the elevated glass windows of an observation room . . .

More curious than alarmed by his vision, Dominique focused on the younger version of the ill-fated zealot and again considered his course of action. Any suggestion would need to be molded carefully to mesh with this fellow's beliefs . . .

In a low silky tone, Dominique spoke the words as an incantation drawing from Mark's psyche to recreate the plan, transferring his visions of the lake into Mark Jarvins' subconscious. Suppressing his hostility, Dominique merely enhanced Mark's conviction and determination while letting the agent see himself walking Veronica on the pier, directing her at gunpoint toward the black skyline. Dull light filtered from the entrance of a boat ramp a distance away, but in his mind, his emotions twisted. Torn between grief and duty, Mark fixated on the black hair glistening in the slight breeze despite the shadow glow. Amplified, the lap of waves slapped against the pilings and sent vibrations through the planks under Jarvins' smooth-soled shoes.

Not missing a beat, Dominique continued to enhance the images of Mark's designed plot. In his mind, Jarvins had, after all, created and carried out this ordeal to remove Veronica from this hotel a few dozen times—no differently than he'd plotted and removed Dominique Jardonet from this same hotel only four days earlier. In the backseat of a dark sedan, Mark had switched the injection from a sedative to a lethal dose of curare to remove the threat of Jade Laquette from the Cause. He'd followed orders, then, to neutralize a threat, and he apparently believed he was following the same orders to remove the wife of his nemesis, believing she knew far more than she should about their plans for a new order.

Fools and zealots, the lot of them, and it took every ounce of Dominique's considerable restraint to view the images in this idiot's mind. Too clearly, he watched Veronica climb from the agent's car . . . and only the absence of her fear prohibited Dominique from unleashing his outrage as the footage continued to scroll through Jarvins' mind . . .

In the pale light, her ivory features glowed, and her immense blue eyes glistened with tears as the revelation of her impending death surfaced in her mind. Until this moment, she hadn't believed, couldn't believe that her old friend could kill her.

Dominique held that moment in Jarvins' mind, barely restraining his own horror—or perhaps, enhancing the same as Mark squeezed the trigger. To Dominique's surprise, the tears exploded over the pale blue eyes across from him in real time. To the sight of Veronica lifting, propelled off the end of the dock, and plunging and splashing into the black depths Jarvins' pain exploded.

"Forgivvve meee . . . I haaad nooo choooice . . ." he cried into the night, lurching—if only in his mind. Barely, Mark refrained from diving into the water after her, then stood watching the lovely pale face sink below the surface, disappearing as the tide dragged her away. Black locks swelled, spiraling over her bulging eyes.

Not remorse, Dominique realized a moment later. Not even genuine grief surfaced in Jarvins' mind. In those final moments, he forced himself to believe he loved Veronica while blaming her for her doom. *If she had only loved him, she would be alive. She'd given him no choice. She'd betrayed him. She deserved to die. She carried another man's child in her womb . . . and there wasn't anything left, now, but to tidy up the details. He needed to cover his tracks, ditch the weapon, an untraceable weapon . . .*

Standing over him, Dominique restrained an overwhelming urge to lean down and snap the agent's limp neck. Too vividly, he had walked with Jarvins through that ordeal. That Veronica slept soundly, dreamlessly in the next room, remained Jarvins' only salvation.

Death truly was too good for this wretch, Dominique nearly spat the words aloud and emitted only a low feral growl.

Exercising an effort of will that threatened to break, Dominique separated his thoughts while leaning and rifling through Jarvins' coat pockets, finding the key to the handcuffs. Hands trembling, Dominique stooped and unlocked the manacles, removing the iron bracelets and returning them to the agent's coat pocket. With a tight rein on his emotions, Dominique ordered Mark to rise and walked him to the telephone. Stooping, Dominique reconnected the phone and lifted the receiver into Jarvins' hand before dialing the number to reach Olden Time. Connecting with the tranced blue eyes, Dominique listened on a dual plane as one of the agents answered.

"Clear out," Mark stated in a firm voice. His eyes misted with an image of a city street in his mind; the scented breeze of the lake in his nostrils. "Leave the books. Tell Mr. Spencer and the woman that Mrs. Laquette was apparently following a blind lead. If they should speak with her, let her know that she's to phone either Agent Devinio or Jarvins as soon as possible. Return to your stations in Pittsburgh and wait for my call. Everything's under control . . ."

Taking the phone as the agent disengaged at the other end of the line, Dominique returned the receiver to its cradle and continued to study Jarvins' strained features. He'd already held the fellow tranced too long. A fine sheen of sweat had formed across the brow; the muscles in the neck had grown taunt. At a deeper level, Jarvins struggled to awaken as if from a dream. There were dreams . . . and there were *dreams*. And Dominique Jardonet wasn't Jade Laquette.

Drawing from his memory, he blasted an image of Veronica into Jarvins' mind, complete with her most loving smile and warm blue eyes, her hair scattered like black silk on satin pillows. Dominique watched the agent's face contort with a conflict of emotions. In a deep silky rhythm, he sent the suggestions into Jarvins' subconscious. "This is the image you will see whenever you think of how it could have been—would have been for you. In every moment, you will know this is the image Jade Laquette carried. An image that could have been yours, should have been yours. Believe with all your being that she would have come to you if you hadn't killed her. And see her now . . ." In his mind, Dominique conjured the image he'd taken from Jarvins, the fantasy of her final moments when Jarvins would have seen her pale, lifeless face sink below the black water. "Know that you have murdered her—your one and only true love. Know that she is dead, and you killed her."

Contorted, Jarvins' face broke into a fine glistening sweat, struggling against the suggestions sinking into his lowest planes.

Smiling slowly, Dominique pushed from his stoop and backed away, speaking in a smooth lyrical command. "Go now. Descend through the service stairs and return to your car. Drive to the dock and see the place where her body sank. There you will awaken fully to what you have done."

Automated, Jarvins pushed off the couch and strode toward the door. He let himself out without looking back, pulling the door closed behind him.

In a split second, Dominique considered the consequences of his actions, but far too rapidly, he considered the sludge inside Jarvins' mind. If ever a mental condition could be classified as a disease, Mark Jarvins was chronically ill. Blindly, he'd obeyed orders from superiors who envisioned a world of superior beings . . . chosen ones. Jarvins was no different than the Taxidermist. Just another follower to believe himself answering to a higher call, spreading his righteous indignation like a disease to fester and destroy. The vision, the ultimate plan was to rise these groomed children into every walk of professional power, whether in the Federal Bureau and other branches of law and order, or the health field. In the new regime, Jarvins would have become a director in the Bureau, and he wasn't too far from his goal even now. His grasp for unraveling and understanding the criminal mind, compounded by his influential family, had risen him swiftly through the ranks. He was, without a doubt, one of the most talented agents working in the field, and his achievements hadn't gone unnoticed by the current leaders.

Well, and sadly, all good things must come to an end. Jarvins' time had come.

Before the phone chirruped its first ring, Dominique knew Spencer hovered at the opposite end of the line. For a fleeting instant, he longed to lift the receiver and chat as he had hundreds of times over the past five years. With no others had Dominique Jardonet ever shared even an illusion of brotherly affection or friendship. Only when he sensed the phone disturbing Veronica's peaceful sleep he leaned, clasping and lifting the receiver. In a nasally high-pitched voice, he announced, "The number you have reached is no longer in service . . ."

Doubtful Tim Spencer would be put off by such a ruse. Inevitably, he'd track down the number or contact Devinio directly, and the Lakeview Inn wouldn't remain a haven for long.

Muttering a curse, Dominique strode to the bedroom door and hesitated unnaturally with the twitch at his nethers. Just the thought of entering a bedroom with her started his blood heating but now was not the time or place.

Alongside the bed, he stood, admiring the long, sprawled length of his anything-but-former wife. His heart hammered a leaden beat with an overwhelming desire to slide onto the colorful quilt beside her, take her in his arms. They'd made love for the first time in a hotel . . . and every ounce of his wicked nature strained to satisfy his selfish desire. He could seduce her . . . as she was seducing him at his very moment. Even asleep, her white light reached toward him, alluring, enticing, nearly daring him to touch her, taste her. In her arms, he had grasped heaven—

"Damn it," he growled, and shook her effects from his mind, searching for a safer direction.

She was exhausted—naturally exhausted. Only exhausted would she drop her natural defenses and succumb to his mentalism. To wake her—even to gain her cooperation— seemed a crime, and he had committed enough of those against her to last ten lifetimes. He couldn't, however, leave her to the mercy of Devinio or worse—his twisted cohorts. . . .

CHAPTER 23

Enlisting talents that had remained dormant too long, Dominique held Veronica in a state of sleep while helping her into her coat, gathering her keys and purse. She knew him. On a far deeper level, she recognized his essence and trusted him. Falling willingly into his arms, she nestled comfortably in his embrace as he carried her down the service stairs. Departing through a side entrance, he whisked her through the nearest shadows, then slid her aground and led her to the Maserati gleaming under bright fluorescent light.

A motel. He would take her only as far as the nearest decent motel . . . or so he believed until he rolled into the shadowy parking lot of a dingy motor lodge. The neon sign under the marquee boasted, ". . .-a-ancy." A string of bare light bulbs burned beneath a sagging awning that strung together a colorful mismatched collection of doors and windows. Five late-model cars and two battered pickups occupied the lot—none newer than ten years old. This wasn't the type of place where a Maserati would blend into the scenery, but it was the type of place where credit cards were neither mandatory nor welcome. Cash only. No identification required.

The white-haired fellow dozing in a lounge chair behind the tall, tattered counter barely glanced at Dominique. Automated, he flopped an old-fashioned ledger open, then turned to retrieve a key from a pegboard on the rear wall. No questions asked, the old man commented, "Thirty bucks for the night, tax included . . ."

Jotting an alias name in a more illegible scroll, Dominique accepted the key, handed over the cash in American currency, offered an amenity, and strode from the office. Veronica hadn't stirred. She remained asleep as he carried her from the car. The motor lodge had only one redeeming quality that likely kept it in business, and after lying Veronica on the dark blue velveteen spread, Dominique glanced through the curtained window.

Beachfront.

A wry smile curled his mustache as he identified the black expanse of the lake between the scattered tree trunks and wild undergrowth. A narrow path might lead to the water's edge, but he needed no second sight to identify the surf slapping boulders rather than sand.

With a fleeting thought, he unlatched the cheap window lock and jimmied the glass upward three inches. If a screen had ever existed, it was long gone. He tasted lake water on the chilly breeze and in his mind's eye, witnessed Mark Jarvins standing, shivering, on the end of a pier. Pulling the paper shade down and drawing the drape, Dominique stole a quick cursory glance of the mismatched veneer furniture—the dresser stood on bent peg legs; the indoor-outdoor carpeting wore more stains than color. Definitely not even a *single-star* accommodation, but the room provided the basics. A cardboard sign taped to the side of the most modern convenience—a television with Bakelite nobs and black convex screen—boasted "cable and HBO." The faint scent of disinfectant offered scant relief. The room smelled like cheap cigars, stale cigarettes, and quick sex.

Muttering a curse, he held the key in hand, locked the door on his way out, and climbed into the Maserati. Cutting between a break in the horseshoe design of lodgings, he pulled the car into thick shadows behind the building, no more than ten steps from the window where the faint glow of light breached the thin window blind and curtain. Mental conditioning, he considered as he locked the car and strode to the window. No one would find them. But whether his safety precaution to conceal the car or other factors confirmed his thought remained a mystery. Forever, impulses and his illusive nature governed his actions from one moment to the next.

What came first—the chicken or the egg?

Picking through vines, he reached the window and jimmied the glass high enough to climb through.

Was he governed by his visions, reacting in the instant to avoid calamity? Or did he govern the visions via his dark dominion and volition?

Did it matter? He stood within the confines of a motel room, gazing down on the loveliest creature he had ever encountered. They wouldn't be disturbed. Hiding the car had seemed reasonable . . . as reasonable as playing with the wires in Jarvins head and unstringing the fellow by a few more threads.

Veronica had repositioned on the bed. She rested on her side with her head pillowed on her arm, her other hand lying flat against the cheap crushed velvet spread. A natural curve tilted her lush lips as if she might be withholding the punch line of a joke. Her long black lashes feathered across her high cheekbones, concealing the dark hollow patches he'd noted beneath her eyes.

If he wasn't already damned, he should be. If for no other reason than for bringing the weariness and sorrow into her life, for putting her through the madness of the past few days . . . For falling so hopelessly in love with this lovely little white witch that he could yet bring her to harm.

He had seduced other women. With a glance, a smile, a word—a touch or a gesture. Not since his first encounter with his mistress in France had he suffered any illusions about women. All too readily, he recalled his reputation in Bentwood . . . becoming known as the most ineligible eligible bachelor in town. He'd dated most of the eligible women in Bentwood. He needed only to consider the series of events to unfold in that small town to wonder again what had come first. The chicken or the egg? Had he been drawn to Bentwood through visions that he couldn't recall . . . or was he even worse the devil to arrive in Bentwood, lured by the black masses and rituals under every full moon. What, truly, had come first? If he'd known eighteen years ago that he would arrive in Bentwood and walk in the footsteps of a killer . . .? Had he taken steps unwittingly to see those moments come to pass? Had he arranged for those events?

Unconsciously, he repositioned the single chair alongside the window and lifted the loose glass to vent the smoke as he lighted a cigarette. His gaze trailed to the woman sleeping so peacefully on the velvet spread. More than anything at this moment, he would love to stretch out alongside her, wrap her in his arms, and breathe the scent of her. But at the same time, he feared to taint her and the child asleep in her womb.

She should hate him. Her hatred, he had seen clearly in the aftermath of her husband's demise. And despite his reaction to his father's news, he had known she would arrive in Cleveland. On some darker distant plane, he had known in advance. Somehow, he had failed to grasp her flying into that hotel room, determined to take to save his wretched life. Was there a glimpse of understanding in that revelation? When she acted out of love for him, were her motives too pure for his grasp? Was he so blasted trapped in the darkness that he could see nothing of the light when his white witch was involved?

Try as he might, any images beyond the immediacy of their situation eluded him. Rooted firmly in the present, he could only gaze upon her. Enamored and as enthralled as ever a moment over the past several months. He could look back. He could see her standing within the white lace and lifting the veil from her face. In hindsight, he considered himself lucky not to have incinerated before the altar in St. John's. But then, perhaps, the old idiom held a grain of truth—God favors fools and small children. He had been a fool to stand before the God of light and make his vow, and therein lay another irony, he considered. Before standing in the church, he had vowed his love within a ring of darkness. In crystal clarity, he recalled, '. . .Heart and soul.'

Those words still applied. Regardless of breaking his vows of matrimony by legally murdering Jade Laquette, he remained bound by that bond spoken over a blood sacrifice. And it was almost amusing, the irony. He had never truly worshiped any deity. He'd attended rituals in his father's house, an unwilling observer of the black arts, as doggedly as he'd sat through the lessons enabling him to be married in the Catholic church. He'd never been baptized into a religious faith. Never christened either a child of light or dark. Neutral. Ambivalent. And yet, he couldn't fully consider himself an atheist or agnostic. He believed in deities. He even believed that some people understood the minds of those deities, whether one followed God or Satan. He was, he suspected, an infidel by desire and by practice, following no religious faith whatsoever and, at the same time, believing in them all. What did that make him? Where did it leave him?

Damned.

Cursed to walk through life with more questions than answers and no anchor to regulate what most people took for granted . . . either decency or decadence. Even Jarvins, misguided and warped as he was, lived with a defined set of rules and principles. Dominique almost envied him. It would be far simpler to have guidelines, to strive toward a goal, however fanatical. Jarvins believed in the superior race, factoring in neither good nor evil, believing he would reap a reward for whatever actions he took to further his cause. Nothing else could have forced him to murder the woman he allegedly loved. She had been a sacrifice, a necessary sacrifice for his warped cause.

His gaze fell on Veronica; Dominique smiled slowly. Maybe he did have a goal, a mission, and a set of rules to abide by, after all. At the heart of his universe, this woman and child existed. Whoever threatened either one would become his enemy. The means justified the end. A fanatic, he mused. All men were fanatics, if not lunatics, toward one cause or another. Some men killed for countries, others for money, others for beliefs. He would certainly not be the first man to kill for a woman, and he would kill for her as surely as he would die for her.

Damn, how he loved her, and how it hurt suddenly to recall those moments when she'd looked at him as if he were a stranger. Physically, she knew he was the same man who had stood before that altar and vowed his love. The difference was internal, and she knew that as well. Whether she could ever love the man who had risen from the ashes, figuratively speaking, was a question burning in his mind. And by no small measure, he considered the duality of that question. He could love her, had never stopped loving her for an instant, but whether he could ever offer her the pure love she deserved, he had no idea. Was it even fair to make the attempt? She would never trust the man he'd become, and for that, he could never blame her. He couldn't even trust himself.

He need only think about what he'd done, how easily he'd walked away, like a blind man, plodding on a course to destroy everything he'd believed himself wanting. With a few lousy phone calls placed from the office in Olden Time, he snuffed his entire future, and he hadn't been Dominique Jardonet when placing those calls. Jade Laquette. The man who had promised his devotion and vowed his undying love had placed those phone calls, arranging for a damned plane, for a nameless corpse to be placed on that plane, for the corpse's fingerprints to be identified as Laquette. His Laquette identification and the clothes he had worn, had been transported from a motel onto that doomed craft.

Insight. Blessed insight. Cursed insight. He had foreseen that plane's demise. Mechanical failure. Without any outside interference, his father's craft had descended and exploded in a ball of fire. In a few lousy hours, Jade Laquette had conspired to have a name appear on an airline manifest and beguiled his French comrades to confirm his arrival in New York. Even if one questioned the other about Dominique Jardonet, none would dispute that he had spent a night in New York.

As Laquette, the man Veronica loved, had destroyed their life, and sooner or later, she would reach that conclusion, if not already. Regardless of what name he wore or what image he posed in her mind, she would never trust him again—and to look too far into the future now would only be painful.

His gaze trailed over the lovely face and down her long slender form. Impulsively, he pushed off the chair and settled carefully on the side of the bed. Not a flutter in the lashes despite the confounding squeal of bedsprings. More carefully, he stretched out, tentatively reaching and touching her hand, covering her hand. The warmth and tingle of contact hadn't changed, and she felt it too. Her lashes fluttered. She muttered inaudibly, and Dominique feared she might recoil even in sleep. Instead, her hand turned naturally under his, and her fingers locked around his palm. Unexpected, the rush of relief and comfort swam over him with a force to lift a sting of tears to his eyes. In a small corner of her mind, she might still love him despite his black heart, and for now, that would need to be enough.

The weariness he'd attempted to ignore since leaving the complex in DC washed over him then, tugging him under a black tide where no conscious thoughts could intrude. She still loved him—maybe just a little . . . and on that thought, his senses lingered in peaceful oblivion.

Waking, Ronnie registered the dull orange glow before ever focusing clearly on the face filling her vision less than four inches away. For an instant, the fan of his long lashes, scattered walnut waves dipping over his dark brows, and the natural curve in his dark mustache stirred her at the core. Reality intruded. The events of the past four days ignited like sparks hitting Mesquite. Her husband was dead! And the weight of his hand enhanced as her anger ascended. The heat of his hand clasped in her palm, their fingers intertwined, only enhanced her ascending anger. This man wasn't her husband! She nearly shouted the words aloud before a deeper emotion surfaced. Silently, she studied the face she had come to know so very well.

As always, in sleep, he appeared content and relaxed. More handsome without the burden of expression to define his nature. Just a man, she caught herself thinking while looking at the sculpted cheeks, aquiline nose, and thick black lashes. With the tumble of walnut waves fallen in a tangle across his forehead, he more resembled the boy she had met only once on a playground. In an odd instant, she overlapped the image of the boy leaning on the A-frame of a swing set, with the man leaning in a doorjamb, pinning Mark Jarvins in an emerald shine—like a large black cat hypnotizing a bird before pouncing.

Far too quickly, the conversation sped through her mind. The mention of a conspiracy, a world war, the implications. How much of what this stranger had told her was fact? How much fabrication? Could she afford to believe him, or had he concocted a grand story? And would she know if he was lying . . .? He was not the man she had married . . .

Mark Jarvins had held a gun on her. Fleetingly, she recalled Mark's desperate attempt to mask the emotions she'd sensed when he'd leveled his Glock at her. He hadn't come to rescue her. He had come to kill her for reasons he failed to divulge other than to admit she would ask too many questions. Mark Jarvins. A federal agent? . . . An alleged friend? He had fully intended to kill her. Assassinate her? Stop her from searching too deeply for answers—answers he believed she already possessed through her allegedly deceased husband.

No longer could she lie still. She barely twitched to extract her hand. the long dexterous fingers locked, and the thick lashes lifted. In a split second, the murky hazel hue sharpened and pinned her with the sheer intensity of his gaze. No doubt about it. He was awake. His contentment vanished, and his lips curved in a deeper smirk. The dimple emerged then; his head canted slightly as if studying her as completely as she'd studied him a moment ago.

"Good morning," she said more sharply than intended.

"Hmm, closer to noon, I think. Did you sleep well, mon amour?"

"Don't," she stated, not entirely certain of what she protested. His mockery of the endearment? Or his attempt to sound natural . . . as if this were natural! When she tugged, he released her hand, and she sat up smoothly, only then waking fully to the scents and strange sights. This wasn't the Lakeview. Not the room where she had laid down and fallen asleep. As she spun her gaze about the shabby surroundings, she dropped her feet to the floor, aware of him rising more naturally to rest on the opposite side of the bed.

Definitely not the Lakeview. Sunlight sprinkled through pinpricks in the thin paper shade and darted, dotting the worn curtains. It was a motel room; that much she identified. Randomly, engine sounds of vehicles passing breached the thin walls. Not a motel alongside a busy thoroughfare. Her gaze pivoted to find him watching her silently. "Where the hell am I?"

"Safe," he said quietly. "You were exhausted. And you would not have slept well at the Lakeview."

"So . . . What . . .? Did you just wiggle your nose and whisk us across the goddamn timeline into the 1950s?" she asked with an edge, intending to wound him. But the very real possibility stifled her hostility. In her belated husband's regard, she had sense to doubt until his smirk deepened.

"A pity I didn't think of that last night," he commented almost idly. "I'm sorry to say, I had energy only enough to drive us a half hour from our starting point."

She snorted a humph of disgust and pushed off the bed. "Suppose that means we're a few hundred miles from Cleveland," she said before her stomach rolled and spots sprayed across her vision. Muttering a curse, she distinguished the bathroom door from the narrow closet and headed in that direction. Tad settled long enough for her to collect her bearings in the small room, and the smell of disinfectant blasted what little resolve she had mustered. The image of drunks dangling over the porcelain bowl turned her stomach, and she veered from her intended target, catching the rim of the sink instead.

As she heaved, she identified the body crowding past her and heard the muttering, cursing, and sputtering at the edges of her mind. Surprisingly, her head began to clear faster than usual, and as she fumbled for a towel, she glimpsed the shaggy dark head at the lower elevation. The strangeness of the moment caught her attention and cleared her head a tad faster. Groping at the spigot, she spun the nobs and commenced heaving breaths, starkly aware of the man stooped at her hip, clinging to the lower bowl. No mistaking that choking sound or the lurching spasms. He sounded almost worse than she felt . . . and if his sputtered curses were any indication, he was no more pleased with his illness than she was. In lightning flashes, she realized the mechanics involved in this ordeal, and despite the situation, a smile crept into her lips behind the towel.

She was recovering—he was getting worse. Maybe there was a God after all! A just and merciful God! Wetting a towel, she stifled a laugh while wiping her mouth. If not for her lingering anger, she might feel a degree of empathy for her allegedly deceased husband. God knows she had suffered enough bouts of nausea in the past few weeks to know his head was spinning like a top in one direction and his stomach revolving just as fiercely in the other. His knee hit the floor, and he lost his balance, landing on his hip as he continued to heave. From her higher elevation, she glimpsed at his hand sliding to cover his waist—which she could attest, wouldn't help. The other arm stretched to the cracked commode tank, offering a wall to lean his head and a shield from her view. He was definitely not a happy man at this moment. Morning sickness had humbled him considerably, leaving him heaving hurt breaths as clearly as curses.

"Cursing doesn't help," she commented quietly, and his fingers gripped more fiercely on the cracked tank. "Don't suppose you thought to pick up a box of crackers, huh?"

His head shook in the negative, and she felt a little sorry for him then.

Stifling a wicked smile with an effort, Ronnie collected the washcloth from the aluminum rail, soaked it, and leaned, handing it over his shoulder into his line of sight. "Here. You might need this in a moment."

In his hissed accented deep voice, it was difficult to determine if he said "Merci'" or "Mercy." Either way, he sounded less than happy with her attempted offer of comfort. His hand lifted off the tank, clasped the cloth, and returned directly to the tank. With his fisted clasp on the cloth, water streamed down the porcelain tank, glowing orange—nearly blood red—with the sunlight glowing through the faded yellow blind.

As an added comfort, she lifted the hand towel—stained nearly gray from faulty laundering—and landed it on his knee. "You'll probably need that, too," she commented and turned from the small room. By what blessing she no longer suffered the ills of morning sickness, she neither knew nor cared, but she wouldn't look a gift horse in the mouth.

To the sound of his continued retching, she meandered in the small room, finding her purse and coat on the shabby dresser. Rifling through her immense purse that could double as a duffle bag, she found her comb. With her thoughts shifting, her hand lingered near the Midnight Special, neatly secured in a side pocket. If she could have reached it last night, she might have shot Mark Jarvins . . . and at the moment, she might not mind landing a telling blow on a tangle of dark waves. Common sense dictated. She recovered her comb and made short work of untangling her hair while looking into the cracked mirror over the dresser. For an instant or an eternity, she saw Jade there. Reflected within the glass, he stood in his tailored Armani, his hands tucked in his pockets, a disheartened smile on his lips, and the warmth of his eyes holding her.

Not a hallucination, she realized as she stood listening to the man recovering in the bathroom. Her husband . . . the man in the bathroom had been her husband, and in another fleeting glance, she remembered seeing him lying in a pool of blood. Not a hallucination, she knew at this moment. He had nearly died physically . . . and he had come to her in those last moments. Whether to say goodbye or to comfort her, she couldn't decide. But he had appeared in a hotel mirror in Elmview, and his image had comforted her.

Turning, she leaned against the dresser, watching him through the door. He leaned at the sink, now, splashing water to his face and using the towel she had provided. He was still swaying slightly, needing one hand on the sink to stay afoot. Morning sickness. This man who was—and was not—her husband stood suffering the megrims that had begun inside of her. Even now, Tad moved in quiet circles within her womb, and Ronnie knew the fellow in the bathroom felt something of that motion.

He still appeared pale when he stepped into the doorway and needed to pause, grasp the frame to stay afoot. His eyes shifted, watery from the effects of his heaving, but no less intense beneath the shade of long lashes. No smile, now. He appeared all too sober despite his natural smirk.

Uncontrollably, Ronnie smiled slightly. "Feeling better?"

"I . . . have felt better in the past," he said carefully.

"Maybe you should lie down for a little while," she said kindly, and glanced at the bed, watching him do the same. Desire flamed in his emerald eyes, but this once, not for coupling. "There's no fighting it, you know," she said quietly. "As I've been told, it's natural."

"You find this ah . . . satisfying?" he asked with a hint of annoyance.

Ronnie stifled her smile, straining. "No, huh uh. Just ah . . . hell," she muttered and averted her gaze as the emotions assailed her. Grasping a more sobering thought, she lanced him. "Satisfying, no. Fitting, hell yes," she admitted bluntly. "Morning sickness is the least of the ills I'd like to rain down on you, Mr. Jardonet. You should consider yourself lucky."

"I think I'd prefer a few of your other curses," he commented and eased off the wall. Staggering a step, he muttered another curse before catching his balance. By the time he reached the bed, he truly needed to lie down, and he wasted no time falling over and closing his eyes.

Her heart tugged with something other than anger as she heard him draw a sighed breath. Too quickly, she remembered all the mornings her husband had delivered a cup of tea and a plate of crackers, appearing as sick as she felt. Damn it. She wanted to hate him. She wanted to despise him. But she pushed off the dresser.

In the bathroom, she rinsed the washcloth, collected the cleaner of the two towels then returned to the room. Settling on the side of the bed, she glimpsed his feral eyes as she brushed the dark waves off his brow. With more sorrow than venom, she smiled faintly, "This isn't natural," she said quietly and held his more wary gaze. "As if anything about our relationship is natural or normal," she continued. "I haven't looked outside. Is there a convenience store anywhere nearby? I could get you a cup of tea and a box of crackers."

"The spinning's slowing," he said carefully. "Few minutes."

"Do you feel up to talking?" she asked and read the dread flash in his eyes. Doubtful he was up to anything at all.

"Depends on the subject," he said. "If you men`tion food, I may have to kill you."

In his drool tone, the words could be mistaken for gospel, but he had intended a jest. Ronnie managed a slight smile. "Seeing you last night . . .? Even half expecting to find you alive and well, I wasn't prepared for it," she said carefully. "You don't . . ." *Know what I've been through*, she meant to say, but the sorrow flashed in his eyes, countering her thought. He did know. He knew exactly what she'd endured at his hands. "Why?" she asked carefully. "Why couldn't you just have confided in me? Why couldn't you have warned me or . . . or given me an explanation? You had to know that I'd see you again. That I'd know you weren't dead. How could you do this to us?"

His hand lifted, clasping her fingers on her drawn knee. "Nothing I could say would be reason enough, Veronique. Even to me . . . the prize seems too high," he spoke quietly, an inflect of French transitioning his c to z. He slipped his hand off hers, brushed his fingertips at her waist, and paused. Momentarily, his focus locked on his hand, then lifted with an echo of the man she'd known lingering in the softer shine, in the sad smile. "For what it's worth, I am sorry," he said quietly. "You de`serve far more than I could ever give you and nothing of what I've wrought against you. For that, I truly am sorry."

"What happened?" she asked while holding his gaze, seeing the curtain drop over his eyes. "What happened after you came to Cleveland?"

His gaze shifted, looking into abstracts that only he could see.

"I know you nearly died," she said bluntly and caught his gaze returning. "I didn't see a plane crash, honey, I saw you lying on a floor bleeding, and I think you saw me then, too. How . . . how did that happen?"

He studied her, canting his head momentarily, and appeared on the verge of answering when his eyes flashed a near emerald and darted away. For an endless second, he stared into space, and the emerald sparks danced in his eyes as if refracted in precious stone.

"Damn it!" he snapped and sat up abruptly. His hand flew to his head as his other hand landed more firmly on the mattress, halting his sway. "Goddamn it!"

"What? What's wrong—"

"My car," he snapped and shoved himself away from her, skidding his feet off the side of the bed. "They're impounding my fucking car," he snapped and climbed afoot, stabilizing his balance with his feet planted firmly, his back to her.

CHAPTER 24

Rising, Ronnie stared at his back. It wasn't a guess nor a ruse to avoid answering her question. His car impounded? "Who? Why would they—"

He pivoted, stable, despite the lingering effects of the nausea in his expression. "You'd think they'd have more important things to do on a goddamn Saturday morning. No. Huh uh. The whole fucking city's in an uproar with the morning news, but . . . damn it," he muttered and glanced around the room. Landing his gaze on the television. His brow furrowed as he sidled to the console and spun the wieldy nob.

Gray fuzz erupted and filled the screen momentarily before the images formed. As the static hiss cleared, he turned and strode to the single chair at the window. Lifting a cigarette pack off the ledge and settling onto the dingy cushion, he caught a butt under his mustache.

Not once in the past four months had he willingly engaged a television. In fact, he hadn't even owned a television before Ronnie had her set delivered from DC. Only on rare occasions, he joined her—almost as if fulfilling an obligation—to view a news broadcast. Generally, he spent those moments muttering curses, shaking his head, or smiling angrily as he glanced at her and offered some wisecrack about poor entertainment. The addition of a VCR had become essential. But he was never too intrigued by movies either. They'd never watched an entire film from beginning to end, although she'd never found fault in the alternatives when they landed in bed—or on the living room floor. Intrigued, she noted him actually glancing at the screen as he lighted a cigarette.

". . . where Dr. William Reddinger was taken into custody . . ."

Ronnie's attention riveted on the screen. Without ever having seen the Cleveland Courthouse, she identified the backdrop.

Front and center, the anchorman, a lean young man with an intensity to match his grave tone, stood on the top marble step. On one of the wide glass doors, the gold etching of Lady Justice loomed over his shoulder as he continued, ". . . We haven't been able to confirm whether the authorities believed Dr. Reddinger was a suspect in the recent homicide of Frances Cummings, the young woman found murdered earlier this week. The mayor's office is expected to make a statement later this afternoon. We do know—no charges were issued against Dr. Reddinger before his release earlier this morning."

From the apparent newsroom, a faceless female voice emitted a deep concern. "Do you know if the police have any other suspects at this point, Rob?"

"According to one source, the mayor's task force may have another suspect, Rhonda. We haven't been able to verify anything yet. But there seems to be a connection between these homicides and a plane crash earlier this week which took the life of entrepreneur," he consulted a sheet of paper in his hand to continue. "Jade Laquette." The anchor's eyes fixed intensely on the screen as if seeing, identifying Ronnie's shock through the camera. "One of our sources indicated earlier that Mr. Laquette may have been fleeing from Federal custody when his plane went down. We've confirmed that the twin-engine plane carrying Mr. Laquette departed from our county airport Tuesday morning, and there's some indication that he may have been wanted by the French government . . ."

"Oh my God," Ronnie uttered and pivoted her gaze to find her former husband already looking at her rather than the screen. In milliseconds, she realized the repercussions of this broadcast even as her name sailed off the lips of the anchorwoman who prodded the on-scene reporter. Shaking her head, a sting of tears lifted at the corners of her eyes. Impossible! They could not suspect her husband of being this maniac! Surely not! But even as her thoughts spun, the anchorwoman raised the mention of the murders in Bentwood, PA, over the spring and summer . . . Bentwood, where he had been living for five years, where she had met him, where they had married—all of which the anchorwoman behind the scenes divulged in her somber narrative.

At the words "Olden Time," Ronnie spun her focus to the screen. By no surprise, she found another on-scene reporter stationed outside their home, her home. The camera panned over the ensemble of friends and neighbors collected on the wide sidewalk, trailing from beneath the burgundy awning shading the wide window displays. Even in the brief scan, she recognized most of the faces.

Ronnie's anger flared at the sight of Jen Andover hovering in the corner of the screen like a frightened rabbit. Her pale face contrasted starkly against the dark eye shadow lending her the appearance of a raccoon. With her neon blond hair, Andover stuck out like an eye-sore against the shaded display of sparkling silver and cut glass. Unnaturally, she wore a conservative checkered blouse buttoned nearly to her throat, a dull-silk windbreaker, and baggy jeans, undoubtedly borrowed or hastily bought at Chauncy's Thrift Store down the street. If this bitch owned anything other than skintight jeans and low-cut clinging tops, she had never flaunted them before today . . . and it was a costume!

If ever Ronnie felt like wrapping her hands around a thin throat, never more than at this moment, and the feeling grew as the anchorwoman spoke.

"There's some indication that Mrs. Laquette fled her home sometime last evening to avoid questioning. As of this moment, no one seems to know where she is, but several of her neighbors have come forth to express concern . . ." The anchorwoman turned, and the camera zoomed in on Jen, who appeared more frightened as the woman addressed her. "Miss Andover, you've told me that you knew Mr. Laquette, personally. Is that correct?"

"Well, sure, I mean we all knew him," Jen said in a quavering voice. But her eyes, sprinting slyly toward the camera, betrayed her reluctance to speak. "He wasn't calling himself Laquette then, though. I mean he was Isaac Bently then."

"I'm going to kill her," Ronnie decided in a low volatile tone and riveted her gaze toward her former husband. His lips quivering, restraining a smirk, he leaned casually in the single chair, his ankle slung over his knee appearing as relaxed as a man could be. "I am, you know? I'm going to strangle her with my bare hands!"

"Temper, temper, mon amour," he said with a musing ring and turned his albeit amused gaze to the screen. "Live entertainment, what more could we ask?"

On the screen, Jen continued, "Well, he was always kind of . . .? Secretive, ya know? He stayed to himself mostly. I mean, he'd spend hours in this old place. He didn't go out too much except . . . well . . . when he went on those trips to other countries."

"You were friends with Mrs. Laquette, is that right?" the anchorwoman said in a sympathetic tone.

Jen forced a rise of moisture into her eyes. "Well, sort of," she said in a quivering voice and darted her eyes away from the camera, then back with a besieging gaze. "When she first came, we tried to make her welcome, and I sort of warned her that she shouldn't get involved with Mr. Bently."

"I can't listen to this shit," Ronnie stated and started toward the set.

"Please, wait, mon amour," he said quietly and held her momentarily with his eyes, his lips turned in a smirk. "We're getting to the good part."

"Damn it, this lying bitch is crucifying you! Us!"

From outside the camera range, a sharp voice cut in. "I think I've heard about as much of this as I can stand."

Meg! Glorious Meg! Meg Price shouldered her way into the camera that jostled and zoomed in on her lovely matronly face, catching the spark of anger in her pale blue eyes as she bounced her focus off Andover to the anchorwoman. "If you believe a word this girl's telling you, you're either looking to make a name for yourself! Or you're working for a tabloid!"

"Ma'am—" The anchorwoman shuffled to stay in the camera focus as Meg faced off against Andover, who attempted to appear stunned. Pictures were worth a thousand words. Nothing could hide the flash of contempt beneath Jen's dipping black eyelashes.

"I don't know what you're trying to prove, Jennifer, but I've just about had it with your mischief and lies."

"Ma'am," the anchorwoman stated. "What is your name?"

"I'm Meg Price. I own that Diner next door. And I'll be damned if I'll stand by and let that young lady—and I use that term loosely," she snapped, flashing an angry glance at Andover. "Soil the memory and ruin the reputation of a few people that I love and respect. I don't know who came up with this hair-brained idea that Jade Laquette was responsible for the murders here—or in Cleveland for that matter—but I can tell you, it's all cow sh—pucky!" she scoffed and sent a scathing glance toward Andover who hovered now at the edge of the screen. Meg's gaze shot toward the anchorwoman as she continued, "I don't know where you people get off twisting the facts, but I can tell you this—for a fact—I was present when those Federal Agents came here to ask for Jade's help to *solve* those murders in Cleveland. He sure as hell didn't commit them!"

A round of cheers erupted from the edges of the camera, and at least one husky voice came clear, spouting, "You tell 'em, Meg!"

Belatedly, Meg realized she stood before a live camera, and a flash of embarrassment lifted the color to her cheeks as she darted her gaze over her audience. The cameraman followed her gaze, panning the cheering crowd in a jostling motion.

Smiling, Ronnie recognized the faces . . . friends and neighbors had assembled in the street, on the sidewalk—likely shutting down Maine. Several faces ducked away from the screen, but Wade, as bold and handsome as ever, stood his ground, watching Meg with an appreciation that the camera favored and enhanced. He was a handsome boy, his rounded face slimming in the first stages of adulthood, his brown eyes as warm as topaz under the sunlight.

"That's all I have to say," Meg stated, and the camera zoomed in as she turned away and accepted a hug from no other than Cy Bender. Protectively, he shielded her with his stout body while turning with her under his arm.

"God, I love that woman," Ronnie huffed and glimpsed the fleeting warmth in the emerald eyes. "You knew that was coming?" she commented as the anchorwoman tried regrouping her broadcast and fumbled a bit over the conflicting images of her story. "Can we turn it off now?"

He shrugged, appearing less than satisfied and only more troubled.

Turning, Ronnie started toward the set again as the anchorwoman in the newsroom announced.

"It has just been confirmed that the mayor will issue a live press release at two o'clock this afternoon. Please stay tuned for further updates . . ."

Snapping off the set, Ronnie turned and leaned against the console. "Why do I have a feeling you're not pleased with that announcement?"

"Perhaps, because I'm not," he said while collecting a cracked ashtray from the ledge, discarding a long cigarette ash.

Studying him, she couldn't decide if he was truly disturbed or merely thoughtful. "What's really going on here? Do you know . . . ? I mean, do you know who the killer is? Is it Reddinger?"

"Knowing is not enough, mon amour," he said quietly. "We live in a material world where only material evidence will confirm or deny, and even then, doubt too often remains."

She pushed off the console, rounding the end of the bed and settling on the crushed velvet spread. "So, how do we catch this maniac? Assuming you know who and where he is."

"We don't," he said with a slight smirk. "You need to return to Bentwood. Though, obviously, not to your home."

"Our home," she snapped.

His gaze said otherwise with a touch of sadness.

"And I'm not leaving until we finish this," she decided. "It would be a lot easier if you'd just tell me what we need to do—" The thought erupted like neon; her attention riveted. "That box. You knew I'd bring it. Maybe arranged for me to bring it. So, what are we doing with it?"

"Veronique . . ." His voice trailed along with his gaze momentarily. When his focus returned, he studied her more intently. "Whitman Reddinger is not the Taxidermist," he said bluntly. "He was ah . . . a red herring, so to speak. Mine."

"I saw him," she said absently, remembering the chill she'd suffered when the police had escorted him to the patrol car and again when she'd glimpsed him through the car window. "It . . . it felt right. He felt right," she admitted. "You're positive he's not the killer?"

"I didn't say he was entirely innocent, but he's not the Taxidermist," he said simply. "At least, I don't think he is."

Slightly taken aback, she studied him more critically. "Excuse me?"

He smiled slightly and shrugged. "Honestly, ma chérie, I am not God. As much as I would love to scry the future, present and past and know all that is, or ever was, I am human. I can't simply snap my fingers and solve this crime—any more than I could pinpoint the killer in Bentwood months ago. One moment leads to another, one insight governed by what preceded it. In twenty-twenty hindsight, I know I've glimpsed whatever is to be, but I don't have a road map to follow clearly from point A to point C. To my current distress, m' love, point B is essential and often as elusive as C."

He appeared less than distressed, and that only kindled her doubt. "You are psychic," she pointed out, searching his eyes for the telltale sign of an outright lie or deliberate subterfuge. "You're telling me you've set this all in motion, and you don't know exactly where it will lead?"

"Do you have any idea what a temptation it would be if I could look into the eyes of a killer and know his guilt before the act? Damned as I am to know I may face such a moment—and have—I don't know how long I'd last in the living realm with such a burden. I have an inkling I'd be more than persecuted by the press, m' love," he said with a smile. "I think in some states, the death penalty lingers on the horizon of any man who takes the life of another man without just cause.

"Perhaps, in the broader scheme of my talents, my impotence in certain situations is a safety device. If I consciously knew the face of this killer, I'd have already killed him for the trouble he's been in my life thus far. In retrospect, had I already killed him, I'd be the man they seek, don't you think?"

The simplicity of the words lifted goosebumps on her spine. He wasn't joking, now, or even attempting to subvert the conversation. He was, in fact, stating a fact. If he could simply know who was responsible for this madness, he would have eliminated the threat before it had become a threat . . . and he would be wanted for murdering an innocent man.

"You're grasping the complexity," he said lightly.

"So where do we go from here?" she asked. "Do you know?"

"Eventually, I'll slip through this window and bring the car around to collect you at the front door. I'd like to think that you'll accept my advice and return to Bentwood to visit with the Spencers but honestly . . .? Where you're concerned, I'm generally left in the dark."

"Excuse me?"

"You're my Achilles' heel, Veronique, and please don't take that to mean I find that reality offensive. Every man has his weakness, and mine happens to be a wondrous black-haired minx. I believe it has something to do with illumination, but I haven't worked that out entirely. Where you're concerned, my insights are never concise."

For a split second, she wondered if his words belied his actions to be free of her, but in the next instant, she glimpsed his hurt and understood his honesty. "I won't apologize for thinking," she said bluntly.

"I wouldn't expect you to," he said in a guarded tone. His gaze returned, slightly chilly. "Any more than I'd expect you to forgive me for what I've done. If you hated me now, I'd understand. No reasons are good enough for the hell you've endured."

"World War III," she said absently, and read his flash of annoyance.

"Who's to say that wasn't a fabrication? A grand prediction based on current trends? And a hoax, by no other definition."

"You," she said while studying him more intently. If nothing else about the past evening rang clear in her mind, his prognosis of an international catastrophe held firm in her mind. He'd taken steps to eliminate that threat, she knew at this moment.

"You would trust me still? After everything I've done?" he asked, sounding genuinely dumbfounded.

"If I choose to believe that you had a damned good reason for destroying our future, that's my business," she stated crisply. "And I think you better stop poking around inside my head," she continued. "That's an invasion of privacy, and I don't like it."

He canted his head, his eyes glittering greener as a smile slid into his lips. He shrugged. "Occupational hazard, mon amour. Afraid it can't be helped. If it's any consolation, I don't judge others by their thoughts."

In an instant flash, she recalled the first time they'd met, remembered sitting four barstools away at Meg's Diner . . . And he had started choking on a gulp of coffee.

"You considered me a homosexual if I recall accurately," he commented with a wry smile. "It took me aback."

Remembering Meg and the two waitresses who had raced to his rescue, she smiled slightly. "I'd imagine it did. I hadn't realized then what a harem you had."

"Don't suppose it would do much good to deny—I wasn't celibate."

Considering her reception in Elmview, she rekindled a few angry thoughts. "No, I don't suppose it would," she said dryly. "Is there anywhere you've gone that you haven't accumulated a following?"

He appeared thoughtful and amused. "Depends on what sort of following we're discussing."

Decidedly, Ronnie snapped, "We're not discussing it at all. Whatever you did before we met was strictly your own business." Jen Andover popped quickly to mind. "You had lousy taste before you met me though."

"True, very true," he said in a silky low tone, his eyes shimmering in the dull orange light and his thoughts not entirely masked behind his smile. "I don't suppose if I moved over there beside you, we would ehm . . .? No, I suppose not," he said with a slightly tainted smile. "It's truly not easy being in the same room with you, mon amour," he said and leaned, collecting his shoes off the floor. "And I think it's time I bring the car . . ."

There might never be another time, another moment to spend with him. With the thought exploding, she caught his eyes. By the speculation and hope arising, he had read her thought. All the reasons why she should not, could not, ran through her mind—only beginning with the fact that he was no longer the man she'd married. Unfortunately, even as her mind protested, her heart leaped toward him. She was as helpless and vulnerable at this moment as the evening he had entered her room with only one thing on his mind. As much as she knew she should hate him and hold him at arm's length, she wanted his embrace. She needed to be wrapped in the strength and power contained within him.

Leaving his shoes on the floor, he slinked from the chair, closing the distance without ever rising to his full height. Settling on the mattress beside her, he reached and clasped her hand. His gaze lowered as he brushed his thumb over her knuckles.

Even that slight touch, a too-familiar touch sent the longing and need deeper. Her heart hammered a quickening beat; the reluctance loomed large in her mind. He was still her husband. Still the same handsome devil she'd fallen in love with a lifetime ago, and his offhanded words months ago spilled through her mind now. 'We are doomed . . .'

His gaze lifted to her. "There is nothing in this world I would rather do at this moment than to make love to you, mon amour," he said quietly and lifted his free hand, cradling her cheek, brushing his thumb over her quivering lips. With a brighter, nearly desperate shine, he captured her eyes. "But I've lost that right, haven't I?"

"I should hate you," she said weakly.

He nodded, "You should."

"But I don't," she said as the sting lifted at the corner of her eyes. "I can't."

He canted his head, leaning, touching his lips down tentatively, and she knew she was doomed. Far more urgently, his mouth descended, and his fingers slid against her neck. Uncontrollably, her hands shifted, one to touch his cheek, the other to grip his hand. Lost. She was lost. The wild abandon unleashed under his touch, in his arms, swam through her as kisses ran across her lips, over her chin and cheek, down her neck. Tingling, heating, her body responded to the familiar desire flaming as his hand slipped beneath her blouse, feathering her breasts, and easing her back to rest in the nook of his arm. Her fingers tugged at his shirt, freeing the cloth at his waist. Gliding her hand over his muscled chest, her palm tingled and tickled against the soft pelt, skidding down the hourglass form to cradle his family jewels. Consciously, she drew him over her, melding to him as his shaft awakened to her touch. If ever she had known restraint, never in his arms, but in a weird epiphany, she identified the difference in him even as he responded, kissing, touching, waking the need to rage more fiercely through her body beneath his gentle ministrations.

She was his . . . but was he hers? Something had changed . . . and she felt it then, the hesitation in his entire body, the restraint coiled through his lean muscles even as he flicked the snap of her jeans and slid his hand over her hips, skidding the cloth away. Whether his control or something deeper drove her, she pushed at him, sliding him backward, shoving him flat with her body moving snakelike to land him beneath her. His eyes glowed emerald, shaded beneath his thick lashes, emitting a feral, wary shine as she slid her hands upward and tugged at his shirt while skidding her shins on the bed, brushing, crushing his legs between her knees.

What had she said only yesterday? What were the words . . .? That she would not let him go! She would not let Jean-Pierre have him! And suddenly, this wasn't just a matter of desire or need. It was a battleground. Anger, pain, frustration . . . Emotions born of grief raged through her mind as she took his mouth, startling him with the ferocity of her assault. She might be his Achilles' heel, but she wasn't his only vulnerability. Mortally wounding him would be no more satisfying than feeling his defenses waning as she nipped his ear and slid one hand down his sides to shove at the cloth at his hips while her other hand played at his ear, his neck. No less active, he tugged at her blouse, and she let him carry it over her head, not missing a beat to nip his shoulder and find his earlobe in her teeth, tugging. Unmercifully, she captured his mouth again, distracting him even as his hands skimmed over her breasts, freeing her from the lace. On his back, he shimmied them onto the velvet spread, and the battle became a test of skill as they stripped in twists and turns, huffing breaths and kisses between contortions.

She wasn't the same innocent woman he'd met and deflowered in June, not the same unworldly female who had succumbed smoothly to his desire. And by God, she wouldn't let him have his way! Not until she knew his desire matched her own with all reservations and restraint blasted from his mind. Only in her mind, she spoke the words over and over, and he heard them, she knew, if only by his urgent kisses sailing over her breasts, tasting and tugging.

'I love you . . . do you hear me! I love you! And I need you! Your son needs you! We won't let you go! Do you hear me! I love you! And I won't let you walk away from us! I don't give a damn who you are! What you are! You're still mine!'

And proving it, she held him ready, felt the tension and need raging like lightning through his sweated limbs, and felt him trembling on the brink of ecstasy. Against her ear, he muttered the words as he had a hundred times before, "mon amour." And still, she held him, heating him, kissing, and touching, refusing him the final instant as he rolled her over and under him. In his eyes, the emotions flamed, his confusion as brilliant as his desire, his thoughts spiraling on thermal waves threatening to whisk her away in her own need.

The distance she'd felt between them closed. The familiar conduit opened and sailed them into that weird and wondrous world of wild abandon. Her heart soaring, she felt the power of his internal battle, the strength of his emotions raging through their physical pores like an electric current. Held, as if captive, she viewed the world as he saw it. Colors exploded. Rainbows twined in a kaleidoscopic frenzy. Streams of brilliant white and liquid black spun like silk on a tapestry to form pictures to shatter and change. Light and darkness, the images flashed at dizzying speeds . . . And this was her husband, a man of incredible magic and mystery, a world apart from the material realm.

Heaving, human, he hovered over her, against her, feather-light and as comforting as a heated blanket. At the nook of her neck, his breath matched her pounding heartbeat; his face buried in the tangle of black hair at her shoulder. She felt him trembling now, the latent tremors of his body spent, her own body equally afflicted to quiver limply beneath him.

"I thought . . . I lost you," he whispered in soft huffed breaths. "I thought I lost you . . . forever, my love."

Never again . . . the words swam through her mind, nearly reaching her lips before she realized those were not her words . . . They were his . . . His words were spoken in a silent vow. Barely, she thought to raise her voice, to confirm her vow, when she realized he wasn't pledging never to leave her, never to lose her. *Never again* . . . could he make love to her. *Never again* . . . could they be together.

Her breath held, caught in her breast. The epiphany struck like a physical blow to take her life away. *Never again* . . . could they live as man and wife . . . Or come close to each other . . . Or soar to the heavens. He had not lost her . . . but she had lost him. He wasn't Jade Laquette . . . could never be Jade Laquette. He was Dominique Jardonet—her husband's half-brother by unnatural law and official documents. And he was right . . . they could never do this again. They could never be this close alone together again . . . because she still loved him. Too much to ever pretend he was someone else. Her eyes, her voice, her heart would betray them . . . And if anyone learned who he was, what he had done . . .? The laws he had broken . . .?

She held him tighter as the tears lifted over her eyes with the revelations pouring like burning liquid through her mind. Not a hoax, not a dream from which she would awaken . . . A nightmare only beginning, she realized as her breath strangled in her throat. To lose him once, to believe him lost forever in a fiery crash even for an instant . . . could hurt no worse than the revelations whipping through her mind at this moment. Jade Laquette was gone. No matter how much she loved the man who had become Dominique Jardonet, she could never again consummate that love or even acknowledge it. He had not lost her . . . but she had lost him.

Jean-Pierre's words rang almost cynically in the hollows of her raging mind . . . 'I already have him.'

He lifted on his elbow, his hand slipping, smoothing her bangs off her sweated forehead, but Ronnie held her eyes shut tight, her head tipped away from his heated gaze. "Veronique . . .?" Jade's voice, his deep resonant tone spoke in a near desperate soft pitch. "I—"

"Don't," she strained softly. "Don't . . . say another word. Just . . . just get up. I . . . I need to get a shower."

No more words were necessary; none were spoken. He moved slowly, carefully, as if he feared hurting her any more than he already had. Without so much as a glance, she climbed off the bed, gathered her clothes, and moved into the tattered bathroom. Somehow, some way, she would get through this . . . but the future had never seemed so bleak.

Forever, she stood under the shower spray, letting the tears mingle with the downpour, her thoughts turning in dull revolutions. Hating him would be so much easier, but that was impossible. She couldn't even blame him for what had just happened between them.

Reality. She was married to a man she loved and would continue to love, but she could never acknowledge that love again. If anyone even suspected that he had been Jade Laquette, the questions would lead to answers which could destroy him. No choice. She had no choice other than to let him go and walk away.

CHAPTER 25

Nothing he could say would ease the pain from Veronica's mind or heart; any more than self-recriminations would relieve the turmoil inside him. Silent and subdued, Dominique washed in the stained sink, not bothering to wipe the steam from the pitted mirror and almost grateful for the thick rubber curtain enclosing the tub. If he were forced to gaze upon that sleek, perfect form submersed in suds, he would surely be doomed as surely as he was damned. No woman, not a single woman in his past, had ever ignited him on sight, but this minx, with just a smile or wink, set his blood afire.

Returning to the bedroom, he dressed in the same ensemble of black jeans and gray sweater that he'd worn the evening of his abduction, laundered, gratefully, compliments of his friends in DC. Muttering a curse, he considered the irony. One would think with his talents, he might plan far enough ahead to replenish his wardrobe. Why bother trying to carry a suitcase or overnight bag? It seemed of late, he was in the habit of leaving the minor necessities to chance. To his credit, he'd deliberately left Veronica's packed bag at the Lakeview. By now, Len Devinio would be half nuts searching for her, while Jarvins would be full-blown with the images playing in his head.

A time bomb, Dominique considered absently. He'd created something of a time bomb, and not even he could decide exactly when the clock would run out. Things were happening. That much, he knew for certain. A great many things were happening in his absence, only beginning with the arrival of one extremely volatile Bentwood police officer, who had tracked down Devinio and, likewise, the Lakeview Inn.

The Want-list books, which Veronica had deemed important, were currently in the hands of the Mayor's task force, but the information contained therein only complemented the press release. Glancing absently at the Bakelite alarm clock on the shabby nightstand, Dominique stole a doubletake, then glanced to the shoddy, glowing window blind. They had missed the live press conference by almost two hours! In another hour, it would be dark, and it was too damned late to worry if this afternoon respite wasn't part of the agenda. No regrets. If the bomb blew up in his face, he had no one to blame but himself.

On the other hand, he needed to trust his nature and hope for the best. That he wasn't consciously in control of the forces moving around him remained a fact he could admit, if only to himself. A safety mechanism, perhaps. His only safety device to conceal the moment-to-moment details. If he concentrated, he could probably see the progression of events . . .

And on a whim, he indulged himself, seeing himself lighting a cigarette, blowing smoke as the bathroom door cracked open . . . and seconds later, he suffered the déjà vu. Through a haze of smoke from beneath his mustache, he watched Veronica step from the bathroom. She wore a towel, turban-style about her hair, and the same clothes she'd worn when he'd carried her from the Lakeview. If she questioned his negligence in leaving her bag at the Inn, she held her thoughts in check.

Her eyes were red, but her resolve had firmed. The fierce spirit he'd seen time and again had surfaced. She met his gaze squarely. "I asked you earlier—what do we do next," she said in a quiet, firm voice. "I'm asking you again, now. What do you plan to do with that box?"

"Deliver it," he answered without a first or second thought.

"To where?"

"A customer," he answered, his gaze unwavering as he read the annoyance flash through her diamond-blue eyes.

"Which customer?"

"Shit," he stated and bounced his gaze off her with a sudden revelation. "My car . . . I'll need to recover my car from the impound yard."

"And you didn't know that would happen, right?" she asked, somewhat skeptically and snidely.

In retrospect—? "Suppose I did. We need to make a phone call." Holding her gaze, he realized, "More accurately, you need to make a phone call. I believe you met Det. Chelsey Davis? We'll need her and Shawn to lend a hand. I uh . . . I think they're my backup."

"Excuse me?"

"M' love, after you make that phone call, you'll need to make another to Agent Devinio and place yourself in his exclusive protective custody."

"Is that a fact?"

"I hope so," he said offhandedly, and continued before she could question him further. "Your husband is officially considered the Taxidermist, according to the national newswire. The Mayor issued a formal press release—supplied to him by no other than the FBI or a facsimile of that revered institution—so stating that Jade Laquette was a bona fide suspect. It is believed that his half-brother possessed information that could have implicated him, and there are rumors that Dominique Jardonet intended to personally extradite him to France. A great deal of speculation has been fabricated, but the bottom line is this . . . you need Agent Devinio's protection as much from the press as from his own organization."

"I . . . I've been almost afraid to ask," she said hesitantly. "What did you do with Mark?"

"We had a chat, and I sent him on his way," he answered honestly. "I don't believe he'll attempt to harm you again, but if you happen to run across him in your adventures, do ask him why you needed to die."

"He'll answer me?"

"You never know," Dominique said with a smirk. "Stranger things have happened."

She considered momentarily, studying him and not trusting him—wisely. "It seems to me I'm a bigger threat to him now. What will stop him from trying to kill me, and uh . . . He does have a great deal of influence in the Bureau. It'll be my word against his, and I'm not even certain how I'll explain what happened last night."

"It may be enough for you to say that you fled for your life when Mr. Jarvins began . . . behaving strangely. You might admit holing up in a dingy motel . . ." A vision of her face floating beneath the surface of dark water, sinking, fading, halted his words and stifled his breath . . . but it wasn't that fabrication to suspend him momentarily.

Darkness spread off the shore . . . Her tennis shoes skimmed over the pavement as she raced through the shadows. Frantic, she glanced over her shoulder, black hair flying. . . Water clapped against stone. Chilly wind clicked the branches and masked the sounds of footsteps racing in her wake. Shrouded in darkness cloaked in the night, and something . . . someone chased her.

An uncanny shiver slid down his spine, his attention riveting on Veronica's pensive gaze. A fabrication? A residual effect of Jarvins' warped mind? Could that lunatic be attempting to recreate an alternate universe where Veronica would escape him? Or was this just another version of his fantasies? "Promise me you'll stay with Devinio," Dominique stated with a soft edge.

"I can't make that promise," she said firmly.

They were running out of time. His gaze slipped toward the window, flashing a vision of a police car halted at the Maserati's bumper. The car would draw attention, and by now, Devinio had issued an APB on that vehicle. There was also the tiny matter of the sedan currently residing in the Cleveland impound yard, and it wasn't exactly an official rental. He'd borrowed the damned car from a gas attendant not far from the municipal airport. Mind-bending just a trifle, he had suggested the fellow was lending the vehicle to a friend, and he'd given the pump jockey more than enough cash to cover the impound fees and inconvenience. Doubtful, the compensation would ease the man's troubled mind when he failed to recall which friend had borrowed his Chevy.

"We need to make those calls," Dominique said abruptly, and motioned to the phone. "Will you dial the number I give you and ask for Det. Davis? I'll take the phone when she's on the line."

She hesitated only a moment, then responded to his growing urgency. Settling on the edge of the bed, she lifted the receiver from the antiquated rotary phone, awaited the number, dialed it, and sat through two rings. If she was surprised by the background noise or the husky voice answering with a simple 'hello,' nothing showed. This wasn't her first foray into making an anonymous call. Masking her voice in a lofty vapid tone, she asked for the detective, then handed Dominique the receiver.

At his ear, the detective snapped, "This is Det. Davis."

"Avoid men`tioning my name or sounding surprised," Dominique commented, and sensed the abrupt tension. "I need a fav`or, de`tective."

"Uhhh . . . Yea, sure. What can I do for you?"

"There is . . . a car incar`cerated in your impound yard," he spoke in heavily accented English. "In the backseat, you will find a sat`shel and a box. I need you and your part`nair to collect those items and ah . . . drive the lakefront road toward Lakefront Beach. Es thot pos`sible?"

"No problem," she answered smoothly. "You're going to give me the details, right?"

He offered the license plate number, color, model, and year, then added. "I will meet you there in one hour."

"Better make it a little longer than that."

"One hour, mon amie," he said bluntly.

"Uh . . . Okay. Anything else?"

"See you then," he stated and leaned, dropping the receiver in its cradle and finding Veronica's critical gaze. On a dual plane, he saw the interior of the task force headquarters. Smoothly, Det. Chelsey Davis turned and snagged her partner, Shawn McAllory's eye, with a silent signal to join her en route to the door. Focused on Veronica, he commented, "You hov Lenny's private numb`air. Phone him now, will you please? Hov him meet you at the Re`jaunzy Restaurant on Bonkfield Rd."

"The Regency?" she asked, studying him more critically. "On Bankfield Rd.?"

"*Oui, mon amour,*" he answered before realizing he'd lost the American pronunciations again. Shrugging, he glanced at the phone. "Phone him?"

"They're hunting for me, aren't they?"

"*Oui,*" he answered smoothly. "But you will be safe."

Her head tipped; her soft blue gaze intensified. "You can say something like that with all the confidence in the world, and you expect me to believe that you don't know precisely how this will turn out?"

"I told you once, Veronique, when I can, I will ans`air you. But I do not always hov the ans`airs on hand. I wish I did. I uh . . . I must trust myself to know whot is . . . essen`tial when et becomes essen`tial."

She studied him more tensely before putting voice to her thoughts. "Are you going to get out of this alive?"

He smiled slightly, hoping to relieve the anxiety he felt in her mind, in her body. "Hov no fear for me, mon amour. I am a sarviv`or. Will you make that call now?"

Not entirely relieved, she turned her attention to the telephone and dialed Devinio's private number.

Dominique needed only a glimpse to know Devinio stood in a private conference room within the headquarters. Relief poured through the line as Veronica stated, "Don't panic, Len. This is me."

No slouch, Devinio need not be told to mask his surprise for the benefit of his audience consisting of the Mayor, DA, and the ranking detectives and chiefs from the Mayor's task force. Devinio had been attempting to convince them that their information was flawed. Too late, Devinio had heard about that press release, and he was still fuming. "How about giving me a number to reach you, and I'll call you back in a few minutes?"

"I'll do one better, Len. You'll find me at the Regency Restaurant on Bankfield Rd. And do me a favor, will you? Come alone. If I even think you have anyone from your agency with you, I'll disappear again."

"How soon?"

"Within the hour," she answered and lowered the receiver, her gaze lifting. Calm, cool, and collected, she held Dominique in a chilly stream. "I'm a survivor, too, Mr. Jardonet. When this is done—regardless of how it turns out—I want you to do me a favor. I want you to return to France or England or wherever the hell you decide to live . . . and don't ever come back. I don't want to know where you are or what you're doing, and I don't want you to try contacting me or my son. For my sake, for his sake—don't ever come near us again."

The finality in her words, the conviction in her eyes, held him frozen. Even knowing she had silently added *for your own sake*, the pain wrapped around his heart and mind. Never again . . . the words were his, but they resonated in her mind, now. Never again could they share the intimacy and abandon of making love—or the joy of life itself. A dual-edged sword, this unyielding love for her. For her sake . . . for the child's sake . . . No other words could touch him more deeply. He would walk through the fires of hell for her, and life without her would be hell.

Nodding, backing a step from an overwhelming desire to take her in his arms, he agreed, "As you wish, madame." Not another moment could he look into her chilly eyes, her closed heart. "I'll bring the car around," he said as he turned, veering to collect his jacket off the back of the chair near the window.

Sliding out the window with an economy of motion, he landed on his feet and collected his balance, tugging the glass down behind him. Upon a time, the motor lodge had probably drawn a decent clientele with the lakefront no more than a hundred yards from the rear walls. Only remnants of that bygone era remained, but he saw it clearly, from the stone footpaths leading through the overgrowth to the gravel roadway ending at a boat launch. Even with the late afternoon sunlight scattered through barren branches, the Maserati remained nearly invisible within the tangle, and doubtful any of the current lodgers had taken a moment to appreciate the rear view. Truckers and a group of local hookers working out of a bar down the block kept the dilapidated lodge in operation, and in the light of day, it was worse than Dominique had first imagined. Mismatched paint, weathered boards over windows, entire sections of wood siding replaced with plywood . . . a testament to the ruin he felt at the moment. Was it any wonder he'd chosen such a wretched place to spend his final hours?

Crunching slate roof tiles, branches, dead leaves, and gravel underfoot, Dominique reached the driver's door, halfheartedly wondering how he had avoided scraping fenders or denting the front bumper. The chrome rested a hair's breadth from a stout sapling that had grown up over the loading dock road. A sixth sense . . . a damned sixth sense to protect him from the minor blows and leave him wide open for the ultimate destruction.

He should have accepted his due years ago, he considered while backing the car smoothly from the shroud of briars. In point of fact, he'd lost track of how many times he'd dodged a stray bullet, a car crash, or a loaded syringe. His damned sixth sense . . . The same sixth sense that had avoided a lethal dose of Curare an assassination team—led by Mark Jarvins—would have administered to Jade Laquette if not for the confusion over a plane crash.

The same damned sense directed him to pull the windowpane glasses and hat from his pocket as he rolled the car in front of the shabby door.

Stunning in the speckled sunlight sinking past the barren trees, Veronica stepped onto the cracked sidewalk, hair glistening, her aura glowing. Never again to experience that white light . . .

A curse, to know he lived now only to protect her from the forces that would attempt to destroy her . . . To know he had fully entrenched himself in the darker realm and accepted the full mantel of his birthright. His own mother had feared him and considered him a monster . . . But she had never hesitated to use what was inside of him. Daring and tempting fate, seduced by the power to exist inside her creation, she had drawn him into her chicanery again and again. A damned thing. A monster to walk the earth in the form of a man . . . that was his curse. To be a prodigy of the dark forces and he truly was damned, had probably been damned from his moment of conception.

As Veronica slipped into the seat next to him, he wondered at his own tiny creation swimming so innocently within her womb.

Already, he sensed the power of his prodigy, a not inconsiderable power for such an insubstantial entity, and for the first time since waking fully into himself, he realized the temptation and seduction that his father undoubtedly suffered.

Damned.

He truly was damned, for if he were merciful, he never would have planted his seed and allowed it to take root inside a woman he loved. He would not wish his life—his curse—on another. Yet, the child flourished. Male. Another male Laquette. A bastard. A warlock. One with a talent to obscure his own future, Dominique knew at this moment. Would this infant even reach adulthood? Would he grow up despising his father and indifferent to his mother? Would Veronique nurture him with all the love she carried inside of her to become something his father wasn't? To be strong in ways his father could never fathom?

Blind. Whatever this infant's future, it remained a mystery. Not even a glimpse of the child's physical image could Dominique conjure, but as he drove, he sensed the third presence within the confines of the car. Almost like a feather brushing against his flesh, he identified this presence reaching out to him. No clear thoughts, no words, just a sensation of curiosity and an insatiable desire to know, to understand the living world beyond the confines of his liquid world.

How much of this material world had the child already discovered? On autopilot, Dominique navigated the course to the Regency Restaurant. Without more than a fleeting thought, he avoided police cars, turned at random, and remained on secondary rather than main thoroughfares.

Did this little wonder already know what dangers lay ahead for him and his mother? Did he already carry the first glimmers of awareness to mold his opinion of his father?

Felicity had tried the ocean tactic. She'd put an ocean between him and his creator, but the bond had never severed. The distrust and despise had grown before Jade Laquette had stepped off a plane and into his father's living realm. Meeting his father hadn't come as a major surprise. What Dominique remembered of those moments was the fear to slide over him, through him, as his father had eyed him from head to heel. He'd known in those moments, the torment he'd foreseen would come to pass, and he'd battled his father with all the ferocity of a raging bull. What he'd failed to see in his innocence was the futility and the result of their conflict. Uncontrollably, the darkness had come over him, into him.

Did such an event linger on his own and this fetus's horizon? Would there come a day when he would look down into a pair of wary, innocent eyes and vow to transform his child into his own image? To make him a child of the night and an instrument of destruction?

A quandary that. Dominique had never simply walked up to another man and struck him dead. He had never killed anyone for the sake of killing or to further a black cause. Not for profit. Not for fame. Not for any sacrilegious goal toward ultimate destruction. He had never practiced the black arts toward an evil end. What did that make him then? A fledgling? Was that still ahead in his future? Would he become as black-hearted as the beast to plague this city? Or had he already become that beast? Could he have removed this maniac as much as three months ago and spared the four victims? If he had arrived in Cleveland three months ago and slain this maniac in his sleep, would he be any more or less damned?

"Assuming you're not just driving in circles," Veronica spoke without a glance and continued with her attention fixed through the passenger window. "Do you intend to drop me off at the restaurant and take the car?"

"Et will be returned to you safely," he answered absently. "If you must off'air an explana'tion, let et be known, you stayed with a new friend," he continued. "Perhaps with a woman you met in a pub. No one will dispute you."

"You have done this before, haven't you?" she asked in a leaden tone.

He followed her thoughts to realize she wondered about his official credentials. It was too late to deny whatever he had done in the past. "Yes," he answered.

"You're a spy or something," she said without effect. "The name changes . . .? It was all part of what you do for a living."

"I am whot I hov always been, mon amour. An entrepreneur. I uh . . . I hov connec'tions, I suppose."

"Is there," she hesitated, then realized the futility of censoring her thoughts. Her gaze tipped toward him, watching his profile as she asked, "Is there anything about you that wasn't a lie since the moment we met?"

He understood her anger, an anger born of pain. "Nothing about me wos a lie with you, Veronique," he said honestly, his gaze held on the highway ahead. "If . . . if I had consciously known this moment hovered on the horizon for both of us, I would nev'air hov allowed myself to fall in love with you. If nothing else, mon amour, believe that."

"Unfortunately," she said quietly, turning her gaze through the passenger window. "I do."

His heart slammed a mean beat, but nothing showed in his expression as he made another turn, and the jutting neon ahead caught his eye. Not another word passed between them as he rolled into the rear entrance of the lounge parking lot. As he pulled near the door, he found her expression masked toward indifference as efficiently as his own. “Veronique—“ Whatever he had meant to say vanished as her eyes lanced him, holding him. No words.

A simple ‘goodbye’ remained her only thought before she clasped the door handle and started out. Pausing she looked back and added aloud, “Be careful.”

“You do the same, mon amour,” he said quietly, wishing he could find words enough to ease the pain behind her eyes.

She pushed the door open and stepped out, not looking back as she slung her purse strap over her shoulder and started across the sidewalk.

In all his life, he had never known a stronger woman. She was walking away, and the finality of her actions could not be mistaken. She was letting him go, making it easy for him to walk away, and he harbored no doubts, she would adhere to her decision. No one would ever learn his identity through this incredible woman.

With an effort, he lifted his foot from the brake, catching a last glimpse of her before she passed through the door. Drawing from her strength, he bypassed every empty parking space and circled the lot. The scent of her hair lingered within the car as surely as her soft perfume . . . an import he’d given her weeks ago.

Distracted, he remained on the secondary roads, navigating random turns until he pulled into a busy shopping plaza. Leaving the Maserati in a space where it would be safe until an observant officer spotted it, he strode across the plaza, passing between parked cars, ultra-aware of his surroundings. As he joined a motley collection of pedestrians awaiting the city transit bus pulling into the parking lot, an attractive young woman holding a lively toddler lost her hold on the bags she attempted to shuffle. Dominique barely stooped to assist when he glimpsed a patrol car rolling into the lot from the opposite direction. In a flashing instant, he knew the officer would run the plates on the Maserati, and the revelation lent him pause to consider how narrow his world had become. The moments were counting down, his insights quickening.

Nodding to the grateful woman, preoccupied, he scanned the lot, watching the patrol car cruise toward the main department store entrance. Behind the woman and child, he ascended the bus steps, deposited the correct change, and slid into a window seat in a position to catch sight of the police car. Only the lightbar across the roof remained visible as the car sped past the storefronts and turned randomly into the row. As the bus pulled away from the curb, the patrol car stopped. Five minutes. Less than five minutes had passed but did that accurately indicate the convergence of future time toward real time? He’d known as much as twenty minutes ago if not a great deal sooner, his sports car would be spotted by a passing patrol car even if the details had eluded him.

Dismissing the analysis, he turned his conscious thoughts toward the immediate goal, not pleased with the revelation. He hadn't lied to Veronica. Even with his insight, he couldn't draw the face of the Taxidermist from his subconscious. He gained only the impression of meeting the maniac at least once in the past, but whether the certainty derived from physical touch or from the events witnessed through the eyes of the victims, he couldn't decide. The fellow had a medical background. Dominique assumed the monster's expertise developed through formal education. Try as he might, he couldn't believe this monster had sat for hours poring over medical books to self-educate himself on the procedures and drugs. On the surface, then, Reddinger certainly fit the profile . . .

The memory came, unfolding within his mind to recall a day—possibly more than two years ago—when the sleek-dressed fellow had meandered into Olden Time. As Isaac Bently had done a thousand times before, he had approached the customer with a welcome smile and the natural line, 'Anything I can help you find?'

Dr. Whitman Reddinger was attracted to things of beauty, drawn like a miller to light toward the cut-glass and glazed oriental pottery in the window displays. The doctor was in town visiting a friend, a college friend who just happened to own a foundry at the edge of town. Only recently, the foundry had opened a division dedicated to perfecting medical equipment. At light speed, Dominique made the connection between Allen Spencer, CEO of Bentrel Industries, a company in which Tim Spencer maintained a financial family interest. Tim's older brother and Reddinger were close to the same age. They'd both completed their undergraduate work at Yale before their interests had carried them in different directions. Allen had returned to Bentwood to run the family business, a company that supplied a great deal of specialty steel products for anything from airplanes to government armaments.

Throughout their conversation that afternoon, Reddinger had admitted his profession as a plastic surgeon and alluded to his preference for male companionship, warming to Isaac's mutual appreciation for art. Whether in a nude sculpt of classic Renaissance style depicting the human body with a stout, hearty physique or in the craftsmanship of a Samurai sword, Reddinger considered himself a connoisseur of Oriental style. By the time Reddinger had departed carrying a half dozen exceptional pieces of pottery, the doctor had added his name to Isaac Bently's mailing list as well as his want files. 'And do be sure to call me if you're ever in Cleveland . . .'

Only in his mind, Dominique cursed his selective memory. Reddinger truly was a red herring, and nowhere even close to the madman in Cleveland. In the broader scheme of things, Reddinger was a pawn, one whose single purpose was to divert the investigation. And what did that say about the dark nature currently cloaked behind the face of Dominique Jardonet? Reddinger's only crime remained his unhealthy attraction to a certain antique dealer who might have harbored a hidden agenda as much as two years ago.

If not Reddinger, then who? Who at this moment might fully believe himself safe from either suspicion or apprehension . . . and on a dual plane, might be outraged to be upstaged by a highly regarded colleague? Self-serving, this megalomaniac. He wouldn't be pleased to hear about another physician stealing the limelight, not after his greatest achievement, and especially not a man of Whitman Reddinger's caliber. Jealousy. The most basic of all vices. By now, this maniac would be raging over the injustice. Most assuredly, he'd hold Reddinger personally to blame for stealing the spotlight . . . and Reddinger was a handsome fellow, all sleek and sculpted, the epitome of male charisma. The Taxidermist wasn't . . .

He was homely.

The Taxidermist was a homely creature and physically flawed, perhaps scarred, and deformed to some degree. And therein lay the root of his rage. Undoubtedly, his monstrous complexion had become the fixation to springboard his murderous intent. Jealousy. At a base level, he envied his victims, and that might be reason enough to take their lives, steel their flawless skin and solid bones . . . but his obsession had not begun in Cleveland.

Abruptly, a window burst open in Dominique's mind. Images, crystal clear, the images animated, and for the second time in just over twenty-four hours, he viewed the crackling movie frames, the same wicked filmstrips that had driven him to the brink . . .

Hour after hour in that wretched theatre where Jade Laquette had been tortured, this madman had been likewise evaluated and destroyed, but in him, the horrors had taken a different turn. Perhaps, programmed to believe himself superior, one of the chosen to be worthy of taking from them, the lesser races. Blond then, and blue-eyed, not unlike Mark Jarvins . . . and just as twisted toward the cause to believe himself instrumental in creating a new order. Twisted. Somehow convinced that he stood on the verge of coronation, conditioned and programmed by his benefactors in the Capital to believe he would be duly rewarded when the moment came.

By what method his benefactors had programmed him, Dominique need not guess. Forced to watch the films, this maniac had reveled in the gruesome tests, enlightening his handlers of his anticipation toward this end. They had merely nudged him in this monstrous direction to fulfill their needs. A test, then, the ultimate test to create this monster and turn him loose.

And Jade Laquette, the child, had informed them of this monster's advent . . . after lying, strapped to the same chair, viewing the same films. Where he had been sickened by the sights, this other had been thrilled and eager to engage in similar tests. In the bows of that unholy laboratory, this beast had learned his skill before graduating to attend a higher level of education.

By now, however, the effects of Asst. Director Lakeland would be taking hold. The lines of communication with this maniac would be severed, and that, too, wouldn't bode well for this maniac's mindset. The financial backing, the promises of his just reward, the creation, and the market for his art withdrawn? Undoubtedly, he already felt the effects of betrayal. Complicate the silence from his contacts in Washington with the announcement that a second, even less than worthy familiar fellow, was now receiving credit for his work . . . a recipe for disaster. To this nut, it probably looked as if his cohorts, his benefactors had conspired against him and supplanted Laquette. Laquette . . . married to the daughter of an important man in Washington. A man who probably boasted a great deal of influence in the political arena in the Capital. If nothing else, this maniac knew a greater design existed. A new order. A supreme order. In his warped vision of reality, he saw himself as the leader of that order, conditioned for that role. He was insane, and that insanity wasn't a mystery to whoever had chosen him for this trial run of chaos.

A member of the medical community, this lunatic, with the white supremacy angle carefully planted at the murder scenes. A test and this lunatic was expendable, no different than the victims in the trial tests for bio-warfare. With only select victims, the leaders of this ultimate plan could monitor the ethnic, moral, and religious effects of this maniac's advent, and doubtful, they were disappointed.

Halfheartedly, Dominique listened to the conversations on the bus, hearing the Taxidermist mentioned at least once. At the edges of his awareness, he felt the tension of an elderly woman who had lost her parents and a brother in the Holocaust. He sensed the distrust of a mid-aged black man toward a young white man seated across from him toward the front of the bus. White supremacy. The words had transcended the airwaves more often in the past week than in the past six months. On the courthouse steps, an ethnic boiling pot had nearly resulted in a riot, and no definitive lines were laid. Christians, Jews, the KKK . . . It was just a matter of time before the battle lines were drawn. The early news release concerning Reddinger—a physician of German descent—had escalated the tension by no small measure. His name, alone, added just a little too much credibility to the Nazi influence, which undoubtedly accounted for Jarvins' arrival the evening past.

A smile slipped into Dominique's lips as he watched the passing scenery. Reddinger was a little too close to the true nature of the beast, despite the doctor's innocence. They had wanted a test, a trial run. Well, and they had it. The public outcry in the early hours had probably accounted for the quick action to find another scapegoat, and Dominique had no doubts, Jarvins had come up with the theory about Laquette's demise. Unfortunately for Jarvins, the lines of communication were truly closing, and his solo decision to implicate Jade Laquette wouldn't bode well for what remained of his future.

Unconsciously, Dominique pushed from his seat and meandered up the aisle, stepping off the bus on a corner not far from his intended destination. On foot, he continued on the sidewalk, aware of the wind whipping off the lake, dropping the temperature a few more degrees. In DC, the lightweight jacket had sufficed. Presently, he could use a warmer coat and the onset of dusk only enhanced the chill.

By the time he stood in the shadow of trees along the lakefront road, he was shivering as much from the cold as anticipation. Something . . . he could feel the advance of something. His gaze fanned over the glimpses of the lake. It was a little late in the season for pleasure boats, even without the choppy water and wind to squelch the avid boater. Farther out on the lake, barely a fleck against the skyline, a considerable-sized ship—undoubtedly, commercial—seemed dead in the water, a tribute to the distance. Nearer at hand, he sensed, rather than heard voices from a collection of teenagers who defied nature to spoil their fun.

The Taxidermist was on the prowl.

With that single thought, Dominique keened his senses, searching the immediate vicinity as if he fully expected to see a lone walker or a van parked in one of the wooded inlets. Nothing. He saw nothing to evidence his belief, but the impression remained in his mind. His conviction needed no material evidence.

The Taxidermist was on the prowl. He'd taken a life less than one week earlier, and that one, less than two weeks after the third. No choice. The maniac needed to strike tonight, needed to relieve his tension . . . and prove himself. Dominique could almost hear him weighing his decision, justifying his need. No matter how this maniac had been born, no matter how he saw himself as an instrument of a greater design, at the base of his psychosis, he remained a serial killer with an insatiable appetite and a need. A need to prove himself in control, to prove himself superior, to set the world straight.

In vivid color, Dominique saw Len Devinio sitting behind the wheel of his dark rental, parked in shadows a half block from the impound yard . . . oblivious of the dark blue van parked at a curb a block away.

The Taxidermist was on the prowl, and he had been watching, waiting, patient, although he'd spotted his next subject days ago. A sign, an omen, that not one—but two potential candidates had come to him. A reward, a sign of his success that he need not even search. These ones had come to him.

His was a talent, an art, and he was the only master of the craft. Once and for all, his benefactors and the world would know that he alone held dominion. *A twofold plan . . . beautiful . . .*

Dominique lost the thought, distracted by the headlights and the sound of an engine approaching. Without conscious thought, he stepped from the shadows ahead of the beam and started walking in the direction from which he had come.

CHAPTER 26

Depressed, Ronnie rested in a corner booth, trying not to stare at the young couple across the room. Without a doubt, they were celebrating a special occasion . . . either a wedding anniversary or the announcement of a first child, an anticipated child. In the candlelight, the young woman's smile quivered, and her mate's eyes sparkled with adoration. Doubtful either noticed her interest. They remained in a world of their own, barely acknowledging the waitress much less other diners. With an iron resolve, Ronnie tugged her gaze from their bliss and suffered a greater annoyance when her attention landed on a silver-haired couple almost equally as absorbed in one another's company. Life wasn't fair. In fact, it could be downright cruel. How dare these people flaunt their marital bliss for all the world to see?

How dare Dominique Jardonet leave her in the type of restaurant where couples dined to celebrate those affairs? Heartless. He was cruel, a cruel heartless . . .

She couldn't finish the thought, not when she recognized the safety of the candlelight atmosphere. Even if her picture had landed on a billboard—or the evening news broadcast—doubtful anyone would distinguish her in the dull light. The hostess hadn't lent her a glance other than to smile and lead her into the dining room. It was still too early for the Saturday night crowd. By six, the elegant entrance would be filled with patrons anticipating an hour's wait, and there was safety in numbers.

Her own wait lasted little more than a half hour, and she wasn't pleased when she recognized the tall, dark-haired fellow who paused in the entryway. Even in candlelight, Tim Spencer spotted her with no trouble at all. He was alone and, if the quick smile flashing in his sober expression were any indication, relieved regardless of the circumstance.

"Funny meeting you here," Tim said as he slipped into the booth across from her.

"Where's Lenny?" she asked bluntly.

"Something came up," Spencer said as he glanced over her as if to judge her health. "Are you all right?"

"Fine," she said bluntly. "What came up?"

"You realize you've had us all about half crazy with worry, right?" Tim asked and barely glanced at the waitress who approached with a pot of coffee. Turning his cup to be filled, he withheld his words while darting his gaze toward her. He hadn't lost his thought with the interruption. The instant the woman passed out of earshot, he continued as if he hadn't paused. "You want to tell me what happened last night? One minute we were talking—"

"What happened at Olden Time?"

"Not a hell of a lot," he answered, his gaze steady. "Now, what happened at that hotel? Why'd you hang up on me and take off?"

"I ran into some trouble," she said carefully, deciding she would keep Tim out of the loop for the moment. She needed to talk to Lenny. If nothing else . . . Lenny? Her heart skipped a quick beat, and she reacted abruptly, "What came up? Where's Lenny, Tim? And don't hedge this one? Why didn't he come?"

For a split second, he hesitated before identifying the renewed tension in her eyes. "How much do you know about what's going on, Ronnie? Have you heard the news or seen—"

"I know the mayor issued a statement that implicates Jade," she said bluntly, and read the anger sparking in his tense eyes. "I'm assuming Len knows it's a lie. And eventually, I want to know how this started. At the moment, I need to know . . . is Lenny with Mark Jarvins?"

"I haven't seen Jarvins," Tim answered. "What kind of trouble did you run into?"

"We'll get into that later. Damn it, Tim—where's Lenny, and what are you doing in Cleveland?"

"I'm in Cleveland because I couldn't get anywhere on the phone and because a certain lady who happens to mean a great deal to me disappeared without a trace. You got off the phone to answer the door . . . let me take a wild stab here. Jardonet showed up."

Something in Tim's gaze suggested the thought made him far more angry. Controlling her reaction with an iron will, Ronnie held his gaze. "And if he did?"

"Look, I don't know what part this character plays in all of this, hon, but I'm beginning to think he might be a little . . . dangerous. And that's an understatement," he muttered and glanced outside the booth, searching and sorting his thoughts. "I've heard he has an uncanny likeness to Sax, Ronnie, but uh . . . that doesn't explain what he's doing here or just what he's up to. Last night . . . you saw him before you called. You want to start at the beginning and tell me what that was all about? How did he contact you? When?"

"You think he had something to do with what happened to Jade," she realized and read the tension in his gaze. He hadn't slept well, if at all. His firm jaw carried a haze of two-day beard stubble that hid nothing of his taut features. Not for the first time, Ronnie sensed the grief belying his expression, knew he'd taken the loss of her husband, his friend, harder than he'd ever admit. He wanted answers, wanted explanations just as badly as she did, and her disappearance had only provided him with the excuse to do what he'd meant to do anyway . . . To come here and find answers.

His gaze returned firmly. "Let's just say, it's a little too coincidental, honey, and I'd really like to talk to this guy personally. Who called him into this? What does he—"

"Jade," she interrupted and held Tim's stopped gaze, her own firm. "Jade brought him here, Tim, and don't bother asking. You know what my husband was even if you don't want to admit it. He knew, Tim. He knew in advance that he'd be asked to consult on this case, and I think he knew how it would turn out."

"Jardonet told you that?"

"In not so many words, yes," she answered. "But there's more to it, Tim. Dominique Jardonet has more than looks in common with Jade," she admitted. "Between you and I, he uh . . . he has a very strong sixth sense. Enough so, that he did know where to find me last night. Not once, but twice, and that's about as much as I'll tell you at the moment. We need to find Len, and I need to talk to him."

"Did you eat yet?" he asked.

"No," she answered, with a hint of exasperation. How could he think about food thinking at a time like this? "And we don't have time for that right now. There's a phone in the lobby—"

"Ronnie, we have about an hour to kill. I promised Len, we'd wait for him here, and I'll hogtie you to keep that promise."

"You don't seem to get it, Tim," she said and leaned forward slightly, glancing outside the booth to verify they were not overheard and drawing Spencer forward to listen. "There's more to this—a lot more to this than meets the eye, and it's too damned possible that Len could be in danger. In fact, a great deal of danger if he's anywhere near Mark Jarvins. His life could be in danger. Now, do we phone him? Or do I dive from this booth and cry rape when you try to catch me? After which, I'll find him myself."

Tim glanced outside the booth as if judging his competition, then looked at her. "Lady, you do drive a hard bargain. Let's go try the phone."

As the car veered to the curb, Dominique stopped, not surprised when both front doors exploded open. Lively, Det. Davis stepped from the passenger door, and her partner launched from the driver's side. As Shawn strode around the front of the car, Chelsey sidestepped almost casually, putting Dominique at the point of a triangle.

He understood their tension, suffered their distrust, and grasped their intentions. Had he known how they would react to his call? Had he sensed the probability of a trap? Without a doubt, he'd planted the seeds of distrust. Within the confines of the task force, it had become known that Dominique Jardonet was related—by blood—to the accused killer.

"How about putting your hands where we can see them," Shawn stated in a controlled, genial tone.

Removing his chilled hands from his pockets, Dominique lifted his hands to either side. "I am not armed, mon ami," he said in a low voice, unaffected when Shawn drew his .45 from under his jacket.

"Just do us a favor, and don't make any sudden moves, Mr. Jardonet," Davis stated. "This is just a precaution," she added while stepping forward. "You won't mind if I just make sure you're not carrying, right?"

"Nat`urally, I will co-op`airate," he said and remained still as Davis moved behind him. Methodically, she patted down his pockets and chest under his jacket, searching his waist. Without reservations, she felt his crotch and skimmed down his legs, but she wasn't pleased with her actions. Head canted, Dominique spied over his shoulder as she rose. "Satisfied, ma chérie?"

With firm resolve, she refrained from answering while pulling her handcuffs from her coat pocket.

"We hov a problem," Dominique said quietly.

"I know how this probably looks, Mr. Jardonet, but we really don't have a choice."

"We're not arresting you," Shawn stated. "But we do have to take you downtown for questioning. There are a few people pretty anxious to talk to you."

In a glance, Dominique guided Davis to snap the cuff on her own wrist rather than his, then turned his gaze to Shawn as the detective distracted, disbelieving his partner's actions. As the pale blue eyes came to him, Dominique locked him in a gaze and ordered, "Replace your weapon in its holster, Shawn."

The detective obeyed, and collectively, Dominique ordered them into the front seat of their car. As they obliged, he climbed into the backseat, grateful to find his possessions awaiting him. To satisfy their curiosity, they'd gone to the impound yard and, undoubtedly, searched his garment bag as well as the box. What he should have asked them to bring was a warmer coat. For a moment, he rested in silence, merely grateful to be out of the wind as he considered how best to gain their cooperation without taking a trip 'downtown.' Without a doubt, at least one federal agent wanted to speak to him, and he couldn't blame this pair for their apprehension in his regard. As the detectives responsible for making Reddinger a suspect with the information he'd provided them, they were not in high standing with their department; after all, Reddinger was threatening to sue the city for defamation of character and false arrest despite the absence of an arrest.

His thoughts turning, Dominique commanded Shawn to drive and find a phone booth. In an enhanced state of autopilot, McAllory obeyed, oblivious to his silent, handcuffed partner and his passenger. Within moments, the detective pulled into an outdated gas station. The pumps still wore the bubble style, and the most modern convenience clung to the Insulbrick wall beneath a silver hood. Leaving the detectives tranced, Dominique climbed from the backseat and dug coins from his pocket. No sooner did he begin to dial the number that stood in the foreground of his mind when his attention divided. On one plane he knew Reddinger's phone had been taken off the hook; on another, he focused on a storefront directly across the street.

Automated, Dominique replaced the receiver and stood momentarily, studying the storefront. If ever he'd believed in coincidences, that time had passed. Distracted, he returned to the car and collected the box from the backseat.

He'd never heard of Gordon's Antiques, not in passing, not in any advertising brochures. A mere hole in the wall of the largest building within sight, the store boasted only one dirty window with a mishmash of used furniture. Dusty glassware and whatnot blocked any view of the interior. To the right of the indented door of smoked glass and heavy mesh, plywood covered the windows—probably a drug store in another era. To the left, a barber shop sporting a candy-cane-style post faced the corner at an angle. The barber shop wore a bold 'closed' sign in the doorway; Gordon's merely appeared closed.

At a glance, awaiting a single car to pass, Dominique realized he stood in one of the more desperate neighborhoods in the city suburbs. Houses—close enough to be considered row houses—extended on either side of the street, inset to accommodate a scattering of barren trees that had long ago breached the sidewalk pavement. Roots jutted from the pavement, scrambling the walk. Many of the houses were in serious need of repair, or altogether condemned, judging by the surplus of plywood-covered windows and stone porches crumbled into heaps of rubble. The atmosphere reminded Dominique of the villages in Europe where the devastation of WWII remained a testament to the dead and cruelty of man. America, he reminded himself. Only Hawaii had suffered a physical assault. The battles here were internal. The bombs were economic strife and social decline.

As he crossed the street, he glimpsed a group of young teens loitering down the block, coats flapping in the wind and cigarettes smoldering between their fingers. White. The neighborhood was predominantly white, he realized while glimpsing a man climbing into a pickup in the opposite direction. Stepping onto the cracked curb, Dominique continued into the inlet entry. A tattered, illegible plastic card boasted the store hours. He relied on his sixth sense to know the store was open for another ten minutes.

The window display hadn't offered a false sense of the interior. Floor-to-ceiling, battered furniture rose in a claustrophobic tunnel effect beneath the dull glow of naked bulbs dangling from single cords. Nothing of daylight touched the interior. Dominique needed only a second for his eyes to adjust and land on the remnants of a bar top directly ahead. With his senses keening, he knew the owner lingered behind that raised counter, fidgeting with a 1930s Bakelite radio. Only the squeal of the door hinges and creak of wood underfoot announced Dominique's arrival, and by the time he rounded the deep wall of broken chairs, the proprietor awaited him.

Harry Gordon, proprietor and operator, rested on a raised stool that he'd probably purchased with the scarred maple bar top. As if he were one with the dust and cobwebbed atmosphere, his dull gray hair wore a sallow yellow haze, and his gray-fuzzed features carried as many shadowed crags and crevices as his walls. He smiled pleasantly and nodded, already glancing at the box and taking in Dominique's features at a glance. Somewhere in the clutter, a mono speaker radio—possibly '40s vintage—played a 50s tune by an artist Dominique couldn't readily identify. Big band. A lot of brass . . . maybe Tony Bennett.

"What can I do for you, Sonny?"

A little more lost than he cared to consider, Dominique sidled to the counter, sliding the box onto the ledge between them and glancing at the folded dirty flaps. It was one of those moments. One of those uncomfortable moments when no glimpses of the immediate future invaded to assist. Past, present, and future converged into the moment. Uncomfortably, Dominique met the older man's gaze. "I am hoping you will ah . . . find a use for this," he said hesitantly, his attention again drawn to the box, his senses straining with an effort to wipe the accent from his words. Wily, this curse of his. Genuinely uncomfortable, he realized he was presently on his own.

Brows furrowed, Harry Gordon glanced at the box. "You have something to sell? Is that it?"

Dominique smiled, relieved abruptly by the simplicity of the words. "Oui, monsieur . . . yes," he corrected and realized the futility of attempting to hide his heritage. He supposed he could pass for Canadian French, but in the next instant, knew the futility of that as well. "I ehm . . . et was my gramma`ma's. When she possed away," he shrugged, glancing warily at the box, then back to Harry with a natural dismay. "I believe et is ah . . . valuable, boot I am . . . not posi`tive. Perhaps, you would know something about et?"

"Well, let's have a look," Gordon spoke with a smoker's gravelly voice and slid off his stool. He stood nearly as tall as Dominique despite his slightly stooped shoulders. With a natural ease, he reached and, undeterred by the black attic dust, he unfolded the limp cardboard. His brow furrowed more as he dipped his hand into the box, and he appeared less than intimidated when he clasped the base in the black depths.

Prickling under his collar, Dominique stood his ground, suffering an almost insatiable desire to step backward as the elder man lifted the obscenity from the box and shoved the cardboard aside. Absently, he reached past the clutter on the counter and spun the nob to silence the scratchy tune emanating from the old radio. Apparently, he needed his concentration.

Even to Dominique, this harmless construct posed as an atrocity, an abhorrence in tribute to the evil which resided in all men. In a matrix of die-cast iron, the claw-footed base—as round as a sandwich plate—boasted a near-renaissance depiction of human forms writhing in what could be mistaken as sexual bliss. Within the dull light, further shaded by the rounded dome of parchment, the human shapes seemed to move, gyrating in agony rather than pleasure. And at the edges of his mind, Dominique heard the screams of terror, the pain. A vision from hell, a living visage of eternal flames. Internally, he shivered as he watched the sturdy fingers turning the base, understood the elder man studying the craftsmanship. Whether Harry Gordon had begun to feel the incubus inside this seemingly harmless object, Dominique couldn't be certain, but the fellow lifted his fingers and wiped his palm on his shirt.

Curious and apparently baffled, Gordon reached to a desk light on a coil and ignited the more intense beam that he used on rare occasions for studying jewelry—and more often when repairing small appliances. Shifting the stream to shine on the parchment, his brow furrowed. Again he began turning the base, oblivious of the figures moving under his fingertips.

With an effort, Dominique blocked the cries at the edges of his mind and steeled his nerve to stand firm.

Dumbfounded, the elder man shook his head. "It's old, I'll give it that," Gordon said in a low voice, his gaze rising to connect with Dominique as he withdrew his hand from the lamp. "It looks like something made in the thirties or forties, but I'll be honest, sonny, I've never seen anything like it. That parchment, it looks uh. . ." His attention wavered to the domed shade; the parchment stretched taut over thin strips of iron, not unlike a Tiffany lamp. Thin threads of apparent rawhide fastened the parchment to the iron in the rendition of an ancient Indian technique for sewing cloth. The parchment itself carried a matrix of designs. Gordon shook his head and continued, "I'm not real sure just what that parchment's made of. It looks like paper . . ." But suddenly, his attention riveted, and he leaned a little closer, his brow furrowing more deeply as he recognized symbols . . . faded ink numbers embedded inside the parchment. “Jesus H. Christ,” he hissed softly and his stricken gaze shot to Dominique with his doubts on high. “Where’d you say you got this?”

“Et ah . . . et was found in my gramma`ma’s attic, monsieur,” he said quietly. Again, looking toward the lamp with a wariness he couldn’t mask. “I hov packed up moost of h`air belongings to ship home, but this—“ His gaze lifted with genuine dismay. “I do not like the look of et, monsieur. Et is ah . . . ugly?”

“Do you have any idea where your grandmother got it? Its providence?”

Dominique started to shake his head but halted, glancing off the lamp and back toward Gordon. “I think et came from Europe boot et is not from my country. My gramma`ma, she tra`veled back and forth from Europe to America many times. Perhaps, she bought et in her tra`vels.” He shrugged uncomfortably and held Gordon’s gaze. “Will you pur`shase et, monsieur?”

Gordon parted his lips as if to reject the proposal, but a clamor of thuds echoed from an open doorway behind him, distracting him. Deciding he better lend this a moment’s thought, he glanced at Dominique. “Let me get that, then we’ll talk about it,” he stated, sending a cursory glance toward the lamp as he turned and disappeared into the tunnel behind the counter.

Tense and suddenly distracted by a thumping in his head, Dominique lifted a hand and rubbed at his temple. Uncomfortably, his gaze fell on the parchment. Under the intense light, the thin material offered a translucent glow which enhanced the symbols as well as the spider web texture embedded in the parchment. His gaze slid down the spiral cast iron column through the center. A cloth-covered cord trailed from between the claw foot base; the woven threads created a diamond pattern reflective of a snake.

From the backroom, Gordon’s husky voice offered a greeting.

Dominique rubbed at his temple, more distracted, more tense. Not in days had he suffered a headache, and abruptly, he understood, his talents working against him. Veronica? Could Veronica be in trouble? Turning, he glanced toward the entrance that seemed further away—as if he truly looked down a tunnel. Only a hint of remaining daylight provided a faint glow through the distant dirty smoke glass. Perhaps, he suffered the effects of holding the detectives in trance. Should he return to them, free them? He started a step toward the door when he glimpsed the motion in the corner of his eye. His attention riveted as another elderly fellow ambled through the door. His heart hammered a painful beat, and for an instant, Dominique suffered the déjà vu, certain he’d seen this fellow before. With the slamming in his head, he couldn’t be positive, and no quick identification touched him.

Silver-haired and reasonably tall, not unlike Gordon without the stoop, his bushy silver eyebrows drew down behind thick glasses. His pale eyes darted over Dominique, and a smile notched his bearded lips. He wore a long dark coat lending an impression of a hardy build despite his apparent age. "Harry said to give him a minute," the man spoke in a growling voice as he continued from the door, rounding the cluttered end of the counter within more shadows.

For a fleeting instant, Dominique glimpsed an image of a wallet held at an angle in large hands, reflecting the light. Before he could fully grasp the content or sort the growing confusion in his mind, he sensed the man still looking at him, coming beside him. Pivoting his murky gaze, he read the thoughts . . . only more confused to find this elder man confirming a preconceived notion of Dominique's physical appeal.

Beautiful?

Handsome, Dominique might accept.

The fellow proffered his hand, smiling, offering, "Jack Black. And you are . . .?"

The name meant nothing. Unconsciously reacting to the friendly gesture, Dominique landed his hand in the grip. Time had just caught up to him. No other thought surfaced as the fire ignited in his palm, as much physical as metaphysical with the lightning-bolt revelation. Behind the thick panes of glass, the pale blue eyes magnified with a flash of amusement, but the focus shot off Dominique and riveted on the glowing lamp. The wave of fire flashed through Dominique's wrist, racing up his arm. He felt it coming, flowing, raging toward his thudding head even as he tried pulling his hand from the grip. Numb. Behind the wave, he'd already lost feeling in his hands. *Make eye contact! Draw him!* "Ah . . ." he started the sound, but his tongue swept under the flames. *Drowning!* Dousing. His insides flashed fire; his knees buckled. Still, the man stared at the object on the counter. In a panic, Dominique groped either to halt his fall or slam his assailant. Frozen, the monster continued to study the artifact while animating to clasp Dominique about the shoulder, drawing him against his sturdy frame. Numbing, collapsing, Dominique knew the world fading as his limbs melted.

A spectator, now, as he had been a million times before, he understood his head rolling against the black cloth. Unable to collect even a partial thought, he squinted through the reflection on the windowpane lenses turned toward him.

"Destiny," the husky voice idled, and fury lips smiled. "I knew it when I first saw you," he said in a less husky voice, a more hushed voice. "Don't be afraid, Dominique . . . You don't mind if I call you Dominique, do you? . . . No, I'm sure you don't mind."

Only an uttered breath and grunted sound escaped as his limbs jostled, struggling to collect within the manipulation of the sturdy arms. He was moving, but nothing of his feet dragging the floor registered beyond the sounds of creaking wood and scraped soles. Hazy, more hazy, the dull light of the cluttered backroom passed through his vision. At the edges of his mind, he understood his body sinking to rest in a heap within shadows—the hulking form shuffling away from him. More desperately, he struggled to lift his head, to move some part of himself. Instead, he spotted the scuffed shoes and ran his focus slowly to the splayed form of another man . . .

In a stopped instant, images overlapped in his mind and sight. Animated, a shadow stooped hurriedly over Harry Gordon as a familiar voice called out. Whether seconds or minutes passed, Dominique lost track. The hulking madman returned, then passed him. A scent of fresh, chilled air stirred the dust as a door opened nearby. Not a muscle moved; not a sound slid off his parted lips as the man swooped down on him. That he might prefer to remain on the floor touched him at a base level, but the hands collected him like a ragdoll, hoisting him onto his rubbery legs.

"Up you go . . . That's it . . . Don't panic, Dominique," the voice soothed and coaxed, drawing him along and supporting him, carrying him. "We're just going for a little ride. We have to hurry though . . . That's it," the words accompanied a gust of cool air, a press of wind, and a glimpse of shadows. "Climb right in there . . ."

Falling, not climbing, Dominique landed in deeper shadows and his scattered limbs followed him onto the raised floor. His body jostled, numb. A door slammed, vibrating through him. The light flickered, vanished, erupted briefly, and another car door slammed before the engine ignited.

As if a window cracked open inside his mind, he recognized the interior of another car and heard the voices sputtering awake. Another—more familiar—voice growled, "Any chance one of you would like to tell me what Jardonet's up to?"

"Wha-at?" Shawn huffed while pivoting his head, blinking spots from his eyes to find the federal agent looming in the opening of his driver's door. In fleeting seconds, he darted his gaze off the agent, scanned the gas station as if just woke, and attempted to collect his bearings. "H-how?"

In the passenger seat, Davis had awoken as well. Cursing and sputtering, hissing in surprise, she identified her manacled hands and recognized her own handcuffs locked on her wrists. "Jesus . . . what the hell? Shawn?"

Far more curious and abruptly alarmed, Devinio leaned lower, spotted the detective fumbling clumsily in her coat, and glimpsed the reflection of iron on her wrists. "What the hell's going on here?" he asked as he backed a step to avoid the swinging driver's door. Shawn launched from the seat, and Devinio read the spooked shine in the detective's eyes. "Did he hold a gun on you?"

"He . . . Christ, I don't know," Shawn sputtered angrily while darting his gaze about the lot, attempting to orient himself or grasp the reality. To Devinio, he stated, "We just . . . we were about to bring him in." The futility of his words struck. Flashing a glance into the backseat, he eyed his partner as she climbed anxiously from the passenger's door. Across the hood, their gazes connected with equal confusion.

"Did he . . . How did we . . . ?" *Lose him? Get here?* Davis's gaze swam around the lot and landed on Devinio. "How'd you find us?"

On the nearer detective, Devinio focused, deciding he'd wasted enough time. "No more games, detective," he stated crisply. "Either you two can cover the back of that store and make sure Jardonet doesn't slip through a crack, or I can have you both busted for obstruction of justice under federal jurisdiction. What's it going to be?"

Shawn bounced his glance over the storefronts across the street, his attention firming with the anger rising in his eyes. "We'll cover the back, and you can bet your ass, if he's in there, he's not slipping through any fucking cracks." Collecting his balance, he slammed the car door shut and locked gazes with his partner as she rounded the car. "I'll go around to the right. You take the side street." His gaze flashed to Devinio as they started toward the street. "You're taking the front door . . . Did you call for backup?"

"I'd like to bring him in quietly if that's possible," Devinio stated and glimpsed the detective pulling his gun. "And alive, detective," he snapped as both detectives took off at a run.

CHAPTER 27

As Tim dropped the receiver in its cradle, Ronnie's heart hammered a quick beat. Something was wrong. All too clearly, she felt the queasiness in her stomach, the tension coiling through her limbs.

"Not answering, hon. He's either extremely busy. Or he has the phone turned off."

"We have to find him," she stated while glancing toward the entrance where a small crowd had begun to form. The evening rush was starting early. Her attention returned to Spencer as she asked, "Where was he when you last saw him?"

"At the courthouse," Tim answered, touching his hand to the small of her back, turning her toward the rear entrance. "The mayor's task force is set up on the third floor. If he's not there, someone will know where to find him."

"Then I suggest we hurry," she stated calmly despite the more rampant tumbling in her gut. "Something's wrong," she said aloud and felt Tim's tension in the flex of his fingers. Her gaze shot skyward to find his deep blue eyes more tense as he glanced off her to the door, shoving it open and passing her through a step ahead. "Tim—"

"I don't like that particular statement," he said in a low voice, gesturing toward the deep end of the lot. Donna's familiar cherry-red Blazer stood under an overhang of barren Maple branches. This far north, with the cool wind coming off the lake, the leaves had changed colors and dropped early. In Bentwood, the livid autumn colors would linger another few weeks. Pulling her coat closed against the chill, Ronnie hurried across the lot, halfheartedly wondering if the chill was in the air or inside her physique. She was shivering by the time she climbed into the passenger seat and watched Tim stride hurriedly around the front end. With no more than another sharp glance, he started the engine and backed out. When he paused at the entrance, he asked, "What made you say that? That something's wrong?"

"A . . . a feeling," she said absently, watching the highway for a break in the oncoming traffic from the right. "After this truck, you're clear."

Tim wasted no time, slamming the gas and rolling onto the highway, apparently headed toward the city. "That's not what I wanted to hear either," he admitted, his attention divided between glancing over and weaving into traffic. Like Jade, Tim enjoyed driving, never needing an excuse to exceed the speed limit or violate a traffic law. If not a police officer, he would have probably done well as a getaway driver for the mob.

How she managed to meet and enjoy the company of men who possessed a dark side, Ronnie couldn't even guess. A curse or something. A flaw in her nature to be attracted to danger. At the moment, she wouldn't mind trading the adrenalin rush for a back porch and a glass of hand-squeezed lemonade. Anything would be better than the tension gripping her muscles and the protest in her stomach. If only to offset the rising panic, she concentrated long enough to ask, "What exactly did Lenny say? Did he give you any hint about what came up?"

For a moment, Tim judged his words, then answered in annoyance, "He didn't say, but I got the impression he saw something that bothered him."

She looked over to judge Tim's tense expression, distracted by how much he and Jade truly looked alike under certain conditions. Tim's hair was slightly shorter and darker, nearly as dark as her own, and his eyes were blue, his mustache thinner and black. Not physical, she realized in another instant. The expressions, from the twist of his lips when he attempted to mask his anxiety behind a smile to the intensity of his gaze when his thoughts turned anxious—that was the likeness. A likeness that hadn't been quite so noticeable before three days ago. Tim had always been more ready with a genuine smile, more laid back and open. Losing Jade, his closest friend, had taken its toll. The grief had brought out a cynicism and wariness that she'd never noticed before. Collecting her thoughts, Ronnie realized, "You know what bothered him."

He glanced over, hesitated, then commented, "I got the impression he's having a little trouble with the local authorities." Again, he glanced over, his gaze critical. "The fact is, he's trying to figure out just how Sax ended up the scapegoat for this mess and to do that, he needs to talk to ah . . . to Jardonet. I think he's pretty sure that Jardonet was involved in your disappearing act, but he didn't think the guy would be with you when he showed up. Bluntly,

I think he was following a hunch. This guy . . . Jardonet. He's a loose cannon, and Devinio's not dumb. If Jardonet's back here, he's not finished with this investigation."

"Would you be if ah . . . if your brother was accused of a crime he didn't commit?" she asked quietly. "For that matter, Tim, what are you doing in Cleveland when you knew there wasn't a damn thing you could do about my disappearing act?"

He fell silent, wrestling with his thoughts.

"I think we all want the same thing, Tim," Ronnie continued quietly and turned her gaze through the glass to hide the pain of her words. "We'd like to know what happened here, and we know there's more to all of this than we suspect. On top of that, we have the privilege of knowing that press release by the mayor's office is pure nonsense, which means that a killer remains at large." Her gaze slid to find Tim glancing toward her. "To prove Jade's innocence, Tim, Dominique Jardonet has to find the killer, the same as you and Lenny."

"You uh . . . you did talk to him. What's he like?"

Considering, remembering, she gazed through the side window as she answered. "It's a little hard to say. His English isn't that great. And my French is limited. He uh . . . he's not Jade," she said with a thudding beat in her heart. The words came easily, honestly. "He's colder."

"He works for the French government," Tim said offhandedly. "Len's equivalent if I understood correctly . . . Did he say where he's been for the past few days?"

Belatedly, she remembered asking, but he hadn't answered. "No. He didn't say," she admitted while sensing Tim's genuine curiosity. Her attention turned to Tim. "Why do you ask? What do you know?"

"Only that Len was trying to find him," he answered. "Sounds like this guy makes a habit of pulling vanishing acts."

If Tim only knew the half of it.

Distracted by the shivering in her gut, her thoughts divided. Tad? Shivering? . . . More than once, Tad had seemed to react to something she was unable to fathom, and this wasn't the exception. On a primal level, their son was connected—already connected to his father . . . And his current distress didn't concern Devinio. Dominique Jardonet . . . her husband. He was still her husband, and he was . . . or would be in trouble. Her senses quickening, she stated, "Drive faster, Tim. We have to find Len . . .." And the detectives Dominique had called for backup.

Devinio had gone through the front door, silently cursing the squeal of the hinges and creak of wood as he stepped into the shadowy aisle. His senses keening for any sound, he ducked his head to peer through cracks in the stacked furniture, seeing only more clutter and cobwebs. Not a sound. Not a single sound touched him as he moved up the aisle, walking nearer the stacks to counterbalance his weight on the planks underfoot. By habit alone, he drew his gun, reacting to an internal alarm, to the silence. A preternatural silence. He supposed Jardonet could have been alerted, could have silenced the proprietor . . . but on the heels of that thought, he remembered Veronica's words the evening past. If she was right, Jardonet knew who the maniac was and intended to meet the fellow head-on.

From his car parked down the block, Len had watched Jardonet make a phone call as clearly as he'd watched the fellow climb into the car with the two Cleveland detectives. On the lakefront road, he'd remained too far away and too deep in shadows to view the details. On a hunch, on a lousy hunch, he'd followed the two detectives when he'd spotted them leaving the headquarters. They'd been in a hurry, and the call from Ronnie had come only seconds before. A hunch, a lousy hunch that Jardonet might have decided to contact them. And it had paid off. Hanging back, he'd followed them to the impound yard and waited as they went inside. Ten minutes, after a mere ten minutes, they'd returned to their car carrying an overnight bag and a box . . . and Ronnie had mentioned a box last evening.

Jardonet.

Rounding the corner, his weapon at the ready, Len scanned the empty counter, the cluttered spaces, and the crowded ends of aisles. Spindle chair legs crisscrossed and tangled like a child's rendition of a high-rise under construction . . . a fire trap if ever he'd seen one. A single match and this place would ignite like kindling. Not a sound. Not a creak in the entire place other than the protest of wood beneath his heels. Far more carefully, he approached the open doorway, his internal mechanisms racing to a greater alarm, a hunch, a sensation of emptiness. Unnaturally, a shiver crept down his spine lending thought to something his grandmother used to say about walking across her grave. He shook the thought aside, nearly cursing aloud as he strained to peer around the corner into the deeper shadows. A single naked bulb dangled at the deep end of the clutter, offering enough of a dim glow to identify the broken plastic sign that had likely glowed neon to designate an exit.

A wave of anger sped through his mind as he realized the probability of Jardonet's escape. And should that be any real surprise? If nothing else, with his newfound belief in psychic phenomena, Len knew this character was as talented as his half-brother. Catching this son of a bitch could compare nicely to trying to catch a bottle of smoke without the blasted convenience of a lid!

Keeping his gun on point, he navigated an indirect route to the light, stepping around jutting crates and over boxes. Jardonet was long gone. And apparently, he'd taken the proprietor with him. As Len started to shove his gun into the holster under his jacket, the rear door sprung wide, shedding light into the interior. Devinio froze as Shawn swung into the opening, gun aimed and ready.

"Hold it!" Len demanded, and the detective started to swing his gaze.

His head jerked back and aside.

Davis came through the opening a half second after McAllory moved, and Len started forward as the detective ducked out of sight. Devinio rounded the corner in time to see the young detective stoop alongside a sprawled body, pressing his fingertips into the carotid artery.

"Come on, old man!"

Davis yanked the handheld radio off her hip, moving toward her partner as the man snapped, "No pulse! Call for an ambulance!"

Devinio glimpsed the wide-open eyes and parted bearded lips before McAllory lifted one of the limbs out of his path and scrambled over the chest. Not wasting an instant, he clasped the shaggy jaw to begin CPR. Ten minutes . . . Jardonet had entered the store less than ten minutes ago, less than a minute after making a phone call. If he'd met someone . . . damn it. Devinio moved through the open door as Davis cited the call signals for an ambulance.

In the fading daylight, Len could barely make out the far end of the alley. Tall wooden fences and indentations designated either garages or backyards. Directly across from the wide span of the collective building, garages stood side-by-side with only the tips of house roofs visible from where he stood. Jardonet had time. He could have fled on foot, but somehow, the man lying inside the store countered that quick theory. Regardless of his personal opinion concerning this misplaced Frenchman, Len couldn't believe that Jardonet had killed that old man. Especially not with two city police detectives resting in a car across the street.

What the hell was going on here!

Turning as Davis came through the opening, Devinio interrupted before she could announce the ambulance on its way. “What did Jardonet say? Who was he calling?”

The young woman’s face screwed up; her eyes flashed in either direction, then landed, resigned and angry. “He didn’t say a damned thing, Agent Devinio,” she huffed. “Me and Shawn were going to bring him in to talk to you. He called me at the headquarters. The last thing I remember is taking out my handcuffs. You can believe that or not.”

“You stopped at the impound yard and recovered his belongings,” Devinio commented.

“Yea, he asked me to,” she said with a steady gaze. “On the outside chance that we might figure out what he was up to, we went to the yard. The car owner was pretty put out with his buddy for leaving the car in a tow-away zone. Neither the name nor the description of the friend who borrowed his car matched Jardonet, and the guy was more than happy to let us remove the contents. In his words, it would serve his pal right.”

“What was in the box?”

“The ugliest damned lamp I ever saw in my life,” she stated without pause.

“A lamp?”

“Yea, at least that’s what it looked like it was supposed to be.” She held her hands about a foot apart, high and low. “About yeah tall. Domed. Heavy as hell, too,” she barely paused. “We went through his bag and ah . . . I do recall frisking him. He wasn’t armed, and there wasn’t anything suspicious in the bag.”

A lamp, Devinio considered as he scanned the shadowy alley.

“Hey,” she stated. “For the record, I really don’t know how the hell we ended up across the street. We were down on the lake road,” she said reluctantly. “How the hell did you find us?”

“I followed you,” he said absently as he reviewed the moments when he’d watched Jardonet stride across the street.

Davis harrumphed and turned into the doorway, undoubtedly, to either assist or offer moral support to her partner. In the distance, a siren wailed, and abruptly Devinio had no urge to face a barrage of either local policemen or reporters. He was missing something. A great deal of something, he nearly uttered aloud as he turned to enter the door.

His attention dropped almost as if drawn and riveted on the dull wood planks, on the layers of dust. Far more slowly, he moved and stoop, not needing more than the dull light to recognize the distinctive dual treads. A chair . . . a chair getting dragged across the floor could make these scuff marks. Turning on the balls of his feet, he followed the drag marks onto the gravel. These were not the telltale signs of furniture . . . not when the drag marks formed near human imprints in the powdery gravel.

"Goddamn it," he uttered and pushed to his feet, his attention once again flying down either side of the alley, landing on the nearest street opening.

In a half second or less, he remembered seeing the van . . . a dark blue van had passed him on the street and turned down this side street. And maybe he had already spent too much time around psychics. Without any rhyme or reason, he knew that van belonged to the killer, knew it had turned down this alley and parked less than three feet from this door . . .

And Dominique Jardonet had neither assaulted that old man nor walked out of this building on his own two feet.

Spinning into the doorway, Devinio heard the young detective heaving a count and saw Davis stooped alongside her partner, coaching him. Her gaze lifted, the doubt and natural dread haunting her lovely eyes as she shook her head. Before she could put her thoughts into words, Devinio snapped, "We have work to do, detective. Find the phone in this place and put in a call to that task force. I want them running a check on Chevy vans, 1982 and 83 models. Dark blue. I want those names cross-referenced with our list of doctors and any names we pulled out of the ledger Officer Spencer brought from Bentwood, PA. After that, find the number for The Regency Restaurant in Coral Park, phone it, and get Spencer on the phone. Have him bring Mrs. Laquette to headquarters and tell him I'll meet him there."

"Sir—" she started while pushing to her feet.

"Get moving, detective. We probably have less than two hours to find Jardonet alive—four if the Taxidermist found a way to keep his victims alive for the whole show."

"... Not much further, Dominique," the husky voice intruded on the images floating in Dominique's head.

Above him, the light flickered on and off, crisscrossing the ceiling like a laser light show or a disco from an earlier era. The engine vibration sent flutters of vertigo through his system, and a groan slid off his lips with a memory flash of nausea.

"That's good . . . You're still awake," the man said in a musing tone. "You don't know what a pleasure it is to have you here. I thought about it, you know? Oh, I'm sure you don't know, but it's true. The moment I saw you . . . I knew you were perfect. I didn't really think this could happen . . . it's fate. It's our destiny. I know you can't appreciate the beauty of this, not right now, but soon . . . You'll see soon. Not much further. Don't be afraid," the voice lowered in a comforting tone. "I won't hurt you, not even you . . . maybe especially not you, my beautiful boy. I'm a doctor, you know? I wouldn't do anything to let my patients suffer needlessly. *Primum non nocere.* You'll see, monsieur. I'll be very gentle with you . . ."

The words only triggered more floating images, confusing images to hold his dull attention. He'd seen those words recently, read them. *Primum non nocere*. Ah, the words were inscribed at the stone entrance of the medical facility in Arlington.

First, do no harm.

This fellow had read that inscription . . . and others had heard those words. Others had laid as he lay now, listening to this voice, watching the lights flashing across the ceiling from an unfathomable source. Fear accompanied the images, but not his fear. He felt nothing as he watched the lights and the visions. As if he floated on a rubber raft, his physical form rocked and swayed, controlled by an external source. The lights . . . the lights stopped flashing, replaced by a constant dull glow that offered no comfort. Dim . . . like the dim light of consciousness fading, and he wouldn't mind falling into the darkness, letting it take him. His reason for living . . . no reason . . . The darkness would be welcome, now. A place to rest and hide, to while away eternity.

"I debated," the voice intruded. "I didn't intend to bring the other one here. I would have left him like the others, though it grieves me to admit it.

There wasn't anything special about him. Oh, he was handsome enough, and his complexion . . . I could have made something of him, I'm sure. But it would have been forced. I wouldn't have enjoyed working with him as much as you. This . . . It truly is karma. We were meant for this, my boy. It's a sign . . . an omen. I knew it the moment I saw you . . . This is going to be beautiful. You'll be beautiful. . . ."

Handsome, Dominique might have corrected if he could lift his tongue. His head lulled with a sway in the raft. Not beautiful . . . only his mother had called him 'beautiful'. . . *'Beautiful bab'be boy'* . . . And it was a lie. She lulled him like this, too, willing him to believe the lie when she wanted him to cooperate. When she wanted him to believe he was something other than a monster. His thoughts floated, losing track of the motion, the sounds. To the voice coming closer, to the stopped sensation of floating, he awoke again slowly, awake as the hands tugged him, pulling him. He groaned and drew sense to attempt a struggle. But his hands hung limp; his body sagged against a sturdy frame. This, too, was familiar. Not a lethal dose . . . not even a near-lethal dose like the one to begin his odyssey in the Arlington facility. Just potent. And as if the Taxidermist heard his thoughts, the maniac spoke again.

"I mixed the herbs a little stronger, but then, it wasn't meant for you . . . You must try to stand now, boy. Come on, on your feet. Just a few steps . . . That's it."

Dull, limp, he struggled to rise, but he needed the arm about his waist. His head thumped against the sturdy shoulder. His hand struggled to find purchase and draw himself up. Stumbling, sagging, he heard the husky idle laugh close to his ear as arms locked more fully around him, holding him up and moving him.

"It's lucky I nearly had this facility complete . . . Here, now. Just lie down and relax."

No choice. Dominique sank sideways, falling over. An immense hand caught his head, lying him down almost gently. Against the dim light, Dominique squinted, barely able to identify the checkerboard pattern within the beige wall before him. His legs lifted, his body flattened, and he glimpsed the unfamiliar face hovering above him, smiling at him. The eyes, something about the eyes . . . blue eyes, magnified eyes. Familiar. He tried to shy from a shadow, but the thumb and finger caught his eye, a familiarity in that, too, although the details eluded him. He tried squinting, His eye watered and blinded under the flood.

"Good . . . very good. You're doing fine, my boy. You just relax now," the confident voice spoke reassurance as the hand lifted, then touched down on his cheek. By impression of weight, Dominique understood the thumb moving over his mustache, over his lips. Blinking, he tried lifting his hand and attempted to turn his head.

"You are beautiful. Every bit as beautiful as your cousin . . . or was he your twin? Was that what the FBI sought to determine? Is that how you fooled them, Dominique? I saw his picture, you know? Not the picture they showed in the press. I saw the picture the FBI have of him . . . and the resemblance is truly uncanny. I am almost sorry that he was lost in a fire. What I could have done with him, with his flesh . . . I could have made him immortal. I could have immortalized both of you. You would have been a matched set . . . like bookends . . . or lamps," he said with a twist of amusement that touched Dominique even in his void.

The voice. There was something familiar about that voice. He'd heard it before. Recently . . . and long ago. Younger. Not an old voice even now, not a voice to match the beard and hair.

"You're not afraid," the husky voice soothed. "That's good. I don't want you to be afraid. Just relax, now. I promise you; I won't let you suffer. I'll make this painless. There's so much needless suffering in the world already. I see it every day . . . people harming other people, killing cruelly, violently. It's so senseless. But we're going to end all of that. It's already begun, you know . . ."

Something was happening, his mind struggled to work out the details, to identify the sensations, and he caught up as he watched his hand emerge from the jacket sleeve. He needed a warmer coat . . . but that thought slipped away with a sense of warmth touching his face, his lips. Not outside. Someone . . . this doctor had brought him in out of the cold wind. He should be grateful. He wasn't grateful. Alarm niggled the edges of his mind as his head lulled, and he watched his other hand slip free of the coat, understanding the material slipping from under him. From the shadow in front of him, he attempted to shy again, but his dull focus landed on the blue eyes watching him, smiling at him. Familiar. He had seen these eyes . . . magnified eyes. Eye contact . . . something about eye contact fleeted in his mind and fled. Around him, the light seemed brighter, too bright. His eyes stung and watered.

"You don't remember me, do you, Dominique?" the husky voice spoke with a chiding note. "I think you know you've seen me before, but you don't know me. I wasn't important enough for you to see me and remember me." As he spoke, he loosened the buttons at Dominique's chest, freeing the cloth, pausing to brush the back of his knuckles against Dominique's muscles and distracting to watch his hand.

"Ah, you are beautiful. One of the beautiful people of the world . . . and so important," he said in a mocking note, a hint of darkness in his voice. "The irony, my beautiful young friend . . . therein lies the irony. You were important back then, but you will be far more important tomorrow . . . or the day after," he added with a musing note, another chiding sarcasm. "With my help, you will be so very important, and I will make you immortal, Dominique. Already, I feel the inspiration of your presence. I will mold you into something far more beautiful. Flawless, I will present you to the world . . . and they will know, my beautiful boy. They will know the mistakes they've made. After we're through, they won't call me such a foolish, derogatory name. Taxidermist," he said with a seething hiss. "They will know the error of their ways. I am an artist. . . and a surgeon," he added as an afterthought and paused, touching Dominique's face, drawing his glazed focus.

"In the dark ages, physicians were considered wizards."

As were warlocks, Dominique countered silently, whimsically.

"Did you know, we were considered sacred, and illness was considered a curse to be banished from the flesh of mortal men. We were like holy men. Revered. Glorified like the high priests of religions today. But the old practices—our very origins—have been forgotten and disregarded. Modern medicine," he said with a musing note as he ran his thumb over Dominique's lips. "We call it modern medicine, but so little has changed. We have the power, all of us, at our fingertips to heal or destroy, to bring life or death . . . to bring immortality. And the world is filled with sickness, my beautiful comrade. It is up to us, the healers, the physicians, to bring change. To heal this illness and plague. Modern man needs modern practitioners, men who are not afraid to act. To make the world a more beautiful place. To find solutions. People, Dominique . . . if there is a surplus on this planet, it exists in the human commodity. Human flesh, my beautiful boy, is the one resource we have in abundance, and I have the answer. An answer to turn these useless shells into something far more beautiful, to breathe immortality into those I touch . . . and to make a profit," he added with a wry note.

"And you know how, don't you? Somehow you . . . or your twin learned about my quest. That's why he was killed. I see that now. I understand what my benefactors meant to accomplish by killing him, by giving him credit for my work. I can't allow that, though, Dominique. My work, my art is too important to me. I am ready. And with your help, I will prove my readiness and unveil the masterpieces I have already created. I will be like the practitioners of old, feared, and adored. Risen beyond the hoi polloi. There will be rebellion," he said as if in afterthought and drew his hand away.

Dominique glimpsed the reflection, a brilliant reflection of light on steel, and his dull focus followed the flickering light like a candle flame in the darkness. Salvation. Redemption. Intrigued more than else, he watched the blade skim up his arm, slice the cloth from his wrist to his shoulder. He felt nothing of the tug against his shoulder as the immense hand wadded the cloth and severed dark gray fur. The soft clump dropped, falling away from his limp arm and brushing his flesh like a feather . . . a feather touch. Veronica. Her essence, the light. A feather touch . . . like the brush of the child in her womb. A smile tugged at his lips with the comfort of his thoughts.

"It is fate," the voice came, hushed, and Dominique's thoughts distracted again as the sensation of touch skimmed down his arm. His head moved . . . a mere twitch of motion, but he saw the palm gliding down his flesh, the heat of the hand reaching him. "You are even more beautiful than I imagined, more than I could have hoped for," the voice continued. "Flawless. As an ivory sculpt, a Greek sculpt of the gods. . . It is a sign. An omen."

With a flutter of thought, Dominique meant to agree. His head moved in a twitch of a nod; his eyes lifted slowly to find the face. Dry, his tongue weighted and numb, he struggled to gain control of his muscles, his throat. "Fate," he heaved, not certain if the word formed in any recognizable language.

The Taxidermist smiled in approval and brushed his hand over Dominique's muscled chest as if he meant to comfort. Gingerly, he passed around the head of the platform and reached the opposite side. Without delay, he sliced the cloth from the shoulder down with the quick, smooth stroke of a genuine surgeon.

In his floating senses, Dominique studied the face, searching, and reaching only one conclusion . . . not a wizard. The man looked like a washed-out Santa Clause . . . a dirty Santa Clause, and in his mind, Dominique remembered that image . . . suddenly tense, as he'd become tense when this image had first assaulted him a lifetime ago.

A deranged Santa Claus! Gray beard, gray hair, thick round glasses, and bushy gray brows! A smile twisted within the beard. His nose shining red with the faintest glimmer of a wart or blemish painted over!

Something of his sudden fear lifted in his eyes, drawing the abomination to look down at him, into him. Whether he found the image truly frightening or vastly amusing, Dominique couldn't decide. A wary, conflicting smile tugged at his lips.

The Taxidermist smiled more curiously, canting his head and studying him more intently.

Something . . . he felt something, not quite understanding anything beyond the discomfort in his confusion.

Patting his shoulder, the doctor shifted his attention, and Dominique heard the clink of metal on metal before the man moved and began tugging at his belt. Working out the sound, Dominique tipped his head slightly more, and even in his dull-witted senses, he recognized the red shine within the reflected glint of surgical steel. Blood. His blood. And this was neither Santa Clause nor a wizard of the dark ages

The Taxidermist.

Dominique's gaze shifted. Understanding filled his drugged mind as the man commenced stripping him of his last material possessions.

And he had lost his suitcase again.

CHAPTER 28

Astride behind Tim Spencer, Ronnie barely dodged a head-on collision with one of two detectives who launched for the opening as she stepped off the elevator. The same man offered a hasty apology and swung about. Flashing a doubletake, he slammed a button on the panel and darted a manic glance at Spencer. As the door started to close, he snapped, "Hey! Stay put! Agent Devinio's—"

The door closed, muffling the remainder of his words.

Ronnie eyed Tim, who appeared likewise curious and alarmed. Devinio was *what?* In trouble?

"The main offices are down the hall," Tim commented, motioning her in the appropriate direction, controlling his hiked tension. "I don't think it's a good idea if I take you back there, but there's a lounge where you could wait while I try to find out what's going on."

"I don't suppose Len mentioned that I have federal clearance, did he?" Ronnie asked and noted Tim's skeptical glance before he realized she was serious. "I suggest we find out what the devil's going on."

Unfortunately, even as they strode through the last door in the corridor, no obvious signs explained the officers' hasty departure.

Ronnie had seen the headquarters of investigations. At least a dozen agents should be at desks, manning phones or shuffling paper. A dozen more should be hammering at computer or typewriter keys to filter the influx of false information. In any big case, agents wasted time and energy scouring through hundreds of phone calls and screening information hoping for the one genuine call that could make or break a case. Presently, only a half dozen officers or detectives—and possibly one federal agent—occupied the immense room. Determined to protect Tad, Ronnie avoided glancing toward the wall across the room. Still, she glimpsed enough of the black and white images to know a forensic display accompanied the living faces of the victims.

Sharing a desk, two young men plucked at separate keyboards of an impressively modern computer. Their concentration drew her focus more readily than the startled glances from two different officers across the room. Spencer moved toward one of the nearest uniformed officers; Ronnie continued only as far as the first desk and leaned at the edge. Ominously, the intensity and tension hovered inside the room like a living entity, enhanced as if the courthouse walls had trapped an energy field.

"Have you heard from Agent Devinio?" Tim's voice carried with the female voice paused.

"He's on his way in," the woman fired back.

"What's going on here. Where is everybody?" Spencer asked.

An unnatural shiver slid down Ronnie's spine, and she glanced toward the door. Her thoughts stopped. Her attention riveted on the stricken pale blue eyes. Before she could form a question or twitch to pull her gun, Mark pivoted and disappeared from the opening, leaving her to wonder der if she'd seen him at all. There and gone, like a retina stain. Her curiosity on high, her heart hammering a quick beat, she glimpsed at the man she'd identified as FBI, a lean fellow with a white-collar look to him. His eyes flashed a similar curiosity from the door to Ronnie, then back to his computer screen.

"Detective, I'd like—"

"Bottom line, I don't have time to bring you up to speed," the woman cut Spencer off before he could ask more. "We have reason to believe the mayor jumped the gun on his press release," she added while stabbing a button on her telephone, engaging a line.

Tim's gaze lifted toward Ronnie, connecting a split second before his attention shot passed her. For an instant, she thought Mark had reappeared. Relief swam through her as Lenny strode through the doorway. Bouncing his dark gaze off her to Spencer, then shooting his attention toward the two-man team across the room, he never raised his voice to snap—"Skyles! How far along are you?"

"Gees man, you have any idea how many blue vans there are in this city?" the younger of the pair shot his gaze from the screen and looked as if he might like to bite his tongue. "Working on it, Sir! We're feeding in the doctors' names now!"

"What's going on, Len?" Spencer asked, arriving nearly at the same moment as Lenny, who clasped Ronnie's shoulder in a simple gesture of relief.

Looking into his intense dark eyes, Ronnie started a sound.

"Are you all right?" He cut her off.

"Fine. What's going on?" she asked without missing a beat.

"We have reason to believe Dr. Frankenstein struck again," he said and included Tim in a sharp glance. "It's not confirmed."

He barely finished his words before another gentleman strode into the room, followed closely by a stocky mid-aged man who scowled in contrast to his apparent leader's pensive expression. By the cut of the suit and the arrogance of the leading man's posture, Ronnie judged him a politician, tempted to believe she was about to meet the mayor. The man flashed her a glance, then a quick doubletake, veering. His stoic expression unchanged, he arrived and wasted precious seconds proffering his hand. "Mrs. Laquette, I'm glad to see you."

The second man lost his scowl briefly, spinning his dumbfound and doubt toward his leader. Clearly, he hadn't recognized her.

"I don't believe we've had the pleasure," Ronnie said as she accepted the firm handshake. Years of social conditioning had honed her ability to control her emotions, but behind her clear gaze, her hostility threatened her resolve. Was he responsible for accusing Jade?

"I'm Adam Macanders, District Attorney," he offered firmly. "I'd like to speak to you a moment if you wouldn't mind," he added, then looked to Lenny with a volatile gaze. "First, I'd like to know what you think you're doing, Mr. Devinio, and on whose authority—"

"I'm trying to save a man's life," Devinio interrupted firmly, his dark eyes glaring with unnatural heat. "As I said this afternoon, Adam, I have reason to doubt the information you received. We already have one man en route to City General, and as soon as we get a lead on the van spotted at the scene, I'm issuing an APB."

"What makes you think this is the Taxidermist?" the DA asked.

Whatever Devinio's reasoning, he hesitated, and the silent pause was interrupted by a near-hushed voice from across the room.

"I'll be damned."

Like every other stopped body in the group, Ronnie saw the lone officer run a hand through his hair, a sure sign of his befuddlement before he realized the stopped silence and his sudden audience. Appearing slightly embarrassed, he flashed his glance over the faces before colliding with Devinio. "I think I might have found something here."

Already in motion, Devinio asked, "What is it?"

"Well, it might be nothing, but I was just going back over the books," the man started and glanced toward Ronnie, then Spencer. Lying open in front of him, Ronnie recognized the simple black binder, the lined filler paper . . . undoubtedly filled. There were three of those books in Olden Time . . . the books her husband had begun to keep five years ago. All three presently rested on the officer's desk; apparently, hand-delivered by Spencer.

"What have you found?" Devinio prodded, advancing on the man, who seemed to realize the threat of the agent's body language.

Far more anxiously, he stated, "The script's not too legible, but I recognize the address. It uh . . . it just strikes me a little weird, sir. Me and Webster, my partner—we had a call about five months ago. Some old lady complaining about weird noises. This is the same address. I'd lay money on it. But uh . . .? It's not a private residence," he said offhandedly, glancing off the ledger to Devinio, who stopped and towered over him. "It's an old grain mill, sir. There's nothing out there but a few metal buildings and falling-down bins. Webb and I checked it out. The place was condemned over a year ago. I think it was sold for taxes. Even if some of these dates in this book are right, there's no way this guy was sending mail out there. That mill's been shut down for over ten years. The farms out there were turned into industrial parks or housing plans."

Devinio had apparently heard enough. "Get over here and show me where it is on the map," he stated and turned from the desk, heading toward an immense wall map where various color-coded pegs designated victims, locations, residences, and suspects. The officer hustled to catch up and reached the map a half second after Devinio, pointing out a location in the upper left corner. "I'll be damned," Devinio stated and spun around, locking gazes with another detective. "You've been waiting for a reason to mobilize your team, lieutenant. The moment's here. I want your SWAT team ready to move in ten minutes."

Without missing a beat, Len connected with the DA. "I think we just found the Taxidermist's shop, Adam. This mill's less than ten miles from where we just had another abduction."

One of the teams at the computer snapped, "Give me that address, Ryan!"

The words relayed in rapid fire, numbers followed by Ridgeway Rd. "Looks like the last name starts with an S or an R. I can't make it out, damn it."

Devinio had moved toward the desk where one of the men worked on the keys like a mad musician playing a medley of Bach. In less than thirty seconds, the man's fingers froze, his eyes riveted, and his lips parted. "Holy shit," he hissed softly.

"What?" Devinio asked as he started around the desk.

"I tapped into the uh . . . the tax office records. It starts with an R," he said as his focus lifted, a sick expression waxing his face. "And I think we're gonna have a problem."

To the light tap on his face, Dominique woke from the floating images, his gaze locking on the windowpane glasses, and in the dull seconds, he suffered the disorientation of a stranger hovering over him. By reflex, he tried to move, to rise. The windowpane glasses . . . light. Bright light. Something had changed in his absence. Whether he shivered physically or mentally, his vision wavered. Something moved. His body twitched.

"I don't mean to disturb you, my boy, but I do like to know you're still with me," the husky voice chided gently. "You should be coming around a little more by now," he said. "I won't let you feel any pain. I promise you; I'll make this as painless as possible, but I do want you to stay with me. I want you to stay awake as long as possible, and I'll try to make you as comfortable as I can."

Not a nightmare or dream image. Not a vision from which he'd awaken unscathed. Motionless, numb, Dominique struggled to bring the face into focus. Something had changed. The face had changed. Rather than a thick gray beard, the bottom half of the face was covered in a stark white mask, and the hair had vanished beneath a tight hood . . . a white hood. Stark white cloth . . . and a green tunic, a surgeon's scrubs. Bright light. Too bright. He closed his eyes against the prickling sensations . . . and saw his surroundings far more clearly.

He'd been moved. He lay on a raised metal platform, a shiny table, or a silver platter like a holiday turkey dressed and served for the carving. A raised edge bordered a concave trough that ran the circumference, enclosing him. No scalloped edges or hand-tooled designs decorated the tray. In a utilitarian style, the tray maintained the integrity of the entire room. Smooth white walls, silver trays, bins, mobile tables, bright lights coiled down from the ceilings . . . covered drains on the tile floor lent him the impression of an immense shower stall. On a high ledge, he focused briefly, identifying the anomaly of the object which didn't belong within this utilitarian room. A camera. . . a video recorder. It stood on a tripod, as high as the light fixtures, angled to pan the length of his splayed anatomy from his head to his toes. He'd never liked cameras. Not still life, not video, not any device designed to project or capture images. Reporters . . . doctors . . . scientists. This film hadn't begun to roll. The device stood waiting, hovering like a mechanical monster prepared to devour the macabre action.

Floating, searching, Dominique understood . . . an operating room. A studio. Even in the afterglow of light, he recognized the slanted windows designed for observation from a balcony overhead. Around him, the supplies . . . art supplies. In the outer edges of the light, in the coves beneath the balcony, he found the plastic boxes stacked on metal carts, found the ledges where spirit gum and latex, glue, and varnish cans stood in neat rows. Chemical smells reached him, stinging his nostrils, but the images . . . his attention riveted on the images within the shadowed cove.

An art exhibit . . . impressionist art. His thoughts staggered as he scanned the constructs hovering in base relief. Like modern impressionist sculpts, the images took on a separate life . . . human bones varnished and molded, spiraling crazily to look like bonsai trees standing no taller than two foot-high on the ledges. Where leaves should cover the limbs to form shapes, parchment stretched like spider webs to billow and balloon off the tiny digits. Hands . . . shadowy human hands hovered behind the gauze, extending as if to beckon or offer . . . to reach through the thin webbed shrouds . . . and he saw the faces. Haunting the human faces stretched over the threads of bones, like double-exposed film laid on the parchment . . . human faces. Empty eye-sockets offered clear glimpses of the tangled bones . . . windows to hell. Empty souls. Lips parted, twisted in ghastly smiles or parted on silent screams; the flesh gnarled as if to impart the agony of mankind. Faces . . . Abraham Lowenstein . . . Erin Demarco . . . Noel Labinski . . . Frances Cummings . . . they were here. Watching, screaming—

To the chilled touch on his cheek, Dominique snapped his eyes open, felt the sting, and snapped the lids shut under the quick flood.

"The light," the doctor idled. "The light's bothering you," he spoke as if offering a clinical assessment. "I should have anticipated your sensitivity to light under the circumstances," he spoke consolingly.

Dominique heard the click, and the intensity of the beam vanished.

"There," the Taxidermist said gently. "We don't need that much light in here just yet. By the time I reach the more delicate procedures, I doubt the light will bother you. Now, open your eyes . . . That's it."

Blinking the sting and tears away, Dominique obeyed, finding the face above him. He could nearly make out the pale blue of the irises behind the glass, but his own reflection distracted him.

"This has to be special, Dominique," the doctor soothed. "You're the first model I've brought here. I didn't plan to open this studio for another few months, but for you, I'm making an exception. This, it must be perfect. You are special. All the signs . . . omens. This truly is our karma. You understand that, don't you?"

"Oui," he drawled, nodding, not certain if he'd spoken a word or uttered a sound.

"I don't want to rush this," he said while running his waxed thumb over Dominique's lips. "I made a mistake with my last model," he spoke quietly, as if to himself. "But you're different. Stronger. You'll stay with me. You'll watch and appreciate what I'm doing for you. You understand, don't you? You know what I'm saying to you. What I'm going to do for you. You've seen my work."

Pictures, images, and visions floated through Dominique's mind as he twitched a nod and uttered a sound, a breath.

"You were hunting for me tonight, weren't you, my boy?" the man asked in a teasing tone. "You wanted to find me, isn't that so?"

Dominique nodded, his eyes shuttered, searching through the lenses.

"You don't really understand my work, though, do you? You don't really understand that I want to help you. Heal you. You are near to perfection, As near to perfection as any model I've ever worked with, but you too, have flaws, Dominique. Do you understand? We have to remove the flaws."

Again, he nodded, his eyes at half-mast.

"I thought I'd want to hurt you," the Taxidermist said thoughtfully. "When I saw you. When I realized who the other was following, I thought I'd want to hurt you, but it's not your fault, is it? You knew the lies in the media. You were hunting for me. You even brought me a gift, but it wasn't to honor me, was it? You were attempting to lure me into a trap with that crude gift, isn't that so?"

His mind had cleared considerably, but his body lay as numb and loose as gelatin, reminding him of the first photo he'd seen of this monster's craft.

Franny Cummings. Young and pretty, sprawled like a jellied mold on Dr. Rhoades—the acting coroner's metal table—

"Answer me, Dominique. Is that what you thought? Is that what you intended?" the Taxidermist asked with a subtle edge.

Twitching a negative against the waxy palm, a palm covered in latex, Dominique struggled to keep the face in focus as he uttered the word in French, then English. "Immm-ortality . . . mmmy karma." On the edges of his mind, he sensed the doctor's attention riveted and struggled to continue, "Mmmy talllisman . . . youuu will givvve me immortality. I hov sssearched for youuu . . ."

"No van," one of the two men at the computer stated. "He has an '85 Dodge—"

"Somebody get me the background on this son of a bitch!" Devinio cut him off shortly. "He could have the vehicle registered under his wife or a kid's name. Find out his mother's name—maiden name—"

"We're pulling up his employment records now!" another man snapped.

"Sir!" the woman Spencer had spoken with snapped, and Len shot his gaze to her. "There's a call for you on line one."

"Unless it's the president, take a message!"

"Sir, he said his name's Director Lakeland."

"Close enough," Devinio stated and sidestepped to an abandoned desk.

Despite the tension and rolling in her gut, Ronnie smiled slightly, watching as Devinio snatched the phone receiver and jabbed the appropriate button. She'd seen him in action before and appreciated his calm, quick efficiency. He was an intellectual, a fellow accustomed to sorting through abstracts and concentrating on facts regardless of how his muscled build suggested a penchant for physical aggression, often more intimidating than his credentials. The rugged image was an illusion. Regardless of what the FBI hierarchy believed, Len was likely responsible for solving the majority of the cases that had boosted Mark Jarvins' reputation. Granted, Mark could profile a killer, but in twenty-twenty hindsight, Ronnie knew why Jarvins' met with such great success in that respect. The man was a maniac behind his quick smiles and arrogance, and in retrospect, Ronnie wondered if Len already knew about his partner's lunacy. How long had Len been covering for him, playing it cool, merely tolerating Jarvins' temperament and idiosyncrasies?

Loyalty . . . the relationship between partners? Out of respect for Mark, Devinio had never pursued any personal relationship with her . . . but all too swiftly, she recalled the moments in the Bentwood Inn four months ago. Mark had admitted to tampering with her files in the federal data banks, changing her religion from Catholic to Jewish . . . allegedly, to subvert Lenny's personal interest. With his family's strict doctrine, he was honor-bound to marry in the Catholic faith. The truth had come out at her wedding. A Catholic wedding that Len had attended without ever mentioning the conflicting information.

An innocent prank? A joke? At the time, Mark had led her to believe he was kidding. He'd suggested she speak a few words in Yiddish or make up words since Len had no grasp of the language. A joke. A prank. She'd believed Mark was teasing, and under his taunting, she'd fallen into hysterical laughter.

Whether the thought of Mark's prank or the thought of Len Devinio being attracted to her, she couldn't recall, but one or the other had struck her funny. Before this summer, Len had always reacted to her as if she were an unwanted guest at his party. In retrospect, she knew Mark hadn't lied about Len's interest and attraction. In deference to Jarvins', Len had never pursued a relationship with her. He was a man of honor and integrity, a man who would never stoop to trickery or deceit to gain the upper hand. With quiet dignity, he'd stepped aside, offering only his friendship to her and, by extension, to Jade.

'Promise me, you will stay with Lenny . . .'

Was there more to those words than she'd believed? Had he meant to give her the freedom and his approval to be with another man in his absence? Did he actually believe that any other man, even one as attractive and honorable as Len, could take his place in her life, in her heart? And in his fantasy world, had he even considered the little detail that Len was currently involved—and probably on the verge of an engagement—with a beautiful young woman who could give him all the happiness and love he deserved?

Devinio was still on the phone, his voice lowered to a pitch to be lost, deliberately, within the gaggle of voices inside the room. In bits and pieces, she heard the conversations, from the computer experts chasing down details through the information network to the burly police chief trying to convince the DA that none of this was possible. They had their killer. The FBI, the senior agent assigned to them, had supplied the information. The mayor had gone on record to assure the public that the threat of a monster had ended with a plane crash in Kentucky. To even suggest that the killer was still alive, to even consider that the maniac responsible for this madness was a paid official of the city . . . *insanity!*

In a low pitch, barely audible, the chief hissed, "This is the same guy who brought in that Frenchman, Adam, and I don't think I have to tell you who he was, how he figured into this mess. Shit, Adam, his own brother knew he was a monster. There has to be someone we can call to get this lunatic out of here. Christ, you said yourself, Dr. Reddinger could sue the city for a bundle over this mess. By the time this agent's done, we're going to have lawsuits coming—"

"Let me worry about the lawsuits, Vince. If this agent's right, we have a person's life at stake."

No obvious words interrupted the District Attorney, and Ronnie turned her listless gaze as Mark Jarvins started into the room, apparently to join the two men closest to the door. His blue eyes darted in her direction, then shot toward Devinio before slicing toward his companions. "Att. Macanders. Chief Dartworth," he said as he addressed them and continued toward Len. Halting, firming in a solid stance, he faced Lenny exclusively. "Agent Devinio, as your senior agent, I'm taking you off this case. I suggest you put the phone down."

Stunned, Ronnie shifted her gaze as Len turned, his hand still holding the receiver to his ear.

The words seemed not to affect Devinio one way or another. His eyes conveyed nothing of his thoughts, and a curtain had fallen over his features. Emitting only the natural tension of the situation around them, he spoke in his quiet deep voice. "You don't want to do this, Agent Jarvins."

Unwavering, Mark spoke in an equally low tone. "Hang up the phone, Devinio. I just got off the phone with the director. I am relieving you of this temporary command." His gaze darted, fleeted off Ronnie, and landed on one of the senior detectives in the room. Steadfast, his sharp, angled features could be carved in granite, but a heaviness haunted his expression, and dark patches, like bruises, underscored his stark blue eyes. As meticulously as always, his dark suit appeared newly pressed, the tie skillfully knotted in a double-Windsor which fitted neatly beneath the collar of a pale, striped Van Hausen shirt. Mark had never bought his clothes off a cheap department store rack. Only the best, from his tailored suits to his soft leather shoes . . . and he looked as if he'd dressed for ultimate effect. His eyes betrayed the calm of his posture, a little too wild, as if crazed, darting even as he ordered the local detective, "Relieve Mr. Devinio of his weapon and place him under temporary custody."

"Sir?" the detective asked, darting his gaze off Mark to Devinio, who continued to hold the phone at his ear.

"You heard me, detective," Mark snapped sharply and lanced the others with his piercing blue gaze as he stated, "This investigation is officially closed." His gaze landed on their associate, ignoring the agent's dumbfound. "Mr. Devinio and I will be returning to Washington. I'm leaving you in charge to tie up any loose ends, Springer."

"Mr. Jarvins?" the DA started with a step.

Mark seemed not to hear him at all. His gaze spiraled off Ronnie to Tim Spencer, who stood alongside her, and landed sharply, briefly. Darting, he lanced another detective in his steady gaze. "I suggest you place Mr. Spencer under arrest for attempting to interfere with this investigation and tampering with evidence. I'll have a list of charges drawn up."

"Mark," Devinio said quietly and drew the heated focus. "I have someone on the phone who wants to speak to you."

"I told you to put that phone down, Lenny," Mark said in an almost disgusted tone, and before anyone could do more than stare, he lifted his lapel with one hand.

Ronnie remembered that same casual action from the evening past when he had pulled his gun and leveled it on her. Insane. He truly was insane! Before she could draw breath, he drew his weapon.

In the military-shooting-stance, he leveled his gaze and gun on Lenny. "Now, put down the phone, Len. It's over," he said in a reasonable tone. "Put down the phone—slowly—and lift your hands to either side where I can see them. I don't want to pull this trigger, but you know I will if I have to."

"Yea, all right," Lenny said in a tempered tone, his black eyes wavering only to locate the phone base as he lowered his hand and the receiver.

Aside from the humming of office machines and the buzz of a telephone ringing, the room had become ghostly quiet. Like her, Ronnie suspected, every pair of eyes bounced off Jarvins to Devinio and back, but unlike her, none of them knew what Jarvins was capable of and how crazy he was. Even holding a gun on his partner, he appeared in complete control, the illusion enhanced by the grim expression and the authority in his deep voice as he ordered, "Detective, I suggest you relieve Mr. Devinio of his weapon." When the detective hesitated yet again, Mark snapped, "Now, mister!" The detective moved, and without missing a beat, Mark turned his gaze to Lenny as he continued, "You've been obstructing this investigation from the start, Len. I wasn't sure just how involved you were with the Laquettes, but after last night, there will be an investigation."

Her attention riveted on Mark, and Ronnie barely realized the rolling and quivering in her gut. Tension . . . the tension in the room could be equated to a generator vibration, and inside her, Tad felt it, too.

"There is going to be an investigation, Mark," Lenny said carefully as the detective nearest him moved closer, intending to follow Jarvins' order despite his apparent confusion. "In fact, there's already an investigation underway," Devinio added quietly. "I suggest you put the gun down, Mark, because you were right. It is over."

"I always knew you were smart, Len," Mark said in a firm tone. "But this won't work. I won't let you complicate this investigation further or pin all of this on another innocent man. You knew Laquette was guilty. We both know we were bringing him here for questioning. I don't know how you arranged that smoke screen with his brother, but we'll find out eventually. In the meantime, we're issuing a warrant for his arrest as well. Put the cuffs on him, mister."

"Mark," Ronnie stated and saw the twitch in his jaw, the wild flutter of his eyes. "Put your gun down," she stated.

Instead, his hand firmed on the weapon, both hands, and his gaze riveted more firmly on Devinio.

The police chief growled in a low voice, "Lawson, get the cuffs on that man."

"Mark," Agent Springer stated carefully. "I think you can put the gun away."

Jarvins shot his gaze toward Springer, fleeting a glance off Ronnie again, piercing the bewildered agent with a glare. "Has there been any word on Veronica Laquette?"

Stopped . . . a pin dropping might have been heard in the silence with the effect of his words. Already, Mark had riveted his gaze on Devinio, but in the ten-second delay, his tension rose, and he fired a glance at the agent. "I asked you a question! Has there been any word?"

"Ahhh?"

The words shot through her mind and slid off her tongue in a soft whispery tone. "Why did you have to kill me, Mark?"

Electric. His blue eyes bounced toward her, started to spiral away, then returned, neon. "Shut up," he stated. "Just shut up."

Whatever doubts lingered in the minds of his audience vanished even before Mark shot his gaze toward Devinio, the gun wavering in his hand. "We will find her, Lenny. One way or the other, we will find her, and you better pray she's all right."

"Why did you have to kill me, Mark?" she asked again, her words firmer, her mind spinning with revelations. Inside her, Tad stilled, merely quivering with his apparent approval. "Why, Mark?" she prodded in a whispery tone, watching the effect on his profile.

Tension knotted the muscles in his cheek as he stared, wild-eyed toward Devinio.

CHAPTER 29

Ahhh and she was beautiful, his love. So wondrously strong, so fierce. *No mercy*, Dominique nearly uttered aloud, a smile playing on his lips despite the drugs weighting his limbs. *No mercy, m' love . . . take him to the limit. Never again will he threaten you or my own.*

Barely, he finished the thought when his attention riveted on the masked face above him. In the corner of his eye, he glimpsed the reflection of steel as the gloved hand lifted a scalpel from the raised tray.

"We're ready to begin," the doctor said in a clinical voice, leaning over and looking into his shuttered eyes. "You are awake, aren't you, my boy? You're alert."

Dominique nodded slightly, the smile still on his lips. "Oui . . ."

". . . We'll make history together," the Taxidermist finished, his eyes flashing madly behind the windowpane glasses. "And you showed me the way," he said in a clinical tone. "I believed I was buying time, taking precautions by closing off the main arteries . . . but we have time. Plenty of time now. I was taking too much . . . cutting too deep. On a corpse, it doesn't matter, but on living tissue . . . I could keep you alive for days or even months. You've shown me the way, my boy—"

Within the soundproof room, the eruption of a mechanical buzz reverberated, startling and drawing the masked face up in alarm. "Impossible," he said quietly. "No one should be contacting me here."

The buzz resounded as if to counter the uttered words, and the Taxidermist hissed a soft curse. A flat-handed pat landed on Dominique's stomach as the doctor leaned over to reassure him in a deceptively warm voice. "Just relax. I'll take care of this."

Relaxed, Dominique closed his eyes, letting his thoughts drift and following the doctor as he sped across the room. With the natural flair of a surgeon, the madman elbowed an electronic door control, a fixture of every critical care ward and emergency room. In mirror reflection of the private clinic on the outskirts of DC, the door opened into a sterile corridor, and the Taxidermist strode through the fluorescent light to a separate room, a combination office and control room. A single desk stood in the center of the stark room, and like all other medical equipment in this facility, the combination of television screens embedded in one of the walls reeked of financial backing. A clinic . . . a private clinic . . . but not one designed for the explicit purpose of entertaining the Taxidermist or promoting his maniacal art.

Eventually, this clinic would have begun operations—discreet operations—in human experimentation. Without a doubt, the madmen in Washington had financed and protected this mad doctor. In the event of exposure, however, only the Taxidermist would be held accountable.

Well, and so it had come to pass. But in reverse order, Dominique considered with a slow-donning smile. The leaders, the benefactors . . . the monsters behind this black machine were already falling.

His thoughts drifting, he grasped the world around him, knowing the details behind the subtle news reports trickling through the media grapevine. Already one prominent doctor in Cleveland had been arrested for charges of malpractice. And in the Nation's Capital, a prominent Washington family mourned the loss of their aging patriarch—an aging aristocrat who had expired in his home office earlier in the day. What the media failed to report—the old goat had self-ingested cyanide as two Federal Agents had stood outside his office door. And furthermore, in the medical world, two esteemed physicians rocked the AMA with their resignation. No mention of the charges pending further investigation or the subsequent incarceration moments after the announcements were made. In the political arena, it was a hell of a day in the Capital with at least four different politicians indicted on charges that the Justice Department had yet to announce, and a member of the President's Cabinet had gone amiss. Linking the disappearance to the federal indictments, one gamey reporter had alluded to the possibility of a conspiracy.

The Taxidermist should have awaited the six o'clock news or the Sunday morning paper. He would have recognized the names.

A lazy smile quivered Dominique's mustache, enhancing the slight dimple that had often driven Veronica wild. If he had waited to capture his fate, he might have spared himself a partial rage regarding another elder sophisticate's demise. Paying the eldest Jarvins an astral visit had certainly stamped paid to that fellow's ticket—and likely the news of his grandfather's passing had twisted the younger Jarvins' mental acuity a notch or two.

Done. It was done. The culmination of his life's work—the only good that could come from the darkness inside of him. Tying up the loose ends, destroying what he had created—that remained his only goal. Eventually, Veronica would sort out her emotions and move on with her life. He'd given her a reason—the greatest reason he could imagine—for fighting for her life. With the white witch to nurture his creation, the child wouldn't become like him. Removing the threat . . . he'd vowed to remove the threat—all threats—and protect his wife and child. No better means existed to fulfill that mission than to lie idle, splayed before this madman.

Idly, he remembered a promise he had made, a promise she'd tricked him into making never to forfeit his life as he had tried to end it months ago. And he wondered now if he had truly anticipated this end. Had he known even then that he was incapable of keeping a promise? Carefully, he had worded his vow with the caveat, '. . . never give me a reason.' And she'd already carried the reason inside of her. The greatest reason he could fathom.

To break the curse, to break the cycle, he had no choice. Understanding. With his full faculties at his disposal, he understood the cycle and knew if he lived long enough, he would become his father's son. The desire to control, to use all that was inside of him, would take over as Jean-Pierre had prophesied. Eventually, he would become a threat to his child. Already, the desire to know this child, to influence him, to teach him . . .? To cast him in his own image, Dominique considered with a near scathing note in his silent voice.

What the hell was keeping this asshole, anyway? Dominique nearly asked aloud. Being skinned alive wasn't the most appealing means by which he might like to die, but he had made a damned promise. Technically, he wasn't taking his own life. Whether his decision to lie still and receive his fate would gain him entry to heaven or hell, he neither knew nor cared, but it certainly seemed a noble enough cause.

Barely, he considered the thought when he felt drawn, the vision unfolding within his mind's eye to see the doctor pulling open a weathered door. Deep shadows enveloped the madman; night chill whipped through open rafters, and a distinct odor of dust permeated the air. The doctor remained behind the door, lost in the darkness, but he wasn't alone. Another man, armed with a gun and a flashlight, meandered through the aisle, moving toward the door, his light bobbing ahead of him to pierce the blackness in the opening the doctor had provided.

"Hey . . . Doc? Are you in here?" the husky voice called quietly, as if afraid the sound might carry beyond the weathered walls. "Damn it, man, I have to talk to you! We have a problem! If you're in here . . ." The man stepped through the opening cautiously. His light beam rotated to pass over empty wooden bins, swinging—

The Taxidermist merely stepped clear and lashed out, jamming the needle gun against the man's neck. The visitor choked a squeak, started to pivot, and dropped like a lead weight at the Taxidermist's feet. Smoothly, the doctor stooped, caught the man by his limp arms, and dragged him onto his rump.

"There, now, no need to worry," the Taxidermist consoled while dragging the limp man afoot. Not large, this second fellow. With no trouble at all, the Taxidermist tugged him upward, nearly lifting him off his feet . . . and Dominique knew abruptly, how Abraham Lowenstein had become a target.

Not wrong, he hadn't been entirely wrong. This doctor had, in fact, spotted the pair, Abraham and Carl Shumaker together on the day Shumaker had sprained his wrist. The Taxidermist was a member of that private club; he'd seen it happen, had followed them, had meandered through the hospital . . . and learned Lowenstein's relationship to two prominent Jewish doctors. Reason enough. Even without the signal from on high, Lowenstein would have become the Taxidermist's first model. Not much longer could this maniac have suppressed his fantasies . . . and Dominique understood the bases of those fantasies. Yes, he did, because he had shared the same theater, watched the same films, introverted the same horrors via an old black and white film smuggled out of post-war Germany.

Conditioning. Programming. Brainwashing.

The Taxidermist had participated in the experiments, had become an experiment. A human experiment gone awry . . . and the man responsible for killing Dr. Carson, the head of the psychiatric testing ground which had created him. The conditioning worked.

Darkly amused, Dominique watched as the doctor half carried his 'patient' or 'model' through a second door which opened smoothly into a larger room. The doctor's van stood in a pale dull light, blocking the doors to the main facility. In mere moments, the doctor landed the lean fellow on a collapsible bed, raised the platform, and wheeled him through the hall.

One more pawn removed from the board. This Agent Springer, who had followed the cause and assisted in the abduction of a Frenchman, wouldn't likely survive to tell the tale.

Seconds later, Dominique heard the mechanical hum of the door, the squeal of rubber wheels on tile, and the dull thud of the mobile bed landing against the wall. "Now, you just rest easy, my friend," the doctor consoled. "I'll get to you in due time."

Almost giddy, the doctor arrived over Dominique, and even through the mask, the smile transcended. "It seems I already have models lining up at my door, but don't worry, my boy, I won't let anyone interrupt us again. Now, where were we?"

"Mark, put the gun down," Devinio said carefully. "I won't move. You have my word, paisano. Just tell me what you want me to do?"

"I'd like an answer, Mark," Ronnie said in a natural pitch, watching his eyes spinning toward her, then away, his gun quaking. "You told me I'd ask too many questions. I wouldn't let it drop. What were you hiding?"

"Shut up," Mark snapped in her direction, then seemed to pull himself up, rivet his wilder intense gaze on Lenny. "You killed her, didn't you, Len? You killed Jade Laquette or arranged for him to get killed—to protect her, didn't you? Not that I blame you, pal, but that doesn't make it right. And you confronted her last night, huh? You realized she'd never accept you, so you had to kill her."

No doubts remained. Every man in the room knew that Mark had slipped off the precious edge of sanity, and the tension notched higher with the revelation. Jarvins was armed, the gun cocked, and with Jade gone, every ounce of his hatred and jealousy had turned on the next likely candidate. If anyone moved too fast, Len Devinio would die.

"I didn't kill her, Mark," Len said in a quiet, careful voice, his dark eyes flashing toward the detective who had drawn out his cuffs. Slowly, Len moved his hand toward the detective to receive the cuff as he turned his full attention to Mark. "If nothing else, paisano, you can believe that. I'd never do anything to hurt her."

"You're a liar," Mark seethed. "She's dead. And you're responsible for that."

"Did you kill her?" Spencer asked in a low voice, and Mark's wild gaze shot toward him, spiraling off Ronnie. "You did, huh?" Tim prodded. "And you arranged for Sax to die, too, huh? You set him up to take the fall for this maniac. That's why you came to Bentwood and dragged him into this, huh, you son of a bitch? You wanted him dead."

With impressive restraint, Mark directed his glare to the officer nearest Tim, not losing his interest in Len even as he commanded, "You have thirty seconds to get that asshole in cuffs and on his way to the county lockup, mister, or you'll be joining him."

"Mark," Ronnie started and her blood ran cold with doubt, fear. Wild fury ignited in the pale blue eyes as Jarvins attempted to ignore her words. "It's over, honey," she said soothingly. "Put the gun down. They all know. We all know, and it's all right, honey," she consoled, unable to say the words to offer forgiveness. He truly believed she was dead, that he had killed her.

His gaze, as well as his gun, turned toward her. The wild craze stopped in a manic shine as he glared at her. "Shut up. Do you hear me? Just shut up."

"Mark," Devinio stated tensely. "Who are you talking to, paisano?"

The gun swung, and for an instant, Mark's blue eyes were as wide as silver dollars. The lashes dropped. His rage returned in force. "What are you trying to pull here, Len? I can always tell when you're trying to mislead me. You and your new pal, Spencer—you think you can put one over on me, right?"

Another phone line engaged, adding another beeping ring to the three or four phones already ringing on the surrounding desks. By habit alone, the woman officer reached to engage the line which had erupted in front of her. Mark swung the gun toward her before her fingers touched the receiver. "Don't answer that," he stated sharply.

"Sir," Agent Skyles interrupted carefully. "Take it easy."

The wrong words, the wrong tone. Ronnie sensed it as surely as Lenny, who flashed a warning glance toward his fellow agent. Mark Jarvins might be over the edge, but he was a trained federal agent who knew how to read a situation. In a single panning glance, he read the faces, knowing at this moment, his audience believed he was insane. That he believed himself sane registered as he turned his gun to Lenny. "I see what you're doing, Len, but it won't work. Regardless of what these idiots believe, I'm not the one with a problem, here. You're good, I'll give you credit for that. You always did know how to turn a situation to your advantage. You did the same thing a couple months ago. You played that one just right, warming up to Laquette, letting Ronnie believe you were her friend. Hell, you probably knew Laquette had killed those old timers even then, but you bided your time, huh? You played your hand close to the cuff, warming to them so you could set them up for this. You've had it bad for her, pal. You've had it bad for her since I first introduced you, but you didn't have a chance. This is beautiful, Len, a really nice plan. But somehow, she got wise to it, huh? She realized you got rid of Laquette, and she hated you for it, Or maybe you were just afraid she'd catch on eventually, huh? And she didn't love you the way you loved her. So, you had to kill her, huh? Now you want me to take the fall for this. But it's over, Len. The gig's up."

"You win, Mark," Len said in a low, resigning tone. His hands shifted in a submissive gesture, lowering slowly to his back where the officer could cuff him. "I should have known you'd catch on," he said with his dark eyes steady on Jarvins. "You're one of the best in the business."

If Mark took Len from this room, Lenny would die. No other thought held firm as Ronnie realized Len's intention, his motive. He wanted Jarvins out of here. He wanted her and her baby, and every other man and woman in this room safe. The only way to ensure their safety was to get Mark out of here. *'Promise me you'll stay with Len . . .'* the deep voice echoed at the edges of her mind.

Not the future. Those words referred to this moment, and unless she acted, she would never see Len Devinio alive again. Mark would never hold it together when the two of them were alone. All too quickly, she recalled the cold indifference in those blue eyes, the eyes of a sociopath. Jarvins was brilliant, but he lacked even a shred of moral consciousness. He would kill Lenny without a second thought, convinced that he could escape the consequences and cover his ass. He would lie. He had lied. He would find a scapegoat, the same way he intended to make Len his scapegoat, now.

Lenny wore the cuffs at his back. In a fleeting glance, he conveyed his intentions, his decision to the man who clasped his arm as if to put him under arrest.

"I'll take him from here," Mark stated and motioned Len with the gun. "Let's go, pal. I have a car waiting downstairs to take us to the airport."

Without another thought, Ronnie started forward, and Tim lashed his hand to stop her.

Reacting to the motion, Mark pivoted the gun.

Ronnie halted, her gaze locked on his manic eyes. "I can't let you do this, Mark. Lenny didn't do this. Len's not responsible for any of this. I'm the one who hurt you, honey. I'm the one you wanted to kill last night. But I'm not dead. I'm right here, Mark."

"You're dead," Jarvins said in a low voice.

CHAPTER 30

Wrong . . . something was wrong. Snapping awake, Dominique found the glittering light overhead, but this was neither reflections off the surrounding surgical steel nor the intense beam from the light fixture above. Weird prisms of color. Rainbow colors—like the sparkle of dust particles in a sun stream. If this was death, it wasn't so bad. But his curiosity betrayed the thought of death as a sense of urgency swam through his veins.

At the clattering sound, Dominique twitched, and his head rocked, his gaze landed on the Taxidermist backing away clumsily. One arm lashed out, and a gloved hand caught a metal cart to halt it from tipping. The shrouded head canted; the windowpane eyes lifted. Only a sense of confusion touched Dominique. The pale blue irises remained masked behind the reflection of glittering light on the lenses. The light. Brilliant light . . .

Living light, Dominique knew abruptly and lifted his gaze. Intrigued and fascinated, he studied the spiraling ball hovering an arm's reach above his head.

With every ounce of his will, he lifted his hand, distracted by the red trails spiraling off his arm, but the light drew him, his attention, his hand. Fingers splayed, he reached and knew when his fingers brushed against the light if only by the warmth spreading, tingling his fingers. Oh, and he knew this essence. He had touched it or been touched by it not that long ago. Light. Warmth. Wondrous. As if a feather stroked his fingers, offering him comfort.

His own creation.

A smile slid into Dominique's lips as he moved his palm to let the light play around his hand. He watched it brush against his palm, touching him. An aura . . . barely a thought in his mother's head, a mere tadpole in a vast lake, and this child's aura was already magnificent.

Was all of creation like this? Was this the beginning of all life? A mere glow of light to be captured and contained within flesh and blood?

He'd seen auras. He'd spent most of his young life attempting to distinguish the beginning and the end of living flesh. Colors. He'd seen all the colors of the rainbow, from the dull sallow shades of fatal illness to the raging blue fires of passion. Never had he witnessed such an opalescence to emit all the most brilliant prisms in the known universe. Beautiful. His little creation was truly beautiful, but even as the thought filled his mind, Dominique saw the transformations, the coagulation of color . . . and he sensed confusion . . . and fear . . . and his own essence reached out beyond his fingers, his light merging, touching, seeking as much understanding as this child had sought when brushing against him in the car.

'. . . Look, Papppa, loook . . .'

Like a melody, a song lyric in the most beautiful voice ever heard, Dominique grasped the words, the notes, his senses swelling with the pure wonder of the sounds.

'. . . Loook . . . ssseee . . .'

Words . . . his child's words. His son's first words, and . . . and Dominique felt the urgency, the fear that he'd only glimpsed in the colors. "Ssseee what . . .?" What did this child want to show him? What could such a . . . a light. The colors unfolded, brilliant colors taking shape within the glowing orb that lighted on his lifted palm. Light. Shapes. The images were taking shape . . . and he'd seen these same images only a moment ago.

The gun, Jarvins held the gun, he glared at . . . not at Devinio. His manic eyes focused on Veronica, and she stood frozen in the line of fire. In the next instant, she reached out, and he heard the blast. In slow motion, her magnificent eyes grew wide as she was thrown by the force of a bullet. The images were fading, darkness closing around him, and he understood the child's fear, understood at this moment, his child was no match for the evil, the insanity. Oh, the infant had the power, and he sought now to understand that power, to use it against the prophecy of this vision, to—?

His son sought the understanding *to kill!* To destroy the threat to his mother! To save her life and his own! And if he used the knowledge he was siphoning from Dominique's essence, the innocence, the purity . . . the magnificence of his aura would be damned no differently than his creator was damned by the power inside of him.

With a snarl of rage to equate nicely with a beast from the very fires of hell, Dominique closed his fist and repelled the light. His essence lashed out, spiraling out of him as the words continued to hiss off his lips, words in an archaic language that his father had taught him more than a decade ago. He knew the words. He knew the forces to call to him. Only a single thought held at the apex of his mind. He needed those forces now! At his command!

"Mark," Veronica said carefully, not trusting the rising shine in Jarvins' eyes, not liking the steadiness of that weapon. And not liking the stillness which had come over her child. All motion had ceased inside her, not a flutter, not a quiver. An emptiness, a vast emptiness that frightened her nearly more than the weapon hovering in front of her. An omen. Her child. Jade's child. The emptiness. The same feeling of abandonment gripped her when she believed her husband was dead. Whether the temperature was dropping inside the room or inside her core, Ronnie shuddered uncontrollably. "Mark, put the gun down," she uttered, shivering internally, externally. The room. A chill. It was coming again! The same chill that had crept into the cul-de-sac months ago!

No! She wasn't about to be shot! Mark Jarvins wasn't about to fire that gun! This was not how her life—her child's life was about to end! With a firming resolve and rising anger, Ronnie reached forward as she stated, "It's over, Mark. Give me the gun—"

Too late . . . too late she realized the finger squeezing. In stunned, slow motion, she lifted her gaze off the weapon, rising to witness the insanity gleaming in Mark's eyes—and in the next second, the explosion, as fierce and powerful as a thunderbolt, pierced the stillness. Staggering backward as if the air blasted through a hole in the floor between her and Mark, Ronnie glimpsed Mark's arm flailing upward as a second explosion erupted from the end of the gun. Wind, the wind came then. As if a tornado touched down within the squad room, chunks of plaster blew off the ceiling above Mark's head and barely started to rain down on them. The wind snatched the particles as easily as it tore papers off the desks and walls. Abruptly, short breaths became more frightened cries. The gun ripped from Jarvins' hand an instant before Spencer's arms enclosed Ronnie, catching her before she lost her balance completely.

Stumbling backward, she glimpsed others ducking, diving behind desks while others drew weapons intending to blast Jarvins or the wind. Landing against Spencer's chest, braced against the wall, Ronnie witnessed Mark's wide stricken eyes as he twirled away as if caught in the wind. His feet lifted off the floor, and his head swung as if a fist slammed his jaw.

"Godddamn," Tim heaved at her ear as papers continued to twist and sail in the wind. Across the room, the reports, the files, the faces of victims and suspects battered and ripped from the clipboards. The map rippled and ripped. Pieces snatched by the wind sailed as far as the door where the chief of this operation cowered and ducked, his arm flying upward to ward off a blow rather than a slice of paper.

As Mark slammed into a desk and tumbled—sending a chair skidding and slamming into a file cabinet—the wind began to settle. Papers floated like confetti in a ticker-tape parade. Dust particles and roof debris dropped like rocks to thud on the terrazzo tiles underfoot. As if catapulted, Lenny launched into motion. One of his hands dangled the loose chain that a wily detective hadn't connected. Before Mark fully landed, Devinio was on top of him, catching his hand, whipping him about to land face-first on the floor.

The stillness came then—an unnatural stillness as Lenny snapped a new set of cuffs to the second of Mark's limp wrists. No one moved. They hovered behind desks peering over the edges and searching for a target. Two stood in the military stance, guns poised and steady in the direction Mark had flown. The district attorney hadn't moved; he stood, lowering his arm that he had thrown in front of his face to shield his eyes from the wild debris. Slowly. Ever so slowly, the bodies animated, and Ronnie's attention fell uncontrollably to find Len's dark eyes studying her, searching her, his fear unmasked before he seemed to realize. . .

"You're all right."

She nodded, feeling the strength of Tim's arms about her, protecting her, holding her afoot, as she again panned the room, watching ashen faces emerge.

From behind the dual computer desk, the younger of the two officers appeared, searching the clutter as he nearly uttered, "What the fuck was that?"

"Is everyone all right?" the DA asked, judging the others in rapid glances. "Do we need an ambulance?"

The stout chief started to rise from his cower, but his knees caved, and he thudded against the wall, sinking. In a pivot, the attorney caught him, supporting him to a chair that had apparently spiraled away from the desk near the door. "Easy, Vince . . . There."

One of the detectives across the room uttered a curse and plucked a pencil from the sleeve of his jacket. "Christ," he hissed as he held it up, and inspected the torn material.

Under Spencer's grip on her shoulder, his persuasion, Ronnie turned partway about and found the piercing blue eyes searching her face, sliding downward to verify what Len had already discovered. Critically, Tim looked into her . . . and the understanding was there. The unspoken knowledge. Her husband had just made an appearance. Whether from the astral plane or a diner down the block, he had just saved her life.

Their child's life.

She felt him then, quivering within the confines of his fishbowl world, and if ever she loved her husband, never more than at this moment. The stillness was gone. The abandonment was replaced by the subtle flutters of life that had awoken weeks ago inside her. *'Your father!'* she wanted to scream the words aloud. Her heart suddenly racing in the aftermath, her eyes lowered to where her hand had come to rest against her. *'That was your father, Tad. That was the man who gave you life . . .'* And the sadness swelled through her mind on the heels of revelation. *'The man you will never know . . . The man who will never know you.'*

"Skyler, see if that phone works, and find out where Springer is. If you can't reach him, put out an APB on him. I want him found and taken into custody," Len stated while pushing off his unconscious former partner.

"Shouldn't we call an ambulance?" the DA asked, glancing off Mark to Devinio.

"Right," Devinio stated and looked to his associate, who hadn't reacted as swiftly as expected. "Maybe you better call Assistant Director Lakeland. Let him know we have Mr. Jarvins in custody and we're transporting him to. . ." His gaze shifted to one of the detectives. "General's the closest, right?"

"Yes, sir."

Without missing a beat, Devinio conveyed more than orders as he continued, "County General, then let him know I've issued an All Points on Springer. While you have him on the phone, I suggest you finish briefing him on the current situation, Ken, and let him know we're rolling with the local SWAT team. I'm just guessing, but I think he probably has our team mobilizing by now. Give him the address to that gin mill."

"It's a grain mill," Skyler corrected as he reached for the phone.

"Same difference," Lenny stated and turned his heated gaze to another. "Call your team, lieutenant. Have them meet us as close to that grit mill as they can get without setting up an alarm." His gaze pivoted toward the man who had located the grain mill. "You mentioned housing plans and industrial parks. Do we have any private residences butting that mill?"

"There's a couple of homesteads—old timers who refused to part with their family homesteads despite the parks. The lady who called us lives about two hundred feet from the fence."

Devinio looked to the computer experts. "Pull up the county zoning maps and get me a list of the nearest neighbors. If you can get me the plat map in two minutes or less, I'll marry your sister."

"If that's a promise, sir, I'll get you that map in under one," the younger mused and yanked his felled chair upright, falling into it and landing his fingers on the keys. "Course, we'll need my ma's consent," he added without losing his thought or slowing his fingers, smiling wryly. "She's only sixteen."

"Deals off," Len fired back. "Just get me those maps."

In motion, Lenny came toward Ronnie, bouncing a glance off Tim as he attempted a smile that fell shy of genuine humor. "You sure you're all right, honey?"

"Don't worry about me," she said bluntly. "Do what you do best, Len."

He nodded and started, "Stay with her, all right. I'll radio—"

Mark's cry interrupted the renewed activity, and Len pivoted. Handcuffed at his back, Mark flopped and screamed, rolling on his head to reach his knees as two detectives dove into action, catching his arms. He tried throwing them off, his deep voice growling and seething as they wrestled him to the floor. "Get offf mmmeee! I'mmm a feddderal agggennnt! Youuu're interrrfeeering in a feddderalll invessstigggation . . . Annn arrressst!"

Len pivoted in a half-turn, addressing Tim. "There's a lounge down the hall."

"I'll show them to it," the DA stated, leaving the ashen-faced chief hunched over the desk, holding his head on his palm.

"Just so you know," Spencer spoke while leveling his gaze on the attorney. "Your questions are going to wait."

"My questions will keep," the man agreed soberly and flashed his glance off Ronnie to Devinio. "I would like to speak with you a moment, however, Agent Devinio. If I have to prosecute this gentleman, I don't want any mistakes."

"As long as you don't intend to ask for a front-row seat, I can spare about sixty seconds."

On the edges of his mind, Dominique felt the Taxidermist creeping up on him, advancing warily with his scalpel poised as if he meant to make a clean slice across an accessible throat. Within the subdued light in the room, the shadow hulked closer, and Dominique sensed the fear escalating inside the man's already tortured mind.

"They were supposed to bring him," the Taxidermist uttered. "They were supposed to bring him to me . . . But you're like him, aren't you? You are his twin . . . his evil twin," the doctor said in a whispery tone, talking more to himself, bolstering his courage. "He was beautiful . . . I remember that most about him. Such a beautiful child. He should have been mine then . . . I should have taken him when I had the chance. You aren't getting away, Dominique. This is destiny . . . our destiny."

Slowly, Dominique turned his gaze and found the masked face hovering at the edges of his sightline. "Your time has come."

The Taxidermist stopped; his knife poised. Undecided, startled by the clarity and simplicity of the words, he hesitated. Behind the windowpane glasses, his eyes magnified considerably, and no reflections could mask the shine behind those lenses. "Yes, my boy," he said carefully. "My time has come. With you, I will rise to greatness."

Dominique sighed and rolled his head in genuine disgust. "There is no escape from the madness. The world is mad, and even with your parting, with my parting, the madness will continue to fest`air. No end to the madness, is there? No cure. The world . . .? Et is not safe, no matter how many of you I hov rent asunder. Always, there will be anoth`air waiting in the wings. Sush is my curse."

"I'll lift your curse," the Taxidermist said as he sidled closer.

Even in the dull light, Dominique glimpsed the blood glistening on the fine edge of the scalpel. His blood. How much of himself had been flayed, he couldn't discern, nor was he entirely put off by the thought. Nothing of physical pain touched him. Almost wistfully, he lifted his gaze from the blade to the maniac who fully intended to finish him quickly. Shaking his head,

Dominique locked onto the lenses, passed through the glass, and connected just as the doctor lunged. “Stop,” he said simply.

The Taxidermist lurched forward, then rocked back on his heels before the scalpel touched its mark. “Nothing is ev`air easy,” Dominique sighed and shook his head. “A shoice I need make now, my mad old friend. Whish ov us is the lesser of the two evils? You . . . *you* is whot my mind tells me. You can be stopped. Wheth`air I stop you or a bull`et finds you, you will not survive long in this world. But moi . . . I am a sarviv`or. Is thot good or bad I am forced to wond`air. Not but havoc could come of my exi`stenze, and yet, I hov touched the sun.”

Veronique, the sun. His child, the orbit of the sun. Veronique was strong in ways he couldn’t fathom, but she was still innocent. She touched evil, she recognized the feel of it, the scent of it, but she was no match for it. His arrival in her life was proof enough in his mind, but she had affected him as well, letting him grasp the sensation of love. Regardless of his confusion over that illusive concept, he did love her . . . and he loved that wondrous ball of light which had cried out to him—and him alone—in that moment of terror.

“Reeeleassse meee,” the Taxidermist hissed.

“A pity I am whot I am, mon ami,” Dominique said wearily. “And dead, I am not,” he added with a slight smile. “Destiny, Dr. Rhoades. Yours is to die. Wheth`air I hov made thot decision or anoth`air has given me the gift ov sight, I will not question. Painless . . . thot is the mercy you hov off`aired your victims but I am not merciful.”

“Youuu wwwon’t kill meee,” the Taxidermist hissed. “Youuu—“

“Hmm, not only are you insane, you are a fool, mon ami,” Dominique said quietly. “Re`moove your mask, doct`air. Use that scalpel as you hov for the oth`airs. We hov time. As you pointed out, often,” he said lightly and directed the hand to run the blade smoothly under the strings to hold the mask in place. He had known the face. At what point, he might have remembered, he had no clear recollection. As a child, he’d seen a younger version of this rugged, pock-marked face. More recently, he’d glimpsed the man alongside the FBI’s forensic doctor as he’d received hasty introductions in the morgue.

The Taxidermist. Remnants of the spirit gum that had held his gray beard hung like peeling skin from his bland face. In a crowd of two, only the noticeable pits of his poor complexion would set him apart. Unobtrusive this lunatic had haunted the chambers of the city’s underworld, undoubtedly, as driven by the madness he viewed daily, as by the demons in his psyche . . . and he’d become addicted to the kill, the torture. Doubtful the chief county coroner's heart attack was a natural phenomenon. As second in command, this fellow had gained the rare pleasure to work with his models coming and going while covering his tracks. Semi-sane then. This monster understood the legal and moral laws to govern society; he merely chose to ignore them.

"If I were as evil as you believe, mon ami, I would hov you experience both ends of your own trade, as surely your victims hov. But alas, I hov no reign in hell. I'll leave thot for anoth`air to decide. Drop your scalpel, doct`air. You will find a gun where you felled your companion. Pick it up, and we will let the fates decide whot becomes of you. Go now, mon ami. Find the destiny you hov shosen for yourself."

The scalpel clattered on the floor at the Taxidermist's feet, and the man hissed a protest, battling internally to break the connection of his will as he started out in lurching steps. Turning, jerking like a ragdoll on strings, he stumbled toward the door.

Dominique closed his eyes, following the staggering, growling man only in his mind. Not a firm hold. In a mind as warped as this lunatic, no firm hold could exist. Wavering and waxing, the Taxidermist lurched and nearly managed to turn about before Dominique blasted a new suggestion into the maniac's mind, mind-bending a suggestion that would surely lend him incentive to obey. Far more smoothly, the Taxidermist lunged through the door, convinced that only a bullet could slay the demon on his table. A bullet to the head, a carefully placed bullet wouldn't damage the flesh that he so badly wanted for his artwork. Nearly giddy with his confidence, with his knowledge that he could outwit this demon and immortalize the flesh and bones . . .

Wrapped in the ecstasy of the creations flying through his mind, the Taxidermist broke into a trot, then a run to pass through the doors and round his van. The gun. He needed the gun—Agent Springer's gun. He could slay the demon! He would slay the demon! His destiny—to have this one's flesh. His destiny—to remold the flesh into a sculpt of such magnificence that the world would bow to him . . .

Well, and the fellow was mad, Dominique considered and heaved a sigh, calling on his internal mechanisms to pull and push himself onto his side. Nothing moved well. The drugs rolling through his system dragged on his muscles, turning his legs to jelly as he swung his feet over the edge of the raised table. Muttering a curse, he let the weight of his feet carry him off the platform. For a second, he held himself aloft on his hands, but his limbs collapsed, dropping him with a splat to blast another curse off his lips. If he had foreseen any of this, doubtful he would have allowed himself to be found in such a wretched state. Modesty. Vanity.

Muttering a curse, he gathered his will about him, calling on the abstract forces around him to lift him onto his knees. He wouldn't be found lying as naked as a newborn on this floor. He refused to have the doors burst open for a troop of strangers to ogle him. Forcing his shins under him, he rested momentarily, head hanging as if on a flimsy cord. If he broke his fool neck over his vanity, it would be his own damned fault.

The sounds came only in his mind. Voices amplified over a bullhorn. Floating, the images sailed through Dominique's mind . . . the doctor scrambling on the floor, searching for the gun. He needed the gun. Needed time to proceed. Needed time to create! These intruders would have to wait!

Lurching, Dominique introverted that last with a flash of concern, then firmed his hold within the maniac's mind, offering another vision . . . another suggestion in line with the madness. Greatness. The doctor sought greatness. Believed himself invincible. Believed himself chosen above all others to become a leader in a new crusade against the illness of the world. Surely these men who hailed him through the horns were his following. He need only address them! He would go to them! His following. He would raise his arms and receive their adoration! They would give him time! They would clear the way for him to slay the demon and create beauty as they could only imagine.

Gun in hand, the Taxidermist ran, shoving through the doors. With the weapon pointed like a flashlight, he trotted through the shadows. He would go to them! His following! And he ran through the doors, an apparition with a blazing white skull, his body clad in the green surgical scrubs with bloodstains glistening under the spotlights. "I'm ready!" he screamed as he flung his arms wide to receive their blessing!

Two dozen armed men poised behind corners, on ledges, behind vehicles. Almost in unison, a half dozen voices shouted, "He's got a gun!"

"Drop your weapon!" a voice echoed, bouncing off the weathered walls. "Drop your weapon and keep your hands in the air!"

The Taxidermist lowered the weapon, turning it, and Dominique felt the connection break as if a cord had wrenched from his hand. Still, he sensed the mind grasping at the shallow remains of sanity. In a flashing insight, the Taxidermist understood these were not followers. They were policemen! The idiot policemen who believed they could stop him, catch him! He was invincible!

He was brilliant! A surgeon! They would never get away with this! His destiny! He would kill the lot of them!

"Drop your weapon!"

The Taxidermist swung his arm, his finger squeezing . . . and the guns opened fire, slamming bullets across his chest, lifting him, propelling him through the brilliant spotlights. Forever he seemed to float through the illumination, his body jerking and lurching, spiraling as the bullets riddled his chest and his blood exploded within the intense beams, a red shower engulfing him as he fell. As a bullet found the doctor's skull, the window snapped shut inside Dominique's mind.

Done. It was done. And no amount of determination would lift Dominique off the floor. Vanity or not, he couldn't rise off his knees or find the strength to locate his clothes. Perhaps, there was some justice, if not consolation, to be found on his knees as if he were a repentant soul. Doubtful. Doubtful, he would repent any time soon. Doubtful, even if he sought salvation from a grand and glorious being, he would be forgiven.

He had a few moments. Even with the flood of officials spreading through the connected buildings, the access routes the doctor had formed would prove a bit of a challenge. With his thought, Dominique struggled again, forcing his hands and body into motion, pausing, distracted by the blood already drying on his arms. Not flayed. Not half-skinned as he had imagined. How exactly he had lost so much blood, he couldn't fathom. Nor did he have time to consider the semantics. If he had any hope of salvaging his pride, he needed to move.

Vanity. Pride. Arrogance. He possessed all the damned vices a damned soul could hope for. And the damned . . . sense to identify a scrape of heels, to recognize the shiny black leather shoes rounding the table.

An uttered hiss, a curse, then the hands clasped his wrist and arm, urging him to the floor as the deep voice commanded in French, "Sit. We do not have much time. Raymonde, his clothes. Pierre, help me with him . . . Steady him."

No match for the hands to clasp his shoulder and head, holding him steady, Dominique recognized the shadowy black image, the cloak of darkness. No genuine relief or surprise accompanied his recognition. Gratefully, he tried to assist as his hands were shoved into the heated soft cloth of his father's coat.

"We don't have much time, Dominique. There is a rear entrance, and we have a car waiting."

"You waited long enough," Dominique noted as he struggled to climb onto his feet, succeeding only with the strength of the hands helping him.

"If you chose to die, who was I to interfere," his father said with a deceptively lighthearted tone, a ring of anger in the undertow. "You are a mess, my own."

"Drugged," he supplied, too aware of his knees buckling, his hands working sluggishly to hang onto the sturdy arm and suit jacket. Muttering a curse, he swayed and would have fallen if not for the arm coming about him.

"Possibly more than drugs," Jean-Pierre said indifferently. "For future reference, exsanguination has its drawbacks, son," he added, and Dominique lifted his gaze enough to see his father's sturdy features in the shadows. The dark glittering eyes panned the operating room as the other two rifled through bins and drawers. Uncomfortably, Dominique followed his father's heated gaze to the operating table. His blood smeared the surface, catching as much light and reflections as the shiny steel. On the opposite side, more definitive trails ran toward the outer edge, and belatedly, Dominique understood the concave trough. A red trickle of water traveled through the trench and carried the blood toward a drain at the deep end of the table.

To the sense of his father's eyes on him, Dominique looked up. By the twist of a smile in the mustache and the lifted brow, Jean-Pierre found this situation vastly entertaining.

"There is such a thing as justifiable homicide, eh, my boy?"

Before Dominique could counter the words, his body tipped under a push. His father dipped, collecting him off his feet, and the lame protest began.

"I wonder if you are more trouble than you are worth," his father commented with a chiding note and started them moving, deflecting the struggle without a serious effort.

"Should we clean up in here?" Raymonde asked.

"Leave it," his father commented. "The Americans can take care of it. They have a grand imagination when it comes to forming theories from collected evidence. It should be entertaining to hear what stories they concoct . . . Shall we?"

"My uh . . . blood and prints," Dominique commented as his father ducked them through an opening he hadn't noticed. "A camera . . ."

At the low deep chuckle, Dominique reconsidered his words, wondering what he had missed to feel so foolish under that musing tone.

In the soft spray of a flashlight beam bouncing back at them, his father's head shook. Even in the dim light, the green eyes glittered. "You have been swallowed by the darkness, my own. A shame, yes, but the Americans will have the film to prove it. About the prints?" he made a sound of dismissal. "The Americans will never trust what their computers tell them, least of all, where you are concerned."

Too tired, too numb to work out those words. Already Dominique suffered the chill of fresh air and tasted a hint of lake water as his father swept them both toward an opening ahead. How long, how far they traveled by foot, Dominique had no idea. Darkness. The soft glow of a flashlight bouncing off stone walls, then wood. The flashlight snapped off with a word from his father, and they passed through a creaking door into the moonlight. Belatedly grateful for the smooth ride, Dominique doubted he could have walked half the distance, and he never could have trotted through the tangle of vines as easily as his father. A dark sedan, as unpretentious as any government vehicle or economy car on the road, waited within a cove of trees, and despite the circumstances, Dominique found the detail amusing . . . that his father should climb into such a bland chariot. Jean-Pierre had never attempted to hide from what he was, who he was, not in Dominique's lifetime. Limousines were his father's choice of transportation; gold and silver, precious metal, and precious stones were his ornamentations by design.

Settled in the backseat, propped between his father's shoulder and one of his escorts, Dominique continued his internal kibitzing as the car sped out, carrying them into a flow of Saturday night traffic, swallowing them. Whether in France or traveling abroad, his father moved with the grace and confidence of a king, the arrogance and authority of the devil himself.

In an archaic language, his father's deep voice reached him, interrupting him. "Have I been so cruel to you, son, that you would rather die than become?"

His father hadn't anticipated an answer. None needed given. In the lingering silence, Dominique closed his eyes and let the darkness take him.

CHAPTER 31

Howling wind and shrieks, cackling laughter, and clattering chains, banging shutters and snarling dogs . . . The sounds amplified through the speakers mounted to the ceiling at each of the four corners within Olden Time's showroom. Ronnie had found the cassette tape tucked in the corner of a box within the office, hidden behind and beneath two layers of classic hits. Her husband had loved classical music . . . Or at least, she thought he did, judging by his collection. Possibly he had been a shrewd businessman, providing ambiance to increase sales, enhancing the desire of antique collectors to recapture the feeling of more gentile eras.

At the moment, the sounds echoing between the highboys and bouncing off glistening crystal challenged even the most avid antiquer to concentrate on cut glass or shined brass. She might see a run on railroad lanterns or oil lamps, pistols or swords, daggers . . . But she doubted she had anything to worry about. Not a single soul had graced the front doors in the past half hour, not since Denny Claymore had dragged Wade away to get ready.

Even that event, no small event when the industrious Denny Claymore was involved, brought sadness to the edges of Ronnie's mind.

In just four short months, Wade Kreider had changed. He was growing up, advancing on his teens with a vengeance. Rather than race headlong, menacing Bentwood sidewalks on his mountain bike, daring the world to step into his path, Wade would soon be thinking about cars and college, and Saturday nights in a backseat out on Shaker Hollow Rd. He was already thinking about girls. And if this afternoon's flood of giggling customers were any indication, the girls in Bentwood were thinking about him. Poor Lynn would have her hands full over the next few years. Doubtful even Denny's persistence and ingenuity would coax Wade into trick-or-treating next year. God knows, Wade had dawdled about the shop, dragging his feet until Denny's conniving had driven him to wit's end.

All too clearly, Ronnie had sensed Wade's desire to stay with her, to skip the childish games, as surely as she'd sensed his reluctance to mention the haunting tape—a cassette tape that her husband had apparently played every Halloween since the shop's grand opening. Like a dark cloud, her husband's demise lingered over Bentwood, and she wasn't immune. Her torment remained as great as the grief of any widow, only more complicated when she looked into the haunted topaz eyes of Wade Kreider or glimpsed the sadness behind Meg's smiles.

For Wade, maybe for herself, Ronnie had tracked down the infamous tape and plugged it into the machine. But whether she would keep it playing throughout the next two hours of business remained to be seen. At another spontaneous shriek, her muscles jumped, and her pen skidded off the lines of the ledger on the counter in front of her. Within his fishbowl, Tad orchestrated a perfect backflip and dove deeper as though he anticipated a gun blast or a windstorm and needed to hide. Shaking her head, she uttered, "Relax, sweety. Nothing to fear. Your mom's just a little on edge . . ." And that was an understatement.

The tension hadn't abandoned her. Far too quickly, she caught herself panning her gaze, falling prey to the howling wind which had begun echoing through the vast empty rooms. If the old magazines started fluttering or glass started wobbling—

A clatter of china clinking on china came from behind an armoire three aisles away, and Ronnie's heart slammed an involuntary beat before Elaine's nervous voice enlightened her.

"Sorry, Ronnie. It's all right. Nothing chipped."

She'd forgotten about Elaine, but the relief came swiftly, as well as the amusement. At least she wasn't the only one reacting to those shrieks and howls. Misery loved company. And listening to this travesty was certainly a little miserable. Wade might need to be disappointed when he arrived in an hour or so. Even though she'd stuffed a few candy bars into his and Denny's pockets, Ronnie had no doubts he would return in full costume; after all, she'd shoved the old clothes and the wig into his hands when he'd attempted to use the lack of a costume as an excuse to avoid this annual event. He would come to show off, along with half the children in Bentwood, she mused and glanced to the mounded cast iron cauldron alongside the vintage 1880s cash register.

Her smile faded considerably as she remembered opening the UPS delivery that had arrived two mornings past. According to the shipping label, her husband had ordered the chocolate nearly a month earlier and confirmed the delivery date by phone more than two weeks past. If nothing else about her former husband, she could never doubt the man had style . . . and class coming out the wazoo. Who else would order imported candy bars—in a quantity to accommodate every Halloween-age child in town?

With the howl of a wolf erupting in the wailing wind, Ronnie's muscles gripped, and abruptly, claustrophobia swam through her mind. Not for the first time over the past few days, she couldn't breathe, as if the walls had closed in. More than once, she had needed to escape the shop and Chateau Laquette. If not for Elaine, Ronnie doubted she would have opened the doors for business. By the time she'd returned to Bentwood the Sunday past, Ronnie had reached only one conclusion—she needed to pack her bags and put this world, this life, behind her.

"Elaine," Ronnie called as she flipped the ledger shut. "I'm going out. I'll be back," she managed, restraining the panic that threatened to quake her voice. Already in motion, she passed through the door into the office, vaguely aware of Elaine calling something after her, only half conscious of the concern she heard in the woman's voice. Her spontaneous exoduses hadn't gone unnoticed in a town the size of Bentwood, and her friends' and neighbors concern was genuine. How she had survived twenty-six years without these folks, she wondered more with each passing day. Between phone calls and visits, it was a wonder she found time to breathe. Getting away, getting out of the shop, out of the rambling walls of her home . . .

No other thought held priority as she snatched a set of keys off the desk and fled through the second hall.

The electronic garage door had lifted high enough to swing the Maserati into the ally. She hit the button to send the door closed behind her without lifting her foot off the gas.

Four blocks from the shop, she rested at a stop sign, catching her breath, trying to calm the tremors flying through her muscles. An anxiety attack . . . just another anxiety attack. If she even mentioned these episodes to her mother, who had begun calling a few times a day, the woman would probably drag a neurologist from the capital. Thanks, but no thanks! Regardless of what methods of persuasion her mother attempted to enlist for her to see a more acceptable gynecologist, Dr. Blackwell was the only physician Ronnie vowed to trust. According to that old sawbones, if she wasn't suffering a few bad moments, she would be in serious trouble. He'd suggested drugs if the episodes persisted or worsened . . . and just for a moment, Ronnie considered paying his home office a visit.

Driving helped. Just driving around town or striking out on a country road had relieved the tension on every prior occasion. This wouldn't be the exception, she vowed and rolled through the intersection without a clear destination.

Over the past several days, she'd arrived at the Spencers' home unannounced and not daring to mention, she had driven on autopilot. Only once, she had awoken from a trance to find herself rolling onto Elmview's main street and it had scared the hell out of her to realize how far she'd driven on autopilot. A subconscious need, she had rationalized after her heart slowed to a normal beat.

In the diner where she and Donna had shared slices of pie a lifetime past, Ronnie had picked up the morning paper. The headlines had heralded the news, 'Jack Trumble's Death Linked To Land Scam.' The subtitle had added, 'Murder Suspects in Custody.' The ensuing article had elaborated to recap everything Ronnie had already known, including the involvement of the county sheriff who had suppressed evidence taken from the scene of Jack Trumble's 'alleged' accident. Algen Industries, the chemical waste company legitimately negotiating to purchase the Ryder land, had been instrumental in uncovering the scam as well as the murder. The sheriff and members of the town council along with at least two of the Ryder heirs, were presently in custody pending an FBI investigation. Indictments would be forthcoming.

In a sidebar, Jason Ryder had recently returned from his duty station in Porto Rico. His input and insight into his grandfather's nature had broken the case. The original Last Will and Testament of John Ryder had been found in a mason jar buried under the back porch of the old homestead—along with a letter that almost assuredly accused his heirs of preempting his death. A few of them, Town Councilman Kyle Ryder specifically, had been 'sniffing around' and 'hinting' at a quick sale of the property. In no uncertain terms, old John Ryder hadn't wanted his farm to become a chemical waste dump.

Algen Industries was currently looking into the purchase of a strip mine twenty miles east of Elmview. Members of the college faculty were pleased to announce that Algen had offered grants to establish a research curriculum dedicated to the conservation and preservation of natural resources.

Not surprised, Ronnie had read the article and several others throughout the paper, but the follow-up on her investigation hadn't brought her to Elmview. It was something more, something Lenny had said . . .

Not one of the pictures from the Taxidermist's house of horrors had Ronnie viewed. She had suffered no desire to witness the madness that had cost her more than all the diamonds in Africa. Her own curse to be an avid eavesdropper had supplied more details than she cared to consider. Even lost and wrapped in the aftershock of revelation, she had overheard far and too many speculations just beyond her line of vision.

Dominique Jardonet . . . he was the last victim. In a hushed voice, Roberta Lincroft, the FBI's forensic pathologist, had concluded that the amount of blood at the scene would indicate that Jardonet could not have survived under the Taxidermist's knife. The absence of a body—which no one wanted to admit aloud—had suggested that the Taxidermist had disposed of the remains, and there were enough methods within the house of horror to verify they might never know for sure. A tape, recovered at the scene, had been hand-delivered to the FBI crime lab via private chopper . . . And judging by those who viewed it, Lenny included, Jardonet hadn't survived.

Stopped. The Maserati had stopped, and Ronnie rested in the first shadows of dusk, feeling the hot tears rolling down her cheeks.

Answers. She had needed answers. If she hadn't needed answers, would Jade have survived? If this once, she had accepted the mysteries . . . but that was impossible even to consider. And foolish. Eventually, she would have demanded answers regardless of whether she'd traveled to Cleveland. They had meant to kill her husband and accuse him of the crime. Ronnie had overheard enough of the partial conversations to realize the conspiracy under investigation in the Capital and Cleveland. The Taxidermist hadn't personally funded his clinic, and the macabre sculpts constructed of living tissue and bone hadn't accounted for the surplus of medical equipment in those sterile rooms. District Attorney, Adam Macanders wasn't about to let those curiosities ride, and he had far more than re-election in mind when he had vowed to mete justice on those responsible.

Brushing at her eyes, muttering an angry curse, Ronnie cleared enough of the blur to glance about at her surroundings, half expecting to hear a horn blasting from behind. No horn. Not likely to be any horn. She rested beneath an immense maple with the dying leaves reflecting fire red and orange in the last rays of sunlight. Not more than three feet from her front fender, a marble slab rose from the dying grass, reflecting the colors between the carved etching of the Blessed Mother cradling the Christ child. Despite Ronnie's haphazard conformity to her religion, the symbol offered comfort. Perhaps, an illusion of comfort, but she warmed to the brilliance of the colors overhead and the promise of life.

Life would go on. Not easily, not joyously, but life would perpetuate, and the stirring in her womb, the quiver of life, only confirmed her belief.

Without lending a thought to her actions, Ronnie reached and tugged on the door handle, a destination in mind. Foolish, she knew. Possible insanity. Not even her husband's remains rested beneath the earth a hundred feet away, but the illusion . . .

Maybe she just needed the proof of the words carved in stone to feel close to him. Whatever the need, she refused to turn back.

The sun rays were deceptive, the promise of warmth an illusion. Perhaps, she was insane. She'd left the shop without more than a lightweight black blazer over a summer blouse. The chill touched her. Internal and external. She passed carefully between rows of raised marble or granite headstones. Visiting a graveyard—even in the light of day—wasn't a comfortable undertaking. Suffering a superstition, she watched where she stepped to avoid the deceptively unruffled patches of grass that concealed the final resting places of a dozen or more strangers. Insanity . . . and the thought of visiting a grave on this of all days . . . the devil's night . . .?

"Damn it," Ronnie muttered and nearly stopped, then cursed again at her foolishness. Restless spirits might walk the earth, but she damn sure doubted they waited for a single day of the year to create havoc on the living realm. Demons though . . .? Did they adhere to certain rules?

"Oh, for God's sake," she uttered angrily. "Do you want to end up in a goddamn straight jacket? Is that it?" she asked only of herself. "Keep this up—Blackwell won't have a choice. He'll ship your ass—"

"There are always choices."

CHAPTER 32

Stopped, frozen, her breath caught, Ronnie stared at the dead grass directly in front of her feet for a full ten seconds before she knew without a doubt, she wasn't delusional. She'd heard that voice as clear as her own, and in slow degrees, she lifted her suddenly calm gaze. Her focus halted, reading the words inscribed in the large black marble stone . . . 'Beloved Husband . . . Jade David Laquette . . . January 8, 1960—October 21, 1989.' For a moment, her thoughts hovered on nothing more, but her focus landed on the soft black leather boot dangling near the inscription.

"It's wrong, you know?" the deep voice offered. "That inscription, I mean."

Her gaze lifted slowly, rising up the slightly kicking boot. Up the black pants cuff. Following the single limb upward and catching on the flash of red within the black draping cloth.

"Almost the entire inscription in fact," the incredibly deep voice commented with a lofty casualness.

If she moved too fast, she might truly need to correct at least one of the inscriptions within her mind—if nowhere else. Twice! That was the only thought filling her mind. This maniac, this apparition, this . . . husband of hers had died not once, but *twice!* Twice, he'd let her believe his physical remains were lost for posterity, but she was definitely not delusional. And she doubted very much that she possessed a talent for seeing spirits. Her gaze lifted, defiantly, and she nearly lost her grip on her rising rage by the pure simplicity of his pose and the wink of a dimple at the corner of his mustache.

Balanced on the four-inch width of the marble headstone—as if sitting on a bench—he rested one boot on the ledge, one arm lying casually over his raised knee. Head tipped, he studied her with a glitter of light in his livid green eyes. A soft breeze brushed at the waves at his brow and collar.

A menace! The man was a menace! Killer smile. Killer eyes! And he . . . he was wearing a tuxedo, complete with a red silk-lined cape that fanned out and draped at his hip.

"Incognito," he said smoothly, his lips quivering, his eyes glittering.

"How dare you," she found voice to utter, her ire rising. How dare he pop up here, blow her away with his presence, and smile with all the innocence of a child! And sit on his own damned headstone! "Get off that stone!"

"It's either sit on it or smash it to ash, m' love," he mused. "I chose the less ostentatious. I'm practical on rare occasions."

"You're a maniac!" she snapped.

He smiled and shrugged. "Suppose I can't deny that, but it's your fault."

"My . . .! How dare you!"

"We have a problem, mon amour," he interrupted, still smiling although a little of the amusement had ebbed from his eyes.

"Oh, just one, right? Just one problem? I'd never have guessed. So, tell me," she started, her eyes glittering with menace, her arms crossing, locking if only to keep from physical assault. Murder. If she murdered him, doubtful he'd just pop back into her life to sit on his headstone. "What is this uh . . . one problem—you seem to think we have?"

"Actually, it's not a serious problem," he said lightly, his head tipped more, studying her in quiet amusement. "Unless you fully intend to carry through with your current thoughts. In that event, it could become a serious problem."

Stopped again, considering her thoughts, the memories fleeted through Ronnie's mind. Murdering him for being alive would be counterproductive. Despite the pain, despite the shock . . . she had known he was alive. The grief she'd suffered after overhearing those words in Cleveland had passed too swiftly. The absence of a physical body had remained in her mind. Nothing had truly changed. To her, to the world, Jade Laquette was dead. Her gaze trailed to the words embedded in the stone, then lifted to his nearly sober eyes. "What are you doing here?" she asked quietly. "Why are you doing this? Haven't uh . . . haven't we been here before? Didn't I tell you not to contact me—"

"Veronique—"

"Look," she said, steeling her nerve, firming her gaze. "I can't do this. We *can't* do this. I . . . I understand why you did what you did. I . . . I can't even blame you." The sad truth of that admission touched her, dimming the anger, the frustration in her mind. "You saved the world," she said with a huff of a laugh, her heart aching with reality. "It's in the news," she continued. "For anyone who knows how to read between the lines, the truth of what could have happened, might have happened, is a little too apparent. So, I really can't blame you. I . . . I knew you had to have a good reason. I knew you wouldn't destroy our life, throw it all away without an extremely good reason. I wanted to make it something simple. I wanted to make it something natural—like maybe another woman—so I could really hate you and get on with my life, all the better for the loss. But I did know it wasn't anything simple. And I knew I wouldn't be able to hate you for it. The truth is, I do still love you. I will probably continue to love you . . . Unless you keep doing this to me," she added quietly, honestly. Fighting a sting of tears, she scanned the length of him, knowing that was a mistake. She still loved him. The look of him. The feel of him. The sound and breath . . .

With an iron resolve, she directed her focus to the inscription and found the strength to look into his hurt hazel eyes. "I warned you to stay away from me . . . Dominique. Now . . . now, I'm asking you. Please, leave. Go back to France. Go to Australia. Go to Kalamazoo. Just don't come back here. Don't make me wonder when you'll pop up behind a headstone or step out from behind a corner. Don't make me keep wishing that things were different. That we could be together again. It's not going to happen. Let me go, m' love. Let me be to cope with this the only way I know how."

"A casual affair with a vampire isn't in the cards, huh?"

Despite herself, she fluttered a dim smile and shook her head. "I'd end up like too many others who've crossed your path, honey," she said with a fleeting thought of Mark Jarvins, currently in residence in Bethesda's psychiatric wing. "I wouldn't be able to explain or hide the joy I'd feel in the aftermath. Eventually, someone would decide that I've slipped over the edge. Think about it . . . I couldn't keep from speaking your name four months ago. Imagine the reaction of our concerned friends and neighbors when I mention a visit from a vampire."

He smiled, no more genuinely amused than she was. "I see your point." With a grace and agility to defy his size, he slipped off the stone, unfastened the cape, and swept it aside, tossing it over the stone. Sexy. He was so damned sexy whether he wore a tuxedo complete with a red silk cummerbund or nothing at all, he was still the epitome of walking sex . . . And by his wry smile, he was well aware of his charisma. "Exit vampire."

She shook her head, tipping her gaze away from him. Too cute. The man truly was a devil. She'd known that at the onset, too, when attempting to keep her distance. Sighing, she found him poised with his hands in his pockets, his head canted as if trying to see a smile where no smile could exist on her lips. “Don’t.”

“I’m in love with you, Veronica,” he said smoothly. “I knew it . . . Possibly as many as eighteen or twenty years ago.”

“Don’t,” she repeated carefully, firmly. “We can’t be together.”

“You wouldn’t elope with a stranger, would you by any chance?”

For a full ten seconds, her heart screamed yes, but her better judgment and practical sense kicked in. “No. I wouldn’t.”

“Not even with your husband?”

She shook her head, her gaze dropping to the headstone, the date of her husband’s death. “A little hard,” she said quietly, all too clear on the consequences if her husband suddenly returned under a new name. Losing him to prison would be almost worse than losing him to death. She shook her head again, colliding with his critical gaze. “I am asking you, Dominique . . . or Jade . . . or Isaac . . . whoever you are, I am asking you to stay away. I will think about you. I will love you. But I don’t want to see you ever again. I don’t want to keep losing you. I couldn’t handle losing you over and over again.”

“Would you consider taking a vacation?”

“God, don’t you get it?” she asked with a touch of frustration, a great deal of pain. “We can’t be *together*. You . . . you knew that before I did. You knew it a week ago when we were making love. That couldn’t happen again. It can’t. I couldn’t play the role you’ve given me to play if you were within arm’s reach, and I’m not leaving Bentwood. This . . . it’s my home. It’s where I want our son to be born and raised. It’s where I fell in love with you and where I want to remain. These people, Jade, they’re as much my family as they were yours. They loved you, and they’ll love your son. I can mourn you here.”

The integrity of her words struck a fierce blow in her mind. She could mourn him here. She could forget he was alive and well beyond her reach. She need only look into the eyes of their friends and neighbors to grieve anew over the loss. Away from here . . . away from Bentwood, she couldn’t be the widow, and it seemed, suddenly, that was the only way she could truly honor the vows she’d made before God, the only remaining vestiges of the life she had meant to live.

Tears stinging the corner of her eyes, she cursed angrily and wiped the water away . . . and stepped back sharply as she realized he stood in front of her. Lifting her angry gaze, her thoughts faltered under the warmth and quiet strength of his gaze. “No,” she said bluntly. “Just let it go. Let me go,” she said, and backed another step, starting a turn.

His hand snagged her arm and whether she pivoted, or he simply closed the distance, he held her against him as he looked down into her eyes. Shaking his head slowly, his gaze sober and intense, he spoke softly, “I can’t, Veronique. I am a selfish, self-possessed man. I am probably a lunatic, greater than you know, and I am in love with you.”

“It doesn’t—“

“I asked you to keep something for me, m’ love. I didn’t understand my own words, not consciously, when I wrote them.”

Hope.

He nodded, his gaze intent. “Perhaps, it’s that spark that attracts me. I don’t know, even now, but I have reached a conclusion, a deci`sion.”

Distracted by the slip of his accent, she nearly lost the thought. Worse, by far, was the distraction of his palm tingling at her back, holding her immobile to feel the heat of him, the vibration of his hammering heart. “A . . . decision,” she uttered, grasping at the thought.

“Life without you would be too dark even for me, m’ love,” he said quietly. “I would die for you. I have died for you. Living . . . I would like to try living for you. That’s the problem, m’ love. Simple. Basic. I’ve spent so many years moving forward and backward, sometimes immobilized by the images that pass through my mind.” He shrugged by his tone. “There never seemed hope enough to live. The thought, so basic, primal, never fully crossed my mind. I am . . . I have always been haunted by death. My own mother . . . I think she was dead to me before she was ever alive. Even now, I don’t know if I resigned to the images of her death, if I loved her too little, if I could have saved her, though I think I tried. Memories are as elusive as my visions. Whether that keeps me sane or drives me mad, I haven’t a clue. What I do know—is that I need you. I need the hope you hold inside of you. I need to be a part of you, of your life. Does that make sense to you?”

She nodded slightly, knowing if nothing else, she felt the same way. Home wasn’t Bentwood or Chateau Laquette. Home was inside this devil’s arms . . . and if he asked her now, she would go. She would vanish without a trace to be alongside him and to hell with the rest of the world. Wherever they went, wherever they ended up, it would be safe as long as they were together. Her life, their son’s life, his life . . . those mattered. Nothing else.

"I can't always control what's inside of me, Veronique. I would like to be ah . . . worthy? Of your love and your trust, but I know enough to doubt. Even if I were to promise you that I would walk away, I fear I would find a way to break that promise. I am extremely good at manipulating circumstances and myself to believe my actions are justified. The only promise I fear I could make and keep is that I will love you forever. And now, I have fully reached the problem I meant to discuss when you first arrived. Knowing what I am . . . what I'm capable of, Veronique, would you have me as your husband?" he asked simply.

For just a moment, she saw it, the glitter of fire within his eyes as if emeralds hovered too near a candle flame. In the next instant, she corrected, not emeralds, jade. Her Jade. And he stood alongside the flames. He was conniving. Manipulative. Deceptive. Illusive . . . And he was still the only man who could heat her blood faster than the sun. Her thoughts tangled, snagged by the chill he allowed to wrap around them, sparking the memory of those hectic moments in the squad room. He'd saved her life. Others in that room might have believed a furnace exploded in the basement of the courthouse and sent a blast of cold air through the ducts, but she knew better. Her husband, by whatever the forces behind his glittering eyes, had saved her life, their son's life.

"Veronique," he said carefully, looking into her with a quiet intensity. "I . . . probably should admit . . . I can't see the future where you are concerned. My life hangs in the balance of your silence. It's not a comfortable position, m' love. If I were to admit to you, I am a . . . well, I'm a . . .." His gaze danced away, his eyes still glittering within the sunspot. Genuine discomfort twitched his smile before he sighed and met her gaze. "I'm a warlock, for lack of a better explanation," he said as if the words disgusted him. "Foolish, archaic term, I know, my own. In such a modern world, perhaps, an alchemist would be more explicit. I didn't choose to be what I am. I never willingly accepted the education, but . . .? That's who I am. Can you accept that knowledge?"

His life, her life hung in the balance, she might have admitted as she judged the integrity of his admission. If any other man alive had offered those words or made that claim, she would question his sanity and her own. The term, however archaic, conjured visions of black masses, covens, harems of women dancing in firelight . . . and far too swiftly she thought about the cult that existed within Bentwood. Once, at the onset of another investigation, Ronnie had questioned the possibility of Isaac Bently as a leader of just such a coven. Before the thought could take a firm hold, she saw the dismay in his eyes and knew he hadn't engaged in that twisted practice. She felt him start to withdraw from her, felt him easing her away, and her hand moved, sliding to his waist beneath the black coat.

Tense and wary, he waited as if he fully expected her to lash out or plunge a knife into his heart.

"You are an enigma, love," she said smoothly, holding him within her fierce gaze. "But if you ever form a coven and stage an orgy in our backyard, you will never live to see another sunrise. If you can live with that threat hanging over your head, m' love, then I can accept you as my husband."

A peculiar smile crept into his mustached lips; his brow arched slightly. "Our uh . . . backyard," he said hesitantly. "How uh . . . how big is it going to be, do you think?"

Studying the wry smile, the spark in his eyes, she decided, "You better consider it about the size of mother earth, sire."

He mocked a mild shock as if she'd struck him, but the expression crumbled, and a laugh slipped from under his mustache. Shaking his head, more genuinely bewildered, he commented, "I do love you, m' lady."

She let him speak no other words. Sliding her hand up his chest, she caught his neck and dragged his head into a bow to capture his furry lips. God have mercy on her, she'd fallen in love with the devil himself, and there was no denying her heart reaching out to him as the fire spread through her veins. Whatever the cost of loving him, she could only trust her instincts to know no price could be too high. They would find another Bentwood. Make new friends. Raise their son . . .

'Tad! Your father's back,' Ronnie ventured silently as the hands drew her closer, folding her within the heat and vibrations of his passion. That she got lost somewhere in that kiss, she had no clear grasp. She rested simply holding onto him, her head buried against his chest under his cheek. Holding onto him, being held by him . . . nothing else ever felt more right, more complete.

"I was born in a brothel," he said quietly, and her attention riveted as much by the words as the reflective tone. Skidding her head, she found his eyes looking down into her, his smile amused. "I was, you know?" he said with a mocked innocence. "In the backroom of one, in any event. A midwife delivered me into this world."

Her thoughts spiked to remember Elmview, the lamp . . . Devinio had mentioned the lamp recovered from the Taxidermist's lair. A relic of the holocaust smuggled out of Germany by a Nazi . . . and made a gift to Madame Savrel.

The question of that lamp had drawn Ronnie back to Elmview to learn more about the grand madame. . .

He nodded slightly; his mustache tipped in a bemused smile. "My grandmother," he commented. "A bit of a rogue as I've heard . . . a story I only half doubted when it was told to me as a childhood tale. My mother . . . she wasn't a very good storyteller. But Maggie Duncan was another matter altogether."

Duncan. She had heard that name . . . seen it. On a gravestone!

"Nan's brother, I'm afraid," he said quietly. "I probably should have gone to the funeral. Maggie was more a mother to me than my own mother more often than not. I did send flowers and a note, but I think I'd like to visit her personally sometime soon."

Something in his casual dialogue piqued her interest more quickly than his words. He was, in fact, disclosing something of himself.

His eyes drifted momentarily, then returned, more intent. "It is nice here, isn't it? Quiet."

"I uh . . . should probably mention, if it were noisy here, I'd be worried."

He huffed a soft laugh. "I meant Bentwood, m' love. If it was noisy in our present location, you wouldn't catch me dead here."

"You are . . . rotten!" she decided.

He smiled smoothly, his head canted, "You started it, mon amour."

"Obviously, I'll need to be careful what I start with you, huh?"

"Did you really like the name Jade Laquette?" he asked almost reluctantly.

"Dominique was sort of nice. I'm assuming it didn't end with an 'ic.' I don't think I could get used to the Jardonet," she admitted.

He nodded, apparently agreeing, then eased his hands away. "I have to leave for a little while. A couple things to take care of, m' love. I'll reach you at Olden Time."

"How much time do I have to pack?"

"I'll let you know," he said, and lifted his knuckles under her chin, brushing another kiss on her lips. Sparks ignited in the instant. "I will hurry," he decided with the promise in his eyes.

"You better," she said and backed from his embrace. The decision was made. Right or wrong, she would follow him wherever he led. That a calm poured over her, through her, she had only a fleeting thought as she watched him swipe the cape off the stone. For an instant, she glanced at the stone, the dates . . . wrong? "Hey," she stated, and he stopped in a half-turn, looking back at her with a smirk. "All right. Go 'head and answer me, smartass."

"October 31st, m' love. At the stroke of midnight in '61, or so my mother always said. I'm guessing, I arrived shortly before that infamous count."

"And?" *His name?*

He smirked and shrugged, "For another time, m' love. See you soon."

The shit! Shaking her head, Ronnie watched him swing the cape over his shoulder as if tossing a topcoat and striding across the lawn toward the descending shadows. If only by her absence of desire to chase after him, she knew he would keep his word. Turning, she strode toward the Maserati, nearly invisible with the evening shadows descending. The sun had dropped . . . and Ronnie sidestepped unconsciously, dodging what she suspected to be a grave. Her husband had suffered no such superstition, she realized with a reflective thought of him striding lengthwise across the neat row of headstones. Was there a message in that detail? He was definitely sensitive to things beyond the material world . . . and he was probably too blasted arrogant to tiptoe around the spirit world. She could almost imagine him defying the dead by treading over their bones.

Shaking her head, Ronnie climbed into the driver's seat. Life . . . would never be dull. She just hoped he wasn't planning to build a fortress in Transylvania . . . or Romania . . . or any other of those ia's. Pennsylvania was close enough.

In honor of Halloween, which made far more sense to Ronnie now than an hour earlier, the infamous Isaac Bently had always extended his hours regardless on which day of the week the holiday fell. That, too, Wade had confided, and Elaine had verified, adding that she could stay to hand out the treats without needing to be paid. Not many children visited her home, she had explained, and it was sort of a habit. Generally, according to Elaine, Isaac had stuck around only long enough to hand out the first few bars, then migrated to Crowley's Bar and Grill down the block.

Barely able to control the anticipation that had begun graveside, Ronnie refrained from dismissing Elaine if only to keep from drawing suspicion to herself. At the slightest indication that she was anything other than depressed, she would probably be inundated with visitors and phone calls. The latest technological advancements in satellite communication couldn't hold a candle to the grapevine in Bentwood, which accounted for her growing concern when the phone rang for the third time in ten minutes. Considering how she had sped out of Olden Time, she shouldn't e alarmed to hear yet another female friend asking, "How's it going? Getting a lot of kids?"

"More than a few," Ronnie admitted, watching as three ghouls and a princess with a tinsel hallo crowded into the main entry where Elaine stood holding the bowl. Safer to keep the cauldron near the door than force the little monsters to race through the aisles. Elaine's laughter and the shouts of "Trick-or-Treat" echoed through the haunting screeches and banging shutters.

"Great night for Tricks and Treats," Rachel stated, then huffed. "Oops, gotta go! Talk to you later."

She should not be alarmed. Such a simple quick call should not create havoc in her system, but with every passing moment, Ronnie felt the strangeness coming, their plans changing. If something happened to him, now . . . no! Nothing would alter her plans. She was leaving with her husband even if she needed to dress as a witch and slip out the backdoor to meet him. Life was too blasted short to waste time worrying about what was lost. What she gained would be just reward, and her feelings hadn't changed for him. If anything, she might love him a little more for the chances he'd taken, for the risks he'd willingly accepted. As much as she loved this town, with its quirks and idiosyncrasies, as much as she loved their friends and neighbors, she loved her husband more. And she did trust him. They wouldn't end up in the back of some brothel or running from the law. Any man who could stage his own death—twice—could certainly provide a life for her and their child. With the certain knowledge that he still loved her, that he hadn't thrown his love away with their life, she'd follow that rake anywhere.

The phone rang yet again, and Ronnie snatched it up, nearly forgetting the words, "Olden Time Antiques and Collectibles. Can I help you?" At the front door, the familiar wig appeared, along with the trench coat, the baggy pants, and undoubtedly the pillow. A single step behind, an elf-like creature with immense, horn-rimmed glasses sprang through the opening, shouting, "Trick-or-Treat!"

In her ear, Donna laughed, "Sounds like you're busy."

"I doubt I've seen this much business altogether in the past two months."

"You okay, Hon?"

"Fine. You?"

"Great," she said. "Any chance you've seen Tim recently?"

"Not yet."

"Have him call me when you do," Donna said then. "See ya later."

As much as she knew people meant well, their concern could be a little daunting. Ronnie shook her head as the phone went dead at her ear. That was definitely one of those, 'just checking on you' calls. Replacing the receiver, she smiled as the hairy hobo sauntered down the aisle.

Lynn had added a layer of shoe polish to Wade's cheeks, but the coating hid nothing of his expression that suggested he felt like a damned fool in his disguise. His eyes rolled, and he smiled a little too wry for his own good. "Tricks are for kids."

"So are treats," she mused. "If I hadn't helped, I wouldn't recognize you."

"Uh-huh," he said. "And I was born yesterday, too. Think I could take a break? It's a real zoo out there."

"I doubt Denny's going to let you rest," she said sympathetically.

"If you don't tell him, he won't even figure out he left me behind," Wade confided, sounding amused. "The kid acts like he's never had candy in his life."

Wade sounded far too old for his age, but he was right. Denny loped out the door without a backward glance. Shaking her head, she mused, "I think you're safe for a moment."

"Not a moment too soon," he decided and reached up, yanking the wig off his head. "This dang thing feels like a wire brush." He raked his fingers through his flattened hair, apparently relieving an itch. "Boy, does that feel good."

The sounds of another troop of children cut short a little too quickly, and Ronnie's heart lurched as Len Devinio stepped into the doorway. Jade! Somehow Len had figured it out! Caught him! Federal surveillance! They might have been following her! Watching her! She hadn't felt anyone watching but her senses . . . Jade's senses were far more accurate. She recovered her fear before Len started down the aisle, but the tension in his face threatened to break her resolve. News. He'd come here with an agenda. Something to say . . . Something like the fact that Jade was currently in federal custody for faking his own death. Something like he had been charged with a million counts of fraud and tampering in federal something or other. He was getting sent to Leavenworth. And if she wanted to see him, she'd need to make arrangements—

"Hiya, hon," Len commented in her direction, glancing to Wade, and reaching almost casually to scuff the mussed blond hair. "Hiya—"

Wade ducked the assault, eying Len a little warily, which had nothing to do with the tussling. Far too perceptive, this scamp.

Devinio seemed to realize he couldn't delay another moment. They both knew something was up. His dark eyes shifted to Ronnie. "There's ah . . . something I need to tell you, hon. Think we could step into your office for a minute?"

"We're fine here," she said in a slightly chilly tone, ignoring Len's glance toward Wade. "What's wrong?"

"Uh," Len hesitated, then sighed and leaned against the counter, studying her more intently. "I really think you should be sitting down for this, hon. What I have to tell you could be a—a little bit of a shock."

"Damn you," she snapped, her tension rising in leaps. "Whatever you have to say—"

"Jade's," he started, and his lips twitched with the tension. "Honey, you know how uh . . . there was some confusion surrounding that crash. We uh . . . Well, we found out what Jade was doing on that plane," he said carefully. "Apparently, he did talk to his brother. They weren't that close, but apparently, Dominique was . . . the fact is, Jade was on his way to meet with someone in Washington. He was definitely on that plane when it went down. He hopped a ride with an executive heading for Knoxville. The uh . . . the other prints we lifted from the wreckage matched up with that guy. The thing is . . . well . . .? He walked away."

Her breath caught, she studied Lenny, anticipating the worst in his next words.

"Apparently, he was thrown clear of the wreckage," Lenny continued with a huff. "He was pretty banged up . . . and he had a concussion. But he . . . Well, he's alive, Ronnie. He turned up in a little town about fifty miles from the crash last night. Actually, he phoned uh . . . you know, if this was anyone but Jade I was talking about, I wouldn't believe half of this. The fact is, he spoke to my director, who he was supposed to meet. We've spent the last twenty-four hours trying to figure this out, and what it amounts to is this—some old timer came across him up in the hills, and your husband had amnesia." *And if she believed that, he had some swampland in Florida*, he might have added with the spark in his eyes. Officially, that was his story, and he was sticking to it. "Anyway, if you want him—"

The man walked like a cat, not a sound under his footfalls. And he still wore the vampire costume. His hand reached out and clasped Wade's swaying blond head, smiling down with a touch of concern. "Steady, lad. I won't bite despite the costume to the contrary," he said lightly, and lifted his haunted gaze. A slightly nervous smile played on his lips. "I uh . . . from . . . hell," he uttered and swept around the end of the counter, catching her from anything but a sway.

Launching into his arms, she met his furry lips halfway, igniting an inferno between them.

"Home," he uttered between kisses. "Light . . . Damn, you're beautiful . . . Missed you. . . Couldn't stand it . . . Love you . . . Forgive me . . . Came as soon as I could . . . Wouldn't believe the red tape! They thought . . . You thought . . . I'm so sorry . . . If I could have. . ."

A devil! The man truly was a devil! Holding her, kissing her neck, their world remained separate and apart from the swiftly filling aisles and hushed startled voices. Against her ear, he whispered, "You haven't had any morning sickness lately, have you?"

The implication, the genuine hint of disgust beneath his musing tone started her laugh, and when his eyes lifted, searching her, Ronnie lost what little rein she had mustered. She could laugh now, no holding back, and as he drew her into his arms, his low laugh and huff only enhanced the pure joy running through her system.

"Mon Dieu," he muttered. "The woman's sense of humor is atrocious . . ." And as a howl erupted from the speaker, he murmured against her neck. "Hmm, and she's playing my song . . ."

Against his ear, she whispered, "Happy Birthday."

EPILOGUE

Five months later . . .

The pain woke him—a quick cutting strike pierced his back as if he'd been skewered. With a startled breath and grunt, Jade pivoted his head and found his love in the shadows. Her head sunk within the white satin pillows, and her hair swept over the silky whiteness of her shoulder. As always, Veronica slept with one arm under her pillow. Not in quite a while had she laid on her stomach. Their joint creation had graduated from a fishbowl to a ten-gallon tank. All of which resided directly in the center of her slender frame despite how often she bemoaned her hips and thighs. Her hips and thighs were perfect. Her face as slender now as when they'd first met . . . but faintly glistening, he noted as the start of another pain moved him uncomfortably.

"Uh oh," he uttered in a hushed voice, not sure what worried him more—the fact that she remained sound asleep or the possibility that when she woke, he would discover the integrity of this alarm? She slept comfortably, peacefully. He felt her warm breaths against his neck and shoulder and saw well enough in the darkness to judge the soft natural smile on her lips. Only in jest, she'd threatened to let him handle the labor pains. But he had a funny feeling, some twist of her magic or his own hadn't accepted the joke. She was still asleep . . . He was wide awake . . . And the pain slipped through his system like hot oil.

"Ahh—Ugh, shit," he uttered and held his breath, nearly biting his tongue as he watched the eyelashes flutter very close to his own. Was it a vision . . . or the genuine article?

His head rolled again, locating the glowing digits of the alarm clock positioned on the headboard for just this event . . . and as his eyes cleared of the fuzz, his heart leaped in his throat.

"Oh, shit," he said more swiftly. He hadn't known the date . . . but he damned sure knew the time! *2,1,4* . . . At two-fourteen, *a perfect seven*, his son would slide into the world, and unless he was suffering a warped vision, it was presently 2:02!

"Oh shit," Jade said again as another slice of pain moved him. Untangling the sheets between them, he twisted and touched Veronica's arm, stirring her gently, "Sweetheart, I think we have to . . . Ow! damn!"

"Huh?"

"M' love, wake up," he strained softly, rocking the bed and mattress as he shook her. "The little devil's up to something, m' love!"

"What?" she asked, tipping her head and squinting against the soft lamplight above the headboard. "What's wrong?"

"The baby," Jade stated. "Your baby—our baby—he's coming."

"Wake me when he gets here," she muttered and dropped her head to the pillow.

"Veronica!" Jade huffed and shook her shoulder, suffering her growl of protest. "The imp's up to something! He's . . . on his way."

"Honey," she said with a lazy, sleepy tone. "Of course, he is . . . Just relax. Go back to sleep."

"Love to! Just as soon as you have our shild!"

Still half asleep, she wiped at her eyes, waking more to look up at him. A curious smile played on her lips as she studied him. "Did you have a nightmare, hon?"

"I most assuredly am having one at this moment . . . and it may get worse if you don't wake up, Veronique. This . . . this is a little out of my bailiwick. Do get up . . . And dress quickly, will you?"

"Uhhh . . . What are you going to do?"

"Probably throw up," he commented calmly as another pain threatened to buckle him. He'd been skinned alive and not felt a thing . . . but the birth of his child would probably kill him. Rolling and shoving off the bed, he rested on the end of the bed, stopped by the pressure sinking through his system, the slice of fire rising up his spine. "This is not nice," he decided and caught his head on his palm, turning enough to find Veronica resting on her elbow. She wasn't looking at him, however. Her focus had lowered toward the blankets covering her middle. "Veronique, please, don't dawdle further. I think we have a . . . ugh, problem."

"My uh . . . I think my water just broke," she said as she looked up with a faintly spooked shine. In a half second or less, she seemed to read the tension and integrity of his distress. "Oh-mi-God," she uttered in a sing-song rhythm. "You're in *labor?*"

"I truly don't like the sounds of that, m' love. If you'll take over, I'll be glad to make the appropriate phone calls—" His breath cut short with a grimace.

"I uh . . . I think I felt something that time," she said almost thoughtfully.

"You're trying to make me crazy, right? You've decreed that I should be driven to bloody madness—"

"You do get testy," she mused, and rolled to her back, reaching and collecting the telephone. "I'll make the calls. Just hang in there a moment."

"The hell if you will," he said, and pushed off the side of the bed, grunting and stumbling clumsily before rounding the bed. He reached her side in time to yank the telephone from her ear. No way in this lifetime would he let her make the damned calls and have the charming town of Bentwood accusing him of sleeping through this event. "Blackwell," he seethed into the receiver as the groggy voice interrupted. "Get your ass over here—"

"Jade?" Spencer asked with waking anxiety.

Dropping his gaze to his smirking wife, Jade shook his head and rolled his eyes. "Get Blackwell over here! We're having a baby!"

"You're . . .? Oh, shit. Hey, just relax, pal. I'll call the doc and have him meet you over at the clinic. You went through the trial runs, right? You have the bag packed? The clothes laid out—"

"I don't need a fucking pep talk, goddamn it! My wife's having this baby right here, right now. Get Blackwell out of bed and get him here! Now! Do you—"

"You're a goddamn psychic, and you couldn't give yourself time to get to the goddamn—"

"I'm getting a lecture," he said in dumbfound, holding out the receiver and looking down at Veronica whose features had lost some of the amusement. She was taking over. He felt the pain ebbing from his system, and his heart hammered a quick beat to realize he'd prefer to feel the pain firsthand rather than watch it. Into the phone, he snapped, "Get the doc or an ambulance, Spence. Now." As he dropped the receiver into its cradle, he caught Veronica's more gentle eyes, her soft smile. "Darlin, let me—"

"No," she said and shook her head, her eyes clear as blue crystal. "If there's one thing I am going to do normal—it's to bring this baby into this world."

"We could try to make it to the—"

She shook her head, flinching, moving slightly. "If we could have made it, you wouldn't have sent for Blackwell or the ambulance. Whether we—" Her words cut short with a breath and a downward glance. "—Wait for either," she strained. "Is the only thing left for debate."

The baby wasn't waiting, Jade could have told her. Cursing his insight in several languages, he swung from the side of the bed and hurried to the bathroom. Grabbing a handful of towels, he returned in time to see Veronica grip the quilt to either side and strain against the start of pain. Nothing of his insight touched him. Frozen, he watched as her eyes closed, her body arched. Not sure which direction to move, either to grasp her hand at her side or move into the midwife position, he could only watch as she swung her head and lanced him with a quick, bright shine.

"Dooo sssommmething!" she seethed, sounding possessed.

Effectively jolted, he dropped the towels at her side and clasped her hand, tugging at the blanket. No doubt! As they had slept, this wily little creation had turned himself about and headed for fresh air. "Damn! He truly is coming—"

"I'm goinnng to killl you if you," she paused to drag a breath through her gritted teeth, heaving breath with her words. "Donnn't dooo sommmething!"

"Mon amour, we have a problem," he said matter-of-factly as he scrambled onto his shins and scooted toward her knees, clasping and shifting her feet. "Bringing life into the world . . .? It's not something I'm good at."

"Dammmn youuu! Ggget goood at it!" she huffed with a short cry and snapped her head up to look at him. "Fast!" she added as a spasm of pain ripped through her. "Goddd!"

"Good, pray," he decided. "We'll need a little extra help here."

"I'm going to hurrrt you! Baaad! If you even—"

"Oh-mi-god," he cut her off as he spotted the anomaly emerging. "Oh-mi-god. Think it's time to push, m' lady. I'll catch—"

"Lunatttic!" she screamed at him as she arched upward, and his hands moved swiftly mechanically into action. That she could swear like a drunken sailor had never occurred to him, and he paused more than once to see if the voice had truly slipped off her lips. Moments—the moments were glorious—his mind locked into the reality, riveted to experience the agony within his hands, enthralled to feel the expansions and contractions of the world around them as the slight living form crept almost leisurely from his haven. Capturing the warm wiggling form in his hands, Jade rested on his shins, rapt in the wonder of creation. He'd seen the rainbow colors before, as he saw them now, sparkling and radiant about the edges of the wet red form. Bathed in blood, the infant squirmed, the tiny arms stretched, and the legs kicked within his palms. By instinct alone, he brought one of the towels to clear the pink round face, to wipe the eyes and blew a breath of utter dumbfound as the little imp sputtered and squeaked a sound. Eyes . . . The windows to the soul, and through the radiance, Jade looked into the off-colored orbs . . . and felt as if the infant had reached into his soul. His creation . . . his son . . . but an entity into himself.

Trembling in the latent shock, Jade lifted his bewildered gaze to find Veronica watching him, felt her love for him as surely as her desire to share this moment of wonder and view what they'd brought into the world. Carefully, he manipulated the squirming form into a towel, not lifting him too far from his mother's body while easing him upward into her arms. Never had he seen her smile more brilliant, her eyes more wondrous. Sweated, tired, and still shaking from the last quake, she looked upon the tiny face while enlisting another corner of the towel to clean the muck from his dark head. Oh, and he had hair. Ringlets of dark hair, although, in the lamplight, no clear shade emerged. And long lashes . . . and soft full lips like his mother, and a pixie nose . . . and all his fingers and toes. . .

Smiling, Veronica looked at him, uttering, "You lied, honey. You're very good at bringing life into the world."

"He's beautiful," he uttered, his gaze lifting toward her. "A wonder . . . just like his mother."

"I uhm . . . I think his name's . . . Thaddeus," she said quietly and looked again to the little bundle squeaking and squirming slightly within the blanket. "Thaddeus. . ." she looked to Jade. "Jade Laquette," she added. "Unless you have another name you'd like to add?"

"Thaddeus," he tested the name on his tongue, knowing their child had been named months ago. "Thad," he considered while bouncing a smirk off the wet tussle of dark curls. "I don't think we should mention to him, he's been named after a baby frog, agreed?"

"I think it's a little late to keep that secret, hon," she said and looked down into the lively green eyes, which even in these moments, seemed to be spying on her, studying her. An illusion, surely, but he'd grown quiet and content within the towel. "You already know, don't you, sweety?"

The shouted, amplified voice through a bullhorn interrupted, and they both looked toward the door as Spencer's voice echoed, "Jade! If you don't come unlock this fortress! I'm blowing the goddamn doors off and waking the whole town!"

Considering the crowd already collected in the street, including Meg in a bathrobe, Donna wearing a pair of sweatpants turned inside out, and others running toward their side entrance, Jade looked at Veronica. "Think we need a wider side door?"

She huffed a laugh, "Not now. I think I just lost ten pounds. You better go let them in before they give Thad a fright."

"Good point," he said, and climbed a little clumsily off the bed, surprised to feel the weariness dragging at his heels. Nearly to the door, he paused at Ronnie's command and looked back to see her bathed in the lamplight, smiling sweetly. "A problem?"

"You uh . . . might want to grab a pair of pants, hon."

Looking down at himself, he shook his head, sighing disgust as he veered and picked up a pair of jeans, commenting. "Another good point." Stepping into a pant leg as the phone began to ring, he glanced toward the bed and caught her looking at him, smiling at his clumsy pose. "A latent case of the nervous father, do you think?"

"Maybe just a little case," she mused as he hopped and stepped into his jeans.

Pulling them up en route to the phone, he paused alongside the bed, ignoring the telephone as he stole another moment to admire his wife and child. They were more than he could have hoped for and worth whatever risks he'd taken, whatever risks he'd take in the future. They were, without a doubt, his life. His gaze caught on the warm weary blue eyes. No words needed to be spoken. Whatever the future, they were in this together, mamma bear, pappa bear, and baby bear. Smirking, he lifted the phone, speaking before Blackwell could utter a word. "You're a few minutes too late. Give me a second to reach the door, and I'll let you in to meet my son. If Tim blasts the doors, I'll blast his jaw. Do mention that to him, will you? See you in two."

Ronnie huffed a soft laugh as Jade dropped the phone. "Who exactly was that?"

"I think it was the doc. Truthfully? No idea," he decided and leaned down, brushing a kiss on Veronica's lips, then dipping further and brushing a kiss on the curly head. Weird, very weird, these feelings tugging and churning inside him. He probably would slam his old pal for the simple act of worrying the infant. The need to protect had only become more fierce, and God pity the poor soul who ever chanced to threaten the son of Jade David Laquette . . . or Dominique Jardonet . . . or Isaac Bently for that matter.

Striding down the steps, he sensed the message had been relayed, and the crowd had fallen silent, waiting anxiously just outside the door. The idiosyncrasies of living in a small town . . .. He loved it. By tomorrow morning, the birth of Thaddeus Jade Laquette would be heralded like the birth of a prince in the villages of another era. Doubtful any king past had ever felt more pride than Jade felt as he unlatched the locks and tugged the fortress door open to announce, simply. "Thaddeus J. Laquette has arrived."

Acknowledgments

A quick hello and thank you to my many nephews and nieces who are more like brothers, sisters, sons, and daughters. In some large or small way, you've all offered inspiration and support for the realization of this and other adventures. Continue to thrive and grow—you are all amazing!

A special thanks to Bruce Sanderson of Sanderson-Decello Design for your patience, your grasp of ideas, and your talent in crafting the perfect haunting moon for the Envy Series. Your eye for detail is both welcome and appreciated!

JKGRUEBER.COM

www.ingramcontent.com/pod-product-compliance
Lightning Source LLC
Chambersburg PA
CBHW030352310726
48979CB00001B/269

* 9 7 8 1 9 6 5 7 9 6 0 7 8 *